Sarah Mason is a full-time writer and lives in Cheltenham with her husband and her West Highland Terrier. *The Party Season* is her second novel. Her first novel, *Playing James*, won the Parker Romantic Novel of the Year Award 2003.

The Party Season

SARAH MASON

timewarner
paperbacks

A *Time Warner* Paperback

First published in Great Britain as a paperback original in 2003
by Time Warner Paperbacks

A CIP catalogue record for this book
is available from the British Library.

ISBN 0 7515 3206 1

Typeset in Berkeley by Palimpsest Book Production Limited,
Polmont, Stirlingshire
Printed and bound in Great Britain by
Clays Ltd, St Ives plc

Time Warner Paperbacks
An imprint of
Time Warner Books UK
Brettenham House
Lancaster Place
London WC2E 7EN

www.TimeWarnerBooks.co.uk

For my brother, Mark.
With my love.

Acknowledgements

My very grateful thanks to Tara Lawrence, Jo Coen and everyone at Time Warner, whose unending patience, good will and encouragement have kept me glued to the computer when I might have been lying on the sofa watching TV. Jo and Tara in particular have both been wonderful and thank you for keeping your sense of humours when mine had already packed and gone to find itself in Mongolia.

Thank you to my agent, Dinah, whose early guidance on the novel proved invaluable, for your continued support and enthusiasm.

As always, my husband has put up with the complex process of writing with patience and humour. Thank you. Also to my Westie, who really couldn't give a stuff what happened just as long as we kept the Bonios rolling.

Friends and family. Useless. All of you. Not a helpful comment to be had among you. Still, at least they were funny.

Thanks also to the country estate and catering company (who shall remain nameless lest they are associated with any fictional happening from the book) for all your knowledge and advice. Any mistakes are of my own making.

Prologue

He's making leaving movements. I recognise the winding-up motions of the hands, the silent platitudes, a body posed for an exit. So I've about thirty seconds in which to say something cool, witty and sophisticated, delivered with a devil-may-care, look-how-far-I've-come intonation. No need to panic, just think of something.

Twenty seconds.

Damn. Damn.

Think, curse you, think. The rush of emotions is making my head swim. The trouble is that on the infrequent occasions I've thought about meeting Simon again, I've always imagined myself rolling up in my fictitious sports car, my Prada bag firmly in my grip and my Manolos even more firmly on my feet. I've entertained images of giving his country estate a sniffy once-over while Simon expressed his disbelief at how glamorous/beautiful/intelligent I've become and how much he now regrets his past behaviour.

I've been waiting for this opportunity for years, but now it's arrived I feel jumpy and uneasy. He had such a momentous effect on my childhood that I can't believe he is standing a few feet away from me now. Shouldn't such events be accompanied by thunderstorms and fireworks, not stuffed sausage canapés? And where are all those saved-up witty and cutting remarks when you need them? I look over to my supposed best friend, Dominic, who is making ludicrous jerking motions with his head and ignoring the two gentlemen hovering in front of his proffered canapé tray. Just as their hands move in for the kill, Dom can't bear it any longer, hoicks the tray out from under their noses and marches over to me.

'Izzy, what are you doing?' he hisses. 'You know who it is, don't you? Go and say something.' He pushes me closer to the door, where Simon Monkwell is shrugging himself into his coat, still oblivious to my presence.

'I don't know what to say,' I nervously whisper back.

'Just start a *conversation*,' Dom mutters and rolls his eyes dramatically. Just start a conversation. He makes it sound so easy, doesn't he? Well, it's pretty easy to start a conversation with a tray of canapés in your hand, isn't it? Would you like the smoked salmon roulade or the mushroom tartlet? Oh yes! Pretty simple then.

Before I can stop him, Dominic puts his tray into my hands and gives me a hefty shove towards Simon. My shoes haven't worn in properly yet and the new soles slip slightly on the polished floor, so that I end up damn nearly on top of him. Simon looks quite surprised to find his arms full of a brunette and several smoked salmon roulades.

Terrific, Izzy. Just marvellous. Now you're actually throwing yourself at him.

'God, sorry,' I mumble, trying to untangle myself. This is my moment. And it isn't going as I planned it. Although I've often wondered what would happen if I came face to face with Simon Monkwell again, I hadn't thought it would happen quite so literally.

Simon takes hold of me by the shoulders and firmly rights me, as though he's putting me in my place. Some things never change. He looks me in the eye with a slightly puzzled expression.

'Would you like a wild mushroom tartlet?' I ask. Bravo, Isabel. You haven't seen him for about fifteen years and that's all you can think of to say?

Simon looks at me quizzically. 'Er, no. Thank you. I was just leaving.' His voice is like a faint whiff of perfume; it fleetingly touches my memory and then it's gone.

'Pancetta and chestnut roll?' I press. Dominic makes throat-cutting gestures behind Simon's left shoulder.

Simon looks at me as though he's trying to place me. I'm not sure he'll remember me from our last meeting: I was eleven and he thirteen. It's only because of his rather meteoric rise to business fame, as tracked by the media, that I recognize him.

'Have we met?' he asks quizzically.

'Em, em . . .' I stutter. My mouth has an increasing tendency to ignore any instruction my brain gives to it. I sometimes wonder whether my brain and my mouth aren't in fact two separate, independent entities.

I don't know why, but I suddenly find myself unwilling to admit my identity. We're at a rather smart party in the heart of Knightsbridge. A launch party for a trendy new trainer called Zephyr, supposedly the Dom Perignon of the trainer world. I organised it – I am a party planner by career – but he'll think I'm a waitress, standing here offering him canapés like an idiot. Dominic is waving at me now from behind Simon's back. I glare at him as Simon glances between us both, completely nonplussed.

Suddenly a light comes on in Simon's eyes. He's recognised me. He knows exactly who I am and stares at me for a second in almost morbid fascination. But the greeting fades from my lips as he bows his head in embarrassment and selects a canapé from my tray, puts it in his mouth and then continues to pull his coat on without any further eye contact. He's recognised me and he's blanked me, without even giving me the opportunity to explain. I'm immediately transported back to the house where we grew up together, and the bad memories of those years fill my mind.

I make one last effort to speak. 'I've been, er . . .' Dom is jumping up and down. 'Er . . . reading all about . . .' Dom now has his hand up like a four-year-old. '. . . you in the . . . CHRIST! WHAT IS IT, DOM?'

'Izzy, you need to come now.' Dom drops his voice to a whisper and says in my ear, 'It would seem that Zephyr's MD's mistress has turned up. I don't think his wife is very happy.' I look over Dom's shoulder to see a woman waving a skewer of fruit around and a huddle of people cowering in the corner. Terrific. Why do things like this always happen on my shift? This will doubtless turn out to be my fault in some way or other.

I turn to apologise to Simon but he's already gone.

Chapter 1

Ten months later

It is very difficult to hold a conversation with a Viking. It's terribly distracting for one thing, the little horns on top of his helmet are practically quivering with indignation and he keeps tossing his cape in my face.

'I just don't feel as though you're giving me enough to work with. How can one be expected to express oneself with this?' He brandishes his stubby plastic sword in front of my eyes. 'How can one's true Nordic inner self be found? Hmmm? Tell me that? And why does Oliver get the pick axe *and* the hammer and I get *this*?'

I glance over to Oliver, who is waiting patiently and in a decidedly un-Nordic fashion by the door. Probably hoping for the off. He lights up a cigarette resignedly.

I turn back to the irate Viking and say quietly, 'Now, Sean, you know perfectly well that you have a much more important role in the proceedings than Oliver. I just thought that giving him a few more props would help him feel he wasn't being left out.' It's plain to everyone except Sean that Oliver couldn't give a toss about being left in or out.

Sean looks slightly mollified. 'I can see your point, Izzy.

Thank you for being so honest. But I really think . . .' he drops his voice to a whisper '. . . that you should ask Oliver to lose a few pounds. I mean, as a Viking one wouldn't have had a lot of food, would one? A few vegetables and a bit of chicken perhaps. One wouldn't look as if one had just swallowed Delia Smith and all her cookbooks.'

'Aahh, but Oliver isn't really your fighting sort of Viking. He's more the bring-up-the-rear sort.'

'More pillaging than plundering?'

'That's right.'

Sean nods understandingly and even manages to shoot the unsuspecting Oliver a nasty look. He sniffs. 'I thought as much.'

I pat his arm reassuringly, but before I can plan my escape he adds, 'Another petit point, Izzy. I was thinking that you ought to call me something like Arnog from now on.'

'Arnog?'

'I think it will help me project myself into character.'

I smile tightly and resist the temptation to look at my watch again. We have been here for over two hours and I know Aidan is waiting to use the room for his own dress rehearsal. Lady Boswell's Nordic Ice Feast is proving more troublesome than first imagined and I've still got weeks of planning to do. 'Fine, er, Arnog. Whatever you think is best. Shall we take it from the top?'

I watch through a gap in my fingers as they take their positions. The door gently opens and Aidan sidles in. He looks around for a second, spots me and then tiptoes around the perimeter of the room.

'How's it going?' he whispers to me with a grimace that shows his vote would be 'appallingly badly'.

'Appallingly badly,' I say and grimace back.

'I think it might be the feng shui in here. I've been having bad rehearsals lately too.'

The proceedings kick off. Oliver nearly takes Sean's eye out with his pick axe within the first two seconds but whether this is deliberate or not it is hard to tell. All I can say is that the Vikings must have been jolly glad they were wearing those helmets. What is supposed to be a show of natural Nordic exuberance is fast turning into a French farce. Along with the fierce battle cries and sword-wielding there are people falling over bearskin rugs amid sing-song 'Sorry, darling!'s, two people have their helmets on back-wards and Oliver has rugby-tackled Sean, wrestled him to the floor and is trying to suffocate him with his cloak.

Aidan leans over to me. 'God, darling, this is more than just feng shui. My rehearsals have never gone this badly. I think you must have a jinx.'

'It certainly would seem that way,' I say dully, wondering how long Sean can hold his breath for.

'Darling, it's only been a couple of weeks. You're bound to drop a few balls after being dumped. It's only natural.'

'Thanks, Aidan. I had managed to forget the state of my love life for a whole two minutes then.'

I think Sean has probably suffered enough and so I rush over to rescue him.

Our rehearsal room is situated in the basement of a large Georgian house which is home to our company. We are one among many identical houses in a square in South Kensington and the only thing that gives us away in all that quiet gentility is a small brass plaque etched with the words 'Table Manners'. Actually we plan all sorts of things: weddings, product launches, corporate events, drinks parties for twenty, masked balls for four hundred, and at any conceivable venue. My friend and colleague Aidan, the Salvador Dali of the party world, has used wigwams, submarines, stables and even a bed manufacture factory.

I really don't see the point in having another rehearsal so I wearily dismiss everyone and they run screaming from the room as though school has just broken up for summer. I'm glad I have such a moralising effect on my staff.

I supervise the return of all props to the huge room next door which is warehouse to our considerable stock of theatrical equipment, glassware, crockery, cutlery, seat covers, tablecloths and napkins and other paraphernalia. Everyone hangs their costumes up on a huge rail which displays the larger-than-life notice: LADY BOSWELL'S NORDIC ICE FEAST.

I start to climb the two flights of stairs towards my desk. On the first landing, Aidan shouts up the stairwell after me, 'Don't tell Gerald where I am.' Gerald is our formidable MD and has no truck with Aidan's artistic temperament.

'Aidan, he knows where you are. You're on the rehearsal board,' I shout back.

'Well, don't let him come down here. I'm not talking to him.'

'Fine. I'll try.' I sigh and carry on with my journey. The company's reception and offices occupy the top two floors of the building. The ground floor houses our kitchens where all the food gets prepared and then shipped out to the required venue in one of our many refrigerated vans. The chefs can be a little volatile so I try not to venture too near them. I clear the last flight of stairs and arrive in the inner sanctum of the national headquarters of Table Manners where Stephanie, our receptionist, is hard at work.

'Any messages, Stephanie?' I ask, only as a matter of habit rather than in any real hope that she will have actually taken any. Stephanie is a firm disciple of the if-it's-important-they'll-call-back school of thought.

She blows out a stream of smoke and screws up her eyes thoughtfully. We have a strict no-smoking policy and Gerald regularly issues written warnings on the matter. Stephanie types them out with a fag hanging from her mouth. But what Stephanie doesn't know about the celebrity world isn't worth knowing. A skill which I have to grudgingly admit is quite useful in our line of work. It is the only reason I can see that Gerald keeps her on.

'Someone did call for you but it didn't sound particularly interesting so I didn't bother writing it down.'

'Right. Excellent. Lady Boswell is coming in later so do you think we could possibly avoid a repeat of last time?'

'She's an old tartar,' Stephanie says sulkily.

'That may be so but she is a rich old tartar and one of our best clients.'

'I hope she catches hypothermia at this ice feast of hers.'

'The way things are going that might be a good bet.'

Stephanie returns her attention to *Woman's Weekly* and I make my way to my desk. It's all open plan on the first floor. The place is littered with sample decorations, theatrical props (which should by rights remain in the basement where they belong but Aidan insists we keep them up here for inspiration), a giant stuffed bear called Yogi who is a remnant from a Davy Crockett party, flower arrangements from the last week's functions, sample books of everything from napkins to ribbons, several different sorts of vases and candelabras as well as a couple of the obligatory computers and laptops. Papers and invites spill out on to every surface.

9

Just as I reach my desk our MD's office door flies open. 'ISABEL. IN HERE,' he announces through his hand-held tannoy which he insists on using even though I could probably reach over and touch him.

Gerald is a sharp-looking man in his late forties. He has dark hair that is always neatly combed into place and sports a slight paunch. He is our much-vilified managing director and deservedly so, for he is without doubt the rudest, most sarcastic man I have ever met. And I quite like him. He doesn't believe in beating around the bush, he says it's tedious. No 'good-morning-how-are-you' stuff for him.

I follow him into his office and shut the door behind me.

'How was the rehearsal?' Gerald demands as I go over to his coffee percolator and pour myself a mug.

'Awful. Sean insisted on swapping all his props with Oliver. Coffee?'

'Please. I need something to get me through this God-awful day. Sean and Oliver will probably end up killing each other. We can only hope. Are you on the Ice Feast all day?'

'Unfortunately. Lady Boswell is in later. It's going to be a very long week.'

'Where's Aidan?'

'In the rehearsal room.'

'He's going through one of his phases.'

I grin. Aidan always goes through one of his phases if he feels some difficult questioning from Gerald coming on. 'Has he blown his budget again?' I ask.

'Into orbit. I don't really know why he bothers doing cost projections at all.'

Gerald eyes me carefully at this last comment. It's a well-known fact in the company that Aidan wouldn't be caught dead next to a cost projection. I think Gerald correctly suspects I do them all for him. 'Nor do I,' I say flippantly.

'Every time I question him about the cost he throws one of his fits.'

'Ah.' This involves Aidan throwing himself down on the nearest piece of furniture and wailing something along the lines of, 'Questions, questions. Why must I deal with so many questions?' Occasionally he compares himself to Picasso or Bach in that genius must be given licence to express itself. I love Aidan's fits; he always has a small crowd gathered around him by the end. 'I'll deal with him, if you want.'

'Do that. Get him to cut down somewhere.'

'I'll try. No promises.'

'Got over being dumped yet?' he asks bluntly. 'You're not exactly a ray of sunshine at the moment.'

My relationship with Gerald is not such that I can weep silently on his shoulder for twenty minutes so I simply tell him that I'm fine.

At lunchtime Aidan reappears, sits eagerly on my desk and crosses his Versace-clad legs. Aidan is my best friend here at the office. When I first arrived at the company I was his assistant for a year before I got to plan parties of my own. He's been here for ages and is the most requested organiser in the company. He is, as he often likes to remind us, creative. It is his get-out-of-jail-free card with Gerald. Any slight misdemeanour and it is put down to his creative nature. Aidan has murdered four clients with a party popper and a tablecloth? Oh, that's because he's creative.

'So how are you today?' he asks. 'I haven't really seen you to ask.' This is accompanied by much face-pulling. You can't have a conversation with Aidan without these facial contortions; you know you've been with him too long when you find yourself incapable of saying a sentence without sucking in your cheeks, rolling your eyes and pushing up imaginary bosoms with one arm.

'Fine!' I say brightly and pull a face back.

'You don't look fine.'

I can't keep it from him any longer. 'Something happened to me on the Tube,' I groan. 'Someone thought I was pregnant and offered me their seat.'

'Oh.'

'Don't you dare laugh, Aidan,' I say sharply, seeing him bite his lip hard. 'Because it simply is not funny.'

'Oh, I'm not laughing, Isabel. I'm merely, em . . . So what did you do?'

'What could I do? Tell them that my *slightly* swollen stomach is due to an excess of Cornettos since Rob dumped me? I did the only thing I could do. I thanked them very nicely and sat down.'

Aidan puts out a comforting hand. 'Darling, you know it always goes on your stomach and never on your breasts. Nature is a bitch like that.'

'Why couldn't I have simply said that I have put on a few pounds since my boyfriend dumped me? We could have had a nice chat about the pros and cons of the Hay diet versus the Atkins and a jolly time could have been had by all. But no, I was too British about the whole thing. Someone accuses me of being pregnant and I am far too polite to disagree.'

'Come on, Izzy. It's only been three weeks. Besides, I think it's very useful to put weight on your stomach. At least it can't sneak up behind you and cunningly slip on your bottom while you're not looking.'

'But then people don't think you're pregnant.'

'No, they just think you've got a large arse.'

'Thanks so much. Why can't I be one of those women who drop four dress sizes when they've been dumped?' I complain.

'Ahhh, ducks, because then you wouldn't be you. I like you being you, apart from the anal cost projections thing of course.'

'I just wish I could figure out why Rob dumped me,' I say. 'We used to have such a marvellous time. Maybe I was too keen, Aidan.'

He snorts derisively. 'Keen, smeen. Darling, we're not in kindergarten any more.'

'Do you think I should call him and ask?'

'No, no and no,' says Aidan. 'We have been over this. Anyone who finishes with someone by telephone, and don't forget that he tried to time the call to get your voice mail because he couldn't be bothered to actually speak to you, is simply not worth the time of day. Also, may I point out, leaving a message on your *work* voice mail is simply the most gutless, horrible thing I have ever heard.'

'I know,' I whisper, my voice wobbling.

Stephanie wanders over to us with a fag in her hand before we can say any more. 'Lady Toss-well is here.'

'Stephannnieee,' I hiss, standing up and smoothing down my skirt. 'I told you not to call her that. Did you put her in the boardroom?'

'Yeah.'

'Thanks.' I pick up my notebook, take a deep breath and march briskly over to reception, up one flight of stairs and into the boardroom. Lady Boswell is sitting bolt upright on one of the chairs with one hand lying gracefully in her

13

lap and the other on top of the handle of a large umbrella she likes to carry everywhere.

'Lady Boswell, how nice to see you,' I say smoothly. 'Did Stephanie offer you a cup of coffee?'

Lady Boswell looks at me as though I have just offered her a cup of cat sick with a couple of teaspoons of maggots stirred in.

'Coffee, Isabel, coffee? You must know that I never take caffeine in the afternoon. We are living in a coffee-obsessed age. Those dreadful bars are everywhere.'

Lady Boswell is fairly typical of some of our more traditional clients. A stickler for the rules and Debrett's, she is also terribly thin, which does not endear her to me at all, and is today dressed in a navy blue suit complete with stockings and gloves. A large handbag accompanies her everywhere and she has been known to take a swipe with it when things aren't going according to plan. Hence my nervousness about the Nordic Ice Feast.

She purses her thin lips, which she always over-paints with cerise lipstick, while I open my notebook. 'Now, how is the party planning actually progressing? Are the Vikings going to look like Vikings? You know I can't have Mrs Sneddon-Wells showing me up. Her Caribbean banquet is still the talk of London.' She pauses for breath and looks me up and down critically. 'Have you put on some weight, Isabel?'

Chapter 2

Party planning hasn't always been my natural vocation. I wish I could claim a childhood of glitzy events had prepared me for it but the closest I had ever got to any excitement was when my father took me to a Don MacLean concert at the age of twelve. The whole thing was a disaster and we had to leave at the interval. My father thought things were getting out of hand because people were throwing their ice cream lids at the stage.

My father was in the army so my sister Sophie and I were continually being uprooted and moved around the world. Perhaps due to my rather chaotic childhood I always craved a very solid career. Once I graduated from university the need for money and ambition took a strong hold of me and I went to train as a financial analyst. I didn't think you could get more solid than reassuring columns of figures and tables. After my training course, a nice City firm gave me my very own office, along with their assurances that they thought I would be very happy with them. I hoped I would be.

On my first day I popped my head out of my office in search of a friendly face and the possibility of sharing a lunchtime sandwich. I was met by a maze of desks and people who were eating their lunch while still talking on their phones. I went back into my office and did the same. It doesn't matter – people who work so hard must play hard too, I thought to myself. We'll all be in the pub on the stroke of six. But as the days went past, we weren't in the pub at all. We weren't even in McDonald's. In fact, the only person who really spoke to me was the girl I bought my sandwich from.

The days plodded on and it came as quite a shock to me when I found myself positively envying the sandwich girl. I envied her mobility. I envied her careless chatter with people. I envied her flexible hours. Things came to a head when I was showing some visitors around the building and we happened to meet the chairman outside his office. Once he had shaken hands with everyone, he turned to me and said, 'I hope we're impressing you!' with great joviality. He thought I was one of the visiting dignitaries.

It was then that I started to wonder whether I hadn't in fact made the wrong choice. How could I be valued if my chairman didn't even know who I was? An uneasy period of indecision followed until one day, while in a conversation with one of our middle-aged employees, I discovered that she hadn't wanted to work in the finance industry at all. She'd taken the job as a stop-gap over eighteen years ago and had stayed because she didn't know what else to do. Peculiar how a conversation like that can shape your life. I didn't want to be her in eighteen years' time.

So I packed up my pot plant and my photographs and left my safe little office in the City. By luck, I answered an ad for Table Manners, and the rest is history. What the advert for an administrative assistant in a trendy party planning firm didn't tell me was that all new employees have to spend a compulsory month being trained in the kitchens, which resembles some sort of boot camp. I was up ridiculously early, peeling and preparing endless mounds of vegetables. I always had at least two of those extremely attractive blue catering plasters on display (that month did nothing for my love life).

But I learned how to make most of the basic sauces, when various ingredients were in season, the best way to cook all kinds of fish and meat; in short, I developed a real sense of food. Not that I hadn't been fairly aware of it before – I always knew immediately if chocolate biscuits were in close proximity – but I came to know instinctively which flavours and textures would work well together.

My knowledge of figures also meant I was good with the foundations of party planning. I could craft into beautiful tabular form the basic costs of an event, so I still had my reassuring figures but without the loneliness of the City. Maybe in a few years' time I might set up my own business because I think I have the foundations to manage it. And I had no idea work could be such fun! Even on a bad day like this one. It seems immoral somehow.

I stomp up the steps to my flat in a thoroughly bad mood and press the buzzer impatiently. I know Dom, my housemate, will be home before me – he always is – and I can't be bothered to fish around in my handbag for my keys. This bugs Dom a lot but I know he will answer because he has learned his lesson from last time when he just picked up the handset and yelled, 'I'm not letting you in, you lazy slut!' Mrs Lawrence was only trying to drop off some Neighbourhood Watch leaflets. It took a card and several bunches of flowers before she would speak to him again.

'Hello?'

'Dom, it's me.'

'Where are your keys?' he demands petulantly.

'Don't know. Pl-ea-se let me in.'

'No!'

'Go on, Dom!'

'Oh, all right.'

He presses the release key in a half-hearted gesture, giving me exactly a second to elbow my way into the hall. Once inside I trot up two flights of stairs, cursing the woman's mag that told me I should do it two at a time or I'll have a backside the size of China, and push open the door to my flat. I bought this flat when I was more profitably employed than I am now and Dominic is my lodger. My period of flush employment didn't run to huge amounts of furniture but Dom claims he likes the minimalist look anyway, with our few well-chosen ornaments of Mouldy Toast on Plate, Dying Plant and Half-Empty Mug. Our bedrooms lead off from the hallway and we share a connecting bathroom. We have a rule that whoever gets any part of their body across the bathroom threshold first in the morning gets preference. This leads to downright dangerous bursts of speed at seven a.m. and even the occasional rugby-like tackle. Dom has been known, after his more drunken nights of revelry, to sleep in the bath in order to guarantee his slot.

The Strokes blare out from the speakers amid much accompaniment of pan-clattering from the kitchen. Dom has probably been home for about an hour.

It was through my job that I first met Dominic. His Aunt Agnes was giving a drinks party – my first solo drinks party.

About halfway into the evening, Dominic sidled up to me and told me that his Aunt Agnes was vegetarian and the canapés were decidedly not. At this point all the blood drained from my head as I looked across the room in time to see Aunt Agnes taking one of the carnivore delights. Before it reached her mouth Dominic made a heroic dash, took it off her and ate it with much lip-smacking, while I brought up the rear and whisked the waitress away before an amazed Aunt Agnes could take another. Dominic then joined me in the kitchen where I was transfixed with fear, wondering how on earth the kitchen staff could have cocked up so monumentally and whether anyone would notice if we were about two hundred canapés down. Dominic simply took every piece of Parma ham off the top of the tarts, began shovelling the ham into his mouth and then sent the waitress back out to the party with the now vegetarian-friendly snacks. And so our friendship began.

He is the most unlikely best friend I could ever hope for. We are undoubtedly the odd couple. I am tidy, Dom is not. I have a Filofax, Dom has the back of his hand and a biro. I schedule the housework, Dom thinks a coaster is something to do with surfing. But I absolutely adore him and I would like to think he feels the same way.

Dominic works in the claims department of an insurance company to supplement his career as a struggling writer (struggling in the sense that he struggles to write anything). This sort of desk job suits Dom just fine. It comes without responsibility – no vying for promotion, no working over-time, no long-term goals because at the end of the day it's just that: a day job. He turns up just after nine, walks a fine knife-edge between doing enough not to get himself fired and little enough to ensure he goes unnoticed, and pisses off home on the dot of five. He looks on every day as a huge adventure and has the amazing gift of taking every ounce of enjoyment out of whatever he's doing. His 'send me a toffee in the post by Tuesday and I'll process your claim' promises are notorious throughout the company. That's notorious in the verbal-warning sense of the word.

'Hello, gorgeous!'

'Hi.' I dump my handbag and leather attaché case on to the kitchen table. 'What are you doing?' I ask him. 'It's not your turn to do the washing up.'

Dom grins at me from behind the soap suds. On the rare occasions Dom does do the washing up he uses about half a bottle of Fairy Liquid. He's even got bubbles lodged in his hair. 'I couldn't find a clean mug. Life can be so cruel sometimes.' He sighs dramatically. 'How are you feeling?'

'Dreadful. How are you?'

'Absolutely fine. I was going to call you at work today,' Dom continues.

'Were you? You never call me at work.'

'That's because you never let me call you at work.'

'Dom, if I let you call me at work you'd be on the phone every half an hour. But I did think about you today.'

'Did you? Did you think ahh, Dom. I do miss him?'

'No. Gerald was asking after you.'

'Was he?'

'And Aidan, come to think of it. What's this sudden fondness my workmates have developed for you?'

'It's because I'm lovable.'

I snort derisively. 'Hardly lovable. They just like you because you get me into trouble. Gerald is still teasing me about my bout of food poisoning that you told him was a hangover.'

'It was a hangover.'

'Yes, well. You see, Dom, this is why I don't let you call me at work – we'd end up having conversations like this. Are you coming up to Aunt Winnie's with me at the weekend?' Dom has visited my Aunt Winnie with me many times – she regards him as one of the family.

'I'll come on Saturday. I've got a stag do on Friday night.'

'A stag do?' This is the first I've heard of it.

'Yep, some bloke from work.'

'Who?'

'Oh, you don't know him.'

'When's the wedding?'

'Not for ages.'

'An all-boys stag do?' I ask suspiciously.

'Is there any other kind? You've got a postcard from your folks, by the way.' He nods towards a pile of post on the table.

I let the surprise stag do go and study a night scene of Hong Kong harbour, then turn it over to see the familiar scrawl of my mother.

Just dashing off to another ghastly party full of diplomats. Honestly, darling, I simply don't know how you do it for a living all day long. Your father sends his love. Will try and call soon but can't seem to remember whether you are ahead of us or behind time-wise. Give our love to Sophie when you see her.
Love Mum.

I drop it back on to the pile and sigh. They seem so very far away from my own reality.

'Have you read it?' I ask Dom.

'Yes. I thought they were coming over to see you and Sophie soon?'

'I think something came up with Dad's work.' I shrug. They aren't the most reliable of parents.

'So what's happened to you today?' Dom asks.

I open my mouth to answer but the phone rings and I rush through to answer it, a small part of me still hoping it could be Rob. It's not even close.

'IZZY!' a familiar voice booms. Aunt Winnie has been calling almost every day since Rob finished with me, bless her. 'You're home! I was hoping to have a jolly chat with Dominic but I suppose you'll do instead.'

'Well, I am actually related to you, Aunt Winnie. Whereas Dominic isn't.'

'That tyrannical boss of yours has let you come home at last, has he? I am absolutely convinced he has Marxist tendencies, Izzy. You want to watch out for that; you could be a communist before you know it.'

'I don't think it's the sort of thing that creeps up on you, Aunt Winnie.'

'Ohhhh, don't you believe it,' she replies sagely. 'They probably slip something into the water.'

'Well, I always try to avoid drinking tap water if I can.'

'That's my girl! I brought you and your sister up well. Much better off with gin. I would ask how you are but you know I detest hearing about other people's health.'

'How's the vicar?' I ask instead. The vicar is Aunt Winnie's new hobby. She adores engaging him in earnest theological discussions. I feel terribly sorry for the man because he simply has no idea what he is dealing with. I remember similar warnings in the *Jaws* film and look what happened there.

'In the middle of a row over the church flowers. Mrs

Harrison did an arrangement last week involving lots of aubergines. I suppose she thought she was being trendy but it turned out quite spectacularly indecent. Lots of phallic bulging purple coupled with some rather unfortunate poppy heads. I thought the vicar was going to have a coronary on the spot. I haven't laughed so hard since one of the Sunday school kids stapled his cassock to the bell rope.'

I giggle. 'Aunt Winnie, you are terrible.'

'Actually, I'm glad I caught you. I didn't want to have to leave a message with Dom as he would probably get the story completely tits-up. Guess who I met today!'

'I couldn't.'

'Go on! Guess!'

'Er, George Clooney?' I say hopefully, praying she would have him at home right now with a large padlock on the door.

'George who?'

'Clooney.'

'Loony?'

'CLOONEY. He's a film . . . never mind. Tell me who you met.'

'Mrs Charlesty!' This really isn't along the same lines as George Clooney.

'No!'

'Yes!'

'Not really?'

'Yes, I was . . . You're being sarcastic, aren't you? Actually, I haven't told you why it's such a big deal so I'll forgive you. I was in the butcher's at Bury St Edmunds. You know, they've had to close the butcher's here in the village for a few days because all the family have gone down with flu. But you needn't concern yourself because I have had my flu jab.'

'Thank goodness.' I remark dryly, wondering if we are ever going to get to the point.

'So I had to go into Bury and I bumped into her there. I was telling her *all* about you and your job. She was absolutely fascinated.'

'Is that it? Why would she be fascinated by me?' I query.

'Of course she was fascinated! You have a very interesting job and I am proud of my gals. Now, have you stopped moping about yet?'

'Well, Dominic has been spared his duties of sitting on the sofa with me and producing tissues from a box like some bored magician, if that's what you mean.'

Aunt Winnie obviously sees this as enormous progress. 'Good, good!' she booms. 'Dom's not having a difficult time at work, is he?'

It is regrettable that I met Rob Gillingham through Dom. The insurance company Dom works for is owned by the Gillingham family and Rob is being groomed to take over from his father in a few years' time. Rob and I met at a large black-tie bash the company threw to celebrate its 150th anniversary. I was there as Dom's guest rather than in the hired help capacity. Rob's not traditionally good-looking but where you might doubt his looks there is no doubting his charm. I fell for it hook, line and definitely sinker.

'I don't think so, he never mentions him.'

'I should think not!' snorts Aunt Winnie. 'Now, chin up and if you feel yourself wanting to phone him just call me instead!'

Dom has finished washing up and is making a pot of tea. 'Who was that?' he asks.

'Aunt Winnie.' I sit down at the table.

He slops the tea into two newly washed mugs. 'What did she want?'

'Just a chat.' I glance down at my stomach, remember the incident on the Tube and sharply draw it in while wincing to myself. 'I really need to go on a diet.'

Dom follows my gaze down. 'Yes, you do a bit,' he says with candour.

'I'm not sure I can face it tonight, I have had an appalling day.'

'Lady Boswell?' asks Dom sympathetically.

'Lady Boswell,' I confirm. 'Or Tosswell as Stephanie calls her.'

'Well then, I think we could declare a state of emergency just for tonight. But tomorrow evening I will personally throw away all the Cornettos and then we can go to Sainsbury's and buy some celery. Or whatever you women eat on these diet things.'

Oh goody. He walks over to the vastly depleted wine rack and pulls out a bottle. 'Join a gym with me too?' I beg.

'A gym?' he questions as the cork comes out of the bottle with a comforting POP. 'Is that really necessary? Oh all right,' he relents in answer to my pleading look. 'I suppose I could do with getting fitter. Although I'm not running any marathons.'

'My body is a temple. That will be our new mantra!'

'More like my body is a shed. Chuck everything in and have a good clear out once a year.' He clinks his glass against mine. 'Cheers! Here's to new beginnings and old endings!'

We sip in silence, then I suddenly say, 'Dom, something happened to me on the Tube today.'

'What?'

'Now, promise you won't laugh . . .'

25

Chapter 3

The next morning, feeling more than a little worse for wear, I ram a pair of sunglasses on to my nose and start the walk from South Ken Tube to my office. At least the weather isn't in keeping with my mood. We are supposedly at the start of summer but this is the first day I have actually seen proof of it. The sun is desperately trying to warm up the tepid air as though making up for lost time and the light throws long shadows on to the bustling, waking streets. The world seems to come into sharp focus which makes me feel more washed-out than ever. I sneak furtive looks at myself in shop windows as I pass. My shoulder-length brunette hair could really do with some highlights and . . . my eyes travel down to my stomach and I pull it in. Yes, it probably is in need of some attention.

At the office, I lean on the buzzer urgently as though I have in actual fact been waiting here quite some time. Stephanie buzzes me in.

'You're late,' she greets me as I reach the top of the stairs.

'I know. Gerald in yet?'

'About half an hour ago. Watch out for him this morning.'

'Why? Is he in a funny mood?'

She shrugs dismissively, 'I don't think his drinks party went too well last night. You look awful, by the way.'

I am just creeping past Gerald's door, hoping to get to my desk, spread a few things out and generally behave as though I have been here for hours, when it flies open and Gerald himself stands before me. I straighten up and try to arrange my features into an enquiring yet intelligent look. This doesn't come out too well as it is painful to move anything too quickly. It is the facial equivalent of flinging myself across the room.

'Gerald!' I say weakly, trying desperately to add a smile. God, the pain.

'Isabel. How nice of you to come to work.'

'Gerald, I'm sorry I'm late. I had trouble with the . . . er . . .'

'Neighbour's cat? Postman? Door handle?'

'No. I, er, lost my, em . . .'

'Walking ability? Tube pass? Mind?'

'Oh look! My canapé samples have arrived!' I exclaim joyfully. Aidan, god bless him, has whisked up behind Gerald and shoves a small tray in my face.

'Sorry, Gerald. Chef said Izzy should try them now while they're hot.'

We both smile patiently at him. We're all petrified of the head chef so this is a safe bet. 'Well?' asks Gerald. 'Are you going to try them, Izzy?'

'Hmm? Oh yes! Of course!' I hastily take one and shove it in my mouth. It's stone cold and tastes vaguely of salmon.

'Deeelicious!' I spit crumbs at them both and wonder if they would notice if I am quietly sick on their shoes. Gerald opens his mouth to say something else, then thinks better of it and shuts it again. He closes his eyes and rests his

27

head in his hands in a Gawd-help-us kind of way. We have a small interval of silence. Then Gerald obviously decides that he cannot be bothered with us anymore, makes an impatient flapping gesture with his hands and returns to his office. We breathe a sigh of relief.

'Thanks, Aidan,' I murmur.

'Sorry about the canapés, at least they're only yesterday's. Coffee?'

'Please,' I bleat. I slump down at my desk and, without even bothering to take off my jacket, rest my head on a very convenient seat cover some wonderful person has placed there. Probably not for this purpose but I am grateful all the same.

It is a matter of minutes before Aidan is back bearing the ambrosial brew. I half-heartedly sit up and manage to take a couple of restorative sips. He has been an absolute rock in these last three weeks. He knows that my current state of dishevelment is very out of character. Normally I am extremely organised and efficient.

'Why are you in such a state? What on earth have you been doing? Was it anything exciting?'

'Just Dominic and me,' I whisper and pull a face.

'Darling Dominic,' says Aidan fondly. 'How is he?'

'Ill, I hope.'

'Izzy, darling, I know this Rob thing has upset you but when can we have our old Isabel back? The anal, everything-has-its-place Isabel?'

'I thought you hated that Isabel,' I mumble into my seat cover.

'Oh, she's not so bad. Besides, my figures don't add up.'

'Leave them on my desk. When I can see again, I'll have a look at them. Who have you got this evening?'

'Mrs Pritch-Bonnington's Arabian Nights party. More Laurence Llewelyn-Bowen than Lawrence of Arabia, I'm afraid. What about you?'

'Nothing until Wednesday.' I raise my head from the seat cover. 'If anyone calls tell them I'm dead. It's not too far from the truth.' The only thing that disturbs me for the next half an hour is Dom texting to ask how he can commit suicide with a paperclip and a Post-it note. He's obviously feeling bad too. Good. I smile to myself as my head drops back down to my seat cover.

Later that morning we gather in the boardroom for our bi-weekly management meeting, where we discuss future projects, assign them to someone if an organiser hasn't been specifically requested and mull over any general problems or ideas. It normally takes all morning; much of it is spent deciding who wants what from the coffee shop next door.

They start without me as I endure a seemingly never-ending call with a client renowned for her absolute hatred of green food at her events. Not even an olive can remain. When I walk in to the meeting Gerald is in the middle of giving someone a big going-over but as soon as he claps eyes on me he's distracted.

'ANYWAY,' he says loudly, 'since the mother ship has finally beamed Isabel back down let's move on to new projects. Does the name Monkwell mean anything to you, Isabel?'

I frown. It does mean an awful lot to me. Great chunks of my childhood are tied up with that name.

'Er, Isabel?'

'Yes?'

'The name Monkwell?'

29

'Well, of course I know the name Monkwell! Doesn't everybody?'

'I mean personally.'

I pause slightly. Gerald is looking very sternly at me. He must have got hold of the fact that I used to be on quite intimate terms with the Monkwell family. I've never mentioned this and contacts are everything in this business. And the name Monkwell would mean BIG business. 'I haven't seen any of them for years,' I say in a very small voice, conveniently forgetting my 'almost' meeting with Simon.

'Simon Monkwell?' interjects Stephanie in wonder. '*The* Simon Monkwell? You *know* him?' This is said in an accusatory tone. She's always in a foul mood in these meetings because Gerald banned her from smoking in here after the time she asked one of us to 'chuck her a fag' and Aidan threw himself across the room with 'Here I am darling!' Gerald couldn't get any sense out of us for about half an hour.

'Em, sort of.'

'How, sort of?' persists Gerald.

'Er, I knew the family as a kid. I grew up on Simon's country estate with him. Why?' I decide to play the innocent.

'Someone called Monty Monkwell called me this morning.'

'Really? That's Simon's father.'

'Yes. Apparently he heard you were in the party planning business through your Aunt Winnie. The one who thinks I'm a communist.' Aunt Winnie is well known to everyone at Table Manners. She has long conversations with anyone in the office who is hapless enough to take her calls.

'Through my Aunt Winnie?' I frown. Aunt Winnie would

have mentioned it if she'd been in touch with one of the Monkwells.

'Well, not exactly through Aunt Winnie. Apparently through a Mrs Charlesty who had been speaking to your Aunt Winnie. I've got all the details. A charity ball is being organised up at the estate—'

'Pantiles,' I fill in.

'Yes, Pantiles. He wondered if you would be able to go along and help out. The fee he's offering isn't much but if you do well, and bearing in mind you actually know the family,' he throws me a nasty look here, 'we might be able to get our foot in the door for the corporate entertaining contract for Simon Monkwell's company. Which, I don't need to tell you, would be massive business. Only last week *The Times* named him as one of the most up and coming entrepreneurs in the country.'

'And *Tatler* named him one of their top fifty eligible bachelors. He's dreamy-looking,' Stephanie throws in. 'That huge country estate. Think of all the money.' She stares off longingly into the distance.

'What does he do exactly?' asks someone.

'Buys companies, tears them apart, sells them off. With their permission or without it. Fairly ruthless by reputation.'

'Not just by reputation,' I murmur to myself. The discussion becomes more animated and everyone leans forward, anxious to add their piece.

'Doesn't he insist on personally firing all the management of the companies he takes over?'

'Something about how he likes to gloat over their failure?'

'Didn't he lay off a thousand workers from his last company?'

'Okay, all right everyone, so the man doesn't exactly smell

31

of roses, but that doesn't change the colour of his money,' Gerald interrupts the proceedings before they deteriorate. 'If we discounted all our clients on the basis of the morality of their money we'd probably only have about two left. I might ask you, Izzy, why you never deemed it important enough to mention here?'

'Simon and I didn't get on.' I shrug my shoulders and stare down at my pad. Simon Monkwell and I were best friends. Note the past tense. *Were* best friends.

'How old were you?'

'Eleven.'

'How can you not get on when you're eleven? Did you steal his mint humbugs? Did you row over who'd had the roller skates last? I don't think he'll hold it against you.'

'When is the ball?' I ask, flipping my huge, stalwart diary, every party planner's faithful companion, open for December.

'Next month.'

'Next month?' I look up in horror.

'Apparently the charity have had to move venue at the last minute and asked the estate if they could relocate there, which is why Monty Monkwell wants you along to help out.'

'But there's not enough time. I can't organise a ball within a month!'

'They might have a lot organised already. I've booked you in for a fact-finding meeting on Monday. So just go along and see what needs to be done.'

'I'm going to see my Aunt Winnie for the weekend; she lives quite near, so she might take me,' I concede. I haven't got a car and Gerald's puritanical attitude towards expenses is ingrained in all of us.

'Mr Monkwell says the estate has never organised anything like this before. It's their first official event.'

'They have never been a working estate. The house and grounds were always strictly private. I can't see Simon Monkwell welcoming anyone with open arms.'

'Well, Simon Monkwell is abroad so you won't see him.'

'Good.'

The Pantiles estate. I never thought I'd be going back there. A rush of memories overwhelms me as I think of it. What a beautiful place it is. The Monkwells own the estate, the village and a couple of thousand of acres of land besides. When I was about eight we moved back to England and we ended up living on the estate in a cottage only a few minutes away from the main house. Pantiles, Monty and Elizabeth Monkwell, Simon and his brother Will became my whole world and, until I turned eleven, I absolutely adored that golden family.

'If this is the first time the estate has done anything like this then we could be in on the start of something highly profitable,' Gerald says, interrupting my thoughts. 'You'll probably need to clear at least the week before the ball due to the timescale problems. Mr Monkwell said you could stay with them if you need to rather than keep going back and forward to London. Wouldn't hear of anything else. It would save us on travel expenses. Whereabouts in Suffolk is the estate?'

'Little village called Pantiles. Quite close to Bury St Edmunds.'

'He said he was looking forward to seeing you again. God knows why you haven't mentioned these people before, Izzy.'

'I've told you. Simon and I just don't get on. In fact, I

don't think it would be an exaggeration to say that he positively hates me.'

'Why? You're pretty innocuous.' This is a compliment coming from Gerald.

I shrug. 'I really don't know.'

'It'll probably be something trivial, knowing kids. Did you get on well with the rest of the family? Would that be too much to ask? How about Monty Monkwell?'

'Oh yes! I loved the rest of the family.'

But most of all I adored the boys. Having one sister, no brothers and a frequently absent father, I found the presence of male company incredibly refreshing. At first Simon and I got on brilliantly; he treated me as though I was his baby sister and I loved every minute of it. We were together constantly, talking in our special made-up language which nearly drove our parents to distraction.

'Anyway, is the date free?' asks Gerald.

I turn my diary to the suggested weekend and frown. 'Mrs Cherington's drinks party.'

'Could you take that Aidan?'

'Not on your nelly! That old battleaxe! I'd rather . . .' He trails off as he catches sight of Gerald's face. 'Yes, of course I can.'

'Good! Simon Monkwell's secretary wants your CV faxed up along with a signed confidentiality agreement.'

'A confidentiality agreement? Why?' A confidentiality agreement is considered perfectly normal if the event is high-profile but not for something like a charity ball.

'Presumably because something might be confidential,' Gerald says in his best morons voice, raising his eyes to the ceiling with a sigh. 'Isabel, it might have escaped your notice these last few weeks but Simon Monkwell is trying to complete a hostile takeover of a rather large manufacturing company. I daresay the family might be worried you could hear something you shouldn't. Pull yourself together, for God's sake. You normally know exactly what's going on.'

I blink at Gerald, realising he's right. Aidan jumps into the awkward silence with both feet. 'Oh look!' he exclaims. 'Here's my smelly pineapple rubber! I've been wondering where that had got to!'

Back at my desk, I try to concentrate on a seating plan for Lady Boswell's Nordic Ice Feast but my thoughts keep straying to Simon Monkwell. Just as I thought I had forgotten all the hurt he caused me, which had been dragged up from the depths of my memory by our recent meeting, the mere mention of his name has brought it all rushing back again.

Simon Monkwell was my best friend when I was eight and in a way our friendship brought our two families together. I don't think we'd have spent nearly as much time in each other's company if Simon and I hadn't been so close. But just after Simon was sent away to boarding school, things started to change.

His first few weekends at home were fine. We'd go fishing. We'd ride our bikes. We'd watch TV. But slowly Simon became introverted and sulky. And spiteful. He played all sorts of unkind tricks on me, locking me in deserted rooms on the estate, abandoning me in the woods at night. Simon was two years older than me so perhaps he outgrew our friendship, but whatever happened it was devastating to me. It got to the stage when any planned visit to the Monkwells' would reduce me to tears and I'd beg my mother not to make me go. I couldn't tell her why so relations became strained between us all. The magic of Pantiles disappeared for me that autumn and the woods held only malice.

The following summer, my father got a new posting to Italy and Sophie and I went to live with our Aunt Winnie so that we could stay at school in England. Both families made the usual pledges to keep in touch and Will and Monty implored Sophie and me to come and visit often, knowing our parents would be in Italy. I was reticent because of Simon, but whenever Sophie suggested the idea to Aunt Winnie something would always come up to stop us from going, until we gradually forgot all about the idea of visiting them at all. In the intervening years, I all but forgot about Simon until newspaper articles started to appear about him. Instead of taking on his birthright and his place at Pantiles, he had decided to go into business. At first the papers focused on his 'dazzling' entrepreneurial skills, his talent for business, his overwhelming affinity with numbers, but little by little I started to see hints of the old Simon. His initial love affair with the press began to dwindle and reports emerged which showed him in a very different light. The thousands of workers laid off from a manufacturing business. His unreasonable demands to the board of directors. The neglected and unloved state of his family seat. It seems he hasn't changed much over the years.

Aidan sits anxiously on my desk. He wants to talk about this latest development.

'Oooh, ducks. Imagine you growing up with Simon Monkwell.' He lifts one shoulder and makes a 'fancy that' face. 'Ooohh, I wonder if he's as bad as they say. I do hope so.'

'Hmmm,' I say, chewing on a fingernail.

'What was he like?'

'Nice until he hit puberty and then he became a younger version of what he is today.'

'Nasty, eh?'

I nod. 'Yep. Pretty nasty.'

'How long were you on the estate for?'

'Em, about three or four years. We arrived when I was eight and left when I was eleven or twelve.'

'God, so quite a chunk of your childhood. You must have a few memories tied up with that place. It'll be strange to go back, won't it?'

I look up at him. 'Yes. Yes, it will be.'

Chapter 4

'Aunt Winnie, do we have to travel everywhere at a hundred miles an hour?' I nervously object as Aunt Winnie takes the racing line around a couple of sharp country lanes. We've been in the car ten minutes and for most of that time I've had my eyes closed in fear, making wincing faces which for some reason seem crucial if we are to reach our destination safely.

I normally drive up here with Dom. He passed his driving test on the third attempt and must have set a world record for the fastest fail ever when he said 'All right your way?' to the driving instructor on his first attempt as they pulled out of the test centre. But despite this, he's good enough for me not to have to worry whether I'm wearing matching underwear or not. It's been some time since I travelled with Aunt Winnie and it is a shock to the system. When I was a kid, it took me a while to work out that cows and sheep weren't actually smeared black and white shapes with startled expressions.

'Oh don't be such a boring old fart,' Winnie booms. Jameson stares over his shoulder at me from the even more alarming view point of the front seat and gives me the sort of look that suggests I should either put up or put out. Aunt Winnie sticks her arm out of the driver's window to tell everyone that we intend to turn left come hell or high water.

'Don't you have to retake your driving test at some point, Aunt Winnie?' I ask, hoping it might already be overdue. Then it would simply be the case of a word in the right direction and a possible lifetime ban. I fasten both hands on to the passenger headrest as we make the left turn so that at least the rescuers will find me easily in the wreckage when I'm still clinging on to it.

'IMPUDENCE!' she roars. 'I'm not that old, it's not due for years!' Jameson turns around and gives me another disdainful look from the front seat. I stick my tongue out at him. At least his seatbelt works. This car is so old that the seatbelts in the back are those you have to tighten manually. I might as well have tied myself in with a pair of tights and an Alice band.

I had opted to catch a train from Liverpool Street tonight along with the rest of the harassed Friday night commuters because Dom has the stag do to attend and I am coming back by train anyway after my meeting with Monty Monkwell on Monday. Aunt Winnie has just picked me up from the station and we are en-route to the supermarket to pick up some essential supplies.

Aunt Winnie dramatically swerves around a parked car and I smack my head on the passenger grip, which I realise I should be clinging on to instead. Jameson manages to get away injury-free as he leans automatically into the turns. I loosen one hand unwillingly from the head rest to give the bump a rub.

'Didn't you want to go to the supermarket?' I ask as we

39

streak past it relentlessly on our way towards another roundabout.

'Bugger,' says Aunt Winnie. She then performs a highly illegal 180-degree turn without the aid of hand or indeed any other sort of signal and zooms into the supermarket's car park. I rather foolishly release my seatbelt before we come to a complete standstill and pay the price by getting lodged between the two front seats with my nose rather too close to God knows how many years' worth of crumbs, fluff and dog hair. Jameson gives my ear a couple of licks in sympathy.

'Jameson! Gerroff!' I mumble into the depths.

'Isabel! Stop messing about with Jameson! You'll get him over-excited,' says Aunt Winnie, seizing hold of my arm and giving a few hefty tugs. 'Evening, Mrs Roffe!' she shouts in response to a lady clipping by. My Aunt Winnie is nothing new to the residents of Stowmarket – a bright pea-green Mini with a rather large Labrador strapped in the front is always hard to miss – but you would have thought the sight of her tugging a tall brunette out from between the front seats might have raised a few eyebrows.

'Do you think Jameson could sit in the back for the return journey?' I ask, still wedged.

'Don't be ridiculous, Izzy, he's too big,' she puffs.

'What am I? A midget?'

'Obviously not. Come on, Izzy, make an effort! It's your ARSE that's the problem!' she bellows. Still no reaction from the good citizens of Stowmarket.

I wriggle bad-temperedly out. 'It is NOT my arse,' I say tartly, standing up and straightening my clothes.

'No danger of you suffering from osteoporosis later on in life?' Winnie says as she locks the car and starts striding across the car park.

'Oh, like you have a problem.'

She laughs and puts an arm around me. I relax and grin back and together we walk into the supermarket.

Aunt Winnie is pretty hard to ignore for many reasons, not least of which is her booming voice which is surprisingly loud given her short stature. Possibly due to her lust for fresh air and long walks, she has a nasty habit of talking to you as though you are a quarter of a mile away in a high wind. However, what she lacks in height she more than makes up for in attitude. I wouldn't go so far as to say she is rude, she's just . . . oh all right, she *is* rude.

For as long as I can remember Winnie has dressed from head to toe in varying shades of tweed, along with stout, plain shoes which add nothing to her height and finished off with a perky hat of some description from her eclectic collection. Today she's wearing a deer stalker with a couple of jaunty pheasant feathers sticking out to the side, which get stuck up us taller people's noses every time she turns around. Her hair is cut short and the look is completed by a pair of glasses hanging around her neck that have been repaired with a Mickey Mouse plaster.

Aunt Winnie has been my second mother for as long as I can remember. As children Sophie and I had the solid dependability and kindness of Aunt Winnie during term time and the extravagant parties and indulgences of my parents, wherever they happened to be, during the holidays. But it was Aunt Winnie who really brought us up. She is the one we run to. She is my mother's elder sister, but two such different siblings couldn't exist anywhere. Where my mother floated, my Aunt Winnie stomped. Where my mother tinkled, my Aunt Winnie guffawed. Due to an unfortunate love affair in her youth which, my mother informed me when I was older, was the reason Aunt Winnie had never ventured into marriage (and Must Never Be Talked About), my aunt had lots of room in her emotional and physical life for us. And fortunate for Sophie and me that she did. She is the sheltering harbour that we are always glad to be welcomed back into.

My parents were, and still are, completely vague. My father was too busy with his work and my mother too busy with her parties and guest lists to bother much with Sophie or me. It wouldn't surprise me at all if we had a couple more siblings wandering about that they simply forgot to pick up from school. I remember when I rang them in Italy to tell them my A level results of two Bs and a C. My mother waxed lyrical for a while about how marvellous it all was and then asked what the Bs and the Cs actually stood for. I told her they stood for Bloody Brilliant and Could Do Better, something she believes to this day. By contrast, people find Aunt Winnie enormously formidable. One of our teachers once asked her at parents' evening about her name.

'Winnie?' he remarked, 'how quaint. As in the Pooh?'

She fixed him with a steely look. 'No. As in Mandela.'

Unfortunately Aunt Winnie operates a shopping trolley in much the same fashion as a car. She charges along the aisles yelling at me to throw various items in but without slowing down an iota, so I end up half an aisle away trying to lob dog food tins into a target moving at about forty miles an hour.

The manager breathes a huge sigh of relief as we leave without injury to ourselves or anyone else. I climb back into the ancient car, clamber over the top of Jameson, who is doing his very best to ignore me by staring stoically out of the window, and settle down in the back. It's amazing how a car can collect years' worth of debris. In the back seat wells there are the compulsory sweet wrappers and discarded lists, but also the torn-off limb from a teddy bear that Sophie and I had a tug of love over, the various hair-bands and accessories of bygone ages and even a punk-like silver lipstick. Memories of my teenage years fill my mind.

Another great advantage of Aunt Winnie's parenting, although not wholly appreciated at the time, was the degree of discipline she exerted over Sophie and me, particularly when we were teenagers. This was due in part to the presence of her set of golf clubs, which still sit innocuously enough by the side of the front door. Legend has it within the family that Aunt Winnie actually killed someone with a golf club (although she maintains that she only knocked them out and it was a complete accident). Aunt Winnie's eyes only had to drift in their direction and Sophie and I would miraculously start behaving again. She's apparently tried this trick with the vicar when he won't put her white elephant stall in the best position for the village fête and she says it works just as well with him too. It wasn't until I was much older that I realised how much Aunt Winnie put herself out for us. Mealtimes were designed around our school timetable, trips and outings were arranged or postponed according to our calendars, the ancient Mini was rowed over as if it were our personal possession. When my mother asked Aunt Winnie to tell us about the facts of life, she spent hours teaching us to play poker and drink whisky.

We roar into the driveway of Aunt Winnie's house and screech to a halt. Jameson is let out of his front seat and runs barking down the garden to scare off any errant black-birds that might have been taking advantage of his absence.

spreads for Aunt Winnie). Finally we're sitting opposite each other at the kitchen table.

'So?' she says eagerly.

'What?'

'Izzy, don't be ridiculous! What do you mean "what"? Tell me about the job at Pantiles!'

'I told you most of it when I called.'

'You didn't tell me anything.'

'But you know as much as I do. They're having a charity ball at extremely short notice.'

'How did Monty sound? Did he mention anything about Simon? Are you going to see him?'

'Simon's away,' I say shortly. I'm tired and not particularly up for any elaborate questioning, especially about Simon Monkwell. Too much time has passed to start telling Aunt Winnie the truth about our friendship now. I haven't even told her about meeting him at that party a while ago.

'Oh,' says Aunt Winnie meaningfully. I munch away and try to ignore her interested gaze. I don't know why I didn't tell anyone about Simon's bullying. Obviously the people around us knew we had fallen out but they just presumed it to be some sort of childish rift. Maybe I was afraid of the retributions from Simon, or just afraid of being a cry-baby. But it felt as though the bullying was somehow my fault for not being tough enough to stand up to him or something. 'And how do you feel about that?' Winnie probes.

I don't quite meet her eyes. 'I wouldn't particularly want to be stuck up at that house while Simon plays lord and master.'

'But you two used to be so close.'

'Not since he hit puberty.'

Aunt Winnie nods. 'He doesn't *sound* very nice, I have

to say, from all those newspaper reports. In fact he sounds quite marvellously nasty! But the press don't tend to be very reliable in that area.'

'I think the facts speak for themselves. Besides, he wasn't very nice as a child either.' This time I meet her gaze squarely.

Aunt Winnie frowns, 'No, I remember your father saying that one of the boys had become quite unpleasant, but I couldn't think whether it was Simon or Will.'

'It was Simon,' I say emphatically, 'definitely Simon. It was before we came to live with you so you probably don't remember it as well.'

'Have you told your parents yet?'

'No, I haven't.'

'What about Sophie?'

'I haven't seen Sophie for ages. Is she coming down this weekend?' I ask, pretty eager to get off the subject and on to slightly more comfortable ground. Sophie is younger than me and works in the City, something to do with currency futures and options. She has explained it to me twice and I really don't feel I can ask again. Unlike her older sister, she has thrived in the City. We share a great deal of similar personality traits but she somehow seems to possess a little bit more of each of them. I like to think I am more social than her, but I know jolly well that her legions of friends would disagree with me. I also like to think that I am more creative than her but I know the fabulous flower arrangements in her trendy Notting Hill flat are all hand-chosen and arranged by Sophie Serranti Inc. But we love each other unconditionally and I know that deep down I wouldn't trade my life for hers despite her spacious pad, boggling salary and wardrobe of designer dresses.

'No, she cancelled. Something came up.' Aunt Winnie pours us both some more tea.

'Oh.' I raise my eyebrows in surprise. It might be me being oversensitive but my sister seems to be avoiding me lately. Normally she loves to come and see Dom and me, but I haven't seen her for weeks. It must be my imagination, I can't think of anything I could have done to upset her.

'How are you feeling about Rob?'

'Better, I think.'

'Maybe going back to Pantiles is a huge blessing in disguise?'

'Yeah, it will be nice to get out of London for a while. And I hope it will be . . . I don't know . . . grounding in a way. To go back to where I grew up, I mean.'

'Yes, yes, I suppose so.'

We drift off into silence and I think Aunt Winnie is probably reflecting on my rather sage and perceptive words. She certainly is looking at me in a thoughtful fashion.

'Dear, what colour is that you're wearing?' she pipes up.

'Hmmm?'

'The colour you have on. What trendy name are they giving it now?'

'Er, pink.'

'I really don't think you should wear it. It makes you look like a marshmallow.'

Chapter 5

'Izzy, darling, come and get me. I'm at this piss-pot station of yours. The only taxi has been taken by a mad Irish nun who has been trying to convert me since Liverpool Street. The porter, who by the way looks as though he's been on some serious drugs, tells me there are no buses until tomorrow. So you are going to have to come and get me. And don't hang about, everyone walks with a limp or has a squint. I'm dying for a pee but I daren't go here as there is obviously something wrong with the water. This is absolutely the last time I use public transport. Izzy, are you there?'

'Yeah, yeah, Dominic, I'm here.'

'Are you coming?'

'I'll be straight down. Except that Aunt Winnie wants to pick up some things—'

'Isabel, if you don't want to start walking with a limp yourself, THEN GET DOWN HERE.'

'Oo-er missus. Keep your Calvin Kleins on. I'm just kidding. I'll see you in five minutes.'

I put down the receiver with a smile. It's late on Saturday morning and although I knew Dominic was turning up today he didn't mention when or how and I never thought to ask. I wander through to the kitchen and pick up an apple. 'Aunt Winnie,' I say between bites, 'Dominic is at the station.'

'That's nice, dear.'

'Hmmm.' I munch in silence for a few seconds. 'I think he might need picking up.'

'You have been more than twenty minutes,' Dominic hisses at me while he swivels his foot on his cigarette. He kisses Aunt Winnie and pats Jameson. 'I had to use the loo in there. Look, I've caught a squint.' He screws up one eye in a thoroughly overdramatic fashion.

'Why didn't you come by car?'

'Because the traffic was so appalling last time I thought the train would be easier. But my mother never told me about the dangers of travelling with Irish nuns.' He puts on an Irish accent, 'Glory be child, he's a great fella that Jesus, absolutely top-hole. You're an eejit for not wanting to be around him, so you are. Have you read the book?' He reverts back to his normal accent, 'Obviously I replied "which book?" which was like a red rag to a bull. You see, public transport. You leave yourself wide open to conversion with Irish nuns. You'd think they'd have a warning about it, wouldn't you?'

'What about the Tube? Don't you count that as public transport?'

'People don't talk to you on the Tube.'

We squash ourselves into the back of the Mini. Dominic is respectful of Jameson's prior claim to the front seat.

'They are a great race, the Irish, aren't they?' comments Aunt Winnie. 'I once sat opposite an Irish bloke on a three-hour train journey. He got out a five thousand-piece jigsaw, started it on the table and then at the end of the journey swept it all back into the box again. I had the sky end. It was jolly tricky.'

'I read in the paper about an Irishman who was dead at his desk at work for five days before anyone noticed,' adds Dom. 'Apparently he was always either really pissed or really hungover and so usually sat with his head cradled in his arms. It was only on Saturday, when they remembered he never came in at weekends, that they discovered he was dead. Now that's the kind of company I would like to work for, not your Mafia-like ex-boyfriend's father's one. So is the vicar talking to you again?' he asks Aunt Winnie.

She grins wickedly and starts to give us the low-down on a new accumulation of village mishaps, climaxing in her nearly running the vicar over. It seems my Aunt Winnie has found a new sport called vicar-baiting. The village's new happy-clappy vicar called Jason arrived about six months ago and made the mistake of calling on Aunt Winnie within a week. So he's not quite as happy-clappy now – in fact, he's probably close to a nervous breakdown. Aunt Winnie says she's sure that God wouldn't begrudge her a little harmless fun, especially since the BBC axed *Eldorado*.

We trundle down to the village pub as Dominic pronounces himself incapable of lasting the whole three-minute drive without a drink to break the journey. We sit in the inglenook by the fireplace of the Oak and Lion, having been led straight there by Jameson who knows his local and his favourite seat well. Aunt Winnie tries to decide where she has got to in the pub's mammoth wall of whiskies. The pub landlord has rather helpfully put them in alphabetical order for her. Aunt Winnie is somewhat fond of whisky, hence Jameson's name, and once she finishes the wall she just starts again.

'I think I was in the "I" section, Izz. Can you remember?'

'I think you were, I remember having a conversation about Islay.'

'So we did. Then I'll have something beginning with 'J', please, Dom. And a bag of crisps for Jameson. Cheese and onion please.'

'His wish is my command.' Dom turns to me, 'Izz?'

'Er . . .' I'm always a bit stuck when it comes to drinking in pubs. I never know what to have. And a white wine spritzer always seems too twee for words in the company of hardened alcoholics like Aunt Winnie and Dom. 'Whatever you're having,' I say bravely, almost instantly regretting the words.

Dominic wanders off to the bar. There's a slight pause. 'Aunt Winnie?' I say, for something has been bothering me since this whole Monkwell thing started, 'how did we come to rent a house on the Pantiles estate and not at the army digs? Was it just because of the stables for Mum?' It's amazing what you don't query in childhood. I remember my parents buying Sophie and me mugs with our names on them when we were about ten, but they had run out of Isabel so they bought an Isaac one instead and sold it to me on the grounds that it was my name in French. If they could get that past my razor-sharp consciousness you can see why it never crossed my mind until now to ask why we moved to the Pantiles estate.

She shrugs slightly. 'Your parents thought it would be good for you and Sophie to be in the country for a while. And as I recall, my dear, you also wanted to ride horses.'

'Me?' I say incredulously. Surely she is thinking of a

different Isabel, or should I say Isaac. This Isabel/Isaac wouldn't like to come within a metre of those smelly, hoof-stomping creatures.

'Your mother rode quite a bit and I think you got it into your head that you wanted to ride too. Of course, as soon as you fell off you decided that you didn't really like it.'

I lean forward eagerly. 'Was I travelling at speed when I fell off? Attempting some sort of jump?'

'No, dear, the horse was standing stock still in the yard at the time. You just lost your balance.'

Ah. This is probably the reason I have conveniently erased the entire episode from my memory. That and the smell.

'But how did my parents know the Monk—' I persist but Dominic's return interrupts us. 'I was feeling inspired by my nun so I got myself a Guinness,' he says.

'I hate Guinness.'

'I know, so I got you a Drambuie and ginger ale.' Obviously.

He unceremoniously plonks two glasses on to the table and then goes back to collect his Guinness, which is breathing or settling or whatever they do to it.

'Are you sure I was on "I" before, Izz?' asks Aunt Winnie. 'Maybe it was "T"?'

'Ho hum, down the hatch anyway!'

We chink glasses and I take a tentative sip of my Drambuie and ginger ale. Interesting mix of flavours. I look over towards Dominic who is talking animatedly with the landlord. He is laughing at something, his head thrown backwards, and I find myself grinning too. Dom has the largest, most infectious smile I have ever seen. He's lovely-looking in a foppish kind of way, not usually my cup of tea, but very appealing when the man in question is as open and unarrogant as Dom. He has dark blond hair which at first I thought was artfully untidy but have since learned is simply untidy, a slim build and an engaging face. Extremely well-connected too; his family is renowned in London circles and Dom is considered to be very much the eligible bachelor. But even if I wanted to marry him, I doubt he would return the compliment. You see, I have just found out he's gay.

Dominic has no shortage of admirers but I have started to see a pattern emerging. He has never actually pursued any of these girls himself. His Aunt Agnes, presumably desperate for great-nephews and -nieces, regularly places girls in his path and Dom dutifully trots them around the block a couple of times and then politely bids them farewell. Girls from work, on the Tube, in the local coffee shop have all at one time or another pressed their numbers into his hand and begged him to call them. But instead of becoming big-headed by this and casually bedding them all, Dom takes them out, shows them a wonderful time, listens to all their problems and then duly deposits them back from whence they came.

I have never probed him about his actions because when your best friend is male it is sometimes difficult to talk about these things, but I did presume he'd had his wicked way with some of them although I never knew for sure because he never brought them back to our flat. Therein lies my error. Dom is a male of the pink-blooded variety. Definitely. How do I know? Because one of his ex-dates told me so. I was busy at a drinks party only a few weeks ago when a girl called Cecily came up to me and re-introduced herself. We stood chatting for a few minutes and then she said, 'It's such a pity about Dominic, isn't it?' I was slightly mystified, wondering what on earth he'd done now, when I noticed she was trying to clock my reaction. Oldest trick in the book. So I casually agreed that it was a bit of a pity and looked meaningfully back at her. Then it all came out in a rush – how he had told her he was gay but was still confused himself about it and could she keep it to herself. Which she obviously couldn't.

I was completely and utterly shocked. Not at Dominic being gay; I couldn't care less if he is or not. I was shocked that he hadn't told me. I like to think I'm his best friend and yet he hadn't said a thing. And then things started slotting into place. The lack of a girlfriend, his penchant for Kylie, his old-fashioned plimsolls, the way he loves to verbally dissect everything and most of all his NICENESS. Yes, all the signs had been blazing and I had failed to see them. That was almost exactly four weeks ago. I remember so precisely because a day later Rob finished with me and things took on a different perspective. There were obviously more immediate issues to think about than Dom being gay. Now everything has settled down again there just never seems to be a good time to talk to him about it – I can hardly say would you mind passing the salt and, by the way, when were you thinking about coming out? over supper. Besides, these things are private and I sort of think that when he is ready to tell me he will.

As Dom wanders back over to us, fishing in his pockets for his cigarettes, his mobile begins to belt out the Batman theme and he retrieves it from his back pocket. He has one of those flash phones where you can pre-programme the ringtone to indicate who's calling. I, for instance, am Hong Kong Phooey. Which is why I forever regret telling Dom the story about how my necklace got caught in a filing cabinet at work and it took them more than ten minutes to free me.

'Hello you!' he answers with an air of familiarity. Now I may be downright insensitive to some things but one thing I can spot is atmosphere. And there seems to be a jolly intimate one between Dom and whoever is on the other end of the phone. Besides which, Dominic obviously knows the person well enough to give them their own ringtone. Jameson and I both prick up our ears; I would like to think it is because he is as interested in Dominic's love life as me but in actual fact it's because Scooby, the pub cat, has just entered the room. I listen intently while ostensibly playing with a beer mat but to no avail. I would challenge Morse, Frost or indeed Poirot to gather anything from the stream of 'Hmm . . . yes, I think so . . . hmmm . . . yeah . . .' Eventually Dom tells the caller to hang on and then walks outside to continue the conversation in private.

'Did you hear that, Aunt Winnie?' I ask in a dramatic whisper.

'Er, what?'

'That.' I spit the word out emphatically.

'What?'

'Dom's conversation with Batman.'

'There wasn't that much to hear, was there?'

'I think he's seeing someone.'

'How on earth can you come to that conclusion from that conversation?' asks Aunt Winnie in genuine puzzlement.

'Now that I think about it, he's been a bit secretive of late. Keeps ending phone calls when I come into the room and then telling me it was a wrong number.'

'Why wouldn't he tell you if he was seeing someone? I thought you told each other everything.'

SMACK! I dramatically punch my fist into my other hand. 'Now THAT, Aunt Win, is the question. Why wouldn't he tell me?'

'Er, I don't know. I've just asked you that.'

I open my mouth to confess all my suspicions but close it again when I realise that Dominic probably wouldn't thank me for telling Aunt Winnie before he has even said anything to me. Luckily we're interrupted.

'Who was that?' I ask innocently as Dom sits down at the table.

'Oh, it was, er, Pete.'

I bob my head around in an oh-so-it-was-Pete kind of way.

'What's for lunch, Aunt Win?' asks Dom.

We wend our way home after we've finished our drinks and Aunt Winnie busies herself putting sausages under the grill while Dom and I choose a bottle of homemade wine from Aunt Win's diverse collection. Ginger, raspberry, apple; the list goes on and on. We eventually settle for rhubarb.

'Two sausages or three, Dom?' asks Aunt Winnie.

'Just the two for me, thanks. On account of me being—'

'A vegetarian,' we both finish. We're used to Dom's idea of being vegetarian, which is selective to say the least and extremely part-time. He seems to think that having smaller portions of meat makes him a vegetarian. It is simply an attention-seeking device that allows him to get his meals before everyone else on aeroplanes. For a long time, whenever he was asked a question such as, 'Excuse me, can you tell me the time?' he would reply, 'No, I'm sorry, I'm a vegetarian.'

With contented sighs Dom and I move ourselves and our beakers of wine towards the window seat. I check carefully between the cushions for the odd bits of chewed bone that Jameson likes to hide there; it took three trips to the dry cleaner's to get a bone stain out of my lovely lilac trousers. Having cleared any debris, I lean with my back against the wall, rest my legs on Dom's lap while he lights up, using his now empty cigarette packet as an ashtray, and take a tentative sip of my rhubarb wine.

'Blo-ody hell, Aunt Winnie,' I say when I've managed to draw a gasp of air. This, I remember, is why I didn't mind too much about the bone stain at the time.

'God,' says Dominic, blinking in surprise. 'You've brewed pure fire and brimstone. It kind of hits you just behind the eyes.'

'Yes, I'm rather pleased with that one,' says Aunt Win, looking proud. We all agree that if ever Aunt Winnie wants to come out of retirement, wine-making should be her new career. 'How's work going, Dom?' Winnie asks.

He wrinkles his nose and pulls a face. 'I'm thinking of jacking it in.'

This is news to me. I sit up. 'Since when?'

'Oh, I've been thinking about it for a while now.' He doesn't quite meet my eyes and I know immediately that some sort of outside influence has been at work. And I could probably guess at 'Batman'. 'I really think it's about time I took my novel a bit more seriously. If I gave up my desk job then I could write full-time.'

'What about money?' I ask.

'Well, actually, I thought I could start working at a few more of your events, Izzy. I could work in the evenings and write during the day. You'd get me a bit of extra silver

57

service here and there, wouldn't you?' Dom often comes and helps out at my events for some extra cash. He's very charming and everyone loves him. 'In fact, will you see if you can wangle me some work at the Monkwell event? I would love to see Pantiles!'

'Of course,' I say, but my mind is elsewhere. I'm thinking that my last link with Rob will be lost.

I spend most of Monday morning supposedly working on my laptop but in reality changing outfits every half hour or so.

'What about this one, Aunt Winnie?' I ask from the top of the stairs.

She looks up from practising her golf swing in the hallway. Jameson is wisely nowhere to be seen. 'Izz, darling, they are all starting to look the bally same.'

'That's because you've already seen this one; it's the first outfit I put on this morning.'

She looks a little fatigued at this piece of information. 'Just don't wear any flowery stuff and then you'll look fine. Tell me what you're trying to achieve and then we'll see.' She abandons her swing and leans on the golf club for support.

'I want to look efficient.'

'The second one then.' She looks relieved at this apparently immediate decision. In days of yore it used to take a good few hours before Sophie would leave the house to go anywhere important. She takes up the golf club again.

'And yet at the same time feminine? I don't want to look as though I'm too aggressive.'

Aunt Winnie pretends to consider this but I know she's bluffing because she obviously lost interest in the subject about half an hour ago. I'm starting to bore myself as well.

'The third one then.'

I nod and disappear to get changed. I am inexplicably nervous at seeing the Monkwells again and I desperately want to make a good impression.

Aunt Winnie shifts down into second gear and urges the Mini on to new heights of speed. I close my eyes and try to think of positive things to say during my meeting with Monty Monkwell. I have an awful tendency to say the first thing that comes into my head when I'm nervous. At my first-ever job interview, when asked what I liked to do in my spare time, I completely lost my usual self-composure and said, 'I like to eat toast'. Not very professional.

'Aunt Winnie? Have you seen anything of the Monkwell family recently?'

'I've only seen the pictures of Simon in the papers. Haven't seen the rest of the family since you left Pantiles. You know that Elizabeth, their mother, died?'

'Yeah, Mum told me. Quite a few years ago though, wasn't it?'

She nods and I stare out of the window, lost in thought. Neither of us has been back to Pantiles for more than fifteen years. Although it is only about thirty minutes' drive from Aunt Winnie's house it might as well be on the other side of the world.

Finally we start the descent into the Monkwells' valley, and I mean that in the proprietorial sense as they own everything as far as the eye can see. Little copses of trees and huddles of cottages dot the plush landscape to the left, separated occasionally by low-slung and sometimes collapsing dry-stone walls. I look over to the right and give a little gasp. Like something out of *Jurassic Park*, animals speckle the pastures.

'Deer, Aunt Winnie!' I cry.

Aunt Winnie glances at me in the mirror. It's the only thing she ever uses it for. 'Yes, darling?'

'No!' I lean between the front seats and point off to the right. 'I mean, they're keeping deer now!' It is always a mistake to distract Aunt Winnie when she is driving. We mount the verge, drive along at a thirty-degree angle for a while and then plop back down on the tarmac.

'They must be trying to make some money out of the estate,' I say, ignoring our little diversion.

'Well, Simon is the eternal businessman! Stags can be very dangerous in season though. Wouldn't want to get caught out in the open with one of those.'

I give Aunt Winnie a look. She says the same thing about all animals. Horses, pigs, cows. I think it's because she and Dominic love to see me running like hell on our walks whenever we come across any wildlife. I can never tell whether she is serious or not.

We arrive at the picturesque village of Pantiles. The Monkwells also own all the houses here. I look around me with interest; after all, this was my stomping ground for a few years. Amazingly, the village of Pantiles has managed to remain completely unaltered. My head swivels from side to side as I recognise and remember. The little village shop that doubled up as the post office, where Sophie and I used to haggle with the proprietor over the maximum number of penny sweets we could buy with our pocket money. The village green with its ancient cherry tree. More than fifty years ago the then vicar grafted a pink blossoming cherry on to an existing white one, and every year the core of the tree blossoms pink while surrounded by a halo of white. There's a gnarled old seat under the tree which is known as the wedding seat, supposedly because the tree looks like a bride from a certain angle, and all couples who sit on it are supposed to get married. The fact that you would need to have taken a kilo of the magic mushrooms that purportedly grow in the local woods in order to see the similarity seems to have completely passed the locals by.

Next to the post office is the little Saxon church, and opposite the church are the giant wrought iron gates which I remember used to be closed every evening by one of the gamekeepers. These gates are the only opening in the wall that encompasses the estate, house and grounds. I lean forward as we pass through them and then get thrown around as we bounce and grunt our way up the slight hill, weaving between the various pot holes, the road flanked by tall poplar trees. In the spring, daffodils wave from the banks either side of us for as far as the eye can see, but these are long dead and gone. We finally pop up over the hill and the house comes into view. If you branch off right at this point, the driveway leads to our old house hidden in the woods, but we mostly went unnoticed as it is hard to draw your eyes away from the Monkwell domicile. We pause for a minute while Aunt Winnie fights to find the appropriate gear. I stare at the grand old house with fondness while Aunt Winnie grunts and thrusts the gearstick in all directions. My reliving of *Brideshead Revisited* is shattered by Aunt Winnie shouting, 'Come on, you bastard car!' into my right ear and we charge forward at quite a lick down the hill.

The house was designed by a former pupil of Lutyens and I can now clearly see hints of the master's trademark style. It sits in a perfect location in the cleft of a gentle valley, protected from the harsher elements and yet accessible to the sunlight. The gardens slope gently away while dozens of mullioned windows dot the house's façade and reflect the perfectly manicured lawns.

Aunt Winnie shoots up the drive, through an archway and into the cobbled courtyard at the back of the house. The front door was only ever used on formal occasions and I'm guessing this isn't one of them. On the other side of the courtyard sits the seemingly deserted stable yard.

'Looks like they don't own horses anymore, Aunt Winnie,' I say and point towards the yard.

'Simon sold them all after Elizabeth died.' She snorts to herself. 'I'll wait here for you. Good luck.' Aunt Winnie leans over and opens the passenger door, undoes Jameson's seatbelt and shoves him out. I push the passenger seat forward and clamber out reluctantly after him.

Chapter 6

As I wait at the back door, I look down at my stomach and pull it in slightly. Five days of dieting has left me a wonderful three pounds lighter and I can already see the difference. Elle Macpherson I am not but I don't think anyone's going to divert me to the delivery ward now. I swivel round to look at Aunt Winnie, whose idea of low profile means heavyweight opera booming from the car. I make a couple of flapping hand gestures at her which she completely ignores.

The door clatters open and I swivel back. A tall lady with a very thin mouth stares expectantly at me.

'Hello! I'm here to see Monty Monkwell.' I beam. She doesn't.

'You are?'

'Isabel Serranti. He is expecting me.'

She attempts a smile but actually just stretches her mouth taut across her teeth. 'Follow me, Miss Serranti.'

She turns back into the kitchen and as I follow her I notice that she is extremely thin and bony. Already we are destined not to get on. Her dark hair is swept back in a severe bun and I would guess she is in her mid-thirties.

I take a good look around the huge kitchen and notice with surprise that not one item of decor has changed. When I was a child it looked fresh and modern with its pale lemon walls and curtains and rustic, farmhouse-style units. Now it just seems faded and shabby, but maybe that's because of my older, more pedantic eye. The same enormous scrubbed oak table sits in the middle of the vast room, surrounded by chairs of all different shapes and sizes. There is a very familiar smell in the air which shoots me back to my childhood more vividly than any photograph could. A combination, I think, of dog, a particular washing powder and the smell of baking. Our progress is arrested by a gaggle of dogs who fall on me joyously. I pat them all, trying desperately to get to a small white one who is constantly being butted out by the rest.

'BASKET!' the woman barks. We all jump and they slope off to their corner. I'm sorely tempted to follow them.

'This way,' she says and sets off at a roaring pace down the labyrinth of corridors. I race to catch up with her.

'Have you been with the Monkwells for long?' I ask politely when I do.

'Long enough.'

I bob my head around and fish desperately for more innocuous comments. 'And you are?' I ask politely.

'Mrs Delaney.' We obviously aren't on a first-name basis here. 'I'm their housekeeper. Have been for the last eight years.' Her chin tilts up and she looks defiantly at me. There's some sort of challenge in those words.

'Well, Mrs Delaney, it's very nice to meet you. I daresay we'll be seeing quite a bit of each other until this charity ball.' I give a cheery smile to intimate how marvellous that will be.

Mrs Delaney gives a snort to indicate exactly what she thinks of the idea. 'Charity ball,' she says in the sort of way you would say 'my arse'. 'You wouldn't have had this nonsense while the lady of the house was alive.' This has more than a slight twang of Mrs-Danvers-talking-to-the-second-Mrs-de-Winter about it.

'I know. Elizabeth always liked the estate to remain strictly private,' I say sweetly, just to remind her that I also have some history with the place.

She looks at me sharply but chooses to say nothing more about the subject.

My Aunt Winnie, although achieving top-class honours in the art of being rude, at least couples it with a form of charm. I suspect Mrs Delaney lacks the latter. We fall into silence as we whistle past numerous closed doors until we reach the heart of the house: an absolutely enormous hallway that connects the several wings. I stifle a small gasp and involuntarily slow down. In my childhood memory this hallway was the largest, grandest thing I had ever seen. It has a huge arched, cathedral-like ceiling separated by several oak beams. An enormous staircase begins in the middle of the hall and then splits into two after the first landing. The grey marble fireplace is at least six feet tall and ten feet wide. But in my memory the hall was warm and welcoming, full of voluptuous velvet curtains and cushions in rich colours along with plenty of lush greenery. Now it is cold and stark. The fireplace is desolate and no fire has been lit there for quite some time. The plants have disappeared, the velvets faded and the place smells of damp. I shiver involuntarily and stop in front of the fireplace. I look up.

There is something bothering me there. Something I can't quite put my finger on.

'Miss Serranti?' Mrs Delaney queries. I look over to her as she stands in front of one of the doors, her hand resting on the handle.

'Sorry,' I say hastily and walk over as she knocks firmly.

'Come in!' calls a voice from within.

'Miss Serranti is here to see you, Monty,' says Mrs Delaney. I feel a smidgen of surprise at her familiar use of his first name but then Monty never had any of Elizabeth Monkwell's frostiness running through him. She steps to one side to let me enter the library.

A much older version of the Monty I remember hastily drops his newspaper and levers himself out of one of the chairs. He seems to have shrunk considerably since the last time I saw him but then I suppose I was shorter then.

'Izzy, me dear!' he outstretches his arms, 'how wonderful! I've been looking forward to seeing you all morning!' He kisses me warmly on one cheek. 'You've grown up into a beautiful young lady!'

I blush slightly, which I hope makes me appear prettily dainty rather than menopausal.

Monty's a terribly distinguished man. I remember regarding him with absolute awe during my childhood but he always had a friendly word for us and some sweets tucked around his person. Like Aunt Winnie, he's overly fond of tweed. His hair is much shorter than I remember it – he used to favour a Hugh Grant floppy style – but there's still plenty of it. He's dressed in faded corduroys, an open-necked checked shirt, a jumper and a tweed jacket which is patched at the elbows, seemingly oblivious to the weather outside. The sun streams in the large bay window at the back of the room, highlighting a little dust storm dancing above an antique desk.

'I was sorry to hear about Elizabeth,' I say gently.

'Bad business.' He shakes his head slowly and looks sad. 'It's a few years ago now. Time is a great healer.'

He takes me by the elbow and we walk towards the middle of the room.

'Could we have some coffee, Mrs Delaney?' he asks over his shoulder. 'Would coffee be okay for you, Izzy? Or would you prefer tea?'

'No, coffee would be lovely,' I say and smile at Mrs Delaney who melts away, shutting the door behind her. Whenever we are doing functions which involve non-company staff, either directly or indirectly, we go to enormous lengths to try to keep them on side. It's less trouble in the long run. I'm not sure how I'm going to pull this off with Mrs Delaney.

Monty plonks me down in a squishy Colefax armchair in front of the un-lit but ready-laid fire and then takes up his recently vacated seat opposite me. The library is a beautiful but relatively small room of oak panels and floor-to-ceiling bookshelves. I take a few minutes to pat the elderly Labrador lying at the foot of Monty's chair. The dog apologises for not getting up with a loud thump-thump of his tail.

'You won't remember old Jasper. I leave the other dogs in the kitchen so he can have a bit of peace and quiet. Doesn't like too much fuss nowadays. Golly! He wouldn't even have been born when you left here! Can it really have been that long, Izzy?'

'It's been a while,' I smile.

'Does the old place bring back memories?'

'Lots!' I say brightly, thinking that he would be horrified to learn that some of them involve his bullying son.

'So tell me about everything you've done since you left here! How are your parents? How's Sophie?' His eyes twinkle at me.

I embark on a halting rendition of everyone's health until Mrs Delaney interrupts us with coffee. She brings in a tray holding a large cafetière, mis-matched china cups, a large jug of milk and a plate of oaty biscuits. She doesn't make eye contact with either of us but plonks the tray on the small coffee table and makes her exit.

'Thank you, Mrs Delaney,' calls Monty to her departing back.

'Thank you!' I echo.

He shifts forward to the edge of his chair, surveys the tray and rubs his hands together. 'Biscuits! She's in one of her good moods!' he announces. Really. One of her good moods. God help us all. 'But no sugar,' he frowns.

'Oh, I don't take it,' I interject.

'Good!' He looks relieved. I wouldn't have fancied my chances if I had. It's obvious neither of us would have had the courage to ask for any.

We chat about my family some more until I tentatively ask how Will is.

'Will? He works here on the estate now.'

'Does he?' I say in surprise. I always thought he would do something wildly exciting. He was the thrill-seeker out of all of us.

'Yes, he's our new estate manager! Got back from travelling a year ago!'

'I expected Will to become an astronaut or a deep sea diver or something!'

'He used to be a bit wild but he's settled down now. Besides, we desperately needed an estate manager. Simon, as you probably know, has been a bit busy with his various companies to worry about Pantiles.'

'Yes, I, er, have read a bit about him.' I glance down at my coffee cup in embarrassment.

'He's not as bad as they say, Izzy,' Monty says softly. 'The press can get things wrong.'

But I've had first-hand experience of him, I want to cry. And I daresay many a mass murderer has an indignant parent sticking up for them.

'He's done awfully well,' I mumble instead. 'So where did Will go travelling?' I add, pretty keen to get off the subject of Simon.

'All over the world! Let's see, we had postcards from Africa and South America – he climbed to that lost city place, 'straordinary how they lumped bits of rock up there, not much oxygen. Then Indonesia and Thailand and Australia. He'd probably love to have a chat with you about the places you've lived in!'

'Yes, that would be lovely, if I can remember back that far! Sophie and I have been in England since I was eight.' I smile back at him. 'And what about you, Monty? Estate still keeping you busy?'

'No! I haven't run the estate for a few years! When Elizabeth died I simply couldn't face it any more. Simon has been in charge since then; after all, it is his inheritance!'

Again I look down at my cup in embarrassment. It seems pretty clear to me, and also to Monty judging by the uncomfortable silence, that Simon Monkwell couldn't give a toss for his inheritance. Monty eventually says, 'I suppose we ought to get on and talk about this charity event!

'Yes!' I say rather too eagerly. I reach for my notebook. 'I was so glad when your company said you were available,' Morty continues. 'Of course, as soon as Mrs Charlesty told me you were a party planner I knew that we couldn't have anyone else! I'm sorry we could only offer you a smallish fee. Because it was such short notice I had to call Simon to ask his permission and he told me it would be ample.' Ample isn't quite the word. 'And because it's for a charity I didn't want to extract too much money from them.'

They should count themselves lucky Simon isn't here then, I think to myself. 'Oh don't worry about that!' I say aloud. 'Gerald, my MD, was perfectly happy to accept it. So what changed your mind about holding an event here? I always thought Pantiles was strictly private.'

'Simon has been talking about trying to make Pantiles more commercial for a while now, so while we haven't been actively looking for business I thought it would be silly not to take the opportunity when it came along. Besides, it'll give an old cove like me something to do! Thought it would be fun!'

I look at him dubiously. He obviously hasn't been stuck up a ladder at three in the morning when a bird of paradise theme isn't working and Aidan is having the screaming hysterics. 'What information has the charity given you so far?'

'Well, there will be about five hundred guests.'

'So a marquee on the lawn then?' Please tell me they've booked it. Please tell me they've booked it.

'They're using the marquee company that they had booked for the other venue.' Phew.

'And what specifically do they want us to supply?'

'Um, everything.'

'Everything?'

'Er, yes. They gave me a list.' He fishes around in his inside pocket for a few seconds. 'Here! They want catering – they've given me a price per head for that – decorations, tables and chairs, cutlery, crockery and glassware and entertainment.'

I scribble all of this down. 'So not much then,' I say with a sigh while cross-checking the requirements against my standard list of questions.

'*Is* it too much?' Monty looks anxious.

'No, no!' I say in what I hope is a comforting manner. 'We've just got our work cut out!'

'You will be able to do it though?' he asks anxiously.

Gerald always gives me carte blanche on whether to accept a job or not. Ordinarily I would think twice about accepting this one but I don't hesitate for a second when I say, 'But of course!' I am rewarded by Monty looking excessively relieved.

'Your fee isn't going to be enough, is it?'

'Don't worry! We have the catering for five hundred to factor in now; we weren't expecting that bonus! Can I meet with the charity to discuss details? Soon?' I endeavour to keep a slightly panicky note out of my voice. Clients don't tend to like it.

'I took the liberty of arranging a meeting this Thursday. The marquee company is coming on Friday. They haven't seen the site yet. You must stay with us, Izzy, I absolutely insist.'

I'll be moving in straightaway, I think to myself. 'Thanks, Monty. That'll help. It's a bit of trek back to London.'

'Oh, by the way, they said they wanted a circus theme.'

'Sorry?'

'You know, big top, that sort of thing! A circus!'

I have a feeling that's what we're going to get with or without my help. 'Marvellous!' I say and smile brightly. 'What will they think of next?' Yes, indeed.

I can't do much more without speaking to the charity first so we get up and wander towards the kitchen. 'Are you parked at the back?' asks Monty.

'Yes, Aunt Winnie brought me over.'

'Winnie did? Why didn't you say, Izzy? She should have come in!'

'Sorry, I always forget you must have met her once or twice!'

We charge along the corridor at a rate of knots. Monty strides across the kitchen and flings open the back door. The pea-green Mini still has opera booming out of it and Monty raps loudly on the driver's window. Aunt Winnie jumps in horror but her face soon spreads into a wide grin and she leaps out as best she can from the Mini.

'Monty, you old dog!' she roars.

'Winnie, me dear, how the devil are you?' he booms.

God, it's like being at a convention for the hard of hearing. They don't know each other very well but Aunt Winnie always makes an impression.

I hang about while they noisily ask about each other's health and generally get skittish until Monty says, 'I've suggested that Izzy comes and stays with us for a few days at the end of the week to sort out this charity malarkey. Will you come and have supper with us?'

'Love to! As long as we're not having pork. Can't abide the stuff.'

'No pig it is then! I'll tell Mrs Delaney. Shall we say Thursday?'

'Marvellous!'

'Izzy, why don't you come over on Wednesday night so you're fresh for the charity folk on Thursday?'

'Thanks, Monty. That would be great.'

The following day I get into work early. I have a ton of stuff to do before I return to the estate at the end of the week. Since the job at Pantiles will involve so much work, I'll hand over all my other events to Aidan, except Lady Boswell's Nordic Ice Feast which no one will take on the pain of death. I daresay Aidan is not going to be very happy; there are some monster clients involved.

Stephanie is puffing on a cigarette and rather dispirit-edly typing with one finger while trying to read the *Daily Mail*.

'Morning!' I say brightly. 'Any messages?'

'Where have you been?'

'Er, in Suffolk.'

'Oh.'

'Any messages?' I repeat.

'On your desk.'

'*On* my desk?' I query. Last time they were found next to the kettle.

She raises her eyes heavenward and mutters something about Hitler which I choose to ignore.

I walk through to the main office. Aidan is having an animated discussion with someone in the corner and waving around what looks like a pair of lederhosen. I turn on my computer and sit down. Aidan has spotted my arrival and comes rushing over, still brandishing the clothes.

'Izzy! What do the Swiss eat?'

I blink for a minute while trying to engage my brain. 'Em, Toblerone.'

'What else? What else?' he demands.

'Er, er' – I blink distractedly – 'I don't know, fondue? Wiener Schnitzel? Or is that German? Why?'

'We're launching a new Swiss cheese and I'm trying to get some ideas together for the launch party. We're having the VIP invites hand-delivered by a yodeller. We've got a couple coming in later to audition,' he giggles and sits down opposite me. 'How was the estate? Has it changed at all?'

'I think it's gone to pot actually. It feels . . . neglected.' Privately I think Simon could do with spending more time looking after his home and less time trying to take over other people's companies. Just a personal opinion of course. Completely unbiased.

'I think you're *so* lucky to get that project. I would *die* for it.'

'Aidan, it's a ball for five hundred and they've decided they want a circus theme.'

'Oh,' he says, not looking quite so enthusiastic anymore. 'A circus theme? At such short notice? Which sick individual thought of that?'

'I don't know but Dominic and I certainly have our work cut out.'

'Dominic's helping you?'

'Yes, I'm going to ask him to be my runner if I can get Gerald to agree.' I look at Aidan suspiciously. 'Why?'

'Oh, no reason. How is he, by the way?'

'Just fine. I'll tell him you asked after him, shall I?'

Aidan smiles a secret smile to himself. 'Send him my regards.'

I open my mouth to find out more but my phone rings and I pick it up.

'Darling! So *glad* to have caught you!' It's my mother

calling from Hong Kong. She still hasn't gathered that through the marvels of modern technology you don't have to speak as though you are talking to a very old, very deaf aunt. She enunciates key words and speaks very loudly and slowly. 'Your *receptionist*, what's her name, *Clementine?*' How on earth has she managed to get Clementine from Stephanie? She doesn't pause to hear my reply but sweeps on. 'She *said* you've been *out* all morning. Now the *important* thing is, and your father is making *frantic* hand signals at me, do you know who *won* the 2.30 at *Kempton?*'

'Er, no.'

She puts her hand over the top of the mouthpiece and shouts, presumably at my father, 'Darling, she doesn't know, please don't go on . . . all right, I'll ask her.' She comes back to me. 'He wants to know who *won* the *premiership.*'

'Mum, I don't know who's in the premiership, let alone who won it. Don't they have English newspapers out there?'

'Yes. But they are always *late*, then we *forget* to look and by the time we've remembered I've *wrapped* the potato peelings in them.' She puts her hand back over the mouthpiece and talks once more to my father. This three-way conversation is starting to play on my nerves. We always talk like this on the phone; the only way to have an actual conversation with my mother is when my father is out. 'No, she doesn't know, darling. . . look, do you want to speak to her? . . . well then, shut up.' She comes back to me. 'Anyway, darling, how *are* you?'

I hesitate for a moment. I could tell them about going back to Pantiles but the dialogue-á-trois would take roughly an hour to complete and I'm not sure I could survive it. I could also inform them of my break-up with Rob but since I didn't tell them I was going out with him in the first place it seems pointless. A few thousand miles isn't the only distance between us all.

'Absolutely fine,' I lie in answer to her question. 'How are things with you?'

On-stage: '*Chaos*. We've got Darth Vole *coming* for *dinner*.'

Off-stage: 'I know he's not bloody well called that.'

'Who?' I ask.

On-stage: '*Local* Chinese *dignitary*.'

Off-stage: 'Of course I will learn his real name by tonight.'

'English food or Chinese?' I ask, trying to keep my side of the conversation going.

On-stage: 'Chinese, *unfortunately*. I still haven't mastered *chopsticks*. I only managed to get three grains of *rice* to eat last night and those were by *flicking* them.'

Off-stage: 'No, it's Isabel, not Sophie.'

'Mum, call me next week.'

'I know, when your *father*'s out.'

'Give him my love.'

'Bye, darling.'

Just as I put the phone down, Gerald pops his head around his office door and yells through his tannoy: 'ISABEL! In here!'

I collect a notepad and pencil and walk over to Gerald's office. He's shut the door again so I give it a light tap and walk in. He's frantically scribbling on a wipe-board.

'Are you okay?' I ask tentatively. 'You look a little, er, tense.' He looks like a rabbit caught in headlights.

'No! Just very alert! Couple of late parties and a few too many espressos. How was yesterday?' he asks.

'Good.' I briefly outline the core points of the meeting for him.

'Are you really going to be able to manage all that work?'

'I'm handing most of my parties over to Aidan.'

'Oh God, Izzy, did you have to? That's going to make him more histrionic than ever. What about Lady Boswell's Nordic Ice Feast?'

'No one would take it. You wouldn't—'

'No. I wouldn't,' he snaps. 'You'll just have to fit that one in somehow. It sounds as though you'll have to spend quite a few days up at Pantiles. I'm not sure the fee is going to be enough.'

'Well, they've already got some things arranged.' I want to go back to Pantiles no matter how much work is involved. 'I'll go and do the cost projection now if you like. Make sure it's viable.'

'You may be anal but at least your figures add up.'

'Thank you, I think. But I think I'm going to need a runner, Gerald.'

'Couldn't you do without?'

'It is a large ball and they do want a circus theme. We do now have the catering for five hundred which we weren't expecting so I think we could stretch to a runner, don't you?'

'You'll nag me until I agree, won't you? You'll drip away like a faulty tap.'

'Yep.'

'Very well. You can have a runner,' he says sulkily. 'But remember your head will be on the block if *anything* goes wrong.'

I smile and make a mental note to call Dom to tell him to book himself some holiday.

After the yodelling auditions, everyone insists on yodelling all their conversations and the office takes on the giggly atmosphere of a three-year-old's party with too much orange squash. I reluctantly leave them all at the end of day and return home.

With rare foresight I manage to locate my keys while on the Tube. Dom is on his mobile phone in the sitting room as I let myself in. As soon as he sees me he hurriedly murmurs something into the mouthpiece and turns it off.

'Hi!' he says brightly. 'How was work?'

'Fine! Who was on the phone?' I ask lightly, my eyes fixed on him. And why was he using his mobile instead of the landline?

'Oooh, no one. Just, er, my mother.' He looks shifty. Dom's mother is an industrious woman who 'does a lot for charities and other good causes'. I take a sneaky look at my watch. There is no way she would be back from one of her afternoon committee meetings yet, but I nod a little. 'Did you have enough holiday left to be my runner?'

'Absolutely! I'm really excited about it!' he says. 'Just think, Izz! I get to see where you and Sophie grew up!' I can't see why this would be so thrilling but I let it pass. 'I might actually give in my notice at the same time, I don't know yet,' Dom continues. 'Working for that company has kind of lost its appeal now.' When Rob and I finished, Dom wanted to hand in his notice as some sort of protest. It was a sweet offer but I knew that, as his landlady, I would be the first to suffer. I nearly point out that there hasn't really been a time when working for Rob's company has ever held an appeal for Dom but I think this might be a little cold-hearted.

My spirits sink only slightly at this veiled mention of Rob. Returning to Pantiles, whatever that means to me, must have had a beneficial effect.

'I just hope Simon doesn't come back too soon.' I bite my lip anxiously.

'You know, Izz, he has probably forgotten all about that ghastly childhood business.'

'He blanked me at that party!'

'Maybe he didn't recognise you?'

'He recognised me all right,' I say grimly.

'Don't worry. Apparently it's a huge takeover he's involved in. I've been reading all about it in the paper. He won't be back for ages.' Dom stretches and yawns, his arms high in the air. 'Can you suggest something to eat with our salad, Izz?'

I think hard. I'm running out of ideas.

'What about some pasta? You could have yours without any cheese?' suggests Dom.

I make suitably appreciative noises. Only a few more pounds to go. Dom gets up to go into the kitchen.

'New trousers?' I ask.

He glances down. 'These? Bought them a few weeks ago. Come and tell me all about Pantiles.' He wanders off into the kitchen.

Peculiar phone calls? New clothes? He's going to have to tell me soon.

Chapter 7

On Wednesday evening I take my straggly set of belongings to Liverpool Street station and catch the next train to Bury St Edmunds. I have realised I am hopelessly ill-equipped for any sort of country estate thing. Whenever we go for walks at Aunt Winnie's we just put on whatever is in her cloakroom. It's not pretty but it does the job and certainly has a scarecrow effect on the cows, pigs and other local wildlife we encounter on the way. Hopefully there will be a similar system in effect at Pantiles as I lack both wellies and any outdoor clothes.

I then discover I don't own very much luggage. I should have thought ahead and borrowed something off Sophie. Dom and I have had to pool together as many hold-alls as we can possibly find, which are misleadingly named as they don't seem to hold very much at all. I don't plan to get caught standing next to them.

I emerge in Bury St Edmunds and find Monty waiting outside in a very much working Land Rover as opposed to the rather clean, bred in captivity ones we have in London.

I dump my bags in the back and rather inelegantly haul myself in. It's not easy in the tight pencil skirt I was determined to wear this morning as it's the first time in over three weeks I've been able to fit into it. 'Hi Monty! Thanks for coming to pick me up!'

'My pleasure, me dear! Good journey?'

'Fine, thanks.'

'Sorry I couldn't get something a bit cleaner to pick you up in; we operate a first-come first-served operation with transport at Pantiles!' This bodes well for the wellie situation. 'Flo's taken me Jag.'

'Flo?' I ask politely.

He glances over at me. 'Actually, come to think of it, I don't think you would ever have met her.'

'No, I don't think so either. I don't remember her anyway.'

'You would remember Flo if you'd met her! She's my sister! Came to live with us when Elizabeth died. She's lived abroad for most of her life. I don't think she visited when you were at Pantiles.'

'No, I don't think she did.' After a small pause I ask tentatively, 'Is Simon home yet?'

'Hmm? Oh, no. Not yet.'

I breathe a small sigh of cowardly relief and get out the long list of questions I had prepared for Monty regarding electricity supplies, staffing arrangements and other such trivialities for the ball. Monty gives me his very distinct views on Porta-loos for the rest of the journey to Pantiles.

'I promised we would go down and collect Will. He's with the deer,' he announces as we turn into the driveway.

'Great!' I say, when I would have been much better off saying, 'Oh shit!' as we plunge off the driveway and rocket down the hillside. I cling grimly to that handy little strap just above the top of a car door that I have never had much use for before and hang on for dear life as we bounce and zoom along, the four wheels rarely in contact with the ground at the same time. Aunt Winnie is a Sunday driver in comparison. Monty seems to know exactly where all the large ruts are and exactly where to hit them for maximum air time. Quite a skill, I'm sure, in some parts of the world. If only I had known to wear my sports bra for such an activity. I seem to be panting unattractively but I don't know whether it's due to an aerobic exertion or an I'm-going-to-die panic.

We eventually draw to a standstill and not a second too soon. I lurch out of the passenger door, sway around for a bit and then rest my hands on my thighs. I wonder briefly, as I manage to persuade my stomach to come out of my boots, whether I'm going to be sick. All in all not a state a girl feels at her best in nor, I think as I watch a rather attractive man stride towards me, one she wishes to be observed in.

'Good God!' exclaims the figure. 'Is that really you, Isabel?'

'Will?' By the time I ask this he has already reached me, seized both my shoulders with, I can't help noticing, two very large tanned hands, and warmly kissed me on both cheeks.

He looks an awful lot like the pictures of Simon I've seen. Handsome and rugged with wide, long-lashed eyes and long, floppy brown hair. The only difference is that Will's personality directly enhances his looks, making him an altogether more attractive prospect than his brother.

'How wonderful to see you again! How's Sophie? And your parents?'

'They're fine, they're all fine.' I smile broadly, instantly feeling that the world is a more friendly place.

'I couldn't quite believe it when Dad told me you were coming back! And as a party planner too! Must have picked up a thing or two about sandwiches on our picnics, eh?' He gives me a little nudge with his elbow and I laugh.

Monty has wandered off to talk to one of his workers so Will links his arm through mine and leads me down to the fence he was inspecting when we pulled up.

'You certainly have grown up well!'

'Thank you. So have you,' I say while fervently thanking Dom for forcing me to lose that weight. My high heels keep sinking into the ground as it is. If I'd been any heavier they would have had to tie a rope around my waist and drag me out with the Land Rover.

'I'm so glad you're here! What do you think? Is it as you remember?' He sweeps his arm out to indicate the scene before us. It nearly takes my breath away. Lush, undulating pastures of an unbelievable green, dotted with ancient oaks, rise and fall before me. I breathe in the unmistakable scent of fresh grass and summer air. It's exactly as I remember.

'Wonderful.'

Monty has joined us at the fence now. 'Can you see the deer?' he asks. He points towards a distant copse of trees. I can vaguely see some shapes.

'Just about. How long have you had them?'

'Only just got them. New venture of Simon's.'

'And what are they, er, you know, used for?' I ask innocently, thinking somewhere along the lines of the country-side equivalent to seaside donkey rides.

'Venison, of course.'

'Venison?' I ask in horror. 'They get slaughtered?' Pictures of little Bambis with their heads on the block come to mind. Like most of the population, I am perfectly happy to eat meat when it comes in little clingfilm-wrapped trays and bears no resemblance whatsoever to the actual animal.

'How else will they make us any money?'

'What sort are they?'

'Disabled.' Oh my God! Not content with slaughtering innocent able-limbed creatures, which is bad enough, Simon has to slaughter disabled animals who can't even run away. Probably cost less to buy them or something, I think to myself grimly.

'Disabled?' I whisper. 'Have they no tail or just one eye? Or have they only got three legs?'

The men are looking at me as if I'm a little disabled in the head myself. 'I said sabled deer, Isabel. Not disabled,' Will says gently.

I feel a bright red flush coming up from my toes. Both of them let out great guffaws of laughter. Really, it isn't that funny, I think to myself as I watch them clutching each other, tears of laughter in their eyes. I give a half-hearted chuckle just to join in. My goodness, do they have to go on so?

'Oh dear, Izzy, you are priceless! Did you think there were little ramps everywhere for their wheelchairs?' asks Will finally, gasping for air.

'Nooo,' I say lamely as though the thought had never crossed my mind.

'And their pens are over there. That's P-E-N-S, Isabel. Where they sleep. Don't want you thinking we're running opium dens or something.'

'Ha, ha.'

'Come on, let's get back to the house. I'm ravenous!' Will rubs his hands together. 'Hopefully Mrs Delaney will have cooked something absolutely marvellous in anticipation of your first night, Izzy.' I wouldn't count on it.

Back at the house, Will takes all my bags upstairs while Monty pours me an enormous glass of wine and I pet all the dogs. Mrs Delaney is busy peeling carrots at the sink so like a creep I ask if I can help and am rewarded with an enormous bowl of French beans to top and tail. Monty leans against the Aga, still chatting non-stop, and Will returns after having changed out of his dirty clothes into a pressed shirt and faded jeans. He is accompanied by a lady I can only assume is Flo. As soon as she enters the room she flings her arms open wide which, to be honest, is a little alarming. She walks towards me, arms still out-stretched, places her hands on my shoulders and kisses me lightly on both cheeks. 'Isabel, my dear! I have heard so much about you and your family! How lovely to meet you!' She has a wonderful husky voice and smells incredibly romantic; I think I recognise jasmine and ylang-ylang. She has an awful lot of soft grey hair, scraped back into an enor-mous bun but with wisps escaping around her face, and her clothes would not be out of place on a Parisian catwalk, divine little bits of floaty material. A huge turquoise stone lies at her neck and her wrists and fingers are positively littered with bangles and rings. She is simply the most exotic creature I have ever met and in my line of work I tend to meet some rather glamorous people. 'I'm so sorry I wasn't here to greet you when you arrived but I was walking in the grounds and completely lost track of the time. I stopped to watch two beetles mating. Absolutely fascinating. Have you ever seen beetles mating?'

'Er, no, I can't say I have.'

'Wonderful. They perform a sort of dance. Next time I see them, I'll come and fetch you.'

'Er, great!'

'You must call me Aunt Flo, like the boys. After all, you're practically family!' This makes me smile broadly with pleasure.

After I have finished my beans, a mere snip for me after my kitchen days, I make the excuse of needing the loo, but take my handbag with the sole intention of touching up my make-up. Aunt Flo is making me feel positively dowdy. 'Just popping to the loo!' I announce. 'Is it still . . . ?' No, Izzy, they've moved the lav just for the hell of it. Quite fancied it in the library.

When I return, Mrs Delaney is ladling the coq au vin on to plates, while Will lays the table by chucking a few mats around, ripping off some kitchen towel for napkins and then dumping a heap of cutlery on the table. Monty looks over at me. 'You'll excuse the informality, won't you, Izzy? I know Elizabeth would have been absolutely horrified!'

'No, it's fine!' I protest, 'I would hate you to go to any extra trouble for me! It's sweet of you to let me stay at all.' I quite like the cosy family casualness of it all, not just because it's the complete opposite to what I do all day.

We all sit down and after the vegetable-passing and claiming of cutlery the conversation naturally settles on the subject of the charity ball.

'I must say, it's terribly exciting!' says Aunt Flo.

'But what next, Aunt Flo?' interjects Will. 'Simon has been talking about making Pantiles more commercial for a while, but now that it's started where will it stop? He's talking about water-skiing on the lake! He's even got hold of a mini speedboat for it! What's next? A theme park?'

'Simon wouldn't do that!'

'Don't be too sure!'

'When exactly is he coming home?' I ask between

86

mouthfuls. The coq au vin is absolutely delicious, especially after the amount of salad I have had to eat this week. I smile appreciatively at Mrs Delaney.

'I spoke to him earlier. He's in Chicago at the moment,' says Monty. 'He's coming home next week sometime. He's not altogether sure when.' This has a curious dampening effect on my spirits. It's almost as though I want the family to myself for a while longer and now he's going to come back and spoil it all. 'This takeover is all-consuming for him.'

'The takeover was announced last week, wasn't it?' I say with an unmistakable air of oh-yes-I-read-the-papers-too. In actual fact I asked Stephanie to give me the low-down before I left the office so my ignorance wasn't neon-highlighted. 'A manufacture company.'

'That's why he's over in America. He's trying to get some of the company shareholders to part with their shares,' says Monty. 'It's a hostile takeover.'

'What does that mean exactly?'

'Well, I'm no expert. From what Simon has told me, it's when a company gets taken over against its will.'

'Can you do that? Take over a company against its will?' This sounds fairly typical of Simon. A corporate bully as well.

'If you own the majority of their shares you can do anything you want. I'm not as much of a businessman as Simon but I understand his company has been buying up shares in this company on the stock exchange. Once they reached a certain percentage they had to announce their intention to launch a hostile takeover – hence the recent press report. Now he's approaching people who already own some of the company's shares and offering to buy these shares at a higher price than they would currently get on the stock market.'

'And will these people definitely sell their shares to Simon?'

'Oh no! They don't have to, but the company he's trying to buy is struggling financially. They have just issued their sixth serious profit warning so understandably the share price is dropping. Long-term the company might end up bankrupt, and then the shareholders would get absolutely nothing for their shares. So they're probably better off selling to Simon now.' Monty shrugs.

'But why does Simon want the company if it's struggling?'

'Because he can see a way for it to make money again. I think he offers the shareholders a stake in the future profit of the company. Obviously he'll have to make a huge amount of change. Sack all the directors and management for a start. But once they start to make a profit again, the share price increases and Simon gradually sells off his shares at a higher price than he bought them for. It's no small undertaking; his company has a huge amount of financial backing from banks and a big team of advisers whose bill will probably run into millions.'

'*Millions?*' I echo disbelievingly. Have those crafty EU people changed our currency into lire overnight?

'He stands to make a huge amount of money from it; it's his biggest deal yet. Very risky though.' Monty takes a sip of wine.

'I've had to ask Daniel to close the gates every night,' says Will. 'The press have started coming up to the house to snoop about. They actually quoted Mrs Delaney in the last article!'

'Last time I ever speak to the press,' Mrs Delaney says

grimly. I involuntarily wince. I feel quite sorry for them. 'I only told them that I didn't know when Simon would be home.'

'Izzy, when he arrives next week, just don't ask!' says Aunt Flo, obviously bored. 'Tell me more about the ball! Do we get to go? I hear they're having a circus theme!'

We laugh a lot during the evening. Even Mrs Delaney, at times, has the corners of her mouth turned up. The wine flows and a cheese board is produced. Will and Monty are on marvellous form.

That night I deliberately leave the curtains open as there are no streetlights to disturb my slumber, climb into my enormous bed and pull the covers right up under my chin. I watch the huge oak trees swaying gently in the distance and listen to the blissful sound of owls hooting. I feel happy again after a very miserable month. I snuggle down and close my eyes, peaceful in the knowledge that I won't be waking up to the grime and dirt of the city but to the greenery of this English Eden. And Simon won't be coming home to spoil it for me just yet either.

Chapter 8

At six o'clock the next morning I am woken by the sound of Monty up and about and clearly wanting everyone else to be up and about with him. I'd forgotten his habit of doing this. You might wonder how one man could wake a whole household, especially in a house as large as this one. Well, it's quite simple. For Making Everyone Miserable fans everywhere, here is an easy guide: first of all, slam all doors, regardless of whether you are going through them or not; then turn on every radio and TV in the house and sing along to anything on them in a loud voice. Even rap if necessary, though not always in tune or in time. If you really want to get up people's noses, take your portable radio outside and teach the dogs some new tricks on the strip of grass underneath everyone else's windows.

After about twenty minutes I decide I can stand it no longer and stagger bleary-eyed out of bed. I normally sleep in just a T-shirt – much as I would like to be a beautiful negligee sort of woman I find that by the morning the straps are always wrapped around various limbs and threatening to cut off my circulation. I grab the first thing to hand to cover my nether regions, which happens to be the grey pencil skirt I was wearing yesterday, and wander downstairs in search of some soothing tea.

'Morning Isabel!' greets an immaculate Will, who clearly has been up for hours. I manage to close my mouth mid-yawn and open my eyes a little wider. I hadn't expected to see anyone else up.

'Morning,' I mumble, embarrassed by my apparently eclectic taste in nightwear. My T-shirt bears the slogan 'Party planners do it all night long' – Gerald had them made for our last Christmas party – which isn't really the impression I want to make with Will.

'I was just making some coffee, would you like some?' He walks off kitchen-wards and I stumble after him. I am immediately pounced upon by dozens of dogs, which nearly brings me down but I manage to grab the kitchen table, pull out a chair and fall into it.

'Why are you up so early?' I ask him.

'We're a bit under-staffed on the estate. Simon's always moaning about the wages so I'm having to put in some extra hours. Do you fancy a tour this evening?'

'Love to!' I exclaim enthusiastically. He turns his back on me while he fills the cafetière and I take this opportunity to rake my fingers through my hair and wipe away the mascara I know will be lodged under my eyes.

He plonks the cafetière on the table along with two mugs. I frown to myself as I notice the flagrant disregard of coasters. Will Mrs Delaney lynch us both or just him?

'Did Dad wake you up?' he asks as he gets the milk from the fridge.

'Nooo, I was already awake.'

'He did, didn't he?'

'Yes.' I can still hear Monty singing tunelessly outside. I

pour the coffee. 'Monty says you've been away travelling?'

'Yes, I went after I finished at Cirencester.'

'Cirencester?'

'Agricultural College. I did always want to be a farmer. I'm good with my hands, you see.' He smiles a teasing little smile and raises his eyebrows suggestively.

God, it's six-thirty in the morning and I haven't even looked in a mirror or cleaned my teeth. Is this how they do it in the country? I look at my coffee mug and fiddle with the handle instead.

'Did you go to university, Izzy?' Will asks.

'Em, yes. I went to Nottingham but I didn't go travelling afterwards. I'd already had my fill of it by then, I think.'

'You and Sophie were moved around a lot, weren't you? Listen, I've got to go and feed the deer. Why don't you throw something more suitable on and come with me and then we can carry on chatting? Much as I like your T-shirt, you night need something a bit warmer. We'll easily be back for eight.'

I hesitate for a second and then nod.

I return to the kitchen ten minutes later dressed in combats, deck shoes and a sweatshirt. Will finds me a pair of wellies from the cloakroom, claims a pair of keys from the dresser and out we go into the fresh morning air. As we soak hay and measure cereal, we fill each other in on what we've been up to since we lost touch. I never got on as well with Will as a child but he always was a joker and a charmer. Always the one to come up with frankly dangerous ideas and carry them out. I had no idea he could be such good company too.

Good to his promise, Will drops me back at the house at five past eight and tells me he'll see me at dinner. I walk into the kitchen via the back door, reeking to high heaven.

A shrill voice hails me: 'Hello! You smell a bit.' Not your traditional sort of greeting but probably fair enough in the circumstances.

A small red-haired boy dressed in a cub's uniform is sat at the table, calmly drinking a glass of milk and eating Shreddies. We're not talking autumnal russet red hair here but bright fluorescent orange.

'Hello!' I reply, 'who are you?'

'I'm Harry.'

I was hoping for a little more detail than that but I'll take what I can get. 'I'm Isabel.'

'The party planner,' he finishes confidently. He's obviously been well briefed. 'You've cut yourself.' I look down at my hand, wrapped in Will's white handkerchief (what a gentleman, no torn-off bits of kitchen roll for him). I had cut it while trying to show off my athletic jumping skills by vaulting a fence. It was only a small cut but it simply wouldn't stop bleeding.

'Yes, I cut it on some barbed wire.'

'Do you want me to swab it for you? I have all my badges in first aid.'

'Er, no, really, it's—'

'Dress it?'

'No, it's em—'

'Lance it?'

'God, no!'

'Splint it?'

'No, really it's—'

'Suck it?'

'Suck it?' I repeat.

'Essential for snake bites.'

'Do you deal with a lot of snake bites at Pantiles's cub brigade?' I ask, thinking this might be the time to find out about any snake population the estate might harbour.

'Ever since Geoffrey Stoats sat on an adder on a day trip to Warwick Castle it's been included.'

'Poor Geoffrey.'

'Yes, his bottom really swelled up. Almost to the size of . . . of . . .' Harry looks wildly around the room until his eyes seize upon an appropriate object '. . . well, almost to the size of yours.' He looks at me earnestly, eyes like saucers, confident of his point being well illustrated.

'Really. I'm surprised he didn't die then,' I remark dryly.

'So am I,' says Harry, supping his milk, oblivious of any social gaffes on his part. Goodness, with this fine line in chit-chat I'm surprised there isn't a queue of Brownies outside just waiting to be swept off their feet by this silver-tongued charmer. Mrs Delaney comes into the room.

'I hope Harry hasn't been bothering you,' she says pertly, mouth pursed. She starts to gather brushes and buckets from underneath the kitchen sink.

'No, no. Not at all. He's, er . . . ?'

'My son. Yes.' Now it's all becoming clear. Harry has obviously inherited his mother's wonderful manner. Let's hope his father has got slightly more going for him than the red hair. Now I come to think of it, I haven't seen any evidence of a father since my arrival. I don't get the chance to ask any more questions, however, as Mrs Delaney makes it abundantly clear that the shutters are down and no one is available for business. She fills a bucket with hot water while Harry finishes his milk. 'School holidays, is it, Harry?' I ask.

He nods happily. 'It's bob-a-job month, starting from next

week. I want to beat Godfrey Farlington. He got more than fifty quid last year. Will you give me some jobs to do?'

'Of course, I'm sure I can find something.'

'You're to keep out of Miss Serranti's way, Harry,' interjects his mother, who in the meantime has started to scrub the kitchen floor.

'No, it's fine, really. He won't be in my way and please call me Isabel.'

'Isabel then,' she gravely acquiesces.

'So do you both live here at the house?' I ask idly.

'Mum and I have rooms over in the east wing. But we're not usually there, we always eat here with Monty, Flo and Will. And—'

'That's enough, Harry.' Damn, just as it's getting interesting. So, his father isn't around. Unfortunately, I've run out of questions I can legitimately ask. 'I'm just going to get changed,' I say to no one in particular and make to walk to the back stairs. Mrs Delaney gives me a long hard look as I try not to step on the bits of the floor she's already cleaned. I walk on tiptoes and make little jumps which don't actually help at all but at least show I'm trying. 'Oops, sorry . . . ooh . . . er . . . sorry,' I gasp, until it occurs to me about halfway across to ask if I should have used the stairs on the other side of the kitchen.

'You're halfway across now, aren't you,' Mrs Delaney says sarcastically, as I stop and gaze at her uncertainly.

I have to concede the point but I don't like the way she mutters bitterly, 'And in your wellies,' under her breath.

'Yes. Absolutely. Sorry.' I make a dash for the back stairwell, sit on the bottom step and struggle to remove my footwear which seems to have become welded to my feet. I'm tempted to ask if Harry has a badge in removing wellies

95

but they come off suddenly and I escape thankfully. In the safety of my room. I shower quickly and scramble into something a little more work-oriented: a black skirt and red top. I throw on some make-up, which is harder than you think with an injured finger, gather some files together and whizz back to the kitchen.

Downstairs, Aunt Flo and Monty have joined Harry and Mrs Delaney at the breakfast table. Monty has his morning broadsheet held up in front of him. He has obviously flipped straight to the obituaries because he suddenly exclaims, 'Good God, Flo! Josephine Bradshaw is dead!'

'Jo Bradshaw? Dead? Are you sure?'

'I do hope so. They've buried her.'

'Morning!' Aunt Flo greets me. Monty lowers his newspaper. 'Izzy! Good morning to you! Did you sleep well, dear? I hope you were warm enough? Do you need an extra dog?'

I reply that I was positively toasty.

'Well, Jasper here makes a wonderful hot water bottle.'

'I'll bear him in mind.'

'So what are you doing today, Izzy? Working on plans for the ball?'

There's a snort from over by the sink. We all glance over. Mrs Delaney has her back to us and is innocently washing dishes.

I look back. 'Well, Monty and I are meeting with the representatives from the charity today,' I reply.

'How too, too thrilling!' Flo beams. Another small snort from Mrs Delaney. It really is most distracting.

'Izzy, toast or cereal?' proffers Monty. I glance over towards the sink again. Any nose issues with that? I help myself to cereal.

At nine o'clock sharp two representatives from the charity arrive for our meeting. Monty and I are waiting for them in the drawing room, which is beautifully elegant and decorated in the palest primrose yellow and a delicate shade of eggshell blue. As with most of the rooms, a huge fireplace dominates one wall. The room is so large that there are several groups of sofas and tables. At one end massive French doors open out on to the lawns. We were never really allowed in here as children as it is full of highly breakable china and dainty little tables which seem to balance precariously on one leg. Someone has thoughtfully placed a vase of roses from the garden on the coffee table in front of the fireplace.

We both stand up as the representatives from the charity are shown in by Mrs Delaney. I watch anxiously as she leaves the room in case she sees fit to throw in inappropriate comment, a snort or indeed a quick cat-like swipe at the back of their heads. Fortunately, she leaves without incident. The appropriate introductions are made between us – the ladies are called Rose and Mary – and we all sit down. I haven't had a great deal of time to prepare for this meeting but I have managed to scrape some menus together. I also haven't had the opportunity to come up with any ideas for the circus theme but that will be easier once I've found out what our clients actually want.

'You go ahead, Izzy,' says Monty. 'You know what to ask.'

'I know this is short notice, Isabel,' gushes Rose before I can even open my mouth, 'but we were hoping that most of our ideas would still be possible.'

'I hope so too,' I say smoothly. Rose and Mary represent a large children's charity that I haven't worked with before and I know that if I can look after them well enough I might be able to pitch for a permanent account.

'Unfortunately our party planner came with the previous venue,' Rose continues. 'We're so thankful that Monty knew of you otherwise I don't know what we would have done. This estate has been a lifesaver all round.'

'So what happened to the last venue, if you don't mind me asking? Why did they cancel?'

'They had a small fire in their kitchens. No one was hurt, thankfully, but they needed to replace some damaged equipment and didn't think they would have everything ready in time for the ball. Considering the numbers involved, they thought it would be best for us to try to find somewhere else.'

'Monty tells me that you have five hundred people coming? Are they confirmed numbers?'

'We've sold just over five hundred tickets, mainly to companies,' says Mary. 'The numbers will probably go up to about five hundred and fifty by the time of the actual event.'

'Have you had any thoughts about food? I've put together some menus for you to have a look at.' I reach for my folder. We spend about twenty minutes going over the menus, including a lively debate instigated by Monty about vegetarians and nut allergists.

'Shall we discuss the circus theme?' I ask eventually. 'Because that might affect some of our other choices.'

'Well, the marquee company we've hired are going to provide a big top!' says Rose excitedly. 'And we did have some jugglers and other entertainers arranged through the other venue; I'll get the names and numbers to you.'

'Thanks. Do you want the marquee arranged in a certain way? Perhaps a sawdust ring in the centre for the performers with the tables arranged around it?'

'That would be marvellous!' breathes Mary. Oh well done, Izzy. Not content with all the work you're already got to do you have to chuck in sawdust rings and the like. You'll be offering yourself up as a performing seal next.

'And you could have a toastmaster dressed like a circus ringmaster, in a top hat and red tails?' Keep digging, Izzy.

'And those shiny black boots?' says Rose with an excited squeak. Monty throws her a worried look.

I'm on a rather unfortunate roll of ideas. 'And how about some usherettes? They could wander through the crowd giving out popcorn and ice cream after the meal. Perhaps even a candy floss machine?'

'I haven't had candy floss for years!'

'I'll need that list of entertainers as soon as possible. You might want to add to it a little: a magician wandering from table to table or maybe a caricaturist? Do you know what age group the guests will be?'

'I'll ask the person in charge of selling the tickets.' Rose makes a note on her pad.

'Do. Now, how about aperitifs?'

'We would like something fun!'

'Absolutely! There are lots of things we could do! How about miniature champagne bottles with straws? Or a cock-tail bar? I'll suggest some ideas in the brief.'

'Thank you! It all sounds simply splendid!'

We go on to discuss table decorations, seating plans, crockery and cutlery, drink arrangements, cloakrooms, portable loos and a hundred other things that are essential for such an enormous bash. I certainly have my work cut out and wonder fleetingly whether Dom and I will be able to cope. After we have scheduled another meeting for the following week, Monty sees the excited ladies out. Despite my worries about resources, I simply can't resist the challenge of making every event the best it can possibly be. I finish writing up my notes and wander over to the French doors. A 'big top' marquee, large enough for five hundred people, will be on these very lawns in just over three weeks. The last event of this size took me over a year to plan and I still get a birthday card from the client's mother. I bite my lip worriedly.

'It sounds an awful lot of work, Izzy! Will you manage?' Monty interrupts my worrying.

'Well, I'll have Dominic with me. He's my runner,' I explain.

Monty notes my dismayed expression and leans over and pats my knee. 'Don't worry, Izzy, we'll all pitch in and help! I know we're asking a bit much of you. I would get you some more help but the problem is we kind of need the money the charity are paying us for use of our grounds.'

'Do you?' I ask, slightly alarmed.

'Simon keeps us a bit short on the old housekeeping and Mrs Delaney does need some new equipment for the kitchen – the fridge is practically falling apart! I was hoping Simon would let us use the money for things like that.' He looks terribly uncomfortable. 'You know, I would never tell a stranger something like that, but you've always been so close to this family, Izzy. That's why I was so relieved *you* were coming to help us . . .' His words drift off and he looks distractedly down at his worn but well-polished brogues. I feel a flash of anger at Simon that he could let his dear father become so distressed.

'Don't worry,' I say firmly and my resolve hardens. 'We'll manage. Whatever happens.'

Chapter 9

I work in the library for the rest of the day, endeavouring to put some meat on the very considerable bones of the ball. By the time six o'clock arrives, I remember with a rush of pleasure that Will wants to take me for a tour of the grounds and that Aunt Winnie is coming for supper. I shut down my laptop and run to change. In the hall, I pause to stare up at the wall above the fireplace for a minute. Something is really bothering me about it and I can't quite put my finger on it.

It feels strange working in the house that formed such a big part of my childhood; I keep spotting cupboards I used to hide in and rooms we used to play in. What's especially bizarre is that most of the rooms look exactly as they did more than fifteen years ago. My mind will be mulling over seating plans and entertainers and I'll suddenly happen upon a dent in the wall caused by Simon playing cricket aged ten. Or I'll spot a replacement pane of glass in one of the doors and recall how we were convinced that if we ran at the door hard enough we would be transported to a Narnia-esque world. Everything feels a little different and yet looks the same; it's quite disorienting.

Once upstairs, I pad down the hall and slosh about in a bath for a while, writing a mental list of things to do. Then I pull on some linen trousers, a little V-necked top and an embroidered cardigan, I quickly touch up my make-up, spray perfume madly around and make my way downstairs.

I try to peep timidly around the kitchen door to check whether Mrs Delaney is in residence but one of the dogs comes up behind me and barges into the kitchen, announcing our presence. Luckily Mrs D isn't there. She's probably upstairs pushing pins into a small replica doll of me. A delicious aroma fills the air, which I hope is tonight's supper and not destined for the dogs – they seem to eat better than we do.

Harry and Will are seated at the table playing what looks like a very violent game of Jenga. I am reliably informed by Harry that this is Speed Jenga; instead of gingerly testing every brick and gently teasing one out, you have a five-second window to locate your brick and whip it out. Chucking said brick over your shoulder also looks to be an intrinsic part of the game. The dogs are hiding anywhere they can; pressed up against cupboards, behind rows of wellie boots, piled up under the table.

'Ahh, there you are, Izzy!' says Will. 'Just need to finish beating young Harry here and then I'll be with you. You'll probably want some wellies, by the way.'

'No rush,' I say. I go through to the utility room, collect the pair I used when I went to feed the deer and pull them on while Will obviously lets Harry win. He gets up from the table, digs into his jeans pocket and hands over a coin to the delighted Harry.

'A pound towards your bob-a-job fund, as agreed, Harry. You drive a hard bargain.'

Harry beams happily at both of us.

'Ready for the off, Izz?'

We say goodnight to Harry and move towards the back door. 'Your father has invited my Aunt Winnie for supper so we need to get back for about eight,' I remind him.

'No problem,' says Will lightly.

'You didn't have the same driving instructor as Monty then?' We are bouncing sedately along a dirt track.

Will looks over at me and grins. 'No! He's scary, isn't he? Look, over there is the old sawmill. Pantiles used to handle its own wood.'

'What happens now?'

'The Forestry Commission comes and does it for us and we sell them the end product. About half the estate is woodland.'

'What about the other half?'

'We let most of that out to local farmers. The rest we farm ourselves.'

'So, do you enjoy managing Pantiles?'

'I would if it were actually mine to manage.'

'How do you mean?'

'Simon owns it all.'

'*All* of it?' This doesn't seem very fair.

'Yep, everything. The eldest son takes all.' There is a distinct note of bitterness in his voice that I can hardly blame him for. He looks over at me and shrugs. We come to the end of the dirt track, go through a wooden gateway and pop out on to a tarmac road. Will points the other way and says, 'We have about ten cottages up there. Unfortunately, some of the tenants are moving out tomorrow so I won't go any closer in case we get rotten tomatoes chucked at us or something. Simon evicted them last week.'

'Why?'

'Said they weren't paying enough rent. Those families have been living here quite happily for the last seven years, until now.'

'God, that seems a bit harsh.'

'I thought so, but you know Simon.'

'Don't I just?'

'Gave you a hard time when we were kids, didn't he?' He glances over at me.

I shrug to try and look as though I can scarcely remember. 'I suppose.'

We turn right along the tarmac road, then take a left and pull up in front of another wooden gate. I leap enthusiastically out of the car to open the gate, eager to show that a city girl can easily make her way in the country, but am so busy trying to impress that I don't focus on the ground and land smack in a cowpat.

'Oooh, yuck! Cow poo on my wellies!' I wail.

Will leans over and grins at me. 'Sorry, Izzy! They bring the cows through here! Forgot to tell you! But don't worry, everyone smells of shit in the country!'

The smell of cow shit fights for supremacy with my sophisticated city perfume and after a small tussle wins easily. I frown to myself. Why does the country have to smell so much?

I struggle with the gate for a while – you need at least a degree in astrophysics to figure out its intricate Krypton Factor-style catches. Will eventually comes to help me and opens the gate with a simple flick of his wrist. We continue on our way.

'What's happened to all the horses? My mother used to

keep hers here,' I ask, mindful of the empty stable block.

'Yeah, I remember. We had to get rid of them. Too expensive. Simon is tight with money and he controls the purse strings now.' But not tight enough to deny himself the large BMW parked quietly in the courtyard that no one seems to drive despite the household's first-come first-served approach to cars. Amazing how the people with the most money always turn out to be the meanest.

'What a shame.'

'I miss them. This is the part of the land we let out, all the way down to that field.' He points some way across the horizon.

'So, did Simon start here straight after school?'

'No, he went to university.'

'Which one?'

'Cambridge. He dropped out in his second year.'

'Why?'

'That's when Mum died. Dad just signed the entire estate over to Simon, felt he couldn't handle it any more without Mum's support. He wanted Simon to finish his degree first but Simon decided not to wait. Just calmly packed up and came home. I guess he was keen to get started but soon after he went into business. Pantiles bores him now.'

I look around at the beautiful countryside surrounding me, the little village up ahead, the subtle greens of the forest bathed in the warmth of the setting sun, and wonder how on earth anyone could become bored of it.

'After I got back from travelling, Simon decided he did need an estate manager after all, so I took the job. I'd like to have my own farm some day though.'

'Couldn't you have the estate farm?'

'To let, maybe.' He sighs. 'They would never split Pantiles

up. It's not fair but quite sensible. You need to keep the estate whole for it to maintain its value.'

'That's very pragmatic of you.'

'Second sons have to be.'

We reach the village and Will pulls over and jumps out. I follow suit. We wander over the green and Will waves to a couple of people while I subtly try to wipe the cow poo off my wellies.

'Is there a great sense of community in the village?' I ask Will.

'Not really. They try hard but the estate used to employ them and now it doesn't. People have had to move away to find more work and so it's getting more difficult for Pantiles.'

We sit on the seat beneath the blossoming cherry tree. 'We should do this again, Iz,' Will says thoughtfully.

'Yeah, it's been lovely,' I say truthfully. 'Most relaxing.'

'I do an estate tour most evenings. Visit the villagers, that sort of thing.'

'Shouldn't Simon do that?'

'I'm the estate manager so it's my job really. Mum used to do it when she was alive though I think she saw it as more of a chore than I do. Look Izzy!' Will exclaims before I get a chance to respond, 'we're sitting under the bridal tree! You're going to have to marry me now!'

When we return to the house, it is with some relief that I find Aunt Winnie hasn't arrived yet. I think it might be a little mean to leave her to the mercy of the Monkwell family when she doesn't really know them that well and I also don't want her drawing any premature conclusions regarding my outing with Will. Although I have a feeling that as soon as she claps eyes on his handsome self they might become unavoidable.

Monty and Flo are digging exuberantly into the gin and tonics, peeling vegetables and chattering madly. I presume Harry has been sent up to bed. They both look up as we come in.

'Good outing?' Aunt Flo asks.

'Lovely!' I say.

'Help yourself to a drink, Izzy me dear! There's wine in the fridge or gin in the cupboard.'

I extract myself from my wellies and quickly wash my hands. Then I pour Will and me a large glass of wine each and locate two coasters from the drawer, earning myself a semi-approving look from Mrs Delaney. A forceful rapping at the back door announces the arrival of Aunt Winnie, who enters the kitchen without pausing and fills the room with her larger-than-life presence. Even Mrs Delaney looks impressed and I nearly go and stand next to my dearest relative with a yes-isn't-she-scary smirk on my face. Instead, I kiss Aunt Winnie on the cheek and make some hurried introductions. She gives Monty a big hug and hands over a bottle of wine (not home-made, I notice with relief) and some berries from the garden. She shakes everyone else's hand. Aunt Flo and Aunt Winnie look hilarious stood next to each other. Aunt Winnie is dressed in a cotton blouse, tweed skirt with thick, pale green tights and sensible solid shoes. Aunt Flo is dressed in a ruffled paisley chiffon dress with beaded flip-flops and bare legs. While they greet each other, Monty leans over to me and murmurs, 'Do you think I ought to tell Flo she's still wearing her dressing gown?'

I laugh at Monty's description of the ultra-trendy long

woollen cardigan Flo has on over her dress. 'I think it's a cardigan, Monty,' I whisper back.

'A cardigan? Are you sure? How 'straordinary.' He goes to get Aunt Winnie a glass of wine, still murmuring 'a cardigan' to himself in a surprised way.

Despite the initial striking differences between their style of dress, Aunt Flo and Aunt Winnie get along like a proverbial house on fire. They bowl the evening along between them (it turns out they have a shared admiration of beetles), aided by a fabulous fish pie from Mrs Delaney and some poached fruit for pudding. Since Monty told me about the shortage of funds on the housekeeping front I have started to notice things. The fridge is indeed starting to fall apart, not to mention the kettle. To my absolute horror I also notice that there isn't a dishwasher. I was so tired last night that I left them all at the table when I went to bed. It didn't even occur to me that someone might have to wash up, which isn't going to improve my relationship with Mrs Delaney. I also note that the vegetables and the poached fruit are from the garden.

Halfway through the evening, on my way back from the loo, I bump into Aunt Winnie in the corridor. 'Do you know where the bathroom is?' I call to her.

'Er, yes.' She waits until I reach her and then whispers, 'Izzy, have you told your parents about coming back to Pantiles?'

'Not yet,' I say, surprised at the seriousness of her tone. 'Why?'

'I just think you should, that's all.'

'Why, Aunt Winnie?'

'Just tell them, Isabel,' she says in an uncharacteristically sharp manner and walks away, leaving me staring after her.

Chapter 10

The next day, after our meeting with the marquee company which involves frantic running around with tape measures, Monty runs me to the station. He kisses me on the cheek and tells me that he'll pick me up next Tuesday night so I'll be in time for my meeting with Rose and Mary on Wednesday. I will have to stay for a few days to try to get through all the other interviews for entertainers and musicians so we have arranged for Dom to join me as well.

Once safely aboard a London-bound train, my laptop and notes spread out on the table before me, I call the office.

'Table Manners?' Stephanie impatiently answers, no doubt disturbed from a riveting article about Tara Fart-Whortle's, or whatever her name is, handbag collection.

'Stephanie, it's me.'

'Oh.' Attention obviously returned to article.

'Er, how's everything?' I ask, my shoulders hunched apprehensively. I always like to test the water first with Stephanie, which prevents any nasty surprises. It's amazing how much trouble you can get into without even being there.

'S'okay.' Phew. I breathe a sigh of relief and settle back down in my seat. 'But he's cross with you.'

Resume hunched position over table. 'Why?'

'Says he's never heard of such a crappy idea.'

'Which one?'

'They couldn't catch one of your doves at the Polynesian banquet and it crapped in the host's drink.'

'Oh God, did it?' I resist the urge to laugh because I know it would just get back to Gerald. 'Were they cross?'

'A bit, but not as cross as Gerald.'

'I'd better speak to him.'

'I'll put you through.'

I wait and eventually Gerald picks up the phone. The first thing he says is, 'Ahhhh, I see the fuck-up fairy has visited us again.'

I grin; he's not as cross as Stephanie made out. 'Come on, Gerald, you can't blame me for a dove's bowel movements.'

'A good party planner is always in charge of everyone's bowel movements.'

'That's quite a responsibility.'

'Are you on your way in?'

'Yeah, just left.'

'Good. I'm expecting a full report.'

Back at the headquarters of Table Manners, a familiar atmosphere pervades. Chaos is threatening to spill out of every corner. Even Stephanie is busier than usual. She has two magazines open in front of her while she sups on a mocha frappé through a straw. She grunts at me and begrudgingly removes the straw from her mouth. 'They're all going mad,' she says and her attention returns to *Hello!*.

'Messages?' I ask hopefully.

She jerks her head in the general direction of my desk, which doesn't instill me with much hope, and adds, 'Lady

Boswell called. I told her you were working up at Simon Monkwell's estate. I then had the old bat waffling on for about half an hour about how she has met Simon Monkwell once, how bloody wonderful he is and how much she would like him to come to her Ice Feast.'

'God, I can't think of a more perfect fate for him,' I mutter.

I walk into the main office where people are indeed going mad. Aidan is standing on a desk in the corner staring thoughtfully at a piece of flex in his hands and looking as though he's thinking of hanging himself with it. For some reason, Yogi the stuffed bear is sitting on the desk beside him. I make my way through the maze of desks and people towards him, ignoring my colleagues who are variously interviewing people dressed up as animals, crawling under desks or wedging flower arrangements with a triumphant, 'That'll hold it!'.

'Hi!' I greet Aidan.

'What's up, Boo-boo?' he says in his best Yogi-bear impression.

'Thinking of ending it all?'

'Christ, I wish someone would end it! Gerald is in a foul mood – did you hear about your dove? Is it true he actually drank the cocktail it pooped in?'

'I don't think so.' I look doubtful.

'Damn, that's what I've been telling everyone.' He leaps down from the desk to join me on the floor. 'So have you got anything on this week apart from the Pantiles thing?'

I shake my head. 'Just some Nordic Ice Feast arrangements, thank God. I've got enough on my hands with this ball.'

'So tell me all! How is the estate? How's the ball coming on? How are you getting on with big bad Simon Monkwell?'

'He hasn't come home yet.'

'But you will meet him?' he demands.

'Yeah, soon.'

Aidan sits down opposite me and looks thoughtful. 'And what about the rest of the family, how are they?'

A wide smile spreads across my face. 'Oh, they're great! I'll tell you more about it later.'

I dump my laptop and bag down by my desk and get back to work on my brief.

Gerald is indeed in a bad mood and roars about for most of the afternoon. A junior party planner tries to get a menu for a teddy bears' picnic approved and he shouts him out of his office with, 'There is nothing amusé about your bouches! Come back when you have something people might like to eat!'

He immediately yells at me to come into his office. By the time I have followed him in and shut the door behind me, he is already slumped at his desk.

'God, it's all so bloody relentless, isn't it?'

'What is?'

'This having a good time malarkey. Goes on and on. How's the Monkwell project? Anything to report?'

'No, everything is fine.'

'Managing not to piss-off the Monkwells?'

'I think so.'

'When is Dominic joining you?'

'Next week.'

'Tell him not to piss them off either. Remember, a closed mouth gathers no foot. And if your mouth . . .'

'. . . is open then you're not learning anything,' I finish for him.

'You can never drum the lesson home too much with Dominic. I'll never forget the time he told a fat guest that she had better not stay still for too long on that yacht of hers in case they mistook her for a whale and harpooned her.'

'Well, she was being annoying and he did say it under his breath.'

'She must have exceptionally good hearing then because, as I recall, she heard him. How is he, by the way?'

I have a sneaking suspicion that Gerald quite likes Dominic. 'He's well.'

'Bearing up, is he?'

I look at him suspiciously. 'He's just fine. Why?'

'No reason. Let's hope we get some more business out of this ball, Izz. It seems like you have been away for ever. Aidan's accounts are deteriorating rapidly.'

'Really?' I ask innocently. 'He's probably having an off day.'

'More like a week of them. So, how is the ball?'

I think of all the work involved – the circus theme, the catering for five hundred and the million other things I have yet to confirm. 'Fine,' I say firmly.

'Seen Simon Monkwell yet?'

'No, not yet. Next week maybe.'

'Will you ask about his corporate contract?'

'If I get a chance,' I say, thinking very definitely not. There is no way I am touting for business from Simon Monkwell.

'Your Aunt, er . . . what's her name? The one who thinks I'm a communist?'

'Winnie.'

'That's it! your Aunt Winnie might have come up trumps on this one! Make sure you're nice to Simon Monkwell next week.'

'I will.' Behind my back, my fingers are firmly crossed.

*   *   *

I begin to enjoy my afternoon, even though I am making arrangements for my bête noire, the Nordic Ice Feast, because I am in the unusual position of being able to leave at seven on a Friday night come what may. Thursdays and Fridays are usually our busiest nights of the week because most of the smart set depart for their country residences at the weekend. People assume our work must be enormous fun, and for a lot of the time it is, but they have no idea what it's like when your table placement hasn't worked out and you know you can't go home until it does.

I spend most of the afternoon on the phone to the ice supplier, smoothing out problems with the ice bar, and then schedule another rehearsal with my mock Vikings and a meeting with Lady Boswell herself for when I am next in the office. Lady Boswell kicks off about Simon Monkwell again but I manage to extract myself from the conversation before she can instruct me to send an invitation to him.

As soon as I let myself through the door of my flat, Dominic leaves, looking remarkably smart. He claims he is going to the cinema with a friend from work but I presume this person to be more than a friend because he would usually invite me along too.

I decide to rent a video and wander through to my bedroom to get changed into my favourite pair of combats before heading off to the video store. I'm just searching for my keys when the door buzzer goes. Dominic must have forgotten something.

'Hello?' I answer.

'Hello?' It's not Dominic but the voice is familiar and recognition stirs slightly.

'Hello?' I say again.

'Isabel. It's me, Rob. Please buzz me in.'

Chapter 11

My finger hesitates on the buzzer, but I push it and the front door opens. I hear him coming up the stairs and then he appears in front of me.

I don't know what to say, so I say nothing. My first thought is whether any of my make-up has survived the day. My second is that Rob must have left something at my flat and come to collect it. Then I notice the bottle of champagne. Little butterflies of excitement start up in my stomach. Do I pretend not to have seen it?

He leans insolently against the door frame and beams at me. 'May I come in?'

'Of course,' I say automatically and step to one side.

I follow him into the sitting room and hastily lurch forward and gather the mugs that litter our coffee table. I take them through to the kitchen and when I return Rob is twisting the foil off the bottle of champagne. I bristle slightly at the presumption.

'You're opening that now? What's the occasion?' I ask.

'Do you have any glasses?'

'No, I don't.'

He laughs at me. 'Come on, Izzy! Have a glass of

champagne with me for the sake of auld lang syne.' I'm stuck between the kitchen and the sitting room, but he smiles up at me with that audacious, lazy smile and I have to admit to a slight softening of heart.

'All right.' I go back into the kitchen and dig out two wine glasses.

We sit in silence as he deftly pours the champagne. He chinks my glass with his, holds my eye for a second and then settles back into the sofa. The sensation of having him here with me again feels dangerously euphoric. 'So!' he says, 'what have you been doing with yourself, young Isabel?'

'This and that. Rob, what's all this about? Turning up unannounced with a bottle of champagne?'

He shrugs and doesn't quite meet my eye. 'I thought you might refuse to see me if I called you first.'

'You're right. I might have.'

'Well, there you are then.' He smiles disarmingly at me once more.

I ignore him and persist. 'But why are you here?'

'Well, Izzy, I've been thinking a lot lately about how good we were together and . . . more champagne?' I hold out my glass as he tops us both up. 'I've been thinking that perhaps I was a little hasty.'

'A little hasty?'

'I've missed you.'

I close my eyes slightly as though to shield myself from the full, slap-in-the-face irony of it all. What I would have given for this a few weeks ago.

'Come on, Izzy,' Rob continues softly. 'I made a mistake. I'm sorry. But don't make one too, just because of your pride.'

I hesitate. This strikes a chord with me. Am I throwing something precious away through sheer bloody-mindedness? After all, what did he do wrong? He didn't cheat on me. We didn't have an enormous row and call each other awful names. He just got a bit scared of commitment, but he's realised he made a mistake.

I take another gulp of champagne and he edges up the sofa towards me and takes my hand. The sensation of his fingertips caressing my palm is not altogether unpleasant.

'Can I take you out to dinner tomorrow?'

'No, I have plans.'

'Next week then?'

'No, I'm away working. In Suffolk.'

'God, what on earth are you doing all the way out there?'

'I'm working up at the Pantiles estate. It's owned by Simon Monkwell,' I add wanting to impress. It has the desired effect.

'Simon Monkwell? Wow!' Rob says incredulously, moving even closer. 'What are you doing?'

'I'm organising a ball for them.'

'That's a pretty impressive job, Izzy.'

'Yes, well, I used to know the family.'

'Did you?' His hand starts to creep up my arm. 'You see, Izzy, I knew I'd made a mistake. You obviously know *all* the right people.' He smiles at me in that way that I used to find utterly charming but I'm not so sure now. 'It must be a difficult job, I've heard he's not terribly nice,' Rob continues, leaning back into the sofa once more and taking a sip of champagne. 'How are you getting on with him?'

'I haven't seen him yet. He's in Chicago at the moment. But no, he's not very nice.'

'How do you know that if you've not seen him?' Rob asks mockingly and a small smile plays around his lips. He starts stroking my hand again.

'He evicts tenants for no reason and deliberately keeps the household short of money.'

'He's sleeping with one of his lawyers, isn't he?'

I look at him sharply. 'Where did you hear that?'

He shrugs his shoulders. 'Around.'

'I wouldn't know or be interested in who he is sleeping with,' I say stiffly.

'So,' Rob continues softly, 'you're having to stay up at the estate? Will I be able to see you during the week?'

'Yes, I'm staying there,' I say shortly, my mind still turning over recent events. Are Rob and I getting back together? Is this what I want? His hand shifts from my palm and starts moving up my arm again. It's rather hypnotic.

'Could you get back during the week at all?'

'I suppose.' His hand has moved across my shoulders and is now playing with a strand of my hair.

'Poor you. Must be ghastly, having to have dinner with all those country bumpkins. What on earth do you talk about?'

'Oh, beetles. Farming. That sort of thing.'

He laughs jovially, thinking I'm kidding, and leans over to kiss me. 'How awful. Can't think of anything worse,' he murmurs. Just then my mobile rings and jolts me from my trance-like state. I frown and lean towards the coffee table to pick the phone up. The display reads a Pantiles number.

'Hello?'

'Izzy? It's Will.'

'Hi Will, how are you?' I say with some relief.

'Good. I'm just calling to see what time your train gets in on Tuesday. I'll come and pick you up.'

I rummage in my bag for my Filofax and reel off the time to him. He says he is looking forward to seeing me and rings off.

I stare at my phone for a second. 'Actually, Rob, can I think about this?' I say firmly.

He looks taken aback but seems to recover quickly. 'Of course, Izzy! Of course. It must seem rather sudden to you.'

'Yes, it does.'

I get up and walk over to the door. He looks at me for a second and then follows suit. 'Can I call you?'

'No, I'll call you. I don't want to rush into anything.' And with this I kiss him on the cheek and firmly eject him from the flat.

Dom is apoplectic with rage when he hears of Rob's visit and I sip the remnants of the champagne apprehensively. I'm quite glad I made Dom neck his first glass now.

'He seemed quite contrite,' I say uncertainly.

'Rob? Contrite? Izzy, those two words have never before been linked in a sentence about Rob without "not the slightest bit" in between them.'

'But he was! Why else would he come round?'

Dom snorts derisively. 'Probably fancied a shag.'

'Well, he wouldn't get one here,' I reply primly.

'Did anything happen?'

'No, nothing!' I say hotly.

'Izzy,' says Dominic sternly. He can read me like a book.

'Well . . . it might have done if Will hadn't called.'

'Will?' he squeaks excitedly. 'From Pantiles?'

'Yes. Will.'

119

'Handsome farmer Will?'

'Yes,' I say with some annoyance, regretting my off-the-cuff description of him.

'Why was he calling you? I thought you were dealing with Monty?'

'He wanted to know what time I was arriving at the station on Tuesday.'

'Oh, so he's picking you up now. Is he the reason nothing happened between you and Rob?'

'Indirectly, I suppose so.'

'That's not what Freud would say. I can see it now. Rob moves in to kiss you; the phone rings and it's Will. Suddenly there's no spark any more. Hmmm.'

Crikey, was he watching from behind the pot plant?

'Give over, Dom. It could have been anyone on the phone.'

'Do you think this Will likes you?'

'I really don't know.'

'God, how exciting! And I can meet him for myself next week!'

I stare at him in horror. I had actually forgotten that Dom was coming with me to Pantiles next week to help with all the work. This does not bode well; Dom fancies himself as quite a shot with old Cupid's bow. Several people lie maimed and injured as a result of it.

I fix him with my most withering look. 'Dom, you are to forget that I ever mentioned Will.'

'Awww, come on, Izzy! I might be helpful.'

'The only way you could be helpful is to forget the entire thing.'

'How can I forget the entire thing when my best friend is in love with a handsome farmer who owns all the eye surveys?'

'I am *not* in love with him and for your information he doesn't inherit. Simon does.'

He frowns. 'Are you sure you've got the right brother?'

He gets a cushion right in the kisser.

When I arrive in Bury St Edmunds on Tuesday evening the dirty Land Rover is once more waiting for me outside the station.

'Will!' I say in delight as I heave open the door and clamber in.

He rewards me with a kiss on the cheek and a huge smile. 'How's tricks?'

'Fine! How's things with you?'

'Good! All set?' He puts the car into gear and we whizz off.

We chatter idly about the weather and then move on to the family.

'How's Aunt Flo?' I ask.

'She and Dad are fine.' He glances over at me. 'Simon is back tomorrow.'

'Is he?' I say, feigning nonchalance.

'Don't worry!' Will says, most likely seeing the slight shadow pass over my face. 'We probably won't see much of him!'

I feel comforted by the 'we' and smile back.

Monty comes charging in at breakfast the next morning, 'Isabel, me dear,' he pants, 'I'm glad I've caught you. Will says you're going to Bury St Edmunds.' I'd asked Will last night if I could borrow the Land Rover to get to my meeting with the marquee company. They want me to approve the final design for the 'Big Top'.

'Er, yes. Do you need anything?'

'Could I come with you?'

'Of course.'

'And Flo?'

'Absolutely.'

'When were you going?'

'Sort of now-ish.'

'Take my car, it's the old Jag. Bring it round to the front while I go and get Flo.' I give Will's keys back to him and pick up my handbag. 'Am I insured?' I ask Monty.

'I'm not sure any of us are, me dear.'

'Yes, all the cars are insured third party,' says Will, smiling at my look of apprehension.

'By the way, Mrs Delaney,' I say. 'My runner, Dominic, is arriving this morning. He's interviewing all the entertainers from about eleven onwards. If he turns up before I get back, would you mind terribly showing him to his room please? He's staying tonight.'

'Of course,' she answers shortly, without actually making eye contact with me. I think she is secretly thrilled that I will be out for most of the morning. Her idea of a happy day seems to be one with at least ten miles between us.

I carefully drive Monty's old car round to the front of the house and soon enough Monty and Flo emerge, accompanied by three dogs. I lean over and open the passenger door for one of them and Flo clambers in.

'Monty, do you want to drive?' I yell through the open door.

'No, me dear. You drive, I'll stay with the dogs.' He waits until all the dogs have settled themselves in the back and then squeezes in beside them.

'Good morning, Aunt Flo. How are you?' I greet her.

'Fine thank you, dear, except that my knee is playing up a little.'

'What's wrong with it?'

'What did you say?'

'I SAID, WHATS WRONG WITH YOUR KNEE?'

'Arthritis, dear.'

There's a loud snort from Monty at this. 'Arthritis? She wouldn't know the meaning of the word.'

'I heard *that*, Montgomery,' says Aunt Flo from the front.

'You should see the doctor about your selective hearing, not your knee.'

'The doctor said my knee must be very painful. More painful than your foot, I would imagine.'

'Your foot?' I ask Monty in concern. I regret pursuing this line of questioning almost as soon as I say it.

'Old war wound, me dear. Can barely walk on it.'

'War wound, hmph! You fell down the cellar steps. You had been *drinking*!' says Flo of the front seat.

'Take that back, Madam!'

'Well!' I say, feeling we ought to stop this little interchange before it gets to bath chairs at dawn or something, 'are the dogs with us for any particular reason, Monty?'

He leans between the front seats. 'They need to go to the vet.' I notice that one of them is the little white Westie that gets pushed about by the others.

'What's her name?' I ask, nodding to the Westie.

'Meg. We haven't had her long. One of the estate workers found her wandering about. I just want her checked over by the vet to make sure she's okay.'

'Poor thing.'

Making conversation never seems to be an issue with Monty and Flo, so they chatter constantly and I drift in and out, thinking of my lists and the things I need to do. We arrive in Bury St Edmunds and arrange to meet back at the car in an hour's time. I spend the next sixty minutes looking doubtfully at a drawing of the Big Top and madly praying that the entire thing won't collapse on top of me and five hundred guests. I arrive back to find Monty and Flo waiting for me by the car.

'How's Meg?' I ask as I climb in. Monty is already in the back so I am assuming he still wants me to play chauffeur.

'Absolutely fine.'

'What have you got there, Aunt Flo?' I ask, indicating her large plastic bag as I reach for my seatbelt.

'Grasshoppers.'

I blink. 'God, sorry, I thought you said grasshoppers!' I release the handbrake, reverse out of the parking space and set off back to the house.

'I did. They're grasshoppers.'

'Oh. And, em, what do you want with those?'

'They're for my pet tarantula.'

I nearly run over a couple of pedestrians. 'Your pet what?'

She looks at me as though I really ought to get my own hearing problem sorted out. And soon. 'My pet tarantula. Poppet.' I have a quick look around my immediate vicinity while we wait at traffic lights in case Aunt Flo has brought her along for the ride.

'Poppet? You haven't mentioned her before.'

'Most people are a little scared of her.' Really? I wonder why that is. 'I thought you might not want to come and have tea with me if I told you.'

Too bloody right. 'Why? Is she loose in your room?'

'Sorry, dear?'

'I SAID IS SHE LOOSE IN YOUR ROOM?'

124

'No, Poppet has her own tank. She comes out now and then.' When she asks nicely? To eat small children?

'Really?' I say weakly. I fish about wildly for something nice to say about a pet tarantula called Poppet. 'She must be a great comfort to you,' doesn't somehow seem to fit. Monty chips in before I can say anything. 'You'd better not let her out when Simon's around.'

'I'll make sure she's kept in.'

'If she escapes there will be hell to pay. Simon doesn't know about Poppet,' Monty confides to me. I look at him in the mirror. Lucky Simon.

'I won't tell,' I promise. 'Maybe it would be best, Aunt Flo, not to let Poppet out until everyone has gone.' Namely moi.

We arrive back at the house at about eleven and the three of us plus dogs walk back into the kitchen carrying our various purchases. I am just about to say, 'Don't drop the grasshoppers!' to Aunt Flo in a jaunty, jokey sort of fashion when one of the dog leads gets twisted around her legs and she falls forward. I grab the bag containing the grasshoppers from her, breathe a small sigh of relief when she steadies herself with the aid of the kitchen table and go to check she's okay. I subsequently trip over one of the dogs and drop the entire bag on to the floor. I stare for a couple of seconds in utter incredulity as one hundred grasshoppers leap forward with the alacrity of escaping prisoners, unable to believe their luck. The next few minutes are mayhem: the dogs make a mad scramble in all directions to escape; Mrs Delaney starts screaming and gets up on a chair while Harry stares in absolute delight; the rest of us get down on all fours and try to catch the buggers.

'Excellent!' cries Harry. 'Does each one I find count as a bob-a-job?'

'Just get on with it, Harry,' roars his mother from her eyrie.

Now normally, if someone were to point a grasshopper out to me, I would say something like, 'How nice!' or, 'Isn't that a cocktail?' or some other such vague nonsense. Never would I lunge forward and actually attempt to pick up one of the little critters. Yet here I am, faced with catching a hundred of the buggers, all of whom are moving at great speed towards freedom.

I snatch a pan and its lid from the draining board and use it as the central holding cell. We leap all over the place, shouting to each other, panting madly at the sheer exertion of it, trying to catch the pesky insects. Until a voice stops us in our tracks:

'WHAT THE HELL IS GOING ON? I CAN HEAR YOU IN MY STUDY.' We all stop short and straighten up. I think Simon might be home.

Chapter 12

Simon impatiently rakes a hand through his hair, which is short at the sides and long on top à la Hugh Grant. He is tall, dark and looks just like Will, but he has an unattractive, arrogant air. He is dressed in faded olive green cords and a thin jumper which is pushed up at the sleeves. I notice that the top of his hair is wet. He must just have had a shower, I find myself thinking, but then he has flown across the Atlantic.

I shove my hand, which contains five wriggling grasshoppers, into my coat pocket and clasp it shut. I gulp, trying hard not to think of grasshopper poop and dry-cleaning costs.

It's amazing how quickly grasshoppers can disperse. Amazing. One of them must have shouted, 'Quick! Run, boys! Run for your lives!' and the others must have taken heed. We have about thirty in the pan which means there are seventy or so more on the hoof. And I can only see about three of them.

I'm glad to say that Simon looks taken aback to find me in the heart of this little group. He moves towards me. 'Isabel? Is that really you?' he says in surprise. 'Dad told me you were coming back. How lovely to see you again!' This is ironic considering our previous meeting. His voice is slightly clipped and makes him sound peculiarly pedantic. He obviously doesn't know whether to shake my hand or not but since he's caught me on the hop and my right hand is holding five grasshoppers in check, I move forward and kiss him on the cheek. He looks abashed at the greeting.

'Good flight?' I ask quickly.

'The old red-eye. But yes, fine, thank you.'

As an afterthought, he moves forward and kisses his relatives too.

Once the greetings are over, I tilt my head to one side, raise my eyebrows and assume an enquiring look, as if to say, 'And is there anything else?'

'So what's going on?' Simon repeats.

With Simon's ignorance of Poppet's existence in mind, I bleat, 'We were . . . em . . . we were . . . er . . .' I am blatantly playing for time here and we all know it. Simon is making me feel incredibly nervous. Perhaps I can continue in this vein until everyone forgets what the original question was? We all follow Simon's eyes as he catches sight of a particularly lazy grasshopper half-heartedly jumping after his fellow ex-cons.

'Racing grasshoppers!' interrupts Monty.

'GOD, YES!' I practically yell in admiration. I have to hand it to the man, it's a stroke of sheer genius.

'Racing grasshoppers,' says Simon in a somewhat disbelieving fashion.

'That's right,' says Monty. 'We were racing grasshoppers. All of us. Apart from Mrs Delaney, of course,' Mrs Delaney is standing on a chair looking ashen so she can't feasibly be included.

'Well perhaps you could race your insects a little more quietly?' he asks dryly. 'I have to get back to work. I'll see you all at dinner tonight. It'll be nice to catch up, Isabel.' He says all of this without any semblance of emotion and leaves the room without another word.

I turn around slowly to face the others. The remaining grasshoppers have legged it a long time ago.

'I stepped on one,' says Aunt Flo, looking distressed.

'Flo, you were about to offer them up as dinner to a spider and you're upset about stepping on one?' Monty says incredulously.

'Ah, yes,' she acknowledges, nodding thoughtfully.

I bite my lip. Somewhere, a grasshopper chirrups to itself. I look around at everyone and we all start to giggle.

Dominic arrives shortly afterwards. None of the family are around so I manage to hurry him through to the drawing room without interruption. I quickly brief him on the list of entertainers he needs to interview and he looks absolutely aghast at the amount of work he has to do. I haven't got the time or the inclination to soften the blow so I give him a couple of pats on the knee and return to the library and my plans.

I had forgotten, however, how seriously Dominic takes his food. He honestly thinks something absolutely heinous will happen to him if he goes without the stuff for more than a couple of hours. He sleeps with a packet of Penguin biscuits by his bed, 'just in case'. (Of what? A hypoglycaemic burglar?) So it comes as no surprise that at some point during the day he manages to locate the kitchen and befriend the most important member of the household: Mrs Delaney. His charm is utterly effortless. When I arrive in the kitchen hoping for an aperitif before my first meal with Simon, Dom is sitting on the table with a packet of biscuits and a glass of wine by his side. There is no mistaking the love light in Mrs Delaney's eyes. He doesn't even have a coaster.

'Evening, Izzy!' he says cheerfully, a huge beam on his face. 'I've just been telling Mrs Delaney here what an excellent place I think the countryside is! Do you know they get post here and everything! Marvellous! Biscuit?' He proffers the packet.

I shake my head and frown. Dominic hasn't been out of London much. He was born a mere brioche-throw away from Harrods and thinks cows only make guest appearances in butter commercials. Someone once told him they didn't have cash-point machines outside of the capital and I think he believed them.

'How were the entertainers?' I ask. 'Any good?'

'Fantastic! I particularly enjoyed the stilt-walker! He nearly took his eye out on the chandelier though. I've booked him, the jugglers, one of the magicians and a sort of balancing thing with a bicycle. Plus all the others that the previous venue had chosen. And don't worry, Izzy, I wrote everything down so you can fill in your precious tables.'

I relax slightly. I've spent the entire day sorting out the food and drink, cloakrooms, loos and numerous other details. Ordering the flowers for the tables alone took me an hour on the phone. I still have to go over the practical arrangements with Mrs Delaney which I'm not really looking forward to.

Will and Monty come in through the back door together, looking fresh-faced and energetic, and pronounce themselves hungry enough to eat the table.

The appropriate introductions are made and the men make a big show of pumping hands and squaring shoulders (which always makes me smile as any minute I expect them to burst into a rendition of 'I'm a lumberjack and I'm okay' with their hands on their hips). I fetch Will and Monty a bottle of beer each from the fridge while Dominic looks sheepishly at the Nancy-boy glass of wine in his hand.

'So you two know each other quite well, do you?' asks Will.

'Dom and I share a flat together.' I can feel Dominic watching us intently and I try to ignore him. Luckily Monty engages him in conversation about the entertainers he has seen today.

'How has your day been, Izzy?' asks Will.

'Oh, fine. How about yours?'

'Equally fine. I suppose you haven't had a great deal of conversation about crop yields though, have you?'

'Not a great deal, no. Were they good?'

'The conversation or the crop yields?'

'Either.'

'The crop yields were average and I'd much rather have a conversation with you.'

'Oh, I wouldn't have a great deal to say about crop yields, I'm afraid,' I say, blushing slightly 'Or any other farming issues, for that matter.'

'Thank God for that! I rarely meet anyone who *hasn't* got an opinion about the estate and how it ought to be run! Can I get you another drink?' He indicates my already empty glass and gets to his feet.

'Thanks,' I say and hand over my glass. Dominic pokes me with his elbow and raises his eyebrows suggestively. I give him a look.

'Good evening everyone,' says a quiet, authoritative voice behind us. We swivel around to see Simon standing in the doorway. Will immediately goes forward to shake his hand.

'Hi Simon! Good trip?' he asks.

'Fine thanks. How are you?'

'Fine. Beer?' Their manner is cool and detached and I get the impression that all is not rosy between the two brothers. Will goes to the fridge to get the drinks and Monty makes the appropriate introductions between Dominic and Simon.

'How's the estate?' Simon asks Will as he hands him a bottle of beer. Will glances at me.

'Nothing to report,' Will answers shortly and hands me my refilled glass. Simon comes and sits down.

'So, Isabel, how's the ball going? I must say I was surprised when Dad told me you were organising it.'

'The ball's going well. We're managing just fine,' I say firmly.

'When is it?' he asks.

'Two weeks on Saturday.'

'And when does the real disruption begin?'

'Only a few days before, when the main marquee goes up.'

It feels strange to be talking so formally to a man I once knew so well. I know about the scar on the back of his leg from where he had a mole removed. I know he absolutely hates mushrooms unless they are chopped up finely. I know he always wants to be the shoe when he plays Monopoly. I watched him cry his eyes out when his first dog died. Yet here we are, talking as though we only met this morning.

Thinking of this, I say suddenly, 'You were at the launch of the Zephyr trainer a few months ago.' I don't want it to go unacknowledged. After all, we are no longer children.

132

He thinks for a second. 'Yes, I was. Did your company manage that one?'

'I did, actually.'

'Did you?' He looks at me, puzzled. 'Were you there?'

'Yes, I saw you.'

'You should have said hello.'

'I was going to but you didn't seem to recognise me.'

'Well, no offence, but you were eleven when I last saw you.'

'Oh.' I feel rather foolish, the wind having suddenly been taken out of my indignant sails. What an idiot I am. I could have sworn he recognised me but that explains why he didn't say anything.

Aunt Flo provides a welcome distraction by floating in and looking like a hothouse flower among us hardy perennials. Dominic looks positively thrilled to meet someone so exotic and they exchange a noisy greeting.

She comes over and lightly lays a hand on Simon's shoulder. 'Are you out of that dreadful work mode yet, Simon dear?'

He grins at her and takes a swig from his bottle of beer. 'I'm ready to talk about anything you want, Aunt Flo.'

She sits down in an adjacent chair. 'You know, you'll never get a serious girlfriend while you work so hard.'

'I don't know that I want one.'

'Did we hear a rumour about you and a certain young lawyer?' Her eyes twinkle merrily at him.

'Did you?' His eyes smile back at her but his mouth is set.

'Are you seeing anyone, Izzy? We haven't asked!' says Aunt Flo.

I'm startled by the sudden swing of the spotlight on to

me. 'Em, I've just come out of a relationship, Aunt Flo.' Cripes, that sounds amazingly serious, as though we were engaged or something. 'But it wasn't anything very significant,' I hasten on, 'more of a fling really!' The word 'fling' hangs jauntily in the air. Sluttishly, even. 'He used to work a lot,' I try to explain. 'It was Rob Gillingham. He's the son of David Gillingham, the insurance people?' Now, I just sound as though I'm showing off. Dear God, someone shoot me, please.

'I know them!' says Monty. God bless him. 'Big company in the city!'

'That's them!' I say in relief and take an enormous slug of wine.

'So was your trip successful, Simon?' asks Monty, changing the subject as he senses my discomfort.

'I think so. A few of the key people are flying over next week to tie the whole thing up.'

He goes on to explain more about his business trip but he is very conscious of the strangers in the household and he glances at me now and then. I'm so wary of him that I'm almost holding my breath and I'm having to fight a desire to cross my arms in front of my body in some form of self-protection.

Will distracts me from my growing anxiety. 'What's for supper, Mrs D? What is that divine smell?' he asks, while peeling the label off his beer bottle.

Mrs Delaney doesn't waste any time in producing a dish from the bottom of the Aga. We all sniff the air appreciatively like the Bisto kids. She plonks the dish on the table.

'Mr Dominic here says he's vegetarian, so I've made some bean stew.'

There's an uncomfortable silence. Vegetarian is a dirty

word in this house. I narrow my eyes and stare fixedly at Dom. Even he looks horrified. He's never had anyone take him quite so literally before.

'Bean stew?' says Will in disdain.

'Are you sure you're vegetarian? Do you think you meant Irish vegetarian?' I ask Dominic pointedly. 'Or perhaps you're not really a vegetarian at all?'

'Er, well. I thought I was. But you know, you can never be sure.' Mrs Delaney is now staring at him too. He looks from one to the other of us, torn between two wraths. Rather sensibly, he chooses to side with the one capable of causing the most misery.

'But bean stew is my favourite thing in all the world!'

'It looks like someone has thrown up on my plate,' says Monty as he is passed his portion. He's the only person in the room who could get away with such a comment but Mrs Delaney still glares at him. I try hard not to laugh.

'What did Harry get?' asks Will wistfully. 'Did he get this too?'

'Fish fingers.'

'Oooh. Fish fingers.'

'Will, Mrs Delaney has gone to a lot of trouble to make one of our visitors feel at home,' says Simon. Will shoots Simon a look at this patronising remark.

'So, Isabel. Have you had a look around the estate? Is it as you remember?' Simon smiles at me.

'It's exactly as I remember,' I reply shortly.

'We must go and visit the lake while you are here. We used to go fishing there a lot.'

'Did we?' I say politely. There is no way I am going to fondly reminisce with Simon as though absolutely nothing has happened. He is going to have to find a more direct way of appeasing his conscience if he wants to do that. Like apologising.

Simon notes my coldness and moves on to other things.

Despite the enforced vegetarian option, dinner is an animated affair. Monty uncorks a few more bottles of wine and the conversation flows along with it. I am sat between Monty and Will, which is undoubtedly one of the best seats in the house.

Simon suddenly says, 'By the way, I keep meaning to ask. Have any of those grasshoppers you were racing escaped?' He fixes his gaze on Monty and me alternately. Will and Dominic look suitably mystified.

Thinking Monty might crack under the pressure, I jump in. 'We released them outside, didn't we, Monty?' Monty nods quickly. 'Why?' I ask, regretting the query as soon as it is out of my mouth.

'I keep thinking I can hear them.'

Suddenly we all develop hearing problems of our own.

'Hear them?'

'Grasshoppers, you say?'

'I can't hear any of them, can you?'

'Pardon?'

'What are you talking about?'

We all look inquiringly at him.

'It's a kind of singing. Like the sound grasshoppers make.' He looks around our little throng.

There's a slight pause as we subconsciously re-group.

'Tinnitus!' I exclaim to almost rapturous applause. 'TINN-I-TUS,' I say a bit louder; after all, he does have a hearing problem.

'Tinnitus?' he questions.

Everyone sees the bandwagon and leaps straight on it.

'Probably stress-induced.'

'Ringing in the ears.'

'You're working far too hard.'

'Mobile phones can do terrible things.'

Pudding suddenly becomes something of supreme fascination for everyone concerned. It's as though none of us has ever tasted ice cream quite like it.

'This ice cream is delicious, Mrs Delaney!' I cry.

'Absolutely gorgeous!' says Aunt Flo, digging in with gusto.

'Yes, where *did* you get it from, Mrs D?' says Monty.

Mrs Delaney looks confused. 'I got it from the supermarket. It's made by Wall's.' Her voice is disbelieving.

'Well, it's just so . . . so . . . *so* creamy.'

At this point Simon excuses himself, saying he needs to do some more work. I visibly relax.

'Anyway! How is dear Sophie, Izzy?' asks Monty. 'Has *she* got a boyfriend?'

'Sophie? Nooo. Sophie is too married to her career, no time for boys!'

'How often do you see her?'

'Oh, every couple of weeks or so. Well, usually, but we've both been a bit busy recently so it's been a while.'

Monty drops his voice and the conversation carries on over our heads. 'I missed you and Sophie when you went. I think the boys did too.' He adds that last bit on rather hurriedly.

'Yes, it's a shame we lost contact.'

He smiles and stares down at his hands. 'I think so too, but some things are better left. Tell me some more about your Aunt Winnie.'

I begin to tell him about her tormenting the vicar but my mind lingers on Monty's comment. Some things are better left. What on earth does he mean by that?

Chapter 13

On Friday morning I get up early, my mind buzzing with all the things I have to do today. Rose and Mary are coming for another meeting so I shower hastily and throw on a smart pin-striped trouser suit. I pick up my clipboard of notes, find Meg the Westie waiting for me outside my bedroom door and together we wander down to the kitchen.

'Morning, Mrs Delaney!' I beam delightedly at her.

'Morning, Isabel.'

'How are you this fine morning?'

She glares at me. 'Busy. I've got a lot of things to plan with all the disruption ahead.'

Ah.

'And I have to go to Bury St Edmunds on top of everything else.'

Most likely for her Chamber of Torture Club. They probably meet Fridays in the town hall.

'I. Have. To. Shop,' she says emphatically and glares at me again.

Breakfast is a hit-and-miss affair in the Monkwell household. It very much depends on the mood of the cook and this morning I'm guessing at 'not good' from all the packets of cereal on the table. I help myself to a bowl and munch away, trying desperately to wake up.

'Morning Izzy! Morning Mrs D! How are we all?' Dominic dances in looking horribly fresh and awake. 'Beautiful day, isn't it?'

'Did you sleep well, Dominic?' asks Mrs Delaney.

'Mrs D, I had no idea that the countryside was so noisy. I seemed to have half a zoo underneath my window. And then this awful screaming started in the middle of the night. Izzy, I thought you were being raped and murdered! I was about to rush into your room, brandishing my wash bag, when I realised it was coming from outside.'

'What if I had been outside being raped and murdered?'

'Oh. I didn't think of that. Well, you obviously weren't, were you? Because here you are looking bright and breezy – well, maybe not bright. Or breezy. You're just sort of here, aren't you?' He's always deliberately provocative in the mornings because he knows I haven't the energy to punch him.

'It was probably a vixen,' says Mrs Delaney.

'Oh, so it *was* you after all, Izzy!' Dominic says this with his ha-ha! face. I do not ha-ha! back. Mrs Delaney already seems to think I am a bit of a harlot. She's been eyeing Will and me suspiciously these last couple of days.

'What do you need me to do today, Izz?' asks Dom.

'Oh, just odd jobs. I need the electricity sorted, so you'll have to call all the suppliers and find out their require-ments. I also need a plan of the inside of the marquee drawn up. Actually, I've written you a list.' I extract the list from my clipboard and give it to him.

Harry comes in while I am saying all of this, sits down

139

at the table and helps himself to some cereal.

'Can you give me a hand today, Harry?' asks Dominic. 'In return for some money for the bob-a-job fund?'

'Oooh, yes please!'

'We need to dib-dib-dob along then!'

My meeting with Rose and Mary takes all morning. They leave at about one o'clock and after I have replied to a dozen e-mails regarding the Nordic Ice Feast I go through to the kitchen in search of some lunch. No one is around so I make myself a ham sandwich and sit down at the table to eat it. On second thoughts, I pick it up and take it outside. I haven't seen our old house since I returned to Pantiles and I have a sudden yen to do so. I set off up the hill towards it, munching as I go.

At the brow of the hill, after five minutes of steady going, our old house comes into view and I pause for breath. The house itself is made of black and white timber and is nestled into the side of the woods, which always made Sophie's and my bedroom at the back of the house extremely gloomy due to lack of light. We used to tell each other spooky tales under the covers by torchlight and then be petrified for the rest of the night and insist that Hector the cat slept with us (although with hindsight I'm not altogether sure he would have been very useful had we been faced with a werewolf, apart from being an appetiser before the main course).

In the summer Simon used to throw stones at the window in the middle of the night and I would dress hurriedly in clothes I had already laid out, drop out of the window on to the garage roof and together we would go fishing by moonlight. I think he knew I was scared of the woods when he wasn't around because he always used to watch and wait for me to climb back into my bedroom window and never left until I was safely inside and had waved at him.

I walk up to the front door of the house, reminiscing some more, and try to peer through one of the front windows without giving the tenants inside a heart attack. To my surprise, the place is deserted. I press my face up against a dirty window and take in the dusty, empty rooms occasionally littered with the old box or newspaper. There's an air of sadness about it, and I shiver and turn to leave.

Will is in a filthy mood when I get back to the house because Simon has imperiously ordered him to make tea. He slams teapots and cups around furiously. Rationing is obviously still in effect at Pantiles because after my first cup I am firmly told by Mrs Delaney that that is my lot.

So when Dominic decides he is in dire need of a cigarette, I accompany him gratefully. We slip out into the balmy late afternoon air and wander lazily into the walled garden. The walled garden was one of my favourite places as a child, only rediscovered a few days ago when I was marking out the pitch for the marquee. It seems nature has been left to her own devices for some time. Somebody has recently mowed the lawn but apart from that mayhem rules supreme in the flowerbeds. All sort of surprises are to be found; a lost lavender plant here and a rebelling fig tree there. It is beautiful. If I had the time I would take a certain pleasure in uncovering the treasures the garden has to offer. I remember that Elizabeth Monkwell used to spend hours out here.

Dominic lights up, drawing the smoke right down into

his boots. 'God, that's better! I've only had three since I got here!'

'So have you decided whether to quit your job yet?'

'Well, I've taken these few days as holiday. I might quit next week, before I have to come back here to help you.'

'Won't you have to work your notice?'

'Normally they send us straight home, but I've got two weeks' holiday due anyhow if they don't.' He takes in another deep lungful of smoke. 'God knows how I'm going to manage the week before the ball with these few cigarettes!'

'Might be a good chance to give up,' I say, idly fingering a leaf. Dom is always going on about how much he would like to quit.

'But then I'll put on weight! I'll just eat crisps all day.'

'A few pounds might be worth it in the long term.'

'Oh give over, Izzy. And it's all right for you, you're not seeing any—' He stops abruptly.

'Anyone? And you are?' I ask innocently.

He opens his mouth hesitantly. 'Actually, Izzy, there's something, or rather someone, that I want to talk to you about . . .'

But he doesn't get any further than that because we suddenly hear the sound of voices getting closer.

'Cigarette,' I hiss at Dominic.

What Dominic should have done at this point is throw the cigarette into the flowerbed and hope it doesn't start a fire. But that of course would be the sensible and mature thing to do. Instead, Dominic panics and hands it over to me (I think we will be bringing up this moot point several times in his lifetime) and I'm stupid enough to take it. We have all had dire warnings from Gerald about smoking in the vicinity of clients. P45s are threatened. He thinks smoking is the most abhorrent thing an employee of a catering company can do. Dominic knows he wouldn't remain an employee for much longer if Gerald found out he'd been smoking in front of clients.

At that moment Simon and an earnest-looking young man wearing glasses round the corner into the walled garden. They survey the little scene before them. I quickly stomp the cigarette into the ground, but then on second thoughts, in case the Lord of the Manor becomes a little pissy about it, pick up the butt.

'Isabel. Dominic,' says Simon smoothly.

'Hi!' I say awkwardly, standing on one foot and then the other as though I am twelve and have just been caught behind the bike sheds.

'I didn't know you smoked, Isabel.'

'Er . . . er . . . er . . .' All three of them are staring at me now, hanging on my every 'er'. It's at times like this that I wish I was French; a bit of shoulder-shrugging, hand-tilting and face-making without actually having to explain anything would work a treat.

Dominic obviously feels he should help out and so he puts in, 'Like a chimney!' and beams.

That does it. I refuse to be friends with Dominic any longer.

Simon stares at me for a second, as though trying to fit this piece of information into what he knows of me, but then turns to the young man next to him. 'I'm sorry, I haven't introduced you. Sam, this is Isabel and Dominic. They're here to help with the charity ball. Isabel used to live on the estate when we were kids. This is Sam, he works at my company.'

143

Sam smiles and extends a hearty hand to each of us in turn. 'I used to smoke myself. About two packs a day,' he remarks. My initial impression of Sam being quite a nice man instantly changes to him being a rather interfering, shit-stirring sort of individual.

'Oh really?' I ask politely, resisting the urge to give him a boot on the shin.

'I've never seen you smoke, Isabel,' says Simon. Are we still on this?

'I'm trying to give up!' I improvise quickly.

Simon raises his eyebrows. 'That's good,' he says encouragingly.

'Yes. Isn't it?' Why aren't we moving on to something else?

'I'm so glad you're trying to kick it.' Sam puts a hand on my arm and looks sympathetically into my eyes. That's not all I would like to kick.

'So, Isabel, you're going back to London tonight?' asks Simon.

'Em, yes,' I say, still seething. 'We both are, but we'll be back next week for a couple of days and then for the entire week before the ball.'

'Well, if I don't see you later, have a good journey.'

'Thanks,' I mutter.

They walk off together and I listen as their voices drift away, '. . . well, if the Americans are good on their promise to . . .'

'You complete and utter git,' I spit the instant they have disappeared and round on Dom who is silently laughing into his jacket.

'Come on, Izzy! It was quite funny!'

'Dom! You are completely irresponsible!' I say crossly.

'Me? Irresponsible? What nonsense! Why, I thrive on

responsibility. I was the milk monitor at school. Besides, better you than me. I would be more expendable than you to Gerald.'

'He thinks I'm troublesome as it is. I am trying to look—'

'What?'

'I don't know. Composed? Sophisticated?'

'But you're not.' Dominic looks confused.

'*I* know that,' I hiss between gritted teeth, 'but he doesn't. And if he says anything about the smoking to Gerald, I'll be lynched.'

Dom puts his hand on my arm, looks deep into my eyes and says in a pained voice, 'I'm so glad you're trying to kick it.'

I suddenly giggle. We walk out of the garden together and I completely forget to ask Dominic what he was going to tell me.

Dominic disappears for most of the weekend and I have to perform at Lady Boswell's Nordic Ice Feast which goes surprisingly well. Sean and Oliver turn up and immediately have a row which turns out to be a blessing in disguise as they then ignore each other for the rest of the evening. The ice bar and vodka luges are a huge success and the only blight on the whole evening is when Lady Boswell manages to get her arm stuck to an ice sculpture. If she will waft bare flesh about when we warned everyone of the dangers then she can't hold us responsible.

The start of the week passes in a blur of Aidan, ribbons, flowers and coffee. Since I have an awful lot of running around to do over the next couple of weeks, I persuade Gerald to hire me a car.

I am due back at Pantiles on Thursday. On Wednesday

night I pack my bags and make my way out of London in my new Smart car to stay with Aunt Winnie before continuing my journey to Pantiles the following day. Aunt Winnie is hosting a whist drive at her house so I help make sandwiches for them all, because apparently they couldn't possibly stop to eat properly, and spend the rest of the evening banished to my room with Jameson and a pile of *Good Housekeeping* magazines.

The next morning, I wrap myself in an old Paisley dressing gown and, once downstairs, find that Aunt Winnie and Jameson have already gone to the village to buy a paper and some bread. I make myself a cup of tea and wander out to the garden, enjoying the warmth of the sun on my neck. A loud bark alerts me to the fact that Jameson has returned, which doesn't always mean that Aunt Winnie has too, and I spin round to find him bounding down the drive towards me, shortly followed by a panting Aunt Winnie. She waves at me. I wave back. She waves again. I frown; it's a bit early for this sort of malarkey, isn't it? I wave again once more in a yes-I-have-seen-you kind of way and she waves furiously back. It takes me this long to realise that she's doing more than passing the time of day.

'Aunt Winnie?' I call. 'Are you all right?'

She seems incapable of speech but then the hill out of the village is quite steep and she's hardly in peak physical condition. She's still waving the newspaper around in a maniacal sort of fashion. She eventually reaches me and, amid much huffing and puffing, hands the paper over. The *Telegraph*. I look at the headline: TUBE STRIKE BRINGS CITY TO STANDSTILL.

'Em, I can catch the bus to work, Aunt Winnie. It's not a problem.'

She grinds her teeth and impatiently shakes her head. She bends over and puts one hand on her thigh, still trying to catch her breath, and holds the other hand up to indicate the number two. At least I think that's what she means – she could just be being rude.

I turn to page two. A headline about halfway down the page screams: MONKWELL'S HOSTILE BID FOR MANUFACTURER IN TATTERS.

'Oh my God!' I say to Aunt Winnie.

She makes an impatient read-on gesture. I read on.

Sensational revelations have made the difference between business and bust for Simon Monkwell. An unnamed American investment bank has decided to back the ailing manufacturing plant Monkwell was trying to buy after some unsavoury disclosures about his business and personal ethics led the bank to believe that various promises and conditions of the sale were unlikely to be met. 'This is a man,' says a source close to the Monkwell family, 'who throws his tenants out of cottages where their families grew up. A man who leaves his family home to rot. He is also sleeping with the family lawyer so don't expect much sense out of her either.'

'Oh my God,' I repeat. I sit down suddenly on the grass underneath the apple tree. The ground is still damp, I notice hazily.

Aunt Winnie, who in the interim has managed to get her breathing under control, kneels down beside me. 'Are these things true?'

'Yes, but the paper makes them sound so awful. I don't

know anything about this lawyer woman though. I think Aunt Flo might have mentioned something the other night. But so what if he is? It has nothing to do with the takeover.'

'I suppose it's a bit like politicians and their personal lives. You could argue that it's got nothing to do with their work, but you get a good idea of their integrity from it.'

'I suppose. I'm not Simon's greatest fan but I still think this is awful. I'd better call Pantiles; it might affect the ball somehow.'

I stand up with this purpose in mind and walk inside. My mobile rings and I leap on it, my stomach filled with butterflies. I have a very bad feeling about all of this and I don't know why. It's Will.

'Hi! Have you seen the news?' I ask anxiously.

'Yes, we got the paper about an hour ago. Izzy, I really think you should get back here . . .' His voice sounds distant and faint.

'I'm just about to leave. Awful, isn't it?'

'Er, yes. Actually, it's worse than that. Simon says he knows who the leak is.'

'Oh really?' I say.

'Yes. He says it's you.'

Chapter 14

I'm keen to make a bolt for the nearest airport but Aunt Winnie persuades me to return to Pantiles. I'm not the bravest person in the world and it's only when she threatens to take me there by force – a coercion she has resorted to in the past (admittedly not at the weight I am now but she does still have the advantage there) – and then looks pointedly at her golf clubs that I relent. She agrees to feed me breakfast first, a sub-clause in our verbal contract that I shoved in at the last minute in order to buy me some time.

Aunt Winnie is cooking me some bacon (she labours under the misapprehension that I need at least three thousand calories to get out of bed in the morning). The smell is making me want to vomit. Perhaps I could throw up into Jameson's bowl and no one would be any the wiser. She shakes the pan vigorously. 'So,' she booms above the noise of the smoke alarm going off and Terry Wogan on the radio, 'why on earth does Simon think you told the press all those things?'

I keep my eyes trained on the butter dish on the table and one hand on the top of Jameson's head. He has already taken up position next to me in anticipation of some pig coming his way.

'Aunt Winnie, I have absolutely no idea,' I say wearily. So far, this has been one hell of a morning. It's not even eight o'clock. I get up, smack the smoke alarm dementedly with a large fish slice and then sit back down again. 'He probably thinks I'm likely to want to extract some sort of revenge on him; we didn't exactly part on the best of terms.'

Aunt Winnie snorts scornfully. 'I doubt that, Izzy. You must be in quite a long queue.'

'Yes, but I'm the only one he has actually let into the house.'

Aunt Winnie shoves half a swine in between four doorstops of bread, plonks the plate in front of me and sits down suddenly, covering one of my hands with hers. 'It wasn't you was it, darling? You didn't call the *Telegraph*, I don't know, for a chat or something and then inadvertently tell them a few things?'

'Why on earth would I call the *Telegraph* for a chat?'

'I don't know. Because of your job?' she offers weakly.

I fix her with a look.

'Er, no. Of course not. I was just wondering how Simon could be so sure.'

I frown. 'Will didn't say "Simon thinks it's you". He said "he *knows* it's you". Do you think Simon will sue me? I signed a confidentiality agreement.'

'He can't sue you if you didn't do it!' Aunt Winnie says indignantly and returns to the stove.

'Want to bet?' I mutter darkly and slip Jameson half a tonne of bacon.

The drive back to the estate is none too pleasant. I call Dominic en-route and babble incoherently at him for ten minutes. After my initial non-stop verbal dysentery, I pause to take in some oxygen and Dominic jumps in. 'Izzy, I'm a bit confused. Why would he think you were the leak?'

'THAT'S my point, Dom. Why? Just because we didn't get on so well when we were younger? Why let me into the house at all if he was that distrustful?'

'Well, Monty actually let you in.'

I ignore this pedantic detail. 'Does he really think I would carry that sort of grudge after all these years? We're not all as petty-minded as him!' I rage hysterically. 'Besides, I would never do that to the family!'

Dom is probably picking his nails or playing Solitaire on the computer by now. 'Now don't get in a tizzy, Izzy. He is probably only thinking of the strangers he has let into the house over the last few weeks. You're presumably the only one.'

'What about you?'

'Oh, everyone always trusts me. I've got that sort of face. You are altogether more shifty-looking.'

'Oh, well, he might as well just take me out and shoot me now.'

'He probably will. It's all rough justice in the country, isn't it? Look, Izzy, just go up there and sort it out. It's probably some sort of misunderstanding.'

I put the phone down and feel much better simply because I have managed to work up a small rage, an infinitely superior emotion to plain lily-livered fear. But as the miles drop away, my courage goes with them. 'Come back!' I want to yell. Where's the old Dunkirk spirit? Rally it fast, please.

Better to walk into the lion's den, I say to myself. But the fear begins to creep in again. How on earth will I defend myself? Does the entire family think the same as Simon? That I am some sort of turncoat and not to be trusted? That would be almost too much to bear. Even if I manage to convince them all that it wasn't me, the rest of my stay will be awful. Actually, I wouldn't be able to stay. Gerald would have to send someone else up in my place and I would have to leave Pantiles, this time for good. Why is that such a dreadful thought?

The estate gates are shut but I shout through them to Daniel, the gamekeeper, who comes and opens them for me. I crawl up the driveway in my Smart car and spend quite some time dawdling in the courtyard before I can drag myself to the back door. I spend a few seconds practising saying 'hello', to see if my voice still works. Just as I'm about to knock the door flies open and Will stands before me. Oh God. He looks incredibly serious. Almost bereft.

'Hello, Izzy. We heard you arrive,' he says stiffly and looks away in embarrassment.

'Hello,' I whisper, probably looking incredibly guilty.

He stands to one side and I creep in. The entire family are seated around the kitchen table. Christ, this is a bit much, isn't it? What's happened to innocent before proven guilty? Jasper is the only dog in the room and the only one who seems pleased to see me.

Monty manages a smile which doesn't reach his eyes. 'Hello Izzy. Simon is waiting for you in the study. What's left of it.'

'What do you mean, what's left of it?' Everyone looks shifty and won't meet my gaze so I turn on my heel and walk quickly down the corridor. I stop short in the hallway and look around me in amazement. Where's all the furniture? Have they been burgled? Do the police know? It would explain the bleak faces in the kitchen a little better. I run towards the study door and open it. This room has also been stripped of all furniture, but odd things are piled up in the corners like rejects from a bric-a-brac sale. Simon is leaning against the mantelpiece, staring into space.

He looks up as I enter. 'Isabel. You're back.'

'Simon, how awful! You've been burgled! Are the police on their way?'

'What were you thinking of?' he asks softly. He obviously has no wish to discuss the burglary which, unluckily for me, isn't going to make his mood any sunnier.

'How do you mean?' I whisper, still looking at the empty room.

'I mean, what the HELL WERE YOU THINKING OF?' His voice rises dangerously at the end. His eyes blaze threateningly at me. He's pretty mad.

'I don't know how the press got hold of that information. It wasn't anything to do with—'

'Oh come on, Isabel! You can't be that stupid!'

'I don't know what you mean.' I bite my lip and try desperately not to cry. It would just be too pathetic.

'I'm surprised you have the nerve to come back here.'

'But I haven't done anything!' A little note of indignation comes into my voice. Thank God. I can rely on Simon to rile me.

'Where do you think the press got the information from?'

'I . . . I don't know.'

'It was completely irresponsible of you not to tell me you still had links with that firm. I suppose you were absolutely desperate for the business. How did you think I wouldn't find out?'

153

'Simon, I honestly don't know what you're talking about.'

'Don't you?'

'No, I don't. I was as surprised as you to see the newspaper article.'

'What about your *ex*-boyfriend? Although I doubt he's that at all. Was he surprised?'

'My ex-boyfriend?'

'Robert Gillingham.'

I bite my lip. 'Rob? But we finished about a month ago. I told you the other night,' I whisper. 'Why? What has this got to do with him?'

'Have you seen him recently?'

'Yes, I saw him about a week ago.' My words slow as my befuddled brain tries to make some sense of it all.

'You honestly don't know, do you?' he says, staring hard at me. 'I couldn't believe it was a coincidence but I think it really is. I wondered why you would blatantly mention him in front of me. I thought it was your way of giving me the subtle two fingers.'

'What?' I ask in distress. 'What don't I know?'

Simon noticeably calms down. 'You mentioned Gillingham the other night?' I nod, still baffled. 'Well, it's been bothering me for days where I've seen that name. Dad said it was just familiar because Gillinghams are a large plc, but I knew I had actually seen it written down somewhere. Then last night I remembered. Rob Gillingham is a nonexecutive director of Wings, the manufacturing plant I was' I wince at the use of the past tense 'trying to take over.'

'What does that mean?' I ask, a small suspicion starting to gnaw at me.

'It means that Rob Gillingham sits on the board of directors of Wings. He doesn't actually work for them but he attends board meetings once a month for a couple of hours and gets paid handsomely for it. It wouldn't be in his interest for me to take over the company because the first thing that usually happens in a hostile takeover is that the board of directors gets sacked. When you saw him last week, did he ask anything about the estate? About me?' he asks quietly.

I think back. 'Em, I think he might have asked a few questions, I can't remember.'

'Did you tell him I was in Chicago?'

'I might have done,' I say in a small voice. 'Why?'

'Because Wings knew which shareholders we were talking to.'

'But he did seem really surprised that I was working for you.'

'Oh, I doubt that.'

'What do you mean?'

'I mean that he was trying to find out what you knew.'

'But how would he know I was working here?'

'Mutual acquaintances? Contacts in the industry? I don't know! There's dozens of ways for him to find out.'

'But he came over to say . . .' My words trail off. He came over to say that he wanted me back, I finish in my head. That he had made a mistake.

'Came over to say what?'

I blush bright red. 'Nothing. So you're saying he came over just to get some information out of me?' The bastard. How could I have been so stupid? Men who finish with their girlfriends by voicemail are not the sort to then say, 'Sorry! Can't imagine what I was thinking! I do love you after all!' But at least I wasn't stupid enough to actually take him back, I think grimly. Thank God for that. What would he have done then? Slept with me until he had all the information he needed?

'But I didn't tell him any of the stuff mentioned in today's article. Well, perhaps I might have mentioned the tenants being evicted but nothing else!'

'From what our PR people can tell, the tenants were a little disgruntled to say the least. Apparently they spilled the beans quite happily.'

'But Rob found out about them from me. Oh God, I had no idea what he was doing, I thought he was just being interested in my work. And I didn't tell him those things maliciously, I never said anything about the takeover. I wouldn't do that – I signed the confidentiality agreement.' Oh well done, Izzy. Bring that up, why don't you? He had probably forgotten all about it until you carefully lobbed the idea into his head. You might as well put a sign over your head saying 'SUE ME PLEASE'. I move swiftly on: 'He just asked me a couple of questions. Could we tell that to the newspaper? Get them to retract the story?'

'Isabel, it's all true. Okay, it's not been portrayed in the most sympathetic light but there is an essence of truth there.' We fall into silence. Simon pulls over two bean bags from the corner of the room and we sit down. One bean bag has pictures of little pigs all over it. I think I recognise it.

'I'm sorry I shouted at you. I just couldn't believe it wasn't a coincidence. Dad said you would never do something like that.'

'He's right, I wouldn't. But I am sorry about Rob. I really didn't know what he was up to.' We fall into an uncomfortable silence. 'When did you find out about the burglary?' I ask suddenly.

'No burglars, Isabel. The bailiffs took the furniture. The bank sent them in.'

'*What?* Bailiffs? The bank?'

'Yep. We personally, as in the house, owe them over half a million.'

'Oh no!' I whisper.

He nods and continues, 'When they read in the paper that the takeover had fallen through, I couldn't persuade them to hold off any longer. They arrived first thing this morning. Some of the furniture is valuable.'

This is my fault.

'Are you okay, Isabel?' he asks in concern. 'You look a little ill.'

I whimper in answer. Simon gets up and goes back to the pile of stuff in the corner and extracts something. He throws a packet into my lap. 'Nicotine patches. I got Dad to buy some to help you give up. The bank didn't want them.' He smiles and sits back down opposite me.

'Why don't you put one on now?' he says after a pause. 'You look like you could do with a cigarette.'

Oh, I could. As a non-smoker I could really do with a cigarette. A drink wouldn't go amiss either. I shakily take out two patches and slap one on each knee. I wonder how he can be so calm.

'So why did you owe the bank all this money? Couldn't you have mortgaged the house or something instead?' I ask.

'It's already been mortgaged. Several times. And if we can't figure out a way to keep the payments up, the mortgage company will take it.'

He sees my bewildered expression and explains further. 'Isabel, when my mother died, I was at university. It was the middle of my second year and I was having a whale of

157

a time. Her death was quite sudden, a heart attack, and I came home immediately. I was devastated – we all were – and Dad didn't want to run Pantiles any more, he just kind of gave up. I thought we could employ an estate manager for a couple of years until I finished university and then I could take over.' He pauses as there is a knock at the door. Mrs Delaney brings in a cup of coffee. For Simon, not me. I wonder if she has had the foresight to put a shot of brandy in it.

'Simon, come through to the kitchen.' There is real affection in her voice.

'In a minute, Mrs D.' He grins up at her. 'They didn't want the kitchen furniture; Mrs Delaney has obviously been ragging it up too much.'

'Good thing too,' she says rather stiffly, without looking at either of us. 'What else would I have to cook on now?'

'Go on,' I urge after she has left because I really need to hear all of this. I need to know the extent of it all. Simon hands his cup of coffee over to me. As he does so, his hand grazes mine and I unthinkingly flinch. Our eyes meet and he looks taken aback.

'Go on,' I say quickly, to cover the discomfort, 'what happened then?'

'Em, well, when I took a look at the accounts, I couldn't quite believe my eyes. Thank God I was doing economics at uni or else we would all have been turfed out years ago. I found that instead of the estate making a comfortable amount of money, enough for everyone to live on, it was losing money and rather a lot of it. The house had been mortgaged and re-mortgaged. We had an overdraft at the bank which we never came out of. Dad has always been not much of a businessman and too much of a philanthropist, but the whole thing really wasn't his fault. Over the last fifty years there has been a huge decline in farming. And the foot and mouth situation hasn't helped matters either; in fact, it plunged the whole estate much faster into bankruptcy.'

I nod at this. I had read about it, of course, seen it on the TV, but I had never had first-hand experience of it.

'Most of our land is farmland,' Simon continues. 'We rent a lot of it out but when things got tough Dad, being the man he is, lowered the rent. He also never raised the rent on the cottages, not in twenty years. The last chunk of our earnings, although it's marginal, comes from forestry and that has also suffered a decline.' I remember the abandoned sawmill on my tour with Will. 'Put all this together and we had virtually no income. Once I realised this, I knew I couldn't go back to university.'

I think of my own carefree existence at university and wonder what I would have done if this had happened to me. I wouldn't have been able to spot a profit and loss account back then if someone had brought it to me on a plate with watercress around it.

'Couldn't you have sold it all?'

'I thought about it. But I knew it would break Dad's heart and I couldn't do that to him after he'd just lost Mum. There were so many people to consider – Dad was beside himself with grief, Will was about to go to Cirencester and then Aunt Flo came to live with us. They all depended on the estate. Besides, I thought there was a chance I could turn it around. I didn't really tell anyone how bad it all was. I had to dismiss every member of staff we had, which left me extremely unpopular in the village, and then figure out a way to keep us afloat. I couldn't do anything in the short-term regarding the farmland and the forestry but I tried to let the cottages out. The problem was they had fallen into so much disrepair. We've managed to restore a couple but I then had to evict the tenants when they wouldn't pay the market rate for them, which is, of course, nearly three times the price they are paying now. I wanted to diversify. Have pheasant shoots, open up the house, outdoor concerts. But when I did the maths, I found that it all needed so much money to start up.'

'What about something like this charity ball? You're making some money from that?'

'Hardly anything, Isabel. Besides, if you do it regularly it needs marketing, which costs more money, and events don't just fall into your lap. And I didn't want anyone looking too closely at the house in case they sussed out how much money it needed spending on it.'

'I just thought you'd neglected it.'

'The maintenance costs are astronomical. So I decided to try to make some money. I had a flair for business so I thought that if I could just make a few hundred thousand then perhaps we would have enough to start again. I had nothing to lose at the start so I took risks. Things went well, I discovered I had a talent for M&A and—'

'What's that?' I ask suspiciously. It sounds vaguely kinky.

'Mergers and acquisitions. Takeovers and so on. Take over a company in trouble, split it up and sell it off. You see, Isabel, it was all a carefully constructed façade. The investment banks were happy to invest their money in me once they had visited Pantiles. I waved a bit of the old school tie and Cambridge blue stuff around as well and used their money to take over businesses. At a healthy profit for them, of course.'

'Couldn't you use them to help Pantiles? Use them to help you diversify?'

'They would want to see the house accounts then. They would have to know how much trouble we are in. They wouldn't touch us after that. People presume you have money if you have a lot of assets. We did have some luck – Will came back from travelling and took on the job of estate manager. Mrs Delaney arrived then and was perfectly happy to live in and take a small wage. She keeps the furniture sparkling while the roof practically falls in around us. We had to close up a couple of wings but no one was any the wiser. And I make sure the gardens are kept up; old Fred tends to them in return for one of the estate cottages rent-free. I own a BMW and a few flash suits, the usual trappings of a successful businessman. There are no obvious signs that anything is wrong.'

'I didn't have any idea,' I whisper.

'You wouldn't have. No one does.'

'But you've completed other takeovers. I read about them in the paper.'

'Any money I made I ploughed straight back into the next takeover, using a little here and there to start making some changes at Pantiles. Repairing some of the cottages, that sort of thing. This was going to be my last business venture. I've ploughed every last penny of the company's money into it. We'd have had enough money to clean our slate, buy the house back and invest in the future.'

He stares down at the floor. I feel quite weak with all this information.

He looks up and misinterprets my expression, 'Don't look so worried, Isabel, I'm not going to sue you. Or tell your company.'

'I'm not worried about that.' Oh no, I'm worried that I won't be able to survive under the weight of all this guilt.

Someone will find me in a few years' time, squashed as flat as a pancake like a cartoon character. Completely selfish, of course.

'But the papers,' I say. 'They always said what a success you were, how much money you had . . .'

'Ahh, the papers. Another carefully constructed spin. The first time they got their facts wrong about something, I found it made my life easier. Every negotiation was less of a trial. It was a bit like the old warlords; they went to huge lengths to frighten their opponents and often found they'd won before any fighting took place. My reputation preceded me. People were bending over backwards to give me money. So the stories were carefully released and I found I could walk into a boardroom and the white flag would already be up.'

'So is the takeover really ruined?'

'It is if the American shareholders really are going to back Wings. We need their shares in order to take over the company. I'm waiting for the head man to call me back.'

'What are you going to say?'

'I don't know. But I need to convince them that parting with their shares would still be a good idea. If they think for one second that I'm not going to perform my half of the bargain, they'll stick with Wings and their promises of a brighter future.' He gets up, walks over to the window and stares out. 'The press will be up here soon, they've been calling all morning. They'll find out about the bailiffs and it'll be splashed all over the papers tomorrow, which is not going to help. It will look as though I can't buy one share let alone half a million, despite what my backers say to the contrary. You'd be surprised how bailiffs panic people.'

Actually, I wouldn't be surprised at all. The mere mention

of their name sent the fear of God through me.

Simon turns from the window and smiles at me. How can he be so calm when his whole world has just fallen around his ears? 'It was my own fault in a way,' he says wearily. 'I was playing a dangerous game with the press. We were careful about what we released to them, but it was only a matter of time before they started digging for some dirt. Rob Gillingham offered it to them on a plate. A pity it had to happen now, that's all.'

'Could you keep up the payments on the house while you organise another takeover?' I ask, desperately fishing about for a solution.

'They take years to set up – you need the financial backing for a start. Besides, I poured all of our money into this one. And if so much rests on reputation, what will mine be like after all this? The bailiffs have removed every single scrap of furniture from my home.' He smiles more faintly. 'Isabel, it's not your problem.'

No, buster. I'm not going anywhere until I feel better. And that won't be until I've done something to help. I struggle for a moment with the irony that I actually want to help Simon but I have to concede that he's not behaving as I thought he would. 'Simon, I grew up in this house. They might not have always been the happiest times of my life' – he has the grace to look uncomfortable at this – 'but I still care what happens to you all. And it's partly my fault because of Rob.'

'He would still have got that information, Izzy.' This is the first time he has called me that since I arrived. 'With or without you.'

'I just made it easy for him,' I say miserably.

'Come on, let's go through to the kitchen. It's a bit of a

163

relief that the family now know. I never wanted to worry them with how bad things were. Poor things, they probably just thought I was being stingy. No fires during the day, insisting the dogs were fed out of a tin instead of with organic chickens. Only Will knew the truth.' He smiles wryly.

'Will knew?'

Simon looks at me curiously. 'Yes, he guessed. I obviously tried to make light of it for him but he's the estate manager, Izzy. How could he not have guessed?'

'But he was saying how . . .'

'How what?'

'Nothing.'

I watch Simon walk out of the room. Will knew and yet still led me to believe that Simon was as bad as people said. Interesting.

I follow Simon but pause thoughtfully in the hall and look up at the wall above the fireplace. I know exactly what is missing. A painting. A very valuable painting. Of course it would have been one of the very first things to be sold. I enter the kitchen where the wake is still in full swing.

'Want to go fishing, Harry?' Simon offers. Harry nods eagerly; the atmosphere in the kitchen is a little oppressive to say the least. He leaps up from the table and goes through to the utility room to collect the gear. I just hope the bailiffs haven't taken it.

'What about your phone call, Simon?' I ask.

'Got my mobile.' He pats his pocket. 'They can still reach me.'

And with this, he and Harry open the back door and walk out into the sunshine.

Chapter 15

Which leaves the rest of us in the kitchen.

'Izzy, what on earth are you wearing?' asks Aunt Flo. Her family home is in imminent danger of being repossessed and she still manages to comment on my fashion faux pas.

I look down at myself. With thoughts of my impending doom rather than my wardrobe most prominent in my mind this morning, I have managed to dress myself in an eclectic mix of clothes. Rather cleverly, I have picked every mismatching piece of clothing I have with me and then put them all on together. A smart mini-skirt teamed with flip-flops and a rugby shirt that I'm not sure is mine.

'Yes. Well. I was thinking of other things,' I murmur.

Personally I would like to retire somewhere private to lick my wounds but the rest of the family are determined to extract all the information they can from me. Thankfully, the bailiffs have left most of the stuff in the kitchen. At Monty's invitation, I pull out a chair and flop into it.

'Simon thought you were still seeing Rob Gillingham?' ventures Monty.

'Yes, but we really did finish about a month ago. However,

I saw Rob the other night and he asked me some questions about Simon. I thought he was just being interested.'

'See?' says Aunt Flo triumphantly. 'I told Simon there must have been a mix-up somewhere! But he kept whittling on about something happening when you were children!'

'I didn't tell Rob those things in the paper,' I press on hastily. 'Simon thinks Rob must have spoken to the evicted tenants and then told the press.'

There's a small pause as everyone digests this information. 'I'll make you some coffee. You look all in,' says Mrs Delaney, getting up and bustling over to the kettle. People can be kind.

'Thanks,' I murmur.

'I blame myself,' announces Monty eventually, breaking the silence. Mrs Delaney plonks a fresh cafetière of coffee on the table and a clean mug in front of me. 'If Pantiles hadn't been in such a bad way in the first place, Simon wouldn't be involved in this takeover. I was never much of a businessman.'

'You couldn't have known that the farming industry was going to decline so dramatically, dear. And you were just trying to be good to the villagers, letting them stay on in the cottages like that,' says Flo, putting a hand over his.

'I always thought I had a duty towards the village.'

'Come on, Dad! None of us knew how bad a state the place was in,' says Will.

I find myself looking at him in astonishment. He immediately colours. He knows that I know. And I know that he knows that I know. And he knows that I know, etc, etc. Suddenly I don't see the handsome young man any more, I see a little boy who is annoyed with his brother.

'You still have the house,' I offer up hopefully, to cover his embarrassment.

'For how long? The place is practically falling in around our ears, and then there's the mortgage payments to be kept up with.'

'How have you been paying them up to now?'

'With Simon's profit, of course. It looks like all that may stop now.'

I bite my lip and feel terrible. Flo notices my distress and leans over to pat my knee.

'Do you think the charity ball will still go ahead?' I ask in general.

'We couldn't let them down again. And we could really do with that money now!' says Monty. 'Have you got any meetings today, Izzy?'

'This afternoon but I'll put them off.'

There's a loud knock at the back door and we all jump. Dominic pokes his head into the room. 'Can I come in? Aren't you amazing, you country folk, leaving your doors unlocked. Are you planning to execute Izzy at dawn?'

'God, Dom!' I say, jumping up and throwing my arms around him. 'I've never been so pleased to see you in my life!'

'And I'm not carrying any food either! Astonishing!'

'What are you doing here?'

'I gave in my notice at work! Just walked out and came straight here!'

'Oh Dom, you shouldn't have done that!'

'Don't worry, I was having a really boring morning until you called. You galvanised me into action at last! Besides, I thought you might want me around.' He links his arm through mine. 'Actually, I feel marvellous!' he pronounces.

He looks at the gloomy faces before him. 'Well, obviously not marvellous about the takeover thing. That's *awful*, simply awful.' He beams and tries not to look too ecstatic about life in general. We don't get out much.

In fact, everyone seems jolly pleased to see him. Monty and Will pump his arm while Aunt Flo plants a kiss on his cheek. 'Do shut the door, dear,' says Aunt Flo. 'People keep not shutting it properly and the postman fell in yesterday. The dogs were so surprised they didn't know what to do with him.'

'So what's happened?' asks Dom.

I quickly explain about the takeover and Rob. Dom looks absolutely incensed.

'Well, I'm bloody glad I handed my notice in now! I couldn't have worked for him any longer! What a louse!'

'You worked for him?' asks Monty, puzzled.

'Only in the claims department. It was my day job. I actually want to write a novel.'

'Oh really? What about?' asks Aunt Flo chattily.

'You didn't mention to Rob that I was working here, did you?' I say suddenly, ignoring Flo.

Dom looks slightly uncomfortable, 'Well, not to him directly. But I might have mentioned it in the office. It's lucky he didn't know *I* was working here too. God knows what I would have told him!'

We all fall into silence. Eventually I whisper, 'What do you think Simon is going to do?'

Everyone looks blankly at each other. I excuse myself, pick up my bag, which is still by the door, and go to my room. I mill about for a while, unpacking my bag, painting my toenails for want of something better to do and thinking. Rob was using me for information. He was using me. I repeat this to myself again and again. He was using me to keep his place on a board of directors. I knew he was ambitious but I had no idea quite how ambitious.

Rob and his cronies must be out celebrating right now. I picture him easing a champagne cork out of a bottle, a grin right across his face. He will be boasting about how he brought down Simon Monkwell almost single-handedly. Almost but not quite, because I managed to play my part too.

I lie on my bed and eye the room. My bag is lying by the side of the bed and on an impulse I drag it towards me. I get out my purse and eye a photo of Rob that I haven't quite got around to removing yet. It's a photo I nicked from his flat – he hated it on sight and threw it away but I carefully fished it out of the bin while he was in the loo. It's thus that Dominic finds me.

'Hellooo, my little dollop of sunshine. The family has just been telling me about the bailiffs! So this is a little worse than it first appears. If that's possible.' He sits down on the bed. 'How are you feeling?' He pulls a face to indicate that his bet would be 'not so good'.

'Not so good.'

'Which bit in particular is bothering you? Your ex-boyfriend wanting to shag you for information or the bringing down of an empire?' You know, sometimes Dominic just isn't very funny.

'Bit of both.'

'It's kind of a double-whammy, isn't it?'

'Simon was nicer than I expected once I'd explained. I honestly thought he was going to go mad and fire me.'

'Well, he could have done. Do you suppose Rob thought about that? That you could actually lose your job?' This isn't a real question, he's just trying to build up the bad feeling in me against Rob.

He looks down at the photo. 'Give me the photo, Izzy. Hand it over.'

'What are you going to do with it?'

'Burn it. I will not have you drooling over a man as despicable as he is.'

'I'm not drooling over him. I'm just trying to make some sense of it all,' I say sulkily.

'You should be furious!'

'I am a bit,' I say crossly, sitting up suddenly and swinging my legs around so I'm sitting next to Dom.

'A bit?' roars Dom. 'You should want to tear him limb from limb! Christ, *I* want to tear him limb from limb! If I hadn't just resigned from his sodding company then I would be doing so now! And I hope you're not going to let him get away with this.'

Actually, that was exactly what I was planning to do.

'No,' I say in a very small voice, shifting position again.

'You are, aren't you? Where is the "hell hath no fury like an extremely pissed-off woman" thing? Eh?'

'What could I do?'

'I don't know! Send him bags of offal, paint his Boxter, anything!'

'I don't want to do stuff like that. Although you're right, I don't see why he should get away with it,' I say, feeling slightly more incensed.

'Well, we'll think about it. There's more than one way to wash a lettuce, as we in the catering world would say.' We would say no such thing. 'Revenge is a dish best served cold. Think Vichyssoise.'

'Okay, let's burn the photo!' I say with more enthusiasm.

After all, this is much more fun than mooching around.

'Atta girl!' Dom leaps up, strides across the room and returns with the metal wastepaper bin. He sits with it between his knees. 'Right! You light it!' He hands me the photo and his lighter.

'Right!' I agree, a large grin spreading across my face. I light the bottom corner of the photo and watch with pleasure as the flames start to lick up the paper, Rob's face bubbling long before the flames reach it. I drop it with satisfaction into the bin.

Unfortunately, the pads of cotton wool that I used to remove my nail varnish go up with a small WHOOSH!

'Oh Christ!' says Dom, looking down into our own miniature version of the *Towering Inferno* and quickly dropping the bin. 'Oh Christ!' I repeat.

'Quick, Izzy! Help me!'

I leap up and look around the room for something to douse the flames. I run from corner to corner but there isn't even a flannel in sight. 'Izzy!! Quick, quick!' shouts Dom, still transfixed by the spectacle.

I pull out three pairs of damp knickers from the top of my travel bag, washed just before I left, and run back. I am debating which pair I would least like to lose when Dom grabs the lot and dumps them on the fire. I watch with resignation as my best M&S pants successfully douse the flames.

'Thank God for your large arse, Izzy,' says Dominic cheerfully.

This really isn't my day.

After a mammoth sulking session I finally agree to go back downstairs because, as Dom points out, it's the only way

I'll get my hands on a stiff drink. I take my mobile with me. A bit of Dutch courage might give me the strength to turn the damn thing on and face the calls I know will be waiting for me from Gerald. He's bound to have read the papers this morning and will want to know the implications of the failed takeover.

Dom holds the door open for me and together we start walking towards the kitchen. 'I think it's probably best, Izz, if we keep the small blaze in your bedroom to ourselves,' he says. 'The family might start to think you don't like them very much if they realise that you just tried to burn the house down on top of single-handedly ruining the takeover. Maybe we should put bells on your ankles to warn people of your approach.'

I ignore him and call the charity instead to cancel our meeting. I tell Rose that I will reschedule as soon as everything is clearer, reassure her that the ball will still go ahead as planned, and then ring off before I can be questioned any further. I switch the mobile off again, still unable to face Gerald, and follow Dominic into the kitchen.

The whole family, apart from Harry and Simon who I presume are still out fishing, are in the same position as we left them – slumped around the kitchen table.

'Will you and Dominic be going back to London?' asks Aunt Flo as soon as we walk into the room. The question has obviously been on her mind. The rest of the family look at us expectantly. 'Where will you hold your meetings for the ball?'

'We'll figure something out. I could meet Rose and Mary in Bury St Edmunds tomorrow. But if Simon doesn't want us here, I suppose we can go back and try to arrange things from the office in London. Otherwise we'd like to stay and help. If we can,' I say awkwardly. Dom meets my eye and nods slightly to indicate his agreement. I probably couldn't tear him away even if I wanted to – he seems to have taken quite a shine to the Monkwell family.

Just as I say this, the back door flies open and Simon and Harry march in looking a little dishevelled. We all perk up.

'I've thought of something,' announces Simon. 'It might not work but it's worth a try. Now, who's for a drink?' The man is a genius. Two winning phrases in one breath.

Our group dynamic now takes on an almost party atmosphere. Monty leaps up, rubbing his hands together, and rushes to get his twenty-year-old malt from its secret hidey hole.

I help Mrs Delaney gather some glasses from the cupboard.

'What have you done to your knees, Izzy?' asks Harry, pointing at my nicotine patches. 'I could have dressed the wounds for you. I have my badge in first aid.'

I blush and glance down at the offending patches. I had forgotten all about them. I am just about to pass them off as plasters when Simon says, 'They're nicotine patches. Izzy is giving up smoking.'

The family look at me in surprise. 'You used to smoke, Izzy?' asks Will.

I open my mouth to reply but Dominic is too quick for me. 'Like a chimney,' he choruses. My hands tighten involuntarily around my glass. I could brain him with it.

Monty pours a shot of his whisky into each glass. I glug mine in one go and feel all the better for it, even though my eyes are watering. I think these patches might be having a beneficial effect on me; I feel positively gung-ho.

We all savour the whisky in silence until Monty

eventually asks, 'So what have you thought of, Simon?'

We all look at Simon expectantly. 'Well, there's no guarantee this will work. I've asked the American shareholders up here to visit. To see if we can salvage this takeover.'

'Up here?' echoes Monty.

'But the furniture . . . ?' says Aunt Flo slowly.

'Well, that's where you lot come in. We need the house re-furnished by tomorrow.'

'Tomorrow?'

'Yes. I'm going to brief our PR agency to invite the press up here tomorrow morning. So they can see for themselves that no bailiffs have visited. The Americans will be arriving at lunchtime.' He looks steadily at us.

'But that's impossible,' says Will.

'Which is exactly why it will work. The quicker we can turn this around, the less anyone will suspect anything is up. If the press see the house furnished there is no way any of them will dare to print that the bailiffs have been here even if the villagers tell them to the contrary. They wouldn't imagine that we could re-furnish the house as quickly as that. The Americans arriving will further refute any rumours, if only in their own minds, and we can try to salvage the takeover at the same time. Any questions?' He looks around the room.

About a dozen are poised on my lips but I don't feel I can ask them since I was the one who got everyone into this mess in the first place. It's an interesting task considering we have two OAPs, a cub scout and a pissy housekeeper on our team. And Dom, who is a bit of a liability at the best of times. I think the others are struck dumb which Simon takes as a sign of assent.

'Great! I've got a ton of work to do! I've called my team

and they're on their way up from London. Are you sure you want to stay, Izzy, Dominic?' asks Simon before he leaves.

Dominic looks completely thrilled by the entire scenario so Simon turns his attention to me. I surprise myself by nodding firmly. He gives me a half-smile, nods and disappears, leaving the rest of us with the task of returning the house to a furnished state. I fish around for some paper and a pen in the hope that I will be positively swamped with ideas.

'Right!' says Monty, 'we need the furniture back!'

'Right!' everyone choruses.

'Right!' says Monty. We all look at each other for a moment. I start a doodle on the corner of my paper. Silence ensues and I can feel the mood of the group begin to deflate like a slow puncture.

'I don't think we're going to be able to get your furniture back from the bailiffs,' I venture. 'They won't release it until Simon has coughed up the money to the bank.'

'Well, we only need to furnish the hallway, the dining room and the drawing room for the visitors. We needn't bother with the library or the rest of the rooms.'

'And the bedrooms are okay, aren't they? They didn't take anything from there?'

'No, they're fine.'

'What about if we hire some furniture?' I suggest.

Monty excitedly slaps the table. 'Yes! We'll hire it! Izz, go and get the Yellow Pages!'

I run all the way down to the study, quietly open the door and find Simon talking animatedly on the phone. I extract the Yellow Pages from the pile of debris in the corner and then run back to the kitchen. We look up furniture hire, dismiss quite a few entries since we are specifically looking for 'period' furniture and then find a discreet advertisement for 'Merritt and Son' who promise quality antiques.

Monty dials the number while we all sit around expectantly. He explains that he has been let down by someone else but needs to furnish three reception rooms by tomorrow. From the various responses we gather this isn't a problem and that the company could deliver tomorrow if wished. We look at each other in relief and I almost lean back in my chair. But when Monty goes on to explain that we have a van and would like to collect the furniture ourselves, the tone of the conversation shifts. We all frown and Monty says he'll get back to them and then rings off.

'They won't let us collect because they need to see where it's going. I suppose we could say we were anyone and then run off with it. Besides which, it isn't insured if we collect it ourselves.'

'Couldn't they deliver it?' asks Aunt Flo.

'Thing is, we don't want them to see where it's going in case they talk to the press. And if the villagers or the reporters see their vans coming up the drive, they'll put two and two together.'

'Aren't we going to have the same problem if we collect it?'

'I was thinking we could hire a van and then take a different route into the estate, which would bypass the village altogether. You can come in through the woods.'

'Can't the hire people come in through the woods?'

'We're still left with the problem of them talking to the press. And it will look very suspicious if we ask them to

176

come up through the woods. They would know they're coming to Pantiles.'

We all slump forward again and think in silence. Nobody says what we're all thinking: can we really pull this off?

Chapter 16

At about three o'clock (which feels about midnight) Sam comes through to ask if refreshments could be brought in for the takeover team, who have been holed up in the study ever since they arrived a few hours ago. I busy myself preparing huge cafetières of coffee and Mrs Delaney finds some biscuits and half a cake as well. I take the tray through to the study. I push the door open with my bum and find a collection of lawyers, accountants and God knows who else sitting on the floor, all with martyred expressions on their faces. I don't want to know what Simon has said to explain the absence of any furniture but I fervently hope he has kept me out of it.

'Thanks, Izzy,' says Simon, looking up and nodding at me.

'You're going to need food at some point; do you want me to sort it out?'

'That would be great, Izzy. Mrs D will have stuff about.'

I nod and gladly escape.

While we have all taken a small break from the furniture replacement problem, I take the opportunity to call Gerald. I access my voicemail to discover he has indeed been trying to get hold of me. Seven messages, the last one talking darkly of P45s and public lynching. I give my nicotine patches an extra rub and dial the office number with a slightly trembling hand. Stephanie doesn't even pause to tell me how much trouble I'm in; she simply mumbles 'Oh shit,' and puts me through.

'Where in the name of God have you been?'

I have to hold the phone away from my ear. 'Er calm down now, Gerald—'

'I have been calling and calling.'

'Well, I only just turned my mobile on—'

'So you found the "on" button, did you? Now there's a miracle.'

'We've been very busy here.'

'Do you think you could occasionally perform a random act of intelligence and actually call in?'

'Well, as you've no doubt seen from the papers, stuff has been going on . . .'

'Is the ball still going ahead? What *is* going on? Lady Boswell has been calling every hour on the hour.'

I have a go at explaining the situation. 'Well, to be honest, not much is going on.' That's the stuff, Izzy, blind him with science. 'The papers have got it all wrong and the takeover is still going ahead. Which naturally means the ball is still going ahead. Simon has also asked me to help with some American visitors who are arriving tomorrow and so I am very busy.' This is said in an imperious, don't-disturb-me tone. I know Gerald will be pleased about the extra corporate work so I cross everything and hope.

It does the trick and slightly takes the wind out of his sails. 'Trust the press to get things arse about tit. I should have known. Next time, however, do you think you could

179

possibly call the office first when something like this happens? You know, the place where you supposedly work? A good party planner excels at communication.'

'Of course,' I say, fervently hoping that there will never ever be a next time. 'It means I won't be back on Friday. How are things at your end?' I ask quickly.

'Fine, apart from the fact that Dawsons have announced they've invited another hundred. They're your clients, you must have got them into bad habits or something. People are wandering about with streamers and muttering four-letter words; it's like hell is throwing a party. How's Dominic?' Everyone is obsessed with Dominic's health.

'He's fine.'

'How's he getting on? Is he annoying anyone?'

'No, the family love him.'

'Good. Keep it that way.'

We hang up.

Feeling vaguely grateful that I am not about to join the ranks of the great unemployed, I head back to the kitchen where Monty and Flo are in the middle of a row about who has received the worst bee sting ever, both being allergic to them. Mrs Delaney is trying to sell tuna sandwiches to Harry on the grounds that Butt Ugly Martians live on nothing else and Dominic is sitting on the floor feeding the dogs Jaffa Cakes – but only after he has eaten the orange bit.

'Have you solved our problem with the furniture?' I ask Dominic, hoping this is the reason that anarchy has broken out.

'Huh? Oh no, we were waiting for you to come back.' I didn't realise I was essential to the solution and the pressure has me reaching for another glass of whisky.

Our little group of vigilantes reconverge at the table. 'Right, where were we?' asks Monty.

'We can't get back the original furniture from the bailiffs and we've tried a hire firm.'

'Any thoughts anyone?'

I don't have any thoughts apart from the one where Simon kills me because we haven't arranged any furniture. We organise ourselves into thinking positions and settle down in silence.

Ten minutes later, with no solution in sight, Will returns from a fact-finding expedition into the village. I sit up, glad for a little distraction.

'What happened?'

He looks depressed. 'Basically, the villagers did see the vans and they did tell the press. Some reporters are hanging about at the front gate. Daniel is driving around the perimeter trying to keep them out.' This is not the news any of us wanted to hear. 'I'd better go and tell Simon.'

I get up. 'I've got to make some food for them, so if you wait five minutes we can interrupt them together.' Mrs Delaney and I make up a pile of tuna sandwiches and Will and I carry them through to the library.

The group is deep in conversation as we walk in. Will pulls Simon to one side and starts to relate his news to him in a low voice. Simon beckons me over. 'How is the furniture solution looking?' he whispers.

'Errmmm . . .'

'Izzy, I don't care how you do it, just get some furniture here for tomorrow. Our PR firm are on their way up here to look after the press situation.'

'We'll get there.' I try to sound as positive as possible. My mobile rings and I walk out to the hallway to take the call.

'Hello?' I answer, my voice echoing strangely in the empty space.

'Me dear, it's me. I've been worried about you and so I've called to see how you got on. You still sound reasonably alive so I presume Simon hasn't done anything heinous to you!' booms Aunt Winnie.

I go over to the stairs, sit on the bottom one and try to explain the events of the last five hours to her. '. . . and I don't know where to get enough furniture to fill three gigantic rooms and I still have to organise the ball and then there are Simon's American visitors arriving tomorrow who are very important for the takeover.' My voice rises danger-ously at the end of the sentence. The act of relating events to Aunt Winnie has made me realise the Herculean task before me. I'm beginning to feel a little hysterical.

'Can see your problem, me dear. Rotten old luck.' Rotten? Old? Luck? Rotten old luck that I happened to be going out with the worst shit in England who was prepared to do anything to keep his stupid seat on a board of direc-tors? Rotten old luck that the house owes trillions of pounds to the bank and they've taken all the furniture away? Or rotten old luck that a tonne of foreign visitors will be descending on the house tomorrow?

'I might have an idea. The old grey cells are whirring,' Aunt Winnie says before I can reply. 'Can I call you back?'

'Sure!' I say in surprise and go through to eat something. Things always look better after tuna sandwiches.

I am just tucking into my third when the phone rings again. It's Aunt Winnie.

'I think I might have the solution, me dear! It came to me in a flash!' she shouts. There is no need to relay the conversation as the entire room can hear exactly what she

182

is saying. 'I was watching that marvellous Hugh Scully! Gorgeous man!'

'What is it?'

'Don't you worry about it. I'll turn up tonight with the furniture.'

'We need it for sure, Aunt Winnie.'

'And you'll have it for sure. Now, which rooms are you talking about and is there anything specific you need?'

I hand the mobile over to Monty so he can issue further instructions. Thank God for Aunt Winnie. A pity they can't clone her and fill the government with her.

'Astounding woman, that,' says Monty as he puts the phone down. 'She says she'll turn up tonight with it. I told her not to use the main gate. One of us will have to go down to the gate in the woods to meet her.'

'Where's she going to get it from?' Will asks.

I shake my head. 'I don't know.' And nor do I want to, I think to myself.

The rest of the afternoon is spent making up the rooms for the foreign visitors. The rooms themselves also look a little shabby and so I spend over an hour collecting flowers and greenery from the garden to brighten them up. Dominic and I will have to move out of our old bedrooms tomorrow and into a twin room in another wing of the house. Oh joy.

At about eight o'clock, I go out to the walled garden to be alone for ten minutes.

'Penny for them?'

I spin round to see Simon standing in the archway to the walled garden. I'm fingering a sprig of rosemary and trying to make some sense of everything.

He walks slowly towards me and I manage a half-smile.

I wish he would just go away and leave me to try to put my tumbling thoughts into some order. I go back to my fiddling as a massive hint that I want to be left alone, especially if he's going to ball me out again. I know I deserve it but perhaps we could save some for later.

'Rosemary,' he says. 'For remembrance?'

'Can I get you anything?' I ask, trying to bring the conversation back to more comfortable, professional ground.

He shakes his head and says, 'Dad says you've sorted the furniture situation?' I nod and he continues, 'The team have all gone. The American investors will arrive tomorrow as scheduled.' He looks absolutely shattered.

'Look, Simon, Dom and I are supposed to be going back to London tomorrow. Do you want us to stay to help with the visitors? I mean, it is what we do for a living.'

'But it'll be over the weekend.'

'That's okay. We don't have a function and we were due back here on Monday anyhow so I won't need to tell the office. I know Mrs Delaney has got the food sorted but I was thinking of the general entertainment stuff. I could take the hostess role.'

'Actually, that would be great.'

'And I thought Dominic could become your resident butler for a few days. Help with the image.'

'Is he okay with that?'

'He suggested it!' Dominic has done no such thing but he deserves it after the cigarette situation. 'I'll run into Bury St Edmunds first thing and hire him a suit.'

'Thanks.'

There's a pause as he also wanders over to the rosemary bush and extracts a sprig. He comes back towards me, sprig in hand, examining it intently.

'This was my mother's garden. She used to spend every minute out here. Sometimes I think she used to prefer this garden to us!'

'You can tell how much it used to be loved,' I remark, looking around at the once tamed and tethered clematis and honeysuckle, now riding roughshod over everything in their path.

'I shouldn't have let it get so overgrown.'

'It just needs some attention,' I say, trying to comfort him for a second as he looks so bereft. Despite all we've been through, I feel a rush of affection for him. Whether I like it or not, a great deal of my past is tied up with this man. He looks up at me and I'm jolted by his eyes. Something passes through them that I recognise but can't put into words. Then it's gone.

'Do you want to walk down to see the deer?' he asks.

'Em, I don't think I'm wearing the right shoes for that.' I look at my neck-breaking flip-flops.

'I'll wait for you if you want to put on something else?'

For a second I'm tempted. I had glimpsed something. Something warm and comfortable and easy to fall back into. But then I remember everything that came after it.

'No, I'm sorry, Simon. I've got things to do.'

He smiles at me and holds my eyes for a second. 'I'm sorry too,' he says lightly and then turns and walks away, leaving me staring after him.

I go up to my room, take off my rugby top and replace it with a clingy pink T-shirt. Meg the dog and Dom appear in my doorway.

'Where are you off to?' Dom asks suspiciously, clocking the different clothes. 'Secret assignation?'

'No, just felt grubby suddenly. Thought I would change for supper.'

'Then why are you putting on lipstick?'

'I always put on lipstick.'

'Not for me you don't.'

Well that's because you're gay, I nearly say, but then wonder what that's got to do with it.

'Have you asked if they want us to stay this weekend and help with the Americans?' Dom continues.

'Em, actually I've just asked Simon and he says that would be marvellous. Did you have any plans for the weekend?' I think I'll save my wonderful butler news for when we have a little more time for Dominic's certain hysterics.

'I can change them. I'll just tell, er, whoever that I can't make it. They'll understand.'

'You know, Dom, I don't care who you're seeing.'

'This is somebody a bit, er, different.'

'Darling, anyone you see would be okay with me,' I say, just to give him the message loud and clear that I will love him whatever.

'We'll talk about it soon, I promise. It's a bit confusing for me at the minute and there's so much going on here with Rob and stuff.'

'I know. Are you coming down for a drink?'

'I thought I might have a bath actually.'

'Okay. I'll see you later!'

I skip downstairs, wondering anxiously if Dom might think our relationship will change or something. He's not normally so backward at coming forward. I then hover in the hallway for a moment, thinking, before running up-stairs, to collect my mobile. I have a peculiar need for some reassurance and so I ring my parents. As the call is to Hong

Kong and on my mobile, I ask them to call me back on the landline and jog through to the now deserted library. I pick up the phone as soon as it rings. 'Hello?' I say cautiously, just in case it isn't them.

'Darling!'

'Mum!'

'What a *lovely* surprise! We've tried *calling* the flat; where *have* you been? Your father *says* where *are* you? Because the *area* code is quite near *Pantiles*, the *Monkwell* estate. Do you *remember*? Where the *horses* were?'

'Yes, I remember. In fact, that's where I am.'

'Where?'

'At Pantiles.'

There's a silence as she obviously sits down and then says to my father, 'That's where she is. At Pantiles.' I wait patiently in the silence until she eventually says, 'Why *are* you *there*?'

'It's the strangest thing. I'm here to organise a party for Monty Monkwell!'

They are not receiving the news as I thought they would. I had thought there would be lots of initial gasps and ooh-ing and aah-ing and then we would settle down to a proper chinwag about our memories of the place and then I could launch into my tale of woe. There is none of that, just another awkward silence.

'Er, Mum?' I finally ask. 'Everything okay?'

'Yes, *fine*, darling,' she says eventually. 'Look, *can* we *call* you back?'

'When?'

'In a *day* or so.'

'Of course, but everything's okay?'

'Yes!' she says in an artificially high voice when she clearly means, 'No!'

Chapter 17

At a quarter to midnight, Will and I set off towards the woods armed with torches and a dog (not Meg, we have decided on a fierce terrier called Albert in case we run into trouble). Part of me cannot help but be thrilled with the secret squirrel theme but the rest of me is tired and would like a long lie down. But I'm glad of the opportunity to speak to Will.

The moon is almost full and very bright so we don't need the torches until we get to the woods. Neither of us have spoken since we left the house, but as soon as we switch our torches on conversation somehow seems permissible.

'All a bit of a shock, isn't it?' I whisper to Will, watching Albert bounding ahead and feeling reassured by his presence. The woods are still as creepy as I remember them being. An owl hoots every now and then and the woods crackle with the noise of things moving about. I firmly tell myself that it is only Albert and resist the temptation to leap into Will's arms like Scooby Doo.

He looks over awkwardly at me. 'I did guess, Izzy. Not to this extent, but I did know,' he says, confirming our earlier exchange.

'But you told me how mean Simon was, and about him throwing those tenants out of the cottages.'

'I couldn't tell you the truth. Besides, I was keeping up the Simon myth.'

I don't think you needed to perpetuate it quite so readily, I think to myself. We both fall silent again, embarrassed.

'I suppose,' Will admits finally, 'that I am jealous of him in some ways.'

'Are you?' I say carefully.

'Well, he gets to defend all of this.' He sweeps his arm around in a circle to indicate the silent trees.

'How do you mean?'

'While I go about my menial day-to-day duties, Simon gets to play . . . I don't know . . . he gets to play superheros.'

I clear my throat uncomfortably. We are straying into decidedly male, not to mention sibling rivalry, territory. 'I don't think it has been that much fun. I mean, I think it looks more grand than it actually is.'

'And I was cross that he had kept the truth about the estate from me all these years, as though he thought I wasn't strong enough to take the truth.'

'He said to me that he wanted you to go to Cirencester and was worried you wouldn't. Maybe after that it was too late,' I offer, wondering why I'm sticking up for Simon.

'I'd only just returned to the estate when all that press stuff started up. It's quite hard to hear someone you resent being talked about in God-like terms. I suppose it made me resent him even more. Then the bad stuff started about him and I think I wanted to believe it.'

This chat with Will is starting to make me think. Something is shifting and I don't like it much. Will still seems like the young boy I last saw over fifteen years ago. It's unclear whether he really is a lesser man than his brother but unfortunately he is starting to behave as such. 'So you don't think the recent press Simon's had is completely fair?' I ask him.

'I don't doubt that he's been a bit ruthless, but then wouldn't you with all this to look after? The bank and the mortgage company breathing down your neck all the time?'

Simon did say that the PR company had deliberately played up his war god image. The uncomfortable thought comes squirming into my mind that Simon might actually be justified in all he has done – is perhaps even a little noble?

'He always was ruthless, even in childhood.' I chuck this in just to bring us both down to earth. I don't want us, or more specifically me, to forget who we are actually talking about.

'He was pretty nasty to you, I guess.'

'Yes! He was!' I whisper triumphantly, glad to know that I hadn't imagined that part.

'I feel guilty. I've been so critical of him, secretly thinking I can run the place better. And I suppose I said all those things about him because I wanted to spend some time with you, and I was worried that as soon as Simon got home things would go back to how they were when we were kids. Despite your tiff.'

'What do you mean?' I query.

'Well, you two were pretty cliquey, Izzy. An exclusive little club for two. You used to push Sophie and me out all the time.'

Even in the dark, I can feel his dejection. I never realised he felt so strongly about it. I reach out and touch his arm. 'God, I'm sorry, Will. I never realised.'

Before he can respond, we see a huge white lorry parked ahead. A hand pops out of the window and waves at us.

'You little beauty,' breathes Will.

Aunt Winnie clambers out of the driver's side, looking very pleased with herself. The lorry is absolutely enormous and I feel a wave of awe wash over me. She has driven that here all by herself, pausing en-route to pick up some antique furniture and subsequently saving my neck. She should be available on the NHS.

'Hello!' I whisper, going up to her, leaning over the gate and kissing her cheek.

'This *is* fun, Izzy! Hello Will!' Will also leans over the gate to give her a kiss. She has obviously thrown herself into the part as she is dressed in a royal blue boilersuit (considering I have never ever seen her in a pair of trousers except on school sports day this is quite a spectacle) and has a jaunty tweed cap perched on her head.

Will gets out a set of keys and, while I hold the torch over them, proceeds to try to find the right one to unlock the padlock on the gate. 'Did you find this okay?' I whisper to Aunt Winnie.

'Fine! The lanes were a little narrow though.' I bet they were; this is probably the first time that a lorry of this size has ever been down them. The route to the back of the estate consists of tiny country lanes and then a couple of tracks.

'Dear, what are you wearing?'

I glance down. 'Em, my clothes.'

'What have I told you about pink?'

'But I wear a lot of pink.'

'I've decided I don't think you should.'

Right. Marvellous.

Will finally gets the gate open and we swing it back as wide as it will go. 'Do you want me to drive the lorry back, Winnie?' he asks.

'Certainly not!'

'You two get in then, I'll close the gate.'

Aunt Winnie clambers back into the driver's side while I make heroic attempts to get into the passenger's. It is tricky to say the least. I manage to make it up the first two steps but end up lying on the seat with my bum pointing skywards. Albert is very anxious to meet Jameson, who is sitting next to Aunt Winnie, and keeps trying to leap in using me as a ladder.

'Come on, Izzy my girl! Stop pissing about with that dog!'

I'm starting to feel a little hysterical. I think I might need a nicotine patch. Just recently I've found myself thinking, 'I could really do with a cigarette'. I am absolutely positive that is not the point of them.

Aunt Winnie starts the engine, which sounds deafening in the silence of the night, and I haul myself into the cab by grabbing on to the gear stick. Albert is settled in my seat, having already scrambled over my head. I shut the door. 'There!' I say triumphantly as though I have just scaled Everest, and squash myself down next to the dogs. Aunt Winnie stifles a giggle, stops making a fuss of Albert and selects first gear. We trundle through the gate, and pause while Will shuts and locks it and then leaps in. He doesn't have my entry problems.

I didn't notice how rutted the track was as we walked down but now I wonder how I could have missed it. The lorry sways back and forth alarmingly and on occasions I wonder whether we're going to topple over completely. There is total silence as Aunt Winnie concentrates on getting us all there safely, with only a few gasps from me as tree branches seem to come out of nowhere at us. Finally, as we reach the relative smoothness of the driveway and Aunt Winnie changes down into second gear, I let go of a breath I didn't realise I was holding.

A few moments later we're in the courtyard, and as soon as Aunt Winnie turns off the engine the kitchen door opens, letting out a shaft of light on to the cobbles. Will has already leaped out.

'Be nice to Simon,' I say to our driver in a low voice. Aunt Winnie hasn't got a very reliable record of being pleasant to people she doesn't think much of and I haven't had time to fill her in. 'He's been through a lot.'

I jump carefully out of the cab; I don't particularly want to miss my footing as it's a long way to fall. Albert leaps out in front of me without any thought for body or soul, swiftly followed by Jameson. I move round to the back of the lorry where Monty, Mrs Delaney, Dominic, Flo, Simon and Will are congregated (Harry is in bed). After Aunt Winnie has made the appropriate greetings to the rest of the family, which feels quite strange in the dark and in whispered voices but we English have to observe our etiquette, Aunt Winnie presses a super whizzy button and the door of the lorry opens and then a tail-lift lowers itself down. We shine our torches in the back to reveal a pile of furniture, professionally packed, looking exactly like a removal van. I'm impressed.

'Where did you get all this, Aunt Winnie?' whispers Simon.

'I borrowed about half of it; most of the heavy stuff is mine.'

'But where from?' I ask.

'The village. Told them I was taking it to *The Antiques Roadshow*. I saw it on the TV while I was talking to you, Izzy, and they said the next one was going to be in Norwich. So I told everyone I was taking it up there.'

Monty has to stifle a particularly loud guffaw.

'You didn't!' I say incredulously.

'I damn well did! I waltzed into their sitting rooms with my pocket antique guide under my arm and picked out what I wanted. The vicar and young Tommy helped me load everything up. I took one or two pieces from almost every house in the village. Obviously when they don't see me on the box and then talk to each other, they'll probably think I've done a bunk but, ho hum, I'll think of something.'

'You're amazing,' says Simon quite genuinely.

Aunt Winnie looks quite abashed for a second and awkwardly says, 'We'd better get this stuff in.'

'No, really,' interjects Monty, shining his torch on to her. 'You are amazing.'

This time Aunt Winnie blushes quite prettily.

The men move all the heavy stuff inside while we women shift things like occasional tables and lamps. It's quite a performance as we daren't use the front door in case anyone sees us so we have to go through the kitchen and down the long passageway into the hall. We arrange the three rooms into some sort of order – they look nothing like they did before but at least they don't look as though the bailiffs have just left. The whimsical mix of styles and eras makes the place look as though it has been furnished by an eccentric aunt, which in a way I suppose it has. The hall looks a little empty but it's such a large space that it's exceedingly difficult to fill it, so we light-finger a few spindly tables from the bedrooms upstairs and dot them around the walls.

'There!' says Aunt Flo. 'That looks quite good, doesn't it?'

It's about two in the morning and a sheep pickled in formaldehyde in the middle of the room would look fairly good to me, but we all agree and retire to the kitchen for a cup of tea. Will goes out to the courtyard to drive the lorry into one of the stables.

'You will stay, won't you?' says Simon to Aunt Winnie. 'Presumably you can't go home if your neighbours are expecting to see you on the box with Hugh Scully any day now.'

'I was going to stay with a friend.'

'Do stay, Winnie,' says Monty earnestly. I open my mouth to add my plea but it's not needed. She looks over at Monty and smiles. 'Okay. I don't think I'd want to miss all the excitement anyway!'

After a bit of fuss about an overnight bag which appears to have been locked in the lorry – the same lorry that Will has just spent ten minutes reversing into one of the stables – Mrs Delaney and Aunt Winnie disappear upstairs together to find a suitable bedroom.

Simon tells us that the press are turning up at nine tomorrow morning, the PR company are here to take care of them and that if we come across any reporters we are to look casual but on no account answer any questions. Simon is looking very long and hard at Monty and Flo when he says this.

We all retire to bed. Meg has obviously decided that since

Albert got to accompany us earlier she now gets to sleep in my room, which is fine by me as a bit of company is much appreciated. I get to my room to find all the windows still open, so the room is freezing cold but still smells faintly of burnt knickers. I can't believe it was only this morning that I was burning Rob's photo; it feels like weeks ago. I crawl into bed feeling absolutely exhausted but then have a small panic that some madman might have come in through the windows while we were all otherwise engaged and is now hiding in the wardrobe. I check the wardrobe by opening the door with a coathanger. No madman. I clamber back into bed and drop off instantly.

A few minutes later, my alarm wakes me at six. I sit bolt upright in bed and wonder why I'm feeling so awful. Then the events of the last few days slowly come back to me and I suppress a small groan. What I would really like to do is crawl back underneath my duvet and dissolve in a pile of apathy; I feel weighed down with guilt at causing such a horrendous mess. At least I have both Dominic and Aunt Winnie with me; I hope Aunt Winnie has brought her golf clubs.

I duly perform my morning toilette which takes much longer than Meg's. Hers consists of stretching and yawning for twenty seconds. If I get a choice the next time around I want to come back as a dog. I pack up my things and strip the bed as I am moving into a twin room with Dominic this evening, and then Meg and I make our way downstairs in search of artificial stimulants. Monty seems to have abandoned his normal morning routine and is sitting very calmly at the kitchen table chatting to Aunt Winnie. Why is it that, however late they go to bed, aged relatives are always up before you?

Even I think it might be a little early for a nicotine patch so I accept Aunt Winnie's offer of a very strong cup of coffee. Besides which, I don't quite know how to explain their presence to her – I think I will just have to tell her they are plasters.

When I am confident the caffeine has actually reached my bloodstream, I fish my files and laptop out of the back of the Smart car, grab a second cup of coffee and wander through to the library, completely forgetting the lack of furniture. I open the door, stand staring at the empty room for a moment, tut to myself and then try the drawing room in the quest for some sort of desk or table to work at. Someone has put a table and a swivel chair in here. There's still an awful lot of work to be done for the ball. It takes me a little while to catch up with my plans but soon enough I am back in the swing of things and have produced an alarmingly long list of things to do today.

For the fifth time in the last couple of weeks I leave a message on my sister's mobile. 'Sophie, it's me. Isabel,' I add, just in case the mobile has distorted my voice somehow. 'You haven't returned my calls and I'm a bit worried. Call me back.' What I really want to do is talk to her about my problems but I don't want to sound selfish.

It's about eight o'clock when I stride back into the kitchen, ready to start some heavy-handed delegation. Harry is about to be catapulted into first place ahead of ruddy Godfrey Farlington in the bob-a-job league tables if I have anything to do with it. Thankfully, most of the family are downstairs and seated around the kitchen table eating breakfast. Mrs Delaney and I have a quick chat about her plans for the American visitors to see if I can help in any way. Despite, or maybe because of, yesterday's dramas, she seems to have relaxed her attitude towards me and we actually manage to have quite a civilised exchange.

After protracted negotiations on how many bob-a-jobs it actually adds up to (we agree on four but I am convinced I could have had him for three), Harry and Aunt Winnie disappear upstairs to finish off the guest rooms while Dominic and I go to the utility room to make a start on the flowers.

'How are you?' Dom whispers.

I bob my head around in an 'okay-ish' way.

'God, you must be feeling absolutely *dire*. I mean, what with the Rob thing and then the awful atmosphere here yesterday.'

I eye Dominic and accidentally break the head off a lily. I'm not quite sure what he's trying to achieve here. If it's the screaming heebie-jeebies from me then this is the most direct route.

'At least you get to have me around.' He starts dancing a little jig in front of me.

'That isn't as much fun as you think it is.'

'But I wouldn't miss it for the world! Simon actually took me to one side yesterday and made me sign a confidentiality agreement. He said that if I breathed a word of what is actually going on to anyone he would wring my neck!' Dom looks absolutely thrilled at this prospect. 'But I told him that you and I were quite close and I wouldn't dream of telling anyone. He didn't look too convinced though – probably because your track record isn't so great.'

I give him another look.

'Izzy, are you sure he was quite so nasty to you in childhood? I mean, it doesn't seem to fit, does it? I know he can be a little abrupt at times – are you sure it wasn't just that?'

'Quite sure,' I say, remembering his spiteful behaviour. 'But you're right. It is strange.'

'Simon strikes me as being quite honourable and he could have made life very difficult for you over the Rob thing. He could have sued you! What exactly did he do when you were eleven?' he asks, piling some roses haphazardly into a vase.

I pause for a second, unwilling to unearth the memories, but then I start to tell Dom and find that I can't stop. The games, the taunts come pouring out until Dom is completely silent.

'Oh,' he says.

'I don't think any of that could be attributed to abruptness, do you?'

'Er, no. Sorry, Izzy. I wasn't thinking.'

We continue our work in silence.

Dom is right, I think to myself as I take the prepared flowers through to the hall. The recent revelations about Simon don't seem to fit with my childhood memories of him. I have no time to ponder this further, however, as the press suddenly appear, on a tour of the house. I can hear the snatches of the PR girl's spiel: '. . . as Mark Twain once wrote, "The report of my death was an exaggeration". As you can see, ladies and gentlemen, no furniture has been removed from the house. The vans yesterday were merely carrying out some work at Mr Monkwell's request.' I sincerely hope God isn't listening and decides to strike the house with lightning. '. . . Mr Monkwell is expecting representatives from the American investment bank later this morning in order to continue negotiations for Wings manufacturers . . .'

I go to the drawing room to deposit the rest of the flowers

and stop to watch Simon as he comes out of the study to meet the press. It's the first time I've seen him today and he looks absolutely pristine in a beautiful suit, complete with immaculately pressed lilac shirt and tie which complement his dark looks. I wonder if his lawyer girlfriend picked them out for him. This is the same man who was such a bully to me fifteen years ago. Does anyone really change? Surely our childhood behaviour truly reflects us, is forever at our core. I shake my head to myself. Dom's right. It doesn't add up.

I don't have time for any more introspection as the American investment bankers will be arriving soon for lunch. I manage to get away with a half hour conversation with Rose on the phone where we rearrange the charity meeting for the start of next week so I can give my full attention to the visitors. Mrs Delaney has planned a menu of rocket salad with Parma ham and blueberries, followed by roasted scallops in a ginger and sesame sauce, with chocolate tart and poached pears to finish. Tonight's feast sounds just as sumptuous and the plan is for all the family, including myself, to eat dinner with the visitors. A frantic hour follows, including minor hysterics from Mrs Delaney on the lateness of the hour, minor hysterics from me as I realise Will has forgotten to pick up Harry from a Scouts trip and then minor hysterics from Dom because he is feeling left out. I am about to stride upstairs at around midday to get changed when I bump into Simon in the hallway.

'There you are! I was just about to come looking for you,' he says, smiling and fixing me with his brown eyes. 'The guests will be here soon. Thank you for offering to look after them.'

'No problem, I do it almost every day! By the way, is Mrs Delaney up to cooking all that food? Some of the recipes are quite complex.'

'Oh yes!' says Simon cheerfully. 'She'll be fine. She was head chef at a restaurant in Oxford.'

'Was she really?' For the first time I wonder about Mrs Delaney's past and how she ended up here. 'Aunt Winnie is helping her, although I hope Mrs Delaney doesn't let her too near the actual food. She tends to tip Tabasco on pretty much everything. Your father is there too.'

'For God's sake, try to keep him away from the visitors. He seems obsessed with his health.'

'I know, he's already told the reporters in great detail about his bunions.'

Simon smiles. 'I hope he hasn't been a pain.'

'No! Everyone's been really helpful. Harry and his bob-a-jobs have been a real boon.'

'First time I've ever been thankful for the mention of Godfrey Farlington.'

'Me too. I was starting to think I might throttle him if I ever met him.'

'Is everything ready?'

'Em, yes. Unforeseen disasters not withstanding!'

'Do you count my family in that?'

'Er, em . . .' He's caught me on the hop with this one. I don't quite know how to answer; I think it might be a little rude to say, 'God, yes, they're an absolute liability.' But his brown eyes are twinkling, so obviously he is just kidding, but somehow this confuses me even more. It is almost as though he's flirting with me. And I think I might be flirting back. I look at my shoes for a second and then risk another glance up at him. He is still staring at me, a slight smile on his face. What on earth is going on? Thank God he continues the conversation as I have completely forgotten what we were talking about.

'Actually, Izzy, I wanted to say thank you. For all you've done. You and Aunt Winnie have been amazing.'

I bite my lip and stare fixedly at a side table. 'Er, well. This is kind of all my fault in the first place, let's not forget.'

'Not really. You didn't know Rob Gillingham was such a shit.'

I blush furiously, pleased he has forgiven me but also thinking that this sounds quite ironic coming from Simon. But Rob is a shit and I hope, more than anything, that this takeover goes ahead and Simon throws him off the board of directors. Dominic is right; revenge is a dish best served cold and I'm thinking Gazpacho.

'Do you think you'll persuade the Americans?' I ask, suddenly quite desperate for him to succeed.

'I don't know but I guess it's worth a try.'

Chapter 18

U pstairs in my new room, I change into a smart lilac suit, throw on some make-up and then swap my white shirt for a black one as throwing foundation around isn't actually a very good idea. Dominic wanders in, yawns widely and throws himself on to one of the beds.

'Have you got a cigarette, Izz?'

I fix him with a look. 'No, but I do have a nicotine patch. Which is a strange position for a non-smoker to be in.'

'Well, if you will get yourself into these situations. Have you got one on?'

'Yes, actually.' I pull my sleeve up over my elbow and show him. 'I quite like them. They make me feel buzzy. Don't you think you ought to be changing into your butler outfit? You did pick it up, didn't you?' I'd sent him into Bury St Edmunds this morning to hire a suit.

'I suppose I ought to try it on.'

'Try it on? You mean you haven't tried it on?'

'Was I supposed to?'

'Oh God, Dom! Try it on. Try it on now.'

He goes over to the back of the door where the suit is hanging, strips off the plastic covering and pulls on the trousers. They're about six sizes too large and there's a big hole in one leg where a grateful moth has filled its boots. He pulls on the jacket to find that it is at least ten sizes too big for him as well. There is no time to do any sewing, much less to take the suit back to Bury St Edmunds. After much wringing of hands and wistfully wishing them to be around Dom's neck, I run down to the study, rifle through the mound of supplies in the corner and run back up to our room clutching a stapler. I staple the trousers and jacket sleeves and with a large black marker pen colour a neat square about ten centimetres wide on Dominic's leg where the hole is. I survey my handiwork and Dominic leaps around the room for a while checking for any position where the paleness of his flesh might show through. I can't focus for long enough to tell whether the hole is there or not.

'Don't keep still for very long and they'll never know it's there.'

'Right. Izzy?'

'Yes?'

'Do you think I could be Irish?'

'Sorry?'

'Irish. I've always wanted to be Irish. I could call myself Dominic O'Leary! Americans love the Irish!'

'Dominic, have you completely taken leave of your senses?'

'Aww, come on, Izzy! Where's your sense of fun?'

'It left, along with my sense of humour, a couple of days ago. I saw them packing. If I hear you speaking with an Irish accent, I swear to God I will throttle you. In front of the Americans.'

'Miserable old cow.'

Fantastic. An Irish butler who looks like he's Mr Bean on speed. Dom marches as manfully as he can wearing an oversize coat and tails down the back stairs.

We all stand awkwardly in the hallway and wait for the American investment bankers to pitch up. Simon's team of advisers look worried to say the least and Simon stands quietly to one side with his hands behind his back, looking thoughtfully down at the floor. The atmosphere in the room is highly charged and suddenly I feel an enormous wave of relief that's it's not going to be me who has to face this and shoulder the responsibility. Simon, probably feeling my eyes upon him, looks up and smiles at me.

I wander over to have a chat with Sam. 'Hello! How are you?' I whisper because the atmosphere is so rarefied it feels like we're in the atrium of a church.

Sam smiles and fiddles nervously with his glasses. 'I'm fine.'

'Have you got a plan?' It must be the party planning bit in me; I always like to know if there's a plan.

'Em . . .' He is frowning and still fiddling with the glasses, probably wondering how much I know about the situation.

'It's okay, I'm a friend of the family,' I say reassuringly, not bothering to add 'and the one who got you all into this mess in the first place'.

He nods slightly at this and then shrugs his shoulders. 'We're just going to try to convince them that we're not such a bad group of people after all. Try to get around the things that Wings have told them and convince them to sell.'

'Is that going to be easy?'

'The press have built up such a bad image of Simon that

it's going to be a tough sell. And they would have spoken directly to Rob Gillingham.' I almost start at the name; it is surprising to hear how easily it runs off Sam's tongue. 'He's a non-executive director of Wings,' he explains, 'the one who we think gave us all the problems with the press.'

I nod dumbly, feeling surprised (and I have to say somewhat relieved) that Simon hasn't told them of my involvement in all this. And Gutless Gertie here doesn't feel much like filling them in; they would probably hang me from the nearest beam.

'Anyway, Gillingham has told them all sorts of things and we need to try to restore their confidence in us and the takeover bid.'

'Why can't they just sell their shares and be done with it? Why all the song and dance?'

'It's not that simple. There will be various conditions attached to the sale and they have to know that we will carry out our side of the bargain.'

I have no time to question Sam further because the radio crackles into life and the gatekeeper announces the arrival of the visitors. Due to the press onslaught we have kept the front gates closed and padlocked, which is a bit of a bummer when you realise you've just left the butter behind in the village shop as I did this morning. Simon has insisted that we carry on as normal and still use the village shop in order to minimise gossip. I'm not entirely convinced that my creeping around the old shop looking as though I'm on the verge of a nervous breakdown, twitching madly whenever spoken to, actually helped.

Dominic swings the large studded door open and we watch as two limousines glide down the driveway and stop in front of the house. The driver of each vehicle gets out and, after opening the passenger doors, starts removing luggage from the boot. Five gentlemen get out. Dominic whisks down the steps to help them.

The five men start walking up the steps towards us like high noon in a cowboy movie. On first impressions, they don't appear to be a barrel of laughs. In fact, collectively they look as though they are having the same sort of week as me. The heat of the day scarcely seems to bother them as they assemble in front of us. Simon stands with the guy in charge whose name I think is Mr Berryman. He is dressed in an olive green suit with an orange tie and is clutching a small wooden box. Simon introduces everyone as the visitors progress down the line until he reaches me: 'This is Isabel who will be looking after you during your stay here. Please ask her for anything you need.'

I shake Mr Berryman's hand. 'How do you do,' I murmur. 'Would you like me to take that to your room?' I ask, indicating the box he is carrying.

He hesitates. 'Er, sure. But it's very valuable to me.'

I try to smile reassuringly, which Dom always tells me looks as if I'm madly demonic. Dom has just come back outside so I imperiously gesture for him to come over and then ask him to take the box to Mr Berryman's room and take great care about it.

Simon leads the five men through to the drawing room and after I have offered them refreshments I dash through to the kitchen. Dominic is still taking the luggage upstairs and Will goes through to help him now that the coast is clear. Aunt Winnie is cheerfully talking to Monty while chopping French beans to go with the scallops and Mrs Delaney is already putting the rocket salad on to the plates that are spread out on the massive oak table.

'Izzy!' Aunt Winnie greets me. 'Are they here?'

'Yep. Just arrived. Have you decided yet whether you are having lunch with them?' I ask, thinking of extra place settings.

'Lord, no!' exclaims Monty. 'House full of foreigners! I need to see what they're up to! And I can't do that if I'm in there eating lunch.'

'Monty and I are going to patrol the house,' states Aunt Winnie.

'Marvellous. Do you think you could lock all the doors to the unusable rooms while you're on this patrol? I don't want any of the visitors inadvertently walking into an empty room. They'll wonder what the hell is going on.'

'I think they're wondering that anyway,' says Aunt Winnie.

'We'll have to wedge the doors shut and escape through the windows, Winnie old girl,' says Monty. I don't know if he thinks this will be more fun or whether in fact the doors here can't be locked with keys in the normal fashion. I thank my lucky stars they're not having lunch with us and go and check the place settings.

Lunch goes off smoothly enough; the Americans aren't terribly talkative but I think they enjoy their food which I have to say is absolute nectar. Everyone seems pretty anxious to get down to business and so as soon as lunch is over they make a dash for the drawing room. I spend the next hour re-setting the table for dinner, adding some extra places for the family, and then gathering the dirty linen to take back through to the kitchen.

The takeover meeting breaks for tea at four and Dominic struggles through to the drawing room with a massive tea tray. Mrs Delaney, in an effort to redress the patriotic balance, has baked miniature Bakewell tarts and Maids of Honour. Simon wanders into the kitchen about five minutes later. He leans against the doorframe and yawns without putting his hand over his mouth, showing off a row of white teeth. Despite this he still manages to look overwhelmingly glamorous.

'How's it going?' I ask.

'Well, they haven't walked out, so I guess we're doing as well as can be expected. We're having a ten-minute break for tea. I came to tell you that lunch was absolutely delicious, Mrs Delaney.'

'Oh, thank you,' she says.

'Tired?' I ask simply.

'Shattered. How about you?'

'The same.'

I haven't really brought a great deal of clothes with me since I was only expecting to stay a couple of nights, so it is with some trepidation that I approach the task of what to wear for this evening's meal. Luckily I have brought with me my one designer suit, which was given to me as a birthday present by my sister Sophie. It is a white trouser suit made by Ben de Lisi but I really don't know what to wear with it as all the tops I have are dirty. In the end, I go along to Aunt Flo's room at the back of the house to see if I can borrow something. I wouldn't normally put so much faith in an OAP but Aunt Flo doesn't have a run-of-the-mill wardrobe. I knock at her door.

'Come in!' her lilting voice calls. 'Ahh, Isabel, my dear! How nice to see you! Come in, come in!' She lays down the book she is reading and peers over her reading glasses. 'How are you?'

'Oh I'm fine, thanks, Aunt Flo. How are you?'

'Never better!' It's only when Monty's around that she seems to get competitive about her health. 'How are you getting along with the Americans?'

'Very well. They seem happy enough.'

'Sorry?'

'I SAID, THEY SEEM HAPPY ENOUGH.'

'Maybe Simon will be able to turn this situation around then.'

'Maybe.'

'If anyone can do it, Simon can. Remarkable young man that.'

'Yes, yes, he is.' It comes out before I have time to think.

'I've always said it's Will that the girls go out with but Simon they want to marry. I didn't show you the beetles mating, did I?'

'Oh no. You didn't.' I try to look disappointed while fathoming the vital link between beetles and marriage. 'Talking of, er, wildlife; is Poppet around or is she having a little nap?'

'She's in her tank. Did you want to see her?'

'No, no! It's fine. She probably needs her beauty sleep. Just wondered where she was – didn't want to step on her or anything!'

'Do you know, I overheard Will talking on his mobile phone this morning. Whoever he was talking to, it sounded very intimate.' She raises her eyebrows suggestively.

I have to say I am interested in Will's love life and so I conspiratorially raise my eyebrows too. 'Did he?'

'Pardon?'

'I SAID, DID HE?' I roar, but most of the accentuation is lost with the shouting and Aunt Flo looks at me as if to say, 'I just said so, didn't I?'

She doesn't seem to have anything else to add to the subject so I clear my throat. 'Aunt Flo? I came to see if I could possibly borrow a top for this evening. To go with my suit. I didn't bring enough clothes with me from London because I was only expecting to stay a couple of nights.' I indicate the white suit that I am carrying over one arm.

She leaps up. 'Of course! Come through to the bedroom.' I follow her through a door. 'Actually, I need to think about getting ready too. What a beautiful suit! Why don't you try it on and we'll see?'

While I change, Aunt Flo rustles about in her wardrobe. She turns back and looks at me for a moment, 'My dear, why aren't you wearing it just like that?'

I look down doubtfully. 'I haven't got anything on underneath the jacket, Aunt Flo.'

'Yes, but if you do all the buttons up then we can't see your bra.'

I duly do so and, sure enough, the jacket cuts down into a V just above my bra line. But literally just above. I look down into the valley of my cleavage. 'I can't do that!'

'Yes, you can! You look very sexy! Try this necklace with it.' She walks over to her dressing table, opens a box, extracts a necklace and puts it around my neck. A perfect drop pearl hangs seductively. 'I have earrings too! We'll put your hair up and with those high strappy shoes you have it'll be perfect!'

I let her dress my hair and put on the jewellery and, I have to say, the results aren't half bad.

I arrive in the kitchen to find Dominic laying out glasses for this evening. 'Wow! You look amazing,' he says.

'Do you really think so?' I ask nervously, straightening the jacket.

His mobile belts out the Batman theme, making us both jump. He looks at the display. 'No signal,' he murmurs and walks outside to the courtyard. Now I know Dominic is on the same network as me and my phone works perfectly well in here. This is neither the time nor the place but I would still like to shout, 'Dominic, I know you are gay and I still love you!' Instead, I concentrate on cutting up limes for the margaritas and worry about why he's uncomfortable with telling me the truth. Does he think I'm too uptight to cope with it?

Half an hour later we are all congregated in the drawing room drinking margaritas as though our lives depend on it. Will sidles up to me.

'You look beautiful!' he whispers.

'Thank you.' I watch Simon walk into the room over Will's shoulder. Simon smiles briefly at me and turns to talk to one of the Americans. I get on with the important job of making each of our visitors feel comfortable and at home. Eventually I notice that Simon and I have worked our way around the room and have managed to end up next to each other. He waits for me to finish a conversation.

'Hi,' he says, side-stepping us out of the group. 'Everything okay?'

'Fine. You?'

'Good.'

We stand awkwardly for a second. I am just about to move on when Simon says, 'I keep meaning to tell you that I found our old den yesterday.'

'Did you?' I ask politely, suddenly watchful. I'm starting to feel a bit more comfortable around him and I'm unwilling to disturb the waters of our complicated past.

'Yeah. I was searching for some torches for your, er,

excursion and I decided to look under the stairs. I don't know why, I haven't been under there for years. Do you know some of our books are still there? You ought to come and have a look.'

He suddenly grins at me and moves as though to take my arm and lead me there.

I instinctively take a step back, more a knee-jerk reaction than anything else. The smile fades on his face.

'Yes,' I force myself to say. 'I must go and look at it sometime.' I try to smile. 'I should get back to your guests though.' And before he can say another word, I move on around the room.

Dominic, Meg and I retire to bed after we've helped clear up. Dominic and I lie in our twin beds and chat about the evening while a grasshopper residing in the chimney provides musical accompaniment. Dom lights up his last cigarette of the night and I take deep, passive mouthfuls of it. Meg lies in the crook of Dom's arm; she seems to have adopted us.

'Can we take her back to London?' Dom asks.

'She's not ours to take.' I would love her to come and live with us but having a dog in London, especially after her experiencing all this space, just doesn't seem fair.

'There's so many dogs here that they probably wouldn't notice.'

'Where would we take her for a walk?'

'There are woods off Lower Richmond Road. But do you think she'd miss the country?'

'Maybe.'

'I could cut out some pictures of trees and stuff from magazines for her.'

'That would do it.' I breathe deeply again, 'Waft a bit over here, Dom.'

'I will not, you don't smoke.' He takes one last drag and extinguishes the cigarette. 'Right! Light off!'

I bristle. I always read for a bit as part of my nightly ritual and every time Dominic and I sleep in the same room it becomes an issue.

'I'm reading for a bit.'

'Awww! Izzy! I can't sleep with the light on!'

'Pull the covers over your head then.'

I try to read for as long as possible (must stay awake, must annoy Dom) but I can feel my eyes slowly closing until eventually sleep overtakes me and I dream of Rob, Simon and all the family in a circus. Aunt Winnie made a particularly marvellous ringmaster.

The next morning, while Simon is holed up with his team checking 'the implications of a couple of conditions', Will, Daniel and I take the visitors down to the lake. It is the first time I have been here since I arrived at Pantiles and I have to say that it looks pretty much the same as it did fifteen years ago. Bulrushes grow densely around the perimeter and the old red boathouse still sits to one side of the lake while a wooden pontoon runs for about twenty metres adjacent to it. When we were young we were absolutely forbidden to come here unless we wanted to be grounded for a year.

Mr Berryman and his colleagues seem to have relaxed since their arrival yesterday. The dinner last night must have gone a long way to soothing their souls and they can probably see now that we aren't such a bad lot to do business with. The newspapers this morning are also painting

Simon in a much more positive light after their visit here yesterday. The suggestion of an hour off for an estate tour and the possibility of water-skiing was met with great enthusiasm over breakfast. A collective stampede for the bedrooms to change into shorts and T-shirts ensued and here we are. The sun is shining as I lay out two tartan picnic rugs on the bank and arrange myself decoratively on them, legs neatly tucked underneath me. I unpack the plastic mugs, the thermos flasks of hot milk and black coffee and Mrs Delaney's white chocolate and macadamia nut brownies and await proceedings, grateful for a few minutes' peace. Fred's old lawnmower whirrs in the distance. Will is standing with the visitors on the wooden pontoon in front of the boat-house, which has been opened by Daniel. Eventually, when they show no signs of moving, I wander down to join them. Inside the boathouse, along with the small rowing boat and the old punt that I remember, sits an amazing James Bond-esque speedboat. Daniel is trying to persuade one of the Americans to have a go at water-skiing.

'Where did that come from?' I whisper to Will.

'Simon had the idea of commercial water-skiing on the lake. Daniel here has just got his licence and Simon managed to persuade the speedboat company to lend us this for a couple of months before we commit to buying one.'

Daniel's voice comes slicing through the group. 'Izzy water-skis. She'll show you how to do it!' All eyes focus on me.

'Er, do I?'

'Yes! Simon told me you did!'

I suddenly remember my mythical CV. Dom made me list water-skiing as one of my hobbies because he said I was too boring and we're two hundred miles inland. I'm holding him personally responsible for anything that happens here today. 'Er, I don't do it terribly well. I've only just got *my* licence! Ha, ha!'

'Come on, Izzy! Mr Tyler here would feel much better if you went first.'

A frantic minute of negotiations follow, but I am absolutely adamant I am not getting in the water. In the end I agree to shout instructions and encouragement to Mr Tyler from the shore line. His colleagues are thrilled with the prospect of Mr Tyler getting wet and being humiliated and chatter excitedly as they retire to the picnic rugs.

I wait on the pontoon while Mr Tyler puts on a wetsuit. Daniel then faffs about with the boat and the skis but just as I'm about to expire from boredom the boat hums into life. Mr Tyler swims a little way out and then waits, skis stretched out in front of him as instructed, for the off. He looks at me for reassurance and so I oblige him with, 'That's perfect, Mr Tyler! You're looking like a real pro!' I still would be shouting the same thing if he were drowning.

We have a couple of false starts as Mr Tyler flails about in the water in grand style. I bandy phrases such as, 'Keep your knees bent' and 'Push your weight in front' about, accompanied by lots of gesticulating and practical demonstrations which sound entirely plausible and wholly apply to skiing on snow. It does seem as though I've done this before, however. Before long, the crowd on the shore is standing very close to the water's edge and shouting like mad. I eye them a little nervously like an over-anxious mother; I do hope they will be careful. The last thing I want to do is wring out an over-excited American. Perhaps we shouldn't have fed them Mrs Delaney's brownies so early in the morning.

I turn my attention back to Mr Tyler, who is now making his fifth attempt at staying upright for more than a millisecond. 'Come on, Mr Tyler! You can do it!' I shout to the surprisingly cheerful figure waving at us. Daniel revs the engine and off they go. At some point Mr Tyler must have taken in my words of wisdom, or perhaps decided to ignore them, because after a shaky start, he regains his balance. A great cheer erupts from the shoreline and, overcome with enthusiasm, I run like mad along the pontoon shouting things like, 'Well done! That's great, Mr Tyler!' until I run straight off the end of the pontoon and fall into the bulrushes.

I squelch with as much dignity as I can muster into the kitchen. I am absolutely mortified. The Americans are finding the whole thing very amusing indeed.

Monty looks up from the crossword. 'Izzy! What the hell happened to you?' His mouth twitches suspiciously.

'Dear God, Izzy! You needn't try to drown yourself!' says Aunt Winnie. 'I'm sure we can sort things out here!'

'I fell in the lake,' I say sulkily.

'You smell!' says Monty.

I open my mouth to utter a stinging reply but words fail me. I have to resort to snorting derisively which I hope conveys my sentiments just as well. Coming from a family who farm for a living, I think this is a bit rich.

Simon strides into the kitchen at that precise moment. 'Dad, have you seen . . . CHRIST! WHAT IS THAT SMELL?'

'It's me,' I say miserably from over by the door.

'Izzy! What happened to you?'

'I fell in the lake.'

'How on earth did you manage that?'

218

'I was coaching Mr Tyler at water-skiing.'

'Really?' His mouth also twitches suspiciously. 'Did you think it would help to demonstrate?'

'I fell off the end of the pontoon.'

'Ah. Tricky things pontoons. There one minute and gone the next.' He shakes his head knowingly. I think he's taking the piss.

'I fell into the bulrushes. There were lots of bird droppings in there and a couple of dead things too.'

'Probably explains the smell.'

I shiver a little and Simon hurries me upstairs to get changed. I could really, really do with a cigarette.

Chapter 19

Apparently, falling into a lake fully clothed is just the thing to get any troubled takeover running smoothly again. It's probably not in the textbook. After I've washed my hair, got changed and flushed repeatedly with embarrassment at the thought of it all, I start organising lunch. Mrs Delaney is busy in the kitchen preparing a feast of crab cakes with a cream sauce of horseradish and dill, roasted sea bass on a bed of Jerusalem artichokes and Dauphinoise potatoes, and iced berries with a white chocolate sauce (complete with sprigs of mint, but then Mrs Delaney is a chef). Harry is sitting at one end of the kitchen table, swinging his legs and eating a French Fancy (this looks shop-bought unless Mrs Delaney has turned into Mr Kipling as well as being a miraculous chef). I might know her a little better now but she still scares the living daylights out of me. Even more so, if that were possible. In my experience, chefs are tricky, volatile characters, prone to picking up meat cleavers.

The visitors have returned from the lake and are now having pre-lunch drinks in the drawing room. Will informs me gleefully that my fall from grace was just the thing to pull the group together and after I left the whole lot wanted to have a go at water-skiing. In fact, the atmosphere was almost party-like. I must remember this for future events.

At lunch I am fallen upon like a long lost friend. The Americans pump my arm repeatedly and laugh a lot. Probably at my expense but I take it all in blushing good spirit; it's difficult not to as they are so good-humoured. With a marginally lighter heart, I go back to the kitchen.

Aunt Flo has lent me a black dress for this evening. It is absolutely beautiful, unspeakably elegant and completely timeless. The straps are very delicate silver chains which link behind my neck in a halter-neck and then hang down my back, ending in diamante balls which knock against my shoulder blades as I walk. The rest of the dress is very plain and exquisitely cut, with slits either side of the skirt that run all the way up to my thighs.

We are running a little behind schedule and I am starting to feel stressed. Mrs Delaney is upset about something and is banging pots and pans around like there is no tomorrow. Monty is making a huge fuss about joining everyone for dinner, something about his health, and Aunt Winnie almost has to lock him in his room to get changed. I haven't seen Flo since she popped in with the dress first thing this morning which is highly unusual and I am hoping that Poppet hasn't eaten her or something.

I hurriedly dress, shove my hair up and then go to put on my pair of very strappy God-send shoes. The same shoes I was wearing when I met Rob, I think bitterly, sitting down and beginning the arduous task of wrapping the leather straps around my ankles akin to ballerina pumps (unfortunately there the similarity ends). In the background, Meg is rustling about in the wardrobe, burying another of her Bonios.

I am just about to slip the second shoe over my heel while admiring my freshly painted toenails when I hear my name being called and turn around to see Dominic throwing himself into the room.

Without so much as a hello, he takes firm grip of my elbow, hauls me up and, like one of those little tugs that pull ocean liners, turns me around and hurries me out of the room. I resist strongly, digging one heeled shoe into the carpet, saying, 'Dom, what on earth are you doing?'

'Izzy. You have to come. Now,' he hisses and pulls at me. He has quite a job on his hands; I am no lightweight.

'What's wrong?' I ask in alarm, 'God, is it Flo? Is she okay?'

'She's fine. The spider has gone though.'

'Gone? How do you mean gone?' I squeal, my first thought being for my cowardly custard self.

'Gone to the pub for a drink with its mates. OF COURSE I MEAN GONE GONE. Aunt Flo has been looking for it all day.'

'Christ! It could be anywhere by now!' I start to frantically limp down the corridor, still carrying my shoe.

'Yes, but that's not the problem.'

'It's not? Are you sure? Because that sounds like a problem to—'

'No. I went up to help her look . . .' he pants as we belt through the doors at the end of the passage and through to the wing where Monty and Flo live '. . . and she was frantic. Apparently she only let it out for a walk and it just disappeared . . .' We arrive outside Flo's room and knock at the door.

'What's the other problem?' I urge.

'Come and see,' he says grimly.

Flo opens the door. 'Hello dear! That dress does look wonderful on you!'

I spy Harry in the corner on his hands and knees. 'I promised him ten bob-a-jobs if he finds it,' Dominic murmurs.

'Only one shoe though? New fashion?' Flo questions.

I simultaneously hold up my other shoe and say, 'Aunt Flo, I hear Poppet has gone missing?'

'Sorry?'

'I SAID, I HEAR THE SPIDER HAS GONE MISSING?'

'Sssssshhhhhhh,' Dominic hisses. 'Someone will hear you.'

'Yes dear. She's done this before,' says Aunt Flo.

'Oh really?' I squeak. 'Em, quite recently? Over the last few weeks at all?' I've read somewhere that you swallow ten spiders a year while you're asleep. The ridiculous thought springs to mind that I might have inadvertently swallowed Poppet while dead to the world. Thinking of my own precious neck again. Dom gives me a sharp poke in the ribs with his elbow.

'I take her out for a little walk every morning.' Another ridiculous image springs to mind of Aunt Flo wandering around the garden with the spider on a red leash.

'Er, sorry?'

'I SAID, I TAKE HER OUT FOR A WALK EVERY MORNING.'

'Sssshhhhh,' hisses Dominic again. I hastily tuck a few inches of my dress into my knickers and balance on one shoe. Don't want Poppet mistaking me for a climbing frame.

Dominic gives me another nudge. 'That is not the only problem,' he whispers, 'look at this.' He leads me over to a chest of drawers and stands me in front of it. I warily lift my foot off the floor again.

'What?' I ask.

'That,' he hisses and points at a very innocuous-looking urn.

'What about it?'

'I've already seen it.'

Has Dom completely lost it? 'Have you?' I ask carefully, still looking around, much more concerned with where the spider is than where Dom is.

'I took it up to Mr Berryman's room.'

I am thoroughly confused by this point. 'So? He's got one just like it. Strange that he would carry it around but—'

'It's the same one,' Dom hisses.

I frown. 'How do you know?'

'I carried the damn thing, stupid. You told me to. This is what was inside the wooden box. Look inside . . .' I lean cautiously over and lift the lid. The urn is full of strange grey stuff. 'His mother's ashes. He told me earlier that he carries them around with him. He pulled me to one side to ask if the house was *safe*.' Dom looks at me wide-eyed at the implication of the last word.

Bloody hell! I drop the lid with a loud clunk and swing around to face Flo, who is prostrate on the floor looking under the sofa. 'Er, Aunt Flo?'

'Still can't see her . . .' she murmurs.

'Aunt Flo?' I say again. 'Em . . .' She is paying no attention to me whatsoever so since we seem to have taken up pole position on the floor I drop down to join her. Could do with a nice lie down actually.

'Aunt Flo? Where did you get that lovely urn thing?' I ask urgently from our horizontal positions.

'Hmmm? Oh that? I found it. Nice, isn't it?'

'When? When did you find it?'

'Today while I was looking for Poppet. It was in a wooden box. Dominic, be a darling and lift up the sofa?'

I leave Dominic to heave up the sofa and hop like I've never hopped before downstairs.

I locate Simon in the drawing room with the rest of his crew. They all look at me in astonishment as I hop in but I have other things on my mind. 'Simon? Can I talk to you for a second?'

'Er, sure.'

'In private?' Eyebrows are raised even higher. I hop across the hallway into his still-empty study and flop on to a bean bag. I gabble away, explaining the sorry situation but missing out the part where Poppet goes walkabout, all the while desperately trying to put on my other shoe.

'So you see, I'm sure she didn't mean to steal it. Or take it. Or . . . or . . . however you want to put it.' I don't really want to accuse his nearest and dearest of being a thief – I'm not quite sure how Simon will react.

'She does have a habit of taking things,' he says slowly.

I blink nervously. 'What do you mean, a habit? Like a, er, kleptomania habit?'

'Well, if you want to get technical about it. We just go and pick up our stuff from her room once a month.'

'She's a kleptomaniac?'

'Izzy, all families have their idiosyncrasies.'

'That's an idiosyncrasy? Actually, now I think about it, I'm missing my white bra.'

'Are you?' He blinks quickly.

'Anyway, don't you think you should have warned me about this?' I jab out quickly, to get off the subject of the bra.

Simon looks surprised. 'I had forgotten about it. It's kind

of second nature to us here. In fact, I thought all aged aunts were the same.'

'Not my Aunt Winnie!'

'Well, she's not really your run-of-the-mill aunt, is she?'

'She's never nicked anything.'

'Oh I wouldn't say that. She's stolen three rooms' worth of antiques.'

'She did not steal them, she borrowed them to save your precious neck!'

He raises his eyebrows at this. 'And yours.'

I nearly laugh out loud. Somehow this little exchange has gotten off track. I swiftly re-direct it by saying, 'I'm not going to start splitting hairs with you on the subject of aunts. What are we going to do about the urn?'

'Oh yes, the urn.'

'Where are the guests?' I ask.

'In the gardens. Having a wander about before dinner. Some of them might have gone to get changed already.'

'So Mr Berryman might have already noticed it's gone.'

'But he might not have.'

'This is not going to look good, is it? A treasured item missing from his room.'

'No, I think we can safely say it is not going to look good.'

'He might want to call the police or something; the urn looks quite valuable.'

'That would certainly put a dampener on the takeover.' Dom arrives in the room with a screech. 'We're just going to have to put it back.'

'Right! What if he's missed it already?'

'Well, Aunt Flo took it out of the wooden box, which is presumably still there, so unless he's checked the box he'll be none the wiser. Besides, I think if he'd noticed it was missing he would have said something by now. If he catches you putting it back we can just say it was taken away accidentally . . . for cleaning.' Out of the thirty-odd words he has just uttered one in particular catches my attention.

'What do you mean me? I'm not putting it back.'

'I can't pretend it was mistakenly taken away for cleaning. He showed it to me and told me it contained his mother's ashes,' says Dom. I narrow my eyes at him. What a weak and feeble excuse.

I look and feel absolutely aghast. 'Me? Why me? Why can't Harry do it? It must be worth at least ten bob-a-jobs,' I bleat. I'm not a terribly brave person but I am perfectly willing to send an innocent boy scout in there.

'Too young,' says Simon.

'What about Monty?' I continue, determined not to be sidetracked.

'Too old.'

'Mrs Delaney?'

'Too busy. She's cooking dinner for twenty.'

'How about me being too scared? Or too jumpy? What about that?'

'Aww, come on Izzy! It's not going to be difficult!' Dom says encouragingly

'Flo?' I counter. 'She obviously managed to take it, she could put it back!'

'She'd probably nick something else while she was in there,' Simon says.

'What about you then?' I demand.

'I couldn't get caught in a guest's room.'

'That's mighty convenient,' I snap.

'Shall I slap you, Izzy?' says Dom hopefully. 'You seem a little hysterical.'

I give Dom a look which suggests that if he even thinks about slapping me . . .

'Come on, Izzy.' Both men are hauling me to my feet.

'What if he catches me? What shall I say?' I whimper.

'Just say you found it downstairs, knew it didn't belong to the household and discovered it had been mistakenly removed from his room.' They are pushing me out into the hallway now.

'Where shall I put it? Where did he leave it?'

'Back in the wooden box which I put in his bedside cupboard for him when I carried it up,' says Dom, 'I'll stand watch outside the door and whistle if anyone comes. We need to wait until he's gone down for dinner.'

'Thanks, Izzy. You'll save our necks,' pants Simon, almost dragging me across the hallway. 'I'll go and see to Aunt Flo while you two are doing that.'

'NO!' Dom and I yell simultaneously and our little party comes to a standstill.

'Em . . .' Dom and I look at each other. Simon doesn't know about the spider.

'It's just that it would be better if she was with us and not wandering the house nicking other stuff,' I stutter.

'Why?'

'Well . . .' I think briefly about covering for Flo but then decide that a tarantula and a dead mother are too much to handle in one evening. If Poppet continues her tour of the house then perhaps it's best if Simon knows about it. 'Flo has a pet.'

'A pet?'

'Yes. A sort of spider.'

'A pet spider?'

'Well, more of a tarantula actually.'

'Poppet? God! I told her to get rid of that bloody thing!'

'She's probably lonely! Old people need pets!' I say defensively.

'Isabel, how could anyone be lonely in this house? Apart from when you're asleep, have you ever had a moment of privacy? And in case you haven't noticed, we have about a thousand dogs littering the place. The spider was supposed to go because Mrs Delaney was refusing to clean in there and kept having the vapours every time Poppet had a walkabout.'

This brings me very neatly to my next point. 'It's very funny you should mention that. You'll laugh at this—'

'It's escaped again, hasn't it?' He looks quite weary.

'Er, yes.'

'It's always escaping.'

'Well, it's probably a bit pissy at being called Poppet, isn't it? Hardly the name for a fierce street-fighting tarantula,' proffers Dom. 'God, it all happens in the country, doesn't it? City life is looking terribly tame!'

'Getting plenty of material for your novel?' I ask acidly.

'Plenty, thank you.'

'Right,' Simon says decisively. 'You two go and put the urn back, I'll see to Aunt Flo.'

After several years working for one of the finest caterers in London, here I am hanging about suspiciously outside a guest's room clutching an urn full of ashes. Life is a funny old thing.

Dom and I pretend to be studying something enormously important out of the window.

'Why is Mr Berryman carrying around his mother's ashes, Dom?' I ask suddenly.

'A good question, Izzy, and indeed, at another time, something that I would love to discuss with you in more depth. But I think we should concentrate on the key issue here and not get sidetracked. Whatever Mr Berryman does with the bloody thing, the point is that you need to get it back to him so he can carry on doing it.'

'Good point.'

'Are you clear about what you're doing?'

'Crystal. Well . . .'

'What's the problem?'

'The plan seems a little simple for my liking.'

'Izzy, love, I know you always want to over-complicate things, and again that's something else we can talk about later, but the plan is simple because it is simple. So, to recap, I will be out here keeping a look-out and if I see someone coming I will whistle. What happens then?'

'I leg it.'

'Any questions?'

'Yes.'

Dominic mutters something and rolls his eyes dangerously.

I don't get to ask him any of the numerous questions on my list because at that moment Mr Berryman comes out of his room and starts to walk down the corridor towards us. In a loud voice I start to explain to Dom various tasks in the gardens that need to be attended to. Thankfully, the fact that it's starting to get dark and I'm in full evening dress doesn't seem odd to Mr Berryman. The urn is hidden behind one of the curtains. We greet each other with a great deal of jollity on his part – lots of shaking of hands and water-skiing references which hopefully mean he hasn't noticed his precious urn is missing.

As soon as he has disappeared down the stairs, I move towards his door, urn in hand. Dominic starts to dust a table of ornaments with his hanky.

I gently open the door to Mr Berryman's room, walk inside and close it behind me. I sprint over to the bedside cabinet, shove the urn inside the wooden box and am about to run for the hills when a thought occurs to me. I hate it when that happens.

Could I find something here which would be of use in the takeover? Help Simon out? An image of myself saving Pantiles single-handedly and thus being free from crushing guilt flashes into my mind.

My eyes narrow as I spot a black leather attaché case on top of the wardrobe. Just a quick peep, what harm could come of it? On impulse, I seize a chair and drag it to the front of the wardrobe. I am just balancing on tip-toe and reaching for the briefcase when a disembodied voice says out of nowhere, 'How are you getting on?'

With a loud parrot-like screech I stumble and then crash to the ground.

'Jesus, Dominic!' I snarl from my sitting position, rubbing my shoulder. God, what is wrong with everyone? Do I look like I need winding up any more? 'What are you doing?'

'Just came to see if you were all right. I thought you might have taken up Buddhism you've been so long.'

'I was going to look in this attaché case,' I hiss, 'to see if there's anything in it that could help Simon.'

'God, Izzy, you're becoming positively immoral! How marvellous! Go on then!'

231

'Go back outside and keep watch!'

He scurries out of the room and I climb back on the chair. In the background, a couple of grasshoppers begin their warm-up, as is their wont at this time of the evening. I silently curse them and get on with the job in hand. Looking up at the door every now and then, I remove the attaché case and try to open it. It's locked. Damn.

After replacing the case, I get down off the chair as softly as I can, return it to its usual position and then have a quick prowl around. I'm just about to give it all up as a bad job when I notice something quite peculiar. By the foot of the bed is what looks like a small furball. I kneel down next to it and instinctively put out my hand to touch it. It flinches. Bloody hell! It's Poppet!

Chapter 20

When he hears my scream, Dominic hurries in. 'God! Izzy! What the hell has happened now?'

I clutch my arms to myself and hop around well away from the vicinity of the bed. I point manically at the bed. My mouth has become paralysed with fear. I'm not that fond of common or garden spiders, let alone ones that are the size of your fist and answer to the name of Poppet.

'What? Is this some sort of happy-clappy hostess dance? I can't see anything. What?'

I stab with my finger in the direction of Poppet until Dominic finally gets the message and peers cautiously at the floor.

'JE-SUS!' he shouts and sprints to join me on the other side of the room. 'What shall we do?'

'Simon!' I manage to mumble and together we scramble for the door in a mess of limbs as though we're joined together in a three-legged race.

Believe me, I can run when I feel like it. And I really, really feel like it. When we reach the study Simon is talking to someone on his mobile phone. He must already have dealt with Aunt Flo. I tug urgently on his shirt and he frowns at me. I twitch madly for a few seconds while he rants on about PE ratios and suchlike. God! To think I almost touched it! Maybe it bit me and in the heat of the moment I didn't notice. I look anxiously at my hand for fang marks. Simon looks at me worriedly but continues his conversation. I pick irritatingly at his shirt again. 'Simonsimonsimonnnnn,' I hiss, looking like I'm about to wet myself. I think he picks up on the note of urgency in my voice because he tells the person on the other end of the line that he'll call them back and rings off.

'*What* is it?'

'It's Poppet. She's in Mr Berryman's room.'

'Are you sure?'

'Positive. She practically devoured my arm!'

'Well, why didn't you catch her?'

I look at him as though he's speaking Russian. Is he on the same planet as me? 'Catch her?'

'With a glass or something?'

'A glass? Simon, it is the size of my hand. What sort of glass did you have in mind?'

'Well, couldn't you have just scooped her up?'

'I'm just plain Isabel. You must be thinking of Incredible Isabel the Spider Tamer. I'm going nowhere near her.'

'God! If you want a job done . . .' He swoops out of the room, muttering to himself. Ungrateful or what?

Dominic and I beetle after him as he takes the stairs at an ambitious three at a time. We catch up with him in the corridor. He taps lightly on Mr Berryman's door and then peers into the room. He looks back at us.

'I'll stay here,' says Dominic. 'I'll whistle if someone comes.'

'But I can whistle,' I protest.

234

am lying with my head at a difficult angle, my cheek pressed up against the wood and the smell of mothballs up my nose. We're not talking about an exceptionally large wardrobe here; it's certainly not designed for two fully-grown adults. My legs are curled under me and my dress is rucked up around my ears. I try to breathe quietly and keep perfectly still but I seem to be taking in great chugs of air and my limbs are already suffering from cramp.

I pray to God, Buddha, Allah and anyone else who could be listening that Mr Berryman doesn't take it upon himself to open his own wardrobe. I mean, what on earth are we meant to say if he finds the two of us inside? Hello, turned out nice again? I bite my lip as I feel a wave of hysteria rise up my throat. But the more I try to stop it, the harder it becomes. Come on, Izzy! Don't let the side down. This is not the time to be overwhelmed with giggles. I manage to find my leg with my hand and dig my nails into it hard. Must think of unhappy thoughts. Must think of dead things and naked politicians and . . . *The Sound of Music*. God, that's not right, is it? The problem is it's not easy to keep your perspective with your face pressed up against the back of a wardrobe. I mean, it's hardly a meditating position, is it? You don't find yoga gurus advocating the inside of a wardrobe as the ideal place to contemplate your inner peace.

I start breathing heavily through my nose. I must think of Simon because I can bet he isn't very amused with this whole situation. He will be taking this very seriously because, let's face it, if we are found in this wardrobe the whole takeover is finished. I suddenly feel a shiver pass through Simon's legs. And another. A sort of shaking. Instinctively I recognise what it is and the wave of hysteria threatens to engulf me altogether. He is desperately trying not to laugh. Absolutely desperately. We both breathe together deeply and I can feel his hand searching for mine. He grabs it and squeezes it hard in an effort to gain some control. I squeeze it back, bury my face in some sort of material and pray for deliverance.

This comes in the form of Dominic who opens the wardrobe door tentatively and whispers, 'Izzy? Simon? Are you in there?' We let go of our breath and indulge in those peculiar little snorts and noises which seem to come from your stomach.

Simon crawls out first, inadvertently kneeing me in the solar plexus, and falls into a heap on the floor. I giggle hysterically to myself and have to be practically lifted out as I seem to have temporarily lost the use of my limbs and can barely breathe. Dominic and Simon put a hand under each armpit and haul me out, knickers flashing wildly, both of then now laughing openly.

'Was it Mr Berryman?' Simon asks.

Dom nods. 'Thank God, he left after a few minutes. I don't know what you would have done if he'd decided to take a nap or something.'

We all remain on the floor and take a few minutes to calm down. Eventually we find the strength to get up, brush ourselves down and go back to the serious business of spider-catching.

Simon peers fearlessly at Poppet while Dom and I look on from a couple of metres away. He moves closer and closer, until eventually he simply reaches out and picks the spider up. My eyes almost boggle out of their sockets. Is there no end to this man's bravery? He's like some sort of demi-god, absolutely fearless of man and beast.

'Izzy, how close to her were you?' He waves Poppet around wildly. I'm not that keen on the old girl but I really don't think Simon should be shaking her like that. It might make her angry.

I manage to pull my eyes away from her jigging form. 'Simon, I really don't think you should be tossing her around like that. Aunt Flo would be—'

'Did you look at this at all? Did you take a really good look?'

'Of course I took a good look at her! She almost bit me!'

He holds Poppet out in front of him. 'Izzy, this is a toupee. Mr Berryman's toupee.'

I take a tentative step forward and look at Simon's hand. It is indeed some sort of hairpiece.

'Oh.'

He replaces the toupee with a sigh. 'Didn't you notice he wears one?'

I look at Dom who is giggling into his hand. 'Er, no.'

Simon walks out of the room, grinning widely. It sounds as though he's saying something like 'stupid', 'fucking' and 'prat' but I am probably mistaken.

'Time to up the medication, Izzy!' Dom says cheerfully and follows him out.

I sheepishly bring up the rear. Oh God, Dom isn't going to let this go for years. A toupee? I could have sworn it actually moved. I only hope the others don't remember that I accused the toupee of biting me.

I look at my watch. God! It's half past seven already. I hope someone has been plying the guests with drinks in my absence. Simon disappears into his room to change for dinner and Dom and I rush downstairs to check on the guests. Thankfully the rest of Simon's team is with them, along with Monty who is doling out the booze and the charm in equal quantities.

I leave Dom to help with the drinks and scurry through to the kitchen to see how Mrs Delaney is faring with dinner. She must be absolutely shattered, especially after preparing breakfast, lunch and tea as well. 'Mrs Delaney? Are you . . . ? Oh.' I stop dead because the room is empty. She must have popped to the loo or something. I wander around, taking note of the open cookery books and the half-prepared dishes.

Ten minutes later I'm a little concerned. Has she drowned in the loo or something? Has she got stuck? I have a quick look under the table just in case she's having a snooze. I am about to go in search of her when Simon strides in. He has changed into some very smart chinos and a pressed shirt and I get a faint whiff of some fabulous aftershave. I give him a wide grin which dies on my face as I note his expression. 'What's up? What's wrong?'

'Mrs Delaney has just called.'

'Where from? The loo?' I ask, rather bemused.

'No, worse than that. She's at the local pub.'

I admire the audacity of the woman. 'Is she? Crikey, talk about sinking ships. Did she go for a quick one? I don't see why, it's not like we don't have any booze here . . .'

'Her husband has just turned up.'

'Mrs Delaney's husband?'

'Yes.'

'Mrs *Delaney*'s husband?' I say again, in order to try to get the concept into my befuddled brain.

'Yes. That would be Mr Delaney.'

'I didn't know there was a Mr Delaney.'

'There kind of has to be a Mr Delaney in order for there to be a Mrs Delaney.'

'I know that, but I thought he wasn't around any more.'

239

'He wasn't. She hasn't seen him since she left Oxford years ago.'

'And he's just turned up?'

'Yep. I think she was a bit surprised.'

'And she's gone to the pub?' Blimey, she obviously developed a thirst that the cellars here simply couldn't handle.

'He's taken her to the pub – I think she was in shock. She said she would come back and finish cooking but I told her to stay there.'

'You what?'

'I don't think he knows about Harry. It was *nine* years ago when they last saw each other and Harry's only eight, so I thought they would both probably need another drink. She doesn't sound as though she's in any fit state to cook anyway.'

'Where is Harry?'

'In bed, thank God.'

'What the hell are we going to do?'

Dominic arrives in the kitchen. 'Any idea when the food might be coming? I think the natives are getting restless.' He looks from face to face. 'Where's Mrs D?'

'In the pub,' I answer dumbly.

'Is she?' Dom asks incredulously. 'Blimey, that's a bit keen, isn't it?'

'I'll tell you later, Dom,' I say quickly. 'What shall we do?' I ask Simon.

'Well, she told me that the pudding and the cheese board are ready in the larder.' We stride over to the larder door, open it and, sure enough, the food is there. On the cold slate surfaces are two enormous cheese plates surrounded by grapes, celery and cape gooseberries, along with three latticed tarts and three bowls of whipped cream. Good, things are looking up.

'Starter and main?' I ask.

Simon mentions something of such mind-boggling complexity that I almost make a run for the pub myself. 'I don't think I can cook that for twenty within an hour,' I say slowly. 'I'll manage the starter but I can't do the main.'

Simon picks up a set of car keys. 'Dom, take my car and run down to the supermarket in Bury St Edmunds. You know where it is?' Simon looks at his watch. 'You'll just catch them. Get whatever you can that's easy. Quiche, salad, whatever. Here's my credit card. Get some cash out.' He reels off a pin number.

Dominic looks confused. 'Cash? Where from?'

'The cash point.'

'There's a cash point?'

'Yes.'

'In the country?'

'Yes,' says Simon with admirable patience. 'Outside the bank.'

Dominic looks at us as though we're having him on but gamely takes the keys and hares off.

'We'll just tell them that the cooker has broken down.' Simon goes to the back of the utility room door, pulls something off it and chucks it at me. 'Here! An apron. You don't want to ruin that beautiful dress of yours. You look gorgeous, by the way.'

'Do I?' I say weakly. I can't imagine this is true. After the experiences I've just been through I suspect my deodorant isn't living up to all its promises. I shake the apron open and fasten it around me. 'Has Poppet been found?' I ask, thinking the last thing we need is for her to wander across the table in the middle of the meal.

Simon is now rooting around in a cupboard. He grins

widely over his shoulder at the mention of our latest debacle and says, 'Aunt Flo and Aunt Winnie are looking for her. I thought it might look too suspicious for all the family to be absent at the meal.'

'What are you looking for?'

'The cooking sherry. Mrs D keeps it in here somewhere. Ah! Here it is! Come and have some.'

I laugh as he uncorks the bottle and takes a swig from it. I take a quick slurp and hand it back to him, noting that he doesn't bother wiping the top before taking another mouthful. 'I'd pop one of those patches on if I were you, Izz.'

'Already have.' I whizz my dress up to show him the one just above my knee. 'I'll slap on another when I get a moment. Do you want one?' I ask seriously.

He laughs raucously as he pops the cork back into the bottle, as though a non-smoker couldn't possibly wear a nicotine patch. He kisses me roughly on the cheek, says 'Thanks Izz. You're wonderful,' and walks from the room, leaving me sniffing the air like a Bisto kid for another whiff of his aftershave.

The evening isn't a roaring success. We have a nasty moment between the drawing room and the dining room when the guests are greeted by Meg the Westie covered in velcro rollers (which are mine, she has a nasty habit of trying to bury them). She's following with great interest the progress of a grasshopper that is jumping languidly across the hall. On top of that, Aunt Flo and Aunt Winnie are both on all fours peering underneath a sofa. Aunt Winnie is wearing yellow rubber gloves and brandishing a coat hanger. The old-fashioned way of protecting yourself against spiders no doubt. I daresay there are pygmies in the Amazon right now who are dressed in similar attire. Simon hurries the Americans into the dining room, explaining that Aunt Winnie had lost her glasses. Lost her marbles more like.

I think our visitors are a little disgruntled at the malfunctioning cooker (which is sort of true; Mrs Delaney's behaviour could be construed as malfunctioning), but then so would I be if I had been revved up by a gallon of booze, and the promise of a feast, only to be told the ambrosial fare was off the menu and cold quiche was on instead. I manage to prepare the starter, which is a sort of far-Eastern bouillabaisse made with chillies, fresh coriander and coconut milk, but it is difficult to tell where Mrs Delaney had got up to in the recipe. At least it tastes all right. Ish. The pudding and the cheese board go down a lot better and finally it is all over and I breathe a huge sigh of relief.

After I have cleared up in the kitchen, I go back to the drawing room to find everyone else sprawled around on the furniture looking exhausted. All the visitors have pushed off to bed. Monty has brought the three open bottles of wine through from the dining room and everyone is now wading through the contents. I help myself to a glass, flop down in an armchair and wonder where Aunt Winnie nicked it from.

The others are having a discussion about which house in Aunt Winnie's village has the best taste.

'You know, Izzy,' booms Aunt Winnie, 'I've decided that the vicar needs to take a wife. His house was a terrible mismatch of styles. I had a peep in his kitchen too, and there were just rows and rows of baked beans. I'm determined to find him a good woman.'

That poor man. God seems to be really testing him.

A very sheepish Mrs Delaney comes into the drawing

243

room. Simon gives her a big smile. 'How is everything, Mrs D? Come and sit down.'

She has the good grace to look very apologetic and spends a great deal of time staring at the floor. 'No, it's okay. I just came to say that I'm sorry about earlier.' Despite her protestations she eventually perches on the end of one of the sofas. 'It was just such a shock to see him. Apparently my name was mentioned in one of the papers when all the fuss about this takeover started and he came to see if it was me. Didn't think he'd still care after all this time.'

'And Harry?'

'He didn't know I was pregnant. That was a bit of a shock for him too, to find a son he didn't know he had.' She manages a wry smile. I sit forward a little in my seat, suddenly curious. I wonder why she left her husband in the first place but don't feel I can really ask. 'I'm sorry I let you down,' she continues and I'm surprised to see a lone tear trickle down her cheek. 'After all you've done for me and then I let you down like that.'

Simon gets up, sits next to her and offers her his handkerchief. The tears are starting in earnest now. 'After all we've done for you? What about what you've done for us? You do more hours than a junior doctor with no decent wage and all of us to put up with. You haven't let us down. Besides, you cook like an angel.'

It's past midnight, the man is coping with a dozen problems, a dodgy takeover that might just claim his family house, and he's still got time to comfort the housekeeper. Where is the nasty Simon that I knew?

'Is Harry okay?' I ask.

'Yes, I've checked on him once and Aunt Flo has too. He's fine. Hasn't even woken up.'

'Where's Mr Delaney?' Monty asks.

'Staying at the pub overnight.'

'Why don't you go to bed? You look done in.' Simon pats her knee and then gets up and stretches his arms over his head. 'I quite fancy a walk down to the lake. Clear the head.'

He wanders over to the door. Monty takes his place on the sofa next to Mrs Delaney and starts talking to her in a low, comforting voice.

'Do you fancy a walk, Izzy?' Simon says casually, barely turning his head. Do I fancy a walk? Rather surprisingly, I think I do. I put down my glass and get to my feet.

'Em, yes,' I say casually. 'That would be nice.'

We wander down the passageway and into the kitchen. We put on a fleece each in the cloakroom and liberate Meg and the other dogs from the utility room where they have been locked up for the evening. Taking Meg with us, Simon picks up a torch and we slip out into the night.

Once outside, I breathe in the cool night air and look up at the stars. The moon shines brightly, bathing everything in an eerie half-light. There is a light breeze which gently kisses my face. Meg scampers along confidently ahead of us as we make our way towards the lake.

After a few minutes, the silence starts to become a little painful and I search about for something to say. I clear my throat. 'It's been a strange few days, hasn't it?'

'Terribly.'

'Are you worried about the takeover?'

'Yes, although I'm rapidly getting to the point where I'm so knackered that I cease to care. She seems to have adopted you,' he says and points ahead to Meg, who is happily darting about in the moonlight, poking her head down rabbit holes, appreciatively sniffing bushes and looking back at us from time to time to check that we are still there.

'Yes. I'll be sorry to leave her.'

'Tell me what you did after you left Pantiles,' Simon says.

Oh God, he wants me to go through the whole Rob Gillingham disaster story in minute detail. 'Well, I got back to London at about—'

'Er, no. I meant fifteen years ago.'

'Oh.' This takes me by surprise and for a second I can't sodding well remember what I've been doing for the last fifteen years. 'Well, Sophie and I went to live with Aunt Winnie when Mum and Dad went to Italy.'

'I like Aunt Winnie. And, er, did you go to university then?' he prompts.

'Yes, I went to Nottingham. I studied geography.' I'm reluctant to say any more as I can't remember what Dominic and I put on my CV. I think it best to change the subject. 'Did you just study economics at university?' I hear myself say and inwardly groan. It's the sort of thing you talk about during university holidays when you've been paired off with the only male in your age group for fifty miles at your parents' drinks party.

'Yep, just economics.'

'How, er, er . . .' I'm about to say interesting but he might think I'm blatantly taking the piss. '. . . useful.'

'What does Sophie do now?'

'She works in the city. Very successful.'

'Is she seeing anyone?'

'Not that I know of; I think she's far too busy with her career!'

'And how did you get into the party business?' he asks gently.

I gabble on for a couple of minutes about my job in the city and how much I disliked it. In the meantime we reach the top of the hill and stand for a second to catch our breath. 'We used to toboggan down this hill,' Simon remarks. 'Do you remember?'

'You and me against Sophie and Will. Used to thrash them.'

'Well, we did wax our toboggan and we were heavier than them.'

'Not that much heavier,' I say indignantly.

'Obviously that would have been all me.'

'Something to do with the ton of potatoes you used to knock back.' Whenever the boys came for supper with us, in the early days when Simon and I liked each other, my mother used to hopelessly overcompensate on the potato front. The amount of potatoes each sex ate was her definition of the difference between little boys (of which she had none) and little girls (of which she had two rather strapping examples).

'Your mother used to think boys needed a small lorry-load of potatoes with every meal in order to survive.' He grins at me. A warm, wide smile that lights up his whole face and makes him look quite gorgeous. I smile back and suddenly the conversation is easy as we remember and laugh. We studiously avoid the more difficult times that we know come later. How different he is now from the last memory I have of him in my head. I look more closely as he talks about the fishing trips we used to take when they all made bets as to how long it would take me to fall into the water. I think that if we had just met for the first time I might quite like this man.

We continue talking about university. 'So have you kept

247

in touch with anyone from Cambridge?' I ask.

He shrugs. 'I did at first. Friends used to visit but after a while we started having less and less in common. They were still drinking and womanising – things I used to do exceptionally well, I might add – but I had suddenly sprouted a family and an enormous estate to look after. It tends to put a strain on things!' He smiles at me once more and I suddenly realise the full extent of his sacrifice. He gave it all up, those irresponsible, halcyon days at university where life-long friendships were made and hearts were broken. He gave it all up but for what? For all this to be taken away from him?

We reach the lake and walk around to the pontoon in silence. Simon sits cross-legged on the edge. 'Come and sit.' He pats the wooden slats by the side of him. 'Talk to me some more. Tell me about your work.'

I try to arrange myself elegantly in my dress. 'My work?'

'Yeah, what do you normally do? What were you doing before this event?'

'That would be Lady Boswell's Nordic Ice Feast.'

'God, that sounds horrific! Actually, Lady Boswell you say? I think I've met her. Very thin. Dreadful woman.'

'Awful.' I go on to tell him about Sean and Oliver and our dreadful rehearsals. We laugh together and Meg comes and lies down next to me.

'How's the ball coming on? Lot to do?' Simon asks.

'An awful lot. The marquee arrives early next week. What have you got on for the rest of the week?' I inwardly cringe; what a crass thing to say. Ohhh, not much, Izzy. Just a hostile takeover and the family home to save. 'I mean, are you around much?'

'Back and forth. The Americans probably won't make a

decision until the end of the week. We'll be right up against the deadline.'

'Deadline?'

'A week on Monday. Midday. All offers for Wings expire then. Unless the Americans agree to our offer, everything has to start over again. But with our money situation we can't afford to restart the negotiations and so the whole thing will bomb. A week on Monday it will all be over, one way or another.'

'God. What do you think will happen?'

'Hard to tell. Are you here all week?'

'I've got to pop back to London tomorrow to pick up some more clothes but then I'll be here until the ball on Saturday.'

'Is it next Saturday?' he asks in surprise.

I nod and bite my lip. And then I'll be leaving Pantiles for good.

We start walking back to the house, talking softly. Simon laughs at how I kept sneaking looks at the top of Mr Berryman's head this evening, thinking I was being oh-so-subtle about it. We reach the back door and, with his hand on the latch, Simon turns and looks at me.

'We're back,' he says softly. 'I really enjoyed this.'

I'm surprised at just how strongly I agree with him.

'This is where we part company,' he says. He smiles at me and my heart suddenly goes into overtime, hammering madly against my ribcage. I truly hope he can't hear it.

He leans slowly towards me, eyes on mine, and I hold my breath. Is he going to kiss me? He pecks me on the forehead, ruffles my hair and says, 'G'night, Izz.'

I watch him walk away. Why am I disappointed?

Chapter 21

'So where did you get to last night, hmmm?' This is accompanied by a good poke in the ribs.

I open one eye sleepily, squint at the perpetrator and roll over. 'Go away.'

'Not until you tell me what happened.' Dom appears on the other side of the bed.

'What time is it? Ooh, tea!'

Dominic holds the mug away from my outstretched hand. 'Not until you spill your guts.'

'Dom, it's too early. Let me drink first and then I'll tell you.'

He looks at me for a few seconds, weighing it up, and eventually hands over the mug. I lean against the head-board and sip appreciatively at the tea. Dom lets me have exactly three sips.

'So?' he demands. 'Where did you and Simon pop off to? All the family raised their eyebrows when you left; I thought Flo had a twitch she was winking at Aunt Winnie so hard.'

'Nothing to report,' I reply. 'We walked down to the lake, chatted about things, walked back and then he kissed me on the forehead and ruffled my hair.'

'Probably checking it wasn't a toupee. So no smoochy looks? No holding hands?'

'Nothing!'

'I take it you wouldn't be adverse to any smoochy looks or hand-holding should the opportunity arise?'

I knead the bedcovers with one hand. 'It's not that. After all, this is Simon we are talking about. Our history is complicated.'

Dominic leaps to his feet in excitement. 'I knew it! Harry owes me five pounds from his bob-a-job fund!'

I look at him in horror. 'You can't take money off Harry! What was it for?'

'The family had a small wager that you and he were . . . you know.' He gives me another poke in the ribs. 'But I knew you didn't fancy him.'

'Me and Simon? What on earth were they basing that on?'

'Just the fact that you two were so close in childhood. My insider information turned out to be extremely profitable and with my smooth city ways to the fore I took full advantage of it. Anyway, explain to me why I can't take money off Harry.'

'Dom!'

'Oh, all right, I'll let him off. But only because we're in the country.' He sinks down on to the bed. 'What sort of lesson are we teaching him if we let him off his debts though?'

I ignore this thinly disguised attempt at morality. 'What are you doing making bets with Harry? Does the whole family think I fancy Simon? Aunt Flo?' I ask, thinking of the clothes and jewellery she's lent me. 'God, you would think they'd have more important things on their minds what with the takeover!'

'Oh come on, Izz! This is much more entertaining!' Dom bounces on the bed.

'Well, I hate to be the bearer of bad news but he doesn't fancy me. Dom, he kissed my forehead. He ruffled my hair. Is this the behaviour of a man who fancies me rotten?'

'Er, possibly not. But, as you say, he does have a lot on his plate at the moment. Maybe after the takeover he'll see you in a whole new light!'

'Unlikely,' I mumble and sip determinedly at my tea. While Dominic goes off about his business I muse about last night and how well Simon and I were getting on. It makes me feel a little odd and, unwilling to think about it any longer, I get up and take a shower. I drag on a pair of tailored trousers and a black top and go down to breakfast.

Most of the family are sitting at the kitchen table. Over the last couple of days we have all been getting up extra early to help Mrs Delaney with the visitors' breakfast. Simon is presumably already hard at work; it's the only opportunity he has before his visitors rise. 'There you are, Izzy! We were just about to start!' exclaims Aunt Winnie.

To make life easier for Mrs Delaney, and as a sort of test run, we've been having exactly the same as the visitors for breakfast. I have to say she is a simply marvellous cook when stretched like this. This morning she looks tired around the eyes after yesterday's little debacle.

'What's this?' I ask, sitting down next to Harry and surveying the concoction in front of me.

'Fresh figs, honey and ricotta!' Mrs Delaney replies brightly, as though she eats this every day of the week. Harry looks aghast.

'Mum?' he questions. Harry's idea of breakfast is a Ready Brek brûlée.

'They have it in London, dear.'

'Oh, well, that explains it,' says Dominic. 'Honestly, what will these Londoners come up with next? At least it's vegetarian.'

The whole table fixes him with a look. 'Dom, you ate sausages yesterday,' proffers Monty.

'Yes. Vegetarian sausages.'

'How do you figure that?' I ask. 'Because the pigs they came from ate vegetables?'

'Izzy, you have a tone.'

'I don't have a tone.'

'I can hear it.'

'Maybe you're tone deaf.'

'I think you need another nicotine patch. You've been wonderfully liberal since you've been on those patches.'

'I'm not sure it's the patches,' I murmur, trying to ignore Dom. 'It's really very nice, Harry. Just try it.'

Everyone picks up their forks cautiously and I make a great show of digging in with huge enthusiasm. Dom takes a mouthful, clutches his throat and falls off his chair. We all giggle. But only after Dominic has mashed the fig mixture up, put it on toast, sprinkled it with sugar and laid banana slices over the top will Harry eat it.

'Do you need anything doing today, Isabel?' Harry asks between mouthfuls.

'Em, not just now, thanks, but there'll be loads of stuff tomorrow.' Meg was given a haircut by Harry as one of his bob-a-jobs because it was getting too hot for her. Now she's walking around shivering as she was shorn to within an inch of her life. The grandfather clock in the hall chimes ten times every hour and Monty only asked him to wind it up every night. So whenever I ask Harry to do something,

I always make sure there is plenty of time to correct the mistakes. 'Off to Scouts tomorrow?' I ask. Harry nods. 'You'll ask how Godfrey Farlington is getting on, won't you?'

'Course I will!' he exclaims shrilly.

'How many more weeks have you got to go?'

'One! But Godfrey always wins – his dad is a plumber and the captain of the cricket team so he is forever getting jobs. Mum won't let me go into the village by myself to ask anyone for jobs.'

'We'll find jobs for you here.'

'I'll never win if I keep losing bets,' he says gloomily.

I glance over at Dom who is looking the picture of innocence. 'Dominic didn't take any money off you, did he?'

'No, he didn't. But Aunt Flo said I couldn't make any more bets after this one.'

'Which one?'

'The one between all of us.'

I narrow my eyes and stare at Dominic. 'Dom? What's this about a bet?' The table slowly goes quiet. 'You TOLD them, didn't you?'

'Izzy, I think the hair-ruffling definitely sounds encouraging,' puts in Aunt Winnie. 'Positively flirtatious.'

'I didn't tell them as such, Izzy. I was just reporting back.'

'Reporting back?'

'They sent me,' he says sulkily.

'God, is nothing private around here? We simply went out for a walk together.'

'Darling, if you want privacy then this is simply the wrong family for you,' says Aunt Flo. 'Think how easy things would be if you were a beetle.'

'But then she wouldn't fancy Simon,' puts in Dom helpfully.

254

'She would if he were a beetle.'

'But do beetles fancy each other?' asks Aunt Winnie.

'I should say so! You should see them mating!'

'Simon isn't a beetle and he doesn't fancy me,' I say sharply.

'But suppose he was!' persists Dom.

'Then Izzy wouldn't fancy him if he were a beetle.'

'She would if she were a female beetle.'

'I'm not a beetle either and I don't fancy him,' I put in. A slight throbbing around my temples tells me that we've taken this discussion further than I wanted it to go.

Mid-morning, after seeing our American visitors off and receiving invitations from all of them to visit if I'm ever in Chicago, I go through to the drawing room to see if everyone is ready for coffee. Simon is talking to his collection of lawyers and accountants. They all give me a brief nod or smile to acknowledge my presence before going back to their notes, utterly absorbed by what Simon is telling them. Just for a second, I see him from another perspective. The silence is so respectful you could hear a pin drop. Whatever detail Simon is explaining to the group, he is passionate about it. It doesn't mean a lot to me but it sounds pretty damn impressive. Where did Simon learn all this? At university? I listen to him some more, quietly impressed.

After a few more minutes, I ascertain that coffee would be very welcome in about half an hour and wander back to the kitchen.

'Cup of tea?' Mrs Delaney offers. 'Kettle has just boiled.'

I nod my thanks. For the first time ever, Mrs Delaney and I have tea together. She sits down opposite me and with floury hands pours tea from the huge ubiquitous brown teapot.

'Em, how are you?' I proffer politely.

'Better,' she says. I get the feeling she would quite like to talk about things.

'Yesterday must have been quite a shock for you.'

'Yes. Yes, it was. I feel pretty dreadful about everything. Believe it or not, I was quite young when we first got married.' She looks me in the eye with a wry smile.

I open my mouth to protest, realise anything I say is going to come out wrong and close it again.

She continues: 'Tom and I had been going through such a bad patch that we both thought it would be a good idea to separate for a month or so, just to think things over. Then I found out I was pregnant. I didn't want us to get back together simply because I was pregnant and of course I knew it would change everything if I told him. The more I thought about it, the more panicky I became. I imagined the dreadful atmosphere our child might have to grow up in and in the end I convinced myself that it would be better if we weren't together. So I left.'

She looks at me defensively as though I might judge her harshly. I try an encouraging smile. 'So you didn't ever tell him you were pregnant?'

'No. I feel awful about it. Always have. But the longer I left it the worse it became until I had absolutely convinced myself that it would never work out. All that weekend visiting for Harry. We had some money problems as well so I thought Tom was better off out of it.'

'And then you got a job here?'

'I don't have any family to speak of so I had to support Harry. Besides, the Monkwells are my family now.'

'I know they feel the same way about you.'

She smiles at me. 'I'm glad Tom knows though. I hope

he's going to be a good father to Harry and not mess him around.'

'I'm sure he'll be a great dad. I think it's hard for a child to be without their father.'

'Do you really?'

'Yes,' I say simply, thinking of my own frequently absent one. 'I don't think you'll regret letting him back into your life.'

'We're seeing him in a couple of weeks. I promised I'd take Harry to Oxford for the day.'

'At least Harry has all the family here. They love having him around.'

Mrs Delaney smiles suddenly, a warm, friendly smile that makes her face seem quite different. 'I was so lucky to find them. They've all been extremely kind. Anyone should count themselves honoured to be attached to this family. I'm sorry I've been a bit defensive about them.'

'That's okay. I understand why.'

She looks at her hands for a second. 'I feel even worse now I know how hard Tom's been looking for me.'

'But he found you,' I say simply. 'That's all that matters.'

I quickly leave a message for the marquee company to check they're going to start work tomorrow and to instruct them that on no account should they leave anything structurally important up to a small ginger-haired boy asking for bob-a-jobs. Then I run up to my room to pack my overnight bag. I have shoe-horned a meeting with Rose and Mary into this afternoon and then I'll drive back to London. I plan to return to Pantiles tomorrow afternoon. Dom comes in while I am packing and lies on his bed.

'Are you coming to London with me?' I ask, thinking a bottle of wine may be in order this evening, along with a long comforting chat.

'No, I'm going to visit someone. Monty's offered to lend me his car.' He doesn't quite look me in the eye.

I stare at him for a second. 'Dom, what's going on?'

He reaches over and plays with the zip on my bag for a second. I don't take my eyes off his face. 'Em, it's difficult, Izzy. I don't want to upset you.'

'You're not going to—' A knock at the door interrupts me. I walk over and open it.

'Oh, hi Harry!' I say in surprise.

He's carrying something. 'You left your cardigan downstairs. I thought you might want it.'

'Oh, er, thanks.' He hands it over to me and there is a slight pause while he stands awkwardly in the doorway. 'Do you want to come in?' I ask. I get the feeling he does.

He shrugs slightly so I leave the door open and he follows me in. I resume packing.

Dominic gets up. 'Well, I must be going. Izzy, I will talk to you tomorrow.' Our eyes meet in implicit understanding. He gives me a kiss, ruffles Harry's hair and leaves.

Harry comes and sits on the bed and starts to swing his legs. Poor little mite, he's had a hell of a week too. 'I'm going to have an awful lot of bob-a-jobs for you tomorrow,' I tell him.

'I don't mind!' he says eagerly.

'Good!' I busy myself with my clothes but find that Harry is looking at me curiously. I wonder if he wants to talk about his father or whether I just look a bit strange. I clear my throat awkwardly. 'So! You met your father yesterday.' I wonder briefly whether I should have a degree in counselling or something before attempting such a tricky subject. Too late now.

Harry looks at his hands for a while. 'First time I've met him!'

'Was it?' I ask in feigned surprise. 'And, er, how was, er, that?' It would help to be able to form sentences properly.

'It was fine,' he says cheerily, seemingly unaffected by this life-changing event.

'Are you going to see your dad again?'

'Yes, we're going to Oxford in two weeks' time.'

'Right.' I nod for a couple of seconds.

'Izzz-zeee,' Harry drawls slowly.

'Yes Harry?'

'How do you know when . . .' He fiddles with his cuff.

'When what?' I prompt.

'When you love someone?'

My arms halt abruptly en-route to my hold-all. Normally this is just my forte – I can spend hours mulling over my relationships with Dom. But when an eight-year-old boy asks me this question I know I'd better not botch it up.

'Em, is there someone in particular you're thinking of?'

Harry blushes bright red. Not advisable with carrot hair. 'Emily,' he mumbles. At least I think he says Emily. It was pretty hard to catch.

'Em, Emily?'

He nods frantically. 'Well . . .' I say, struggling for something sensible to offer him. 'Do you like being around her?'

'More than anyone!' he says enthusiastically. 'Most girls are stupid. They whisper and giggle but Emily talks to me. She doesn't have a father either. I get this funny feeling. In my tummy.' He looks at me for answers. If only he knew I'm the last place on earth he's going to find them.

I would love to tell him that he's just eaten something funny and it will wear off but sadly I know that these crushes never really do.

'In your stomach?' I query, suddenly struck by something.

'Yes. Do you get them too?'

'A sort of butterfly thing when you see them, or if you think you're going to see them?'

'Yes!'

I sit down suddenly next to Harry. Actually, that is a slightly familiar feeling. A fairly recent one too. Was it with Rob? Will? The answer strikes me right between the eyes. Shit.

'Izzy?'

'Yes, Harry?'

'What do you think about me and Emily?'

'Well, it sounds as though you like her an awful lot.'

He nods slowly and seems satisfied with this completely inadequate answer. I wish I could add something more comforting but there's nothing to say to Harry or myself.

I look at my watch and realise I really do have to leave in order to get to my meeting on time. I also need to be by myself to think about this new development.

'Let's go and get you an ice pop,' I say, holding out my hand to Harry, and we wander slowly down to the kitchen. My walk may be nonchalant but my heart is going ten to the dozen. This sudden change of heart, I tell myself, for someone who until a few days ago you couldn't stand the sight of, and had regular fantasies about giving a swift kicking, may just be due to the fact that you're very, very tired.

I deposit Harry into the arms of Monty and Aunt Winnie

and an ice pop and return to the hall. I pause at the bottom of the stairs.

'Izzy!' a familiar voice calls behind me.

I spin around to find Simon hurrying towards me. 'Simon, hi!' I raise my eyebrows and fix a smile on my face.

He halts in front of me and frowns. 'What's up with you?'

'With me?'

'Yes, you look strange.'

'Strange?'

'Are you going to repeat everything I say?'

'No, of course not. That would be strange when I am, of course, feeling perfectly fine.'

'Fine?'

'Now you're doing it.'

'Where are you off to? I wondered if you wanted to take a walk down to see the deer?' A walk? Again? What is it with all this walking? Is it a country thing?

'I can't,' I say quickly. 'I'm going to London.'

'When are you back?'

'Tomorrow.'

He looks disappointed. 'Well, I'll be working right up to next weekend but I'll give you a hand with the ball on Saturday if you like.'

'Great! Thanks! I'll see you later.' I turn away and run up the stairs, feeling the need to put as much distance as possible between myself and Pantiles. This latest turn of events is making me very confused. Very confused indeed.

I collect my stuff from my room and rush down to the kitchen via the back stairs. I leave a note for the family, give Meg a quick pat and zoom out to the car.

My feeling of claustrophobia lifts slightly as I put some miles between me and the estate. What am I thinking? Am

I losing my tiny mind? Why not fancy Will? Ah yes, Will. A carbon copy of his older brother but not a patch on the original. Great fun to be around but lacking the depth, charisma, attractiveness and sheer magnitude of his sibling.

But therein lies the problem. It certainly will be an uncomfortable state of affairs if history repeats itself. It's as though I've sneaked a look at the exam questions and know all the answers. I know how this is going to end up. It's not going to be pretty.

After a brief meeting with Rose and Mary in Bury St Edmunds, I race down to London with my mind on one thing and one thing only. I dash up the steps to the flat and call Aidan. Although it is Sunday, he agrees to meet me at a little Italian restaurant on the Kings Road which is a lunchtime favourite with all of Table Manner's staff. The waiters know us well and always attempt to teach us pidgin Italian while we instruct them in the complexities of the English language.

After we have 'Ciao bella!'-ed like mad, perched ourselves on the highly uncomfortable bar stools and equipped ourselves with a bottle of house white, Aidan encourages me to start my story. I think I confuse him somewhat with tales of stolen furniture, killer spiders and urns containing dead people's ashes. My tale of woe culminates in my moonlight walk with Simon and the rather unfortunate fact that I think I fancy the pants off him.

'You mean Will,' Aidan puts in helpfully at this stage.

I narrow my eyes. I wonder if he has been listening at all. 'No, I mean Simon.'

He looks patently bewildered by this. 'But Dom said you fancied Will.'

'When did you talk to Dom?' I ask suspiciously.

'Does it matter? He said you fancied Will.'

'Nooo,' I hiss, impatiently waving my arm about and damn near punching the nearest diner in the face. 'I fancy Simon.' I don't like the way this is making me sound, especially as the diners nearest to us have stopped talking to each other in an effort to tune in to our conversation. Giuseppe, the head waiter, opens his mouth to say something but I silence him with a look.

'Simon? You fancy Simon? Not Will?' Aidan says incredulously. I'm starting to wonder if he has some sort of mental deficiency. Even the diners by the door are looking interested now.

'I'm trying not to think about it,' I mutter. Easier said than done. All I can remember about Pantiles is how wonderful I think Simon is. How much he loves his family. How hard he is working to save his home. And how much I used to love him.

'Bloody hell,' Aidan adds for good measure, pulls a face and then stares into his wine glass for a minute.

While he recovers from this latest revelation, I have one of my own and discover that the wine bottle is empty. Before I can open my mouth to order another, Giuseppe plops one down in front of me. 'On the house!' he announces grandly. I suppose I'm cheaper entertainment than a magician. Maybe I should have a sign saying 'Also available for weddings and bar mitzvahs'.

I refill both our glasses and wait for Aidan's response.

'But I thought you *hated* him,' he says eventually.

'I did. But things have changed slightly. He's actually a very nice person. Considerate. And he's been doing all the business stuff for a very noble reason: to save his family home.'

'So?'

'I just started to fancy him. *Really* fancy him.' I lean forward to illustrate my point and nearly fall off my stool. I struggle back on again.

'But doesn't he have a girlfriend?' Aidan asks. Giuseppe looks suitably aghast at this and I wonder if he has given up serving food completely for the evening. I try to ignore him.

'I think so. A lawyer.'

'Is he still going out with her?' Aidan asks. Giuseppe lets a small tut escape his lips. We both look at him and he makes a magnanimous carry-on gesture with his hand. 'Have you asked him about her?'

'No! I don't want to look desperate.'

'Well, how would you like things to proceed from here?'

'Past stuff aside, I want to, er—'

'Boff him?' Aidan puts in helpfully.

He is so uncouth. Wearily I say, 'I don't know what I want. Maybe I just need to get this whole job over with and come back to London.'

'But past stuff aside?'

'That's the confusing bit. I mean, he was pretty nasty to me when we were kids.'

'Of course, you've known him for years,' Aidan murmurs thoughtfully.

'Yes! I've known him for years!' I repeat loudly so that the people at the back don't think I'm a complete and utter slut.

'Everybody is nasty when they is kids,' Giuseppe puts in. 'I once cut sister's hair when she asleep and—'

'This was a bit more than just childish pranks, Giuseppe. This was quite an intense campaign of bullying.'

264

Giuseppe mulls this over and helps himself to a glass of wine. The other waiters are scurrying about like billy-o and throwing him nasty looks but I'm actually quite keen to hear his opinion now.

'Give me example,' he says.

I tell him about the time Simon collected all the insects he could find, including some hefty spider specimens, threw them over me and then locked me in a cupboard for several hours. I was petrified.

'Ah,' he says at the end of this sorry tale.

'That doesn't sound so good, Izzy darling,' says Aidan.

'But do you think people change?' I persist, looking from one face to another.

'Yes!' says Aidan.

'No!' says Giuseppe. 'I think you have to ask, why he so nasty?' Giuseppe adds on helpfully.

'Because he didn't like me?' I answer in a very small voice.

Nobody says anything for a second. I can see they're struggling to find something positive to say. 'How's Dominic?' Aidan asks eventually.

'He's bloody buggery fine!' I damn near shout, almost falling off my bar stool again with the exertion. 'Why does everyone want to know how he is?'

'Who else wants to know how he is?'

'Eh?' My drink-sozzled brain is struggling to keep up.

'Who else wants to know how he is?'

'EVERYONE wants to know how he is. Why is that?' I pause and stare at Aidan. 'You're jealous, aren't you? You're not seeing him, are you?'

'Not jealous, Izzy. Just . . . well, it's too complicated to explain. He obviously hasn't said anything so I'm not saying anything either.' He crosses his arms.

On this subject he will not be drawn and eventually Giuseppe disappears behind the bar for another bottle of vino.

The next morning I'm not sure whether it's the insights of last night or the amount of alcohol I poured down my throat that make me feel so bad. I drag myself unwillingly into work. Gerald decides he is on a sales drive and insists on a total clearout of the offices because he says they don't look professional enough. He shouts instructions through his hand-held tannoy while we all spend the best part of an hour trooping up and down the stairs, returning all the props to the basement. It takes three of us to move Yogi the stuffed bear and every time I pass the kitchens I'm smacked in the face by garlic fumes. I'm feeling so nauseous by the time Yogi has been released into his natural habitat that I have to lie down in the basement for five minutes.

Aidan is obviously as awful as me and refuses to take off his *Top Gun* aviator shades, which makes it very hard for anyone to know whether he's listening to them or actually having a quick snooze. Every time one of us makes a visit to the coffee machine we return with a cup for the other in some sort of silent salute to our night together. Gerald is still charging about so, after a visit to the kitchens to confirm the food deliveries for the ball, I gather my things together and set off once more to Pantiles.

On the motorway, I delve into the underworld of my bag in search of my mobile and end up emptying the contents all over the passenger seat while dangerously swerving around lorries. No mobile. I come to the conclusion that I've probably left it on my desk at work. Gerald is going to kill me. I pull off at the next service station and call it from a payphone. Aidan answers. Damn. I make him promise to Fed-ex it to me at the estate that very minute and hang up.

I hesitate for a second before calling Dom on his mobile to let him know I'm on my way back. I also want to be pre-warned if anything disastrous has happened.

He answers on the second ring.

'Dom, it's me.'

'Darling! How are you?'

'Fine.'

'I know it's a difficult situation.'

'Oh Dom. It is,' I say in relief and wonderment at Dom's ESP virtues.

'As I told you last night, I'm going to tell Isabel about us today. I promise,' he continues.

There is a pause. 'I am Isabel,' I say slowly, for my benefit as much as his.

This time the pause is on his end of the line. Eventually he says, 'Izzy?'

I look down at myself, just to double-check, and then say, 'Yes.'

'This is not your ringtone though. Where are you calling from?' he says in a strange voice.

But I'm not listening. I'm trying to think of someone whose voice he might have confused with mine.

I can only think of one person.

Chapter 22

'Dom, can I see you for a minute?' I ask the second I clap eyes on him. Most of the family are sitting at the kitchen table playing cards and Harry has a huge pile of coins in front of him. They are playing with the big jam jar full of old pennies that we used to use when we were young. Mrs Delaney is bustling around in the background. Dom looks up from his hand of cards.

'Could it wait a second, Izz? Just until I've—'

'No, it couldn't.'

'We found Poppet!' trills Harry. Thank God for that, I was starting to fear for the life of the grasshopper in my chimney, not to mention my own. 'I found her upstairs! They gave me ten bob-a-jobs for it!'

'That's marvellous, Harry!'

Dominic follows me up the back stairs, along various corridors and into our bedroom. I swing around to face him. 'Dom, you could have told me.'

He looks sheepish and stares at his feet for a second. 'I was going to tell you that time in the garden but we were interrupted. You know, you sound exactly like each other on the phone. Uncanny.'

'How long has this been going on for?'

'About six weeks.'

'Six weeks!' Actually that does add up. 'I thought you were trying to tell me you were gay!'

His head whips up at this. 'Gay? Me?' I nod. He starts to swagger around. 'Why on earth would you think I was gay?'

'I thought you were going out with Aidan! He kept asking me how you were!'

'Well, Aidan kind of knew.'

'Aidan *knew*? Why would you tell him and not me?'

'I didn't tell him! We were at the Lacey-Steele function a few weeks ago. Do you remember it?'

I try to think back that far. 'Er, vaguely.'

'You'd only just broken up with Rob. You disappeared back to the office to collect something and I was on my mobile. Aidan grabbed it off me, thinking it was you, and then found out it wasn't. Only the person sounded very much like you. So I had to tell him.'

'I think he probably told Gerald too; they've both seemed obsessed with your health lately.'

'I don't look gay, do I?' Dom asks anxiously.

'It was just that, well, you dated all those girls and you didn't sleep with any of them!'

'Izzy, just because I'm nice and don't sleep around does not mean I'm gay! Besides, I slept with a couple of them.'

'Did you? Which ones?' I ask with interest.

He opens his mouth to reply and then, in the light of my relationship with his new amour, closes it again. 'So you thought I was trying to come out all this time, did you?'

'Cecily told me you were gay.'

'Cecily?' He sits down on the bed.

'Yes, I met her at a drinks party.'

'Oh God. Cecily. She invited me to have dinner at her house – it was one of those ghastly dates my aunt keeps setting me up with. At some point in the evening she must have decided she quite fancied me because when I popped off to have a pee I came back to find she'd taken her top off!'

'What? Her bra too?'

He giggles and nods. 'I mean, Christ! It was one hell of a shock! I didn't know what to do. I sat back down at the table and then she started to lean across it, tits dangling in the pavlova, and I panicked! Told her I was gay and had been trying to come out for years. I thought it was the only way I would get out of there alive! I didn't want to hurt her feelings and it was all pretty embarrassing anyway considering she was topless at the time. I asked her not to tell anyone because I hadn't officially come out yet. God, what were the chances of her meeting you?'

'What about when you pointed out boys you thought were good-looking?'

'I was just trying to divert your incredibly blinkered eyes away from Rob.'

'But why didn't you tell me about you and Sophie?'

'She's your sister! I thought you might be really funny about it.'

'I wondered why she'd been avoiding me lately.'

'I wanted to wait and see how serious it was before I said anything.'

'How serious is it?'

'Serious enough. And it was quite confusing; why do I fancy her and not you?'

'A good question.'

He looks amusingly uncomfortable. 'I don't know,' he says in a small voice.' 'Maybe because we know each other too well? Besides, you don't fancy me.' His voice gets stronger as he reaches dry land.

'Don't I?' I demand, unwilling to relinquish this point just yet.

'No. You don't.'

'You're right, I don't. How did it all start?'

'We got to know each other quite well through those weekends at Aunt Winnie's. Then, late one night when you'd gone to bed,' he shrugs and looks sheepish, 'we were chatting and . . . I don't know . . . we just started kissing and . . .'

'TOO MUCH INFORMATION!' I bellow, putting my hands over my ears.

He stops and grins. I tentatively take my hands away from my ears and walk over to the window. Sophie and Dom! Who would believe it? My eyes suddenly fill with tears and I wipe one away. Dom notices the movement and gets up and puts an arm around me. 'Now, don't tell me you're going to get upset about this.'

'I'm not upset, I'm happy for you.' I give him a hug. 'I think it's lovely. Strange but lovely. But why didn't you tell me?'

'I'm sorry I kept it from you. And I'm sorry that you had to find out like this. You've enough on your plate at the moment.'

My shoulders sag. 'How's the takeover going?'

'I don't know much, but everyone is very subdued. I only got back myself about an hour ago.'

There's a knock at the door. 'Izzy, dear!' booms Aunt Winnie from behind it.

271

I walk over and let her and Jameson in. 'Have you told her?' I ask Dom.

'Aunt Winnie!' he greets her. 'Don't get too excited but we're probably going to be related!'

'Bloody hell,' says Aunt Winnie faintly.

After several slugs from the cooking sherry, which I have to liberate from the kitchen while Mrs Delaney isn't looking, and several reassurances that it was Dominic and Sophie we were talking about rather than Dominic and me (although I'm not quite sure she wouldn't have preferred it the other way around), we finally manage to coax the revered old relative out of her trance-like state and away from the bottle.

'Did you want me for something, Aunt Winnie?' I ask.

'Oh! Just to say hello, and to see if you've spoken to your parents yet?'

'They're calling me back.'

'Make sure they do.' She gets up and walks over to the door. 'I'm going to find Monty,' she says and marches out.

'Can I call you Mom?' Dominic shouts after her.

She turns and faces him at the door. 'You can call me something close, Dom. You can call me Ma'am. Like the Queen.'

The next few days pass in a haze. Rose and Mary seem to take up permanent residence at the house. While I wrestle with electricity supplies, stroppy performers and waiters who have suddenly had the opportunity of a lifetime to go to Africa and 'we wouldn't *mind*, would we?', Dominic oversees all the rehearsals and persuades the fireworks company that the site they've chosen really is too near to the house. I have no opportunity to talk to Simon as he is also working long hours on the takeover.

We're not the only ones who are run off our feet. Fred, the gardener, works from dawn till dusk to get the gardens looking as nice as possible. The plan is to have preliminary drinks on the back lawn if the weather permits. Mrs Delaney continues to cook madly every day, feeding not only the family but Simon's team of lawyers and accountants as well. I think Mr Delaney is still staying at the pub in the village; Harry and Mrs Delaney slipped out last night to meet him.

I at last manage to get hold of Sophie on the phone and we have a long chat. It's such a relief to be able to talk normally to her again; I hadn't realised what a strain our relationship had been under. She is so thrilled about her relationship with Dom that I haven't the heart to dampen her spirits with my rather more depressing tale of woe.

On Friday morning I get up early to supervise the delivery of the portable loos. It's the only time the company can do and if they are left unsupervised the loos usually end up at least half a mile from the marquee. The day is bright and cool. Dom barely stirs as I get dressed; Meg looks at me dozily but elects to stay with Dom. Even Monty isn't up yet.

Once the delivery has been made I wander into the kitchen, trying to ignore the siren call of my nicotine patches. I find Simon sitting at the kitchen table reading yesterday's paper.

He lowers the paper as I walk in. 'Izzy! Why on earth are you up at this ungodly hour?'

I start at the sight of him. He's wearing a pair of old jeans and a thin V-necked jumper. He looks utterly delectable.

'Nothing very exciting, I'm afraid. The portable loos have just arrived. I was showing them where to park the trailers. What are you doing?' I ask.

He shrugs. 'Not much. Couldn't sleep.'

'Worried?'

'A little. Come and sit down and tell me how the ball is going. It feels like I haven't seen you for days! Any problems?'

I don't quite meet his eye. 'No, no. Nothing really.'

'Tomorrow's Saturday; I can be yours all day if you want me. Do with me what you will.'

'That would be nice,' I say dreamily. 'I mean, er, that would be very useful.'

The day of the ball dawns and I immediately run to the window and peer through the curtains. I breathe a sigh of relief; it looks as though it's going to be a fine day. I wake up Dom, get dressed, slap on two nicotine patches, argue with Dom about why exactly I'm not going to bring him a cup of tea and then run downstairs clutching my clipboard. I'm high on adrenalin. There is nothing quite like the buzz of a huge party to get me going.

'So what do you want me to do today?' Monty asks while we have tea together in the kitchen, after I persuade him that teaching Jasper to bark whenever he hears the phrase 'Richard and Judy' isn't terribly worthwhile. Not to mention extremely annoying.

I look down at my clipboard. 'The car park valet is turning up at midday. Could you show him exactly where to park all the cars? And put together some signs for the guests?'

'Consider it done.' I scan down my A4 list and tick off those two items. 'This is an awful lot of fun, isn't it, Izz?'

'Hmmm.'

'God knows what Elizabeth would have said about the whole thing.'

'You don't think she'd approve?'

'She thought the estate should always be kept strictly private. She'd have hated the idea of people coming to gawp at her home. But you've got to move with the times, haven't you?'

There's a small silence as I absorb myself in my list. Monty interrupts my thoughts once more.

'Izzy? I know this is none of my business . . .'

'What's that?' He clearly has something he needs to get off his chest.

'You and Simon. Is there . . . ? Because, you know, if there was then that would be wonderful.'

I open my mouth to reply but just then Albert the terrier pokes his head around the kitchen door – from about three feet off the ground. I know it's Simon because it's something we used to do as kids to cheer the other up.

I grin widely as he pokes his head around the door a few seconds later. 'Morning!' he says cheerfully, putting Albert down. 'How are you, Izz? Dad?'

'You're up early again!' Monty says.

'I said I'd help out so Albert and I are raring to go!'

I can't help it, I love him to bits. 'Thank you, that's really helpful,' I smile.

'Well, you did so much to help with our American visitors. It's just a small way of saying thank you.'

'But that was a disaster!' I protest.

'Not compared to what it could have been. I think we probably got off quite lightly.'

'Cup of tea?' I ask, indicating the pot with my head.

'Yes please. Where are your coasters, Izzy?' He grins as we survey the minefield of mugs and milk bottles.

'Completely forgot.'

'Anarchy has broken out in Mrs Delaney's kitchen. It must be your patches.'

'How is the takeover?' I ask as I get him a mug and pour the tea.

A small cloud crosses his face. 'The American investors say they'll have a decision for us on Monday morning.'

'But isn't that the deadline?'

'Yep. Make or break. They want to be left alone to make their decision so I've decided to take today off in honour of Pantiles's first ever event. We'll have to work tomorrow to prepare for the press conference on Monday. Anyway, enough about all that. Who are you taking to the ball, Dad?'

Monty clears his throat. 'I thought I might ask Winnie actually.' He looks anxiously at me for a reaction. 'Do you think that might be all right?'

I beam at him. 'I think it will be marvellous!'

'Absolutely,' adds Simon, smiling too. 'Is Mrs Delaney coming?'

'I don't know, I think Mr Delaney is still around.'

'She could always bring him.'

'I'll tell her.'

'Come on, Izz, let's get started. We'll come and have breakfast later with everyone else.'

Monty stays put while Simon and I go out into the court-yard, Albert and Meg trotting behind us, and walk round to the marquee.

'So do you and Dom wear evening dress too?'

'Oh yes, I brought something back with me specially.' It's a dress I always bring for these occasions, again donated to me by the Sophie Serranti fund. 'I only hope Dom has had his dry-cleaned since the last event!'

'Is he still in bed?'

'I woke him up and I hope he hasn't gone back to sleep. His list of things to do today is almost as long as mine!' Thinking of Dom makes me anxious. After my initial euphoria I am now nervously hoping that I won't become too jealous of Sophie and Dominic's new relationship. Dominic and I have been so close for so long that it feels a bit like he's being taken away from me.

'What's wrong?' asks Simon, looking at me.

'Oh nothing! Dominic's just told me that he and Sophie are seeing each other.'

'Dominic and Sophie? Your sister, Sophie?'

I nod. 'I thought he was trying to tell me he was gay!'

'Dominic? Gay? You should have asked me, I could have told you that he wasn't gay. God, that's excellent, isn't it? Keep him in the family. But it must feel strange too – he's been yours for so long.'

I look up sharply at this perceptive comment. Simon holds the flap open to the entrance of the marquee and smiles at me. It suddenly strikes me that you could have said the same thing about Simon and me over fifteen years ago.

I think today must be the nicest pre-event day I have ever had. Watching this calm, supremely capable man in action makes me realise what a formidable opponent he must be in the boardroom. Everything seems to get done in half the time and with half the fuss. When the band arrive mid-morning and announce that they are going to need extra electricity which our generators simply won't cover, Simon doesn't even blink. He simply gets on the phone and another generator arrives within half an hour. He doesn't throw his weight around with anyone, he doesn't raise his voice (and I have to say that on occasion pre-event days have found me screaming like a banshee), he just coolly negotiates and people find themselves doing what he wants. There is no doubt that I am watching a very talented man at work, which just serves to make me fancy him more than ever. There is something very sexy about a man who is good at what he does.

'What's next on the list, Izz?' he asks after managing to convince an entertainer that tonight really wouldn't be the occasion to perform for the first time without a safety net.

The Big Top is looking absolutely magnificent and I am thrilled with the results. We have hired an authentic ring-master for the night, complete with huge handlebar moustache and shiny black boots (Rose will be ecstatic). We have managed to rig up a tightrope and a trapeze, where the performers will perform their acts at intervals during the meal. The tables are placed around the sawdust ring in the centre of the marquee and we have used very bright colours for the flowers and decorations to suit the circus theme.

While the staff lay the tables, Aunt Winnie, Monty and Harry place the favours on each table – toffee apples, juggling balls and lottery tickets. I watch them for a second, chatting and smiling between themselves.

'I suppose they'll never be short of something to wear; they must own half the nation's tweed between them!' Simon whispers in my ear and I laugh. 'Nice to see though,' he continues. 'I haven't seen Dad looking so happy for a long time, despite all this trouble with the house. Your Aunt Winnie hasn't been married before, has she?'

'No, I think she was too busy looking after Sophie and me. My mother told me that there was someone once though.'

'What happened?'

'I don't know. I've never talked to her about it; it was always a bit of a closed subject.'

One of the waiters tells us the Table Manners vans have arrived and we go out to meet them. We show the chefs round to the catering tent where they immediately start inspecting the equipment. I look at my watch. It's five o'clock already.

'How are we doing?' Simon asks.

'Okay, I think. I just need to fix some of the flower arrangements – I noticed there were a few holes in some of them – but I need to check off this delivery first.'

'I can do that; have you a list for it?'

'Thanks, Simon.' It's been simply marvellous having him with me today. I rifle through my folder and hand over the delivery list to reconcile. 'I'll be in the garden getting some greenery. Then I simply must go and get changed.'

'No problem.'

We go our separate ways, I find a pair of secateurs and make my way out into the garden. There's a huge laurel bush to one side of the house that I am intent on using. I trot around to it and indulge in a frenzied bout of chopping which would probably give poor old Fred a coronary on the spot.

Back in the marquee, Simon is nowhere to be seen so, after I have hastily filled in the holes in the floral arrangements, I quickly double-check on all the staff and our chefs and then rush upstairs to get changed.

I hook my dress off its hanger on the back of the door and notice that Dominic's suit carrier is already empty. It me feel marginally better that someone from the company is at least on the scene. He's probably being useless, but he's there all the same.

279

My dress is the ultimate confidence booster and I thank Sophie from the bottom of my heart for it every time I put it on. From some eminent fashion house, whose name I can't even pronounce much less afford, it's a deliciously figure-hugging and wonderfully luxurious dress. The top loops over one shoulder, there is a split to the top of my thigh at the front and all around the split and the bottom of the dress is an exquisite crocheted lace hem. I add a pair of specially purchased jet drop earrings and a bracelet that Aunt Winnie gave me. Piling my hair on top of my head, I draw a line of black kohl under each eye with a slightly shaky hand, smudge them with a cotton bud and then add a dash of scarlet lipstick.

Rose and Mary are already standing in the marquee, dressed in their regalia and chatting excitedly to Dominic, when I return.

We greet each other with suitable oohs and aahs at each other's attire and then move on to the state of the marquee.

'It looks simply marvellous!' breathes Rose, looking up at the vast space.

'Thank you.'

'Is it all ready?'

'Well, Dom and I are about to do our last-minute checks,' I smile at them. 'But why don't you help yourselves to some drinks on the lawn? The guests will start arriving in about half an hour.' Dom hands my radio receiver over to me.

With great alacrity Rose and Mary bustle off drink-wards, pausing en-route to admire the ringmaster who is already dressed for action. Dom is in radio contact with most of the staff, which is probably the highlight of the night for him. He insists everyone has handles and I leave him to make contact with all of them. I check the tables, have a last-minute chat with the chefs and then walk out to the back lawn to ensure the drinks are ready to be served with canapés as soon as the guests start arriving.

I am busy foraging underneath one of the serving tables when someone lightly taps me on the shoulder. I swivel round on my heels to find Simon bending over me and so I very hastily stand up. I have no wish for him to see me squatting, tits squashed and arse a-dangling.

'Simon!' I say in delight. 'Gosh, you get ready quickly!'

'No one gets undressed quicker than me, Izzy.'

'Er, really?' I say faintly and blink quickly to try to banish the images that have sprung to mind.

'You should remember that from when we used to swim in the lake!'

'Em, no. Not really.' You know, children really ought to take more notice of their parents. I should have listened to my mother more when she told me to pay attention.

'You look stunning. That's a beautiful dress.'

'Thank you,' I say, feeling suddenly gauche. 'You look good too.'

'The rest of the family will be down soon. Do you want me to do anything?'

'No, we're all fine. You enjoy yourself.'

'Are you going to be working all night?'

'I might get half an hour off later.'

'I'll save a dance for you. Make sure you eat something.'

'I'll try,' I say, suddenly feeling absurdly happy. No one has cared whether I eat or not for a very long time.

'See you later,' he adds before wandering off, hands in pockets, towards Will who had just appeared on the other side of the lawn.

Guests start arriving in twos and threes and I spot Aunt

281

Winnie looking resplendent in burgundy taffeta. A very proud Monty is standing next to her. They give me a wave. Even Mrs Delaney and a nice-looking gentleman with red hair, who I presume is Mr Delaney, are looking happy and as though they are enjoying themselves.

Suddenly the majority of guests seem to arrive in a huge wave and from then on things start moving at an alarming pace. Someone breaks a glass and cuts their finger. The head chef has a fit because people aren't moving through to the marquee quickly enough and his first course will be ruined. One of the trapeze artists feels ill and isn't sure about going on. Dominic and I gradually start to move the group through to the marquee before the chef has a nervous breakdown altogether. There isn't a seating plan as such – each table is assigned to the appropriate company. The waiters and waitresses scurry about, dishing up the first course while some stragglers bring up the rear.

'That's the lot,' whispers Dom to me.

I frown as I look around the marquee. 'Who's taken those seats?' I ask, pointing at two empty tables.

Dominic consults his clipboard. 'A company called Maida Insurance. They might turn up later.'

I shrug and wander over to the Monkwells' table. As I weave my way through the maze of furniture, twisting my hips this way and that, I notice that they look as though they are having a marvellous time. Although, if we're being honest, park some booze and half-decent food near the Monkwells and they will always have a good time. Will is looking very handsome but he can't eclipse his older brother.

I eventually reach their table and Simon smiles at me. 'I can't believe you put all this on! It's simply amazing! Is it better than Lady Boswell's Nordic Ice Feast?'

'Definitely!' I smile back at him appreciatively. 'Thanks,' I say simply.

'Are you tired?'

'My feet are killing me!'

'Izzy?'

'Yes?'

He glances at Aunt Flo, who has her back to us but her ears tuned in to our conversation. 'Did you know that our old friend Gussie is looking for a cat?' he says casually, without taking his eyes off me.

My brain vaguely stirs in recognition. He's talking to me in our secret language, I think slowly to myself. The problem is, I haven't heard it for fifteen years and I am absolutely amazed that he remembers it.

Gussie means us. Any reference to cat means that we need to talk (I think originating from the fact that the French for cat is chat).

'When are you seeing Gussie?' I ask, meaning where and when shall we talk.

He smiles at me and reaches out to take my hand. An extra shot of adrenalin starts to pump around my body.

But the smile dies on his face and he suddenly drops my fingers. He is staring at something behind me and I swivel round to see what it is. I gasp because there, very calmly taking his seat at the vacant table in black dinner jacket and tie, is Rob Gillingham.

Chapter 23

The next thing I spot is Dominic haring towards me like a maniac. He has gone quite pale.

'Izzy,' he hisses. 'Rob is here.'

'I know,' I snap back, 'I can see him.'

Simon stands up. 'What name is he booked under, Dom?' He inclines his head towards Dominic's clipboard.

'The table is under the name of Maida Insurance.'

'That must be them,' I say, watching the rest of the table take their places.

'I recognise some of them,' whispers Dom.

'It's the whole of the Gillingham board,' Simon says grimly. 'They're trying to intimidate me. I'm the only representative from my company here. Bugger.'

'They must have bought tickets,' I say in wonderment. 'They must have been planning this all along.'

During our little interchange, Rob looks around the marquee. As soon as he spots us, he gives a charming little wave as though we are all the best of chums and gets up.

'Christ! He's coming over!' Dom says incredulously.

I glance at Simon. He looks calm but I can see a little muscle ticking in his neck. This is clever. To catch Simon at his most vulnerable, at his family home, without anyone from his company to support him and when he is supposed to be relaxing and having a good time.

'Simon, Isabel and Dominic,' Rob greets smoothly. 'How nice to see you all!' He extends a hand to Simon, who shakes it grimly. 'May I call you Simon?'

'Why are you here?'

'We thought it would be a nice evening out for all of us. After all, these last few weeks have been a bit of a strain. We thought we'd celebrate the failure of your takeover, Simon. You did say I could call you Simon?'

I try to stand closer to Simon. I can feel every muscle in his body tensing and for one awful moment I think he is going to hit Rob.

'After all,' Rob continues, albeit a little less confidently, 'it wasn't until Isabel here said she could get us tickets for this event that we thought we would treat it as a sort of final farewell to the whole ridiculous idea.'

'What did you say?' I manage to stammer. 'I didn't suggest anything of the sort.'

'You know, I have never seen you perform before, Izzy.' He gives a little laugh. 'Well, not in public, my love. But I have to say, I am very impressed.' He looks around at the marquee. 'You have been a little gem these last few weeks. You know, Simon, I don't think we could have won this takeover without this little diamond here.'

'There are no winners in this,' Simon says in a hard voice.

'We'll see,' Rob says softly, 'we'll see,' and with this he turns and goes back to his seat.

I spin around to face Simon. 'Simon, I haven't seen or spoken to Rob Gillingham since that night I told you about, I swear. He's just—' The rest of my words are drowned out as the family crowds around Simon, demanding to know who Rob is and what all that was about. And then one of the chefs taps me on my shoulder to inform me there is a problem in the kitchen.

The rest of the evening passes in a blur. I fight the desire to go over and kick Rob firmly in the goolies as some sixth sense tells me that any sort of showdown won't help Simon or the takeover. I try my best to ignore Rob, even though he has the audacity to raise his glass to me every time I walk past his table. In contrast, Simon won't even make eye contact. Things on the Monkwell table are decidedly tense but everyone is uncomfortably holding their ground. When I finally have five minutes to myself, I walk anxiously over to them.

'Simon, can I talk to you?'

'What about?'

'The Rob Gillingham thing, obviously.'

'Izzy, I'm exhausted and I don't want to give Rob Gillingham the satisfaction of us looking as though we're rowing. Can we talk about this tomorrow?'

I really want to clear the air between us but Simon is right, Rob has already caught sight of us talking together and is watching us with interest. I nod and get back to work.

Rob manages to grab me later in the evening. He neatly sidesteps me as I make to walk past him and blocks my way.

'Izzy, you never called me,' he says gravely but with a distinct air of piss-take.

'Rob, you complete shit. I can't believe—'

'Now, now, Izzy. People will start to talk,' he says, putting his hand on my arm.

I look over to one side to find Rose and Mary watching me. I concentrate very hard and smile at them. They relax slightly, smile back and look away.

'So what's the score between you and Simon Monkwell?'

'Why? Do you want to ring a newspaper with that information?'

'Don't be bitter, Izzy, I did what I had to do. You would have done the same in my position.'

'I doubt it, Rob. I could never bring myself to sleep with you again for anything.'

'Don't say that. Your lover is looking for you, by the way.'

I glance over my shoulder to see Simon staring at us. There is no disguising the look of distaste on his face.

It is about four in the morning by the time I have supervised the general clear-up operation but, despite my tiredness, I am completely incapable of sleep. Dominic is already gently snoring by the time I reach our room. I play the whole Rob scene over and over in my head, rehearsing what I want to say to Simon and what he might say back. Does he really think I have been feeding Rob information all this time? The sun has already risen by the time I drop off into an uneasy slumber.

The next morning, I creep down to breakfast to be greeted by the sight of a very hungover Aunt Flo and a frighteningly cheerful Aunt Winnie and Monty. I try unsuccessfully to avoid eye contact with any of them.

'Hello Izzy! What a marvellous party! Well done!' Aunt Winnie greets me. Is she mad? Was she at the same party as me? 'Apart from the Rob thing. That obviously was dreadful. Poor Simon. I could have gone over there and punched him myself.'

'I wish you had done,' I rejoin gloomily.

'Simon wouldn't say anything about it. Just told us to ignore them.'

'He didn't mention anything about me?' I ask hopefully. That doesn't sound too bad.

'No. But whatever did you see in that Rob character? Dreadful-looking youth.'

I slump down at the table. This is all I need – a cheerful half hour reminding me where I've gone wrong in my love life.

'Are you okay, Izzy?' asks Aunt Winnie in concern.

'Yes, I'm fine.'

'You don't look fine,' says Monty. 'Are you ill? Which one of the girls was always ill, Winnie?'

'I'm fine.'

'Was it Izzy who could only sit in the front of the car because she always got car sick?'

'I don't get car sick.'

'I don't know because both of them always had to sit in the back with me.'

'I don't get car sick.'

'Always a bit of a hypochondriac, like Flo. Quite endearing.'

'But I don't get car sick.'

'Actually, I think that might have been Sophie, Monty dear. But you're right, Izzy doesn't look at all well. Have you been travelling in a car this morning, Izzy?'

'I DON'T GET FRIGGING CAR SICK!' I'm quite anxious to get this point clear – the only reason I don't look well is because they are steadily winding me up.

They both look at me in surprise. 'Do you want to go back to bed?'

'Aunt Winnie, much as I would like to go back to bed and stay there indefinitely, I have to help with the clearing up.' I try to say this with as much dignity as I can muster. It's not much.

'I'm making scrambled eggs for Simon's team, Izzy. Would you like some?' asks Mrs Delaney from over by the Aga.

'Simon's team? Are they here?'

'All in the drawing room,' says Monty. 'I think they're preparing for the press conference tomorrow. Marvellous do last night, by the way. Haven't had so much fun for years!' Everyone noisily expresses their agreement.

I frown to myself as Mrs Delaney bustles about and hands me a plate of scrambled eggs on toast. I am desperate to see Simon again, if only for a minute, but God knows how long they will all stay in the study for.

The morning passes quickly. I have to oversee the clear-up operation in the marquee as well as the removal of various bits of equipment. Gerald also calls to demand a report. I walk hopefully past the solid wooden door of the drawing room at least ten times in the vague hope that Simon might come out and I would have a chance to speak to him. My opportunity comes about halfway through the morning when I glimpse him disappearing into the kitchen ahead of me. I accelerate, calling out, 'Simon!'

The figure in front of me hesitates and then turns around. The body language is not good. It's awkward and bristly.

'Isabel. Good morning.'

'Er, morning.' I halt in front of him. 'Simon, I need to talk to you about last night.'

He sighs. 'I suppose we have to talk about this some-time. Come on then.' He takes my elbow resignedly and leads me into the deserted kitchen. We sit down at the table. I look around me nervously. The kitchen isn't a very good place to be. It scarcely remains deserted for long, especially with Dom around.

I jump in first. 'Simon, surely you didn't believe anything that Rob Gillingham said last night?'

Simon's eyes remain fixed on the ground. He stares unseeingly at a slab of flooring. 'I don't know,' he says finally. 'You tell me.' At last he looks up at me.

'Of course not! After all we've been through these last few weeks, do you really think I'd still be in contact with him? He was just shit-stirring!'

'Isabel, let me ask you a question. Before you came back to Pantiles, how did you feel about me? Really feel about me?'

I blink; the query has taken me completely by surprise. 'Well, I, er, suppose that, em . . .' His eyes are fixed on my face. 'I didn't like you very much,' I finish in a small voice.

'Really, Izzy? Just "didn't like"? That's a bit mild for someone of your strength of character. Are you sure you didn't hate me? Don't forget that I was there when we were kids. I remember it just as well.'

I inhale sharply. This is the first time we have openly talked about his bullying. 'Okay, I hated you. Is that what you want to hear? Does that make me guilty of feeding information to Rob Gillingham?'

'Was that ever the plan?'

'What do you mean?'

'Did you come back to Pantiles to extract some sort of melodramatic revenge? I mean, you have to admit that you going out with a non-executive director of the company I am trying to buy is a pretty big coincidence.'

'We *had* finished by the time I got here and, yes, it was a coincidence. You're going to have to accept that. Are you also saying that I managed to arrange for a ball for five hundred people to happen here at the same time?'

'I'm saying that you and Rob might have seen an opportunity. Something that you could both get something out of. And you know, Izzy, I wouldn't blame you. I really wouldn't.'

'What are you trying to say? That my behaviour has been a sham?' My heart is pumping in my ears. I don't like the turn this conversation is taking; it feels terribly dangerous.

'Maybe not. Maybe it was all for real. Maybe you and Rob didn't plan anything at all.'

'We didn't!'

'But my point, Izzy, is that somewhere very deep inside me, I doubt you.'

'You doubt me?' I say disbelievingly.

'Yes, and that makes me feel guilty as hell. Because of our past. Because of what happened fifteen years ago. I did all that stuff to you but I still doubt you.'

'I can't believe you would think I would do anything to hurt you or your family.'

'I'm sorry, I can't help it.'

'You're the one with the nasty streak, not me,' I snap.

He flinches slightly at this and I look down at the table, ashamed of myself.

'That stuff won't go away, will it?' he says quietly. 'You'll be watching all the time for some glitch in my character. Some small-minded act or thought that might signify a return to that time.'

I hesitate just for a millisecond – he has touched a nerve.

'I would if I were you,' he adds.

'Then tell me why, Simon. Tell me why all that stuff happened fifteen years ago.'

He looks at me for a long time and reaches out a hand to touch my face. I smile hopefully. 'There's nothing to tell, Izzy,' he says simply and walks from the room.

It is a few seconds before I manage to gather myself together and flee up to my room, Meg trotting after me. I stand in front of the mirror staring at myself. A very pale and scared-looking Isabel stares back at me. Don't you cry, I threaten myself, don't you dare. I think about finding Dom or Aunt Winnie but realise that if I do I will have to relate the whole conversation and that will well and truly open the flood-gates.

Earlier there was no doubt in my mind that Simon and I shared some sort of intimacy. It was the same intimacy we had over fifteen years ago, until the bullying started – which I can't explain the reason for. So maybe I don't know this man at all. Maybe I have been imagining things that simply aren't there. Maybe some leopards don't change their spots. What the hell am I going to do? Go home, says a small voice inside me. Go home where you can cry your eyes out and eat Cornettos to your heart's content.

I close my eyes and rest my forehead against the cool glass of the mirror. There's a slight problem in all of this. The slight problem is that I think I love him. Almost as much as I did all that time ago, but this time it's a different sort of love. More intense, more fierce. But, reason tells me, I loved him fifteen years ago and look what happened there. Am I so stupid as to risk all that again?

And as tough as that is to handle, I think I have also fallen in love with his family. I not only want him, I want his family to be mine too. But how is this going to work, Izzy? Your Aunt Winnie and Monty look as though they might be forming some sort of an attachment and so you'll be forced to occasionally return to this house and this family and watch Simon at the heart of it. Watch him get married, watch his children growing up, chatter idly to Aunt Flo while wishing so hard that it was you at the centre of it all. I clench my hands into fists. It is almost too much to bear.

I go over to the bed and lie on it. Meg hauls herself up next to me and settles down in the crook of my legs with a contented sigh. For the next half an hour or so I remain exactly like that, staring numbly at the ceiling, taking a small amount of comfort from the furry body next to me. Eventually, I pull the duvet over me and close my eyes in an effort to blot out the pain. I suppose I must have dropped off – Lord knows how little sleep I've had over the last few days – because the next thing I know there is a loud knocking at the door. I awake with a jolt. 'Izzy? It's Dom. Can I come in?' he calls.

'Of course!' I reply.

He pokes his head around the door. 'Here you are! I've been looking all over! What's wrong?' he asks in alarm, seeing my miserable face.

'Simon,' I mumble.

'What about him?'

I feel tears prick at my eyes again. Dom comes over to the bed, sits on one side of it and gives me a big hug. This little piece of humanity is too much for me and I succumb. When my sniffles eventually calm down, Dom makes me tell him everything.

'So let me get this straight. Simon doesn't want to be with you because of your childhood—'

I interrupt him. 'He didn't even say that he wanted to be with me.'

'Oh. So even if he did, he wouldn't because of your past together.'

'I think so.'

'What do you think?'

'I don't know.'

'Would you be able to trust him again?'

'He hurt me pretty badly. I suppose he broke my heart really. I think he's right; we couldn't ever be together.' Tears fill my eyes once more. 'Our childhood will always be between us, won't it?'

'What are you going to do?'

'Go home, I think.'

'That would be the smart and sensible thing to do.'

'You really think so?'

'When we're back in London, I'll buy you a Cornetto.'

He pats my knee and finally says, 'Do you want me to go and find you some chocolate?'

'There you go. You can see now why I thought you were gay, can't you, Dom?'

'I am merely in touch with my feminine side,' he says with as much dignity as he can muster and sets off, his feminine side telling him that he doesn't need an answer to the chocolate question either.

I don't think I have ever been so miserable in my entire life.

Oh yes, silly me. I have.

Chapter 24

A hideous evening ensues where Simon refuses to make direct eye contact with me, even when Aunt Flo starts a lively debate as to the attractiveness of short hair or long hair on men. After a while I leave them to their arguments and go to bed. I lie awake until about four, listening for the chimes of the grandfather clock in the hall until I belatedly realise that the bailiffs have taken it away. This agitates me so much that I have to turn the light on, check the time and then Meg and I pace up and down for a bit while I try to persuade myself that the events of the last few days do not justify my taking up smoking for real. Although I fail to rouse Dom, who can sleep through anything, I do wake a sodding grasshopper who begins to chirrup happily. I feel as though this is all part of a giant jigsaw puzzle but all the pieces haven't been given to me yet – if I could just understand what's missing then maybe everything will be all right.

I must fall asleep at some point because when I wake up Dom's bed is empty, stripped of all its covers, and his bags are sitting in a neat pile at the end of the bed.

There's a knock at the door and Meg bounds into the room. Dom follows with a cup of tea. 'You know,' he says,

'I think I'm going to miss this place. Our flat will seem quite empty after all this.'

'What are you going to do now?' I ask, conscious of his current state of unemployment.

'Write my novel and live off the money from this job for a while, I suppose.'

'So you'll be at home all the time?' I take a sip from the cup.

'Shall we ask if we can take Meg with us?'

'Just what I was thinking,' I smile, hugely comforted by the fact that we could possibly adopt her. Otherwise it would have been yet another loss.

'I'll go and ask now. You get dressed and packed and I'll see you downstairs.'

'Who's down there?' I ask. I'm not sure if I want to see Simon.

'All the family except Simon. He's preparing for the press conference this morning. Then we're helping load up the furniture for Aunt Winnie to take back. After that, I suppose it's the office for you and home for me.'

He smiles and leaves me to it. After I've got dressed, I start to pack up my belongings and then spend the best part of ten minutes staring out of the window. You'll feel better when you leave, I tell myself firmly, and then spend another ten minutes staring out of the window. There's another knock at the door. 'I'm just coming,' I yell at Dom and start frantically stuffing my bags with clothes.

'No, it's me, Izzy. Aunt Winnie. Can I come in?'

I walk over and open the door. Aunt Winnie and Jameson practically fall through it.

'Hello dear! Just came to see if you're all right! I've been worried about you.'

I frown. 'I'm fine, just packing up.'

Meg tries to play with Jameson but Jameson, being older and wiser, is having none of it. He curls up in the corner with a dignified air. Aunt Winnie closes the door behind her. I make a great show of actually folding my clothes up to pack rather than my usual practice of just stuffing them all in.

I'm fine until she actually speaks. 'So you're leaving, are you?'

I feel the tears well up in my throat. 'What else can I do?' I ask, practically choking with the effort of keeping my emotions at bay.

Aunt Winnie thinks I'm suffocating and gives me a couple of hefty slaps on the back. I eye her warily in case she starts the Heimlich manoeuvre.

She sits down on the bed. 'You could stay. Stay and see what happens.'

'Simon and I have talked about it. We don't think it's smart.'

'Smart?' snorts Aunt Winnie. 'I think of you as many things, Izzy, but smart isn't one of them.' I look at her sharply. Is that what she meant to say? 'Look, Izzy. After you went to bed last night, Dom told me what happened.' What happened when? This is the problem with having so much history in one place. She sees me looking doubtful and adds, 'When you and Simon were kids.'

'Oh.'

'I think Dom was worried about you and needed a second opinion. I kind of knew something had happened anyway. I mean, you were always really funny when Simon's name was brought up and I could see that you never wanted to come back here to visit after you'd left.'

297

'What was your second opinion?'

'History is a funny thing, Izzy. If you had met Simon Monkwell for the first time a couple of weeks ago, would you still be in this situation? Of wanting to be with him, I mean? Or would you have had an altogether different impression of him?'

'Er, I don't know. Are we going anywhere with this, Aunt Win? Anywhere specific?' I could really do without the philosophy lesson.

'Think of old school friends.' I think of the few I made when Sophie and I were living with Aunt Winnie. 'If you met them for the first time now, would you be friends with them? Or is the bond that you share simply common memories?'

'Are you questioning how I feel about Simon?' I tentatively ask, to try to find the point to all this.

She looks relieved and nods slightly. I come and sit next to her on the bed. 'Aunt Winnie, I love him because I know him so well. Not because we share common memories. In fact, it's the common memories that are keeping us apart.'

Aunt Winnie pats my hand for a second and looks down at the floor. 'Izzy, since we're talking about shared history, I think there's something I should tell you.'

I look at her uncertainly. Is this the link I have been missing? The thing that will make everything fall into place?

'I meant to tell you ages ago.'

'What?' This comes out a little more tersely than I intended.

'Well, Monty and I used to . . . how do you say it? We used to see each other.'

I get my timescale all mixed up and say in horror, 'He had an affair?'

'Oh no! No, it was before he got married.' I relax minutely. 'That was how we knew the Monkwells.'

'So what happened?'

'Oh, it was silly really. We were both too young. Only in our twenties. No, Izzy, that wasn't during the war,' she says as I open my mouth and close it again. 'Anyway, both families were heavily against our relationship, which made life pretty difficult. We had a big row one day, I can't even remember what it was about now but it seemed like the end of the world at that age, and I huffed off saying I never wanted to see him again. I was due to go to America for a few weeks to visit some relatives and so I left without saying goodbye I was so mad at him – he could be absolutely infuriating, you know. But then, so could I. It was the biggest mistake I ever made. I returned home to find him uncomfortably engaged to Elizabeth.' She stares off into the distance, lost in a private world. 'I remember it so well; it was summer, one almost as hot as this. I was wearing a beautiful new twin-set with my pearls and I danced over to the estate, longing to see him. Thinking our silly row would all be forgotten. And there she was. Sitting on the lawn in the middle of a picnic rug, sipping champagne with the rest of the family. I didn't find out until later that they were actually engaged. The family didn't like me much. Thought I was a disruptive influence.' She leans over and whispers conspiratorially, 'I was a bit of a wild child back then. Rode horses bareback and swam in the swimming pool naked.'

'They had a swimming pool?'

'The first thing Elizabeth did was to dig it up and put a rose garden over the top of it. Of course, my behaviour means nothing now, it's probably called spirited or something, but back then it was very non-PC for the prospective Lady of the Manor. The Monkwells wanted someone with more dignity. Someone who would treat the servants as servants, not chums to have a good gossip with in the kitchen garden. Elizabeth fitted the bill beautifully. The family loved her and apparently shoved Monty at her so hard he was engaged before he knew it. Poor love; when I think back, he did look a little dazed that day.'

'So what happened when he saw you?'

'He didn't see me. I came around the side of the house and saw them all sitting on the lawn. Monty was holding Elizabeth's hand with his back to me so I just turned and ran. I couldn't have gone over to him, not with all the family there – it would have been far too embarrassing. I never knew whether he found out I'd been there. His mother saw me but I doubt she ever mentioned it. I sometimes used to wonder if things would have been different if he had seen me.'

'Didn't you try to contact him?'

'Pride, Izzy, my dear. The downfall of many a relationship. I was furiously angry with him and didn't really believe the marriage would happen. If I had taken it more seriously I think I would have stayed and fought for him. When you're so young, you don't realise how decisions like that can change lives.'

'Do you think he loved her?'

She looks pensively into the distance, somewhere over my shoulder, and then says quietly, 'Yes, I think he did. The boys were born, and then you and Sophie were born, the happiest days of my life.' I lean over and squeeze her hand appreciatively. 'I started to hear less and less of them. Started to lose contact with the people who told me about them. Time moved on for all of us.'

'But you never married, Aunt Winnie.' It suddenly strikes me that this is the unfortunate affair that my mother mentioned to me. It was Monty. Winnie looks down at the table for a second and then says quietly, 'No. But I'm not sure we would have been happy together. We've both mellowed a lot now but back then we were pretty fiery and we used to have some dreadful rows. Elizabeth was a very settling influence on him. You always need one rock in a relationship.'

'That's very pragmatic of you, Aunt Winnie.'

'Well, you can't spend your life mooning around. You have to get on with it and extract what you can when you can.' She pats my hand quite forcefully.

'So how did my parents come to live at Pantiles?' I ask.

'A little masochistic of me. When your father was stationed here and your mother decided she wanted to keep her horses somewhere, I suggested the Monkwell estate before she'd even finished the sentence. I wanted an excuse to go there and see how they were all getting along. So, there your parents settled for a few years, and naturally the Monkwells were getting along just fine without me. Anyway, I'm glad I've told you at last. I've been meaning to for years but never found the right time.'

We both sit in silence for a second, me in slight regret that none of this is the answer I am looking for about Simon. It does, however, explain some of the peculiar behaviour going on around here.

'Funny how two families can be so inextricably linked together, isn't it?' I say softly. 'You and Monty, me and Simon.' Aunt Winnie pats my hand again. 'Neither of them worked out, did they, Aunt Winnie?'

'That's not all, Izzy.'

'How do you mean?'

'Stay until after the press conference?'

I nod and she leaves me to finish my packing.

Our last breakfast at the estate is very subdued. Everyone is exceedingly concerned about the takeover negotiations and we all leap for the phone whenever it rings, hoping it might be a decision from the American investors before the deadline. But it's either a fellow boy scout for Harry, or a newspaper reporter wanting a quote from Simon, or a sultry female voice wanting to speak with Will (I had no idea he was such a ladies' man). I am quite thankful for the repressed atmosphere as I can just blend into it without much comment. Aunt Flo returns from taking Poppet out for a walk and I make a mental note to check my luggage later to ensure Poppet hasn't crept into it while I wasn't looking. We then make Harry run around in a last-minute flurry of bob-a-jobs as he is driving us all insane with how he, Harry Delaney, has only managed to raise forty-six pounds and thirty pence while ruddy Godfrey Farlington, who seems unbearably precocious and in need of smacking with a large stick, has raised so much more.

I look at Monty in a new light after Aunt Winnie's revelations. I try to picture them when they were younger but I can only see them as they are now, not just in terms of how they look but also in their responsibilities and attitudes. I can't imagine either of them being young and carefree. I look over at Aunt Winnie. Nope, it's no good. I just can't do it.

The press conference is scheduled for eleven a.m. Simon's PR firm thought it would be a good idea to have it here at the house in order to bury the bailiff rumours once and for all. Dominic and I have absolutely nothing to do as the PR firm sweep in to organise it. An efficient girl called Victoria bustles in and out of the kitchen while we lounge around on the furniture, drinking coffee and waiting for some news. Mrs Delaney is baking some sweet treats for the press which is completely unnecessary but she seems to enjoy doing it.

I take a careful look around me. Dom is chatting to Aunt Winnie, Mrs Delaney and Harry, and Flo has disappeared with Will. Monty and I are the only ones left sitting at the table. 'I had a chat with Aunt Winnie this morning,' I say to him quietly.

'Yes, she told me,' he replies. 'It's funny but after all this time she hasn't changed a bit. She's just mellower.'

'She said she used to be a bit fiery.'

'A bit! We used to have rows every second day! At least this time they'll only be once a week.'

I raise my eyebrows. 'This time?' I query.

'Well, we'll see what happens.'

'So you're going to see more of each other?'

He glances over at me. 'Next week. I said I'd take her out to dinner. That's if we're not busy moving out! Do you mind?'

'Of course not! I'm delighted!' I beam at him. That's the best news I've heard in quite a while. Mind you, that wouldn't be too difficult.

'Dom asked me if you two could adopt Meg. I said of course you could – she seems to have taken a big shine to you both anyway. But I was sort of hoping, in fact we all were, that we might be seeing a bit more of you after all this?' He raises his eyebrows suggestively.

I reach over and pat his hand, shaking my head slightly.

'Thank you for Meg, Monty.' And with this I wander out into the walled garden and call the office.

'Hi Stephanie,' I say dispiritedly.

I hear her blow out a long stream of smoke. Or she might just have been holding her breath. 'You'll be wanting to speak to Gerald then?'

'Er, yes. If he's there.'

Eventually Gerald comes on to the line. 'Are you actually returning to the office at any point today or have you taken it upon yourself to declare a public holiday?'

'I've had to tie up a few things, I'll be back later. Do you need me?'

'I'm not sure our insurance company can afford you. Unless you come under the force majeure heading, along with other naturally occurring disasters.'

'Now, now, Gerald, don't be like that.'

'How's Dominic?'

'Going out with Sophie.'

'He told you then?'

'So you did know.'

'Aidan told me.'

'I thought Dom was trying to tell me he was gay.'

'Dominic? Gay? Are you going out of your mind, Izzy?'

'I think I probably am. Aidan isn't straight too, is he?'

'No, he definitely is gay.'

'By the way, I haven't got any parties scheduled for this weekend, have I?'

'No, no. I thought you could do with the weekend off.'

'Thanks, Gerald.'

'Bugger off now. And don't call if you need anything; you'll be better off talking to the Samaritans.'

I grin to myself and ring off.

'Any news?' I ask Monty when I return into the kitchen.

'Yeah, Sam has just been in. He says the Americans want to extend the deadline so they can have more time to decide.'

'Is that a problem?'

'I'm not sure, but Sam didn't look too pleased. They're going ahead with the press conference though. The press are starting to arrive. Shall we sneak in the back?'

At about a quarter to eleven we wander through to the drawing room, where the PR company has set up a large table surrounded by fifteen chairs at the front of the room and then rows of chairs facing it. The room is already buzzing with activity; people are huddled together drinking from mugs and eating Mrs Delaney's biscuits. A large buffet table has been erected and Dom and I help ourselves. Every couple of minutes the numbers swell until we almost have to shout over the din. Flo and Will join us, both of them looking unexpectedly thoughtful.

'Are you okay?' I ask Aunt Flo in concern.

'Yes, dear. Just a bit worried for Simon.'

'I'm sure he's faced worse than this,' I say comfortingly.

'Yes, but I haven't. They might take our house, Izzy.' She whispers the latter in my ear as though she is only just grasping the concept.

'He'll find a way,' I say, knowing full well that he probably won't be able to this time.

Our little huddle stands nervously at the back until the door opens again and Simon marches into the room, head held high and proud. I stifle a gasp. He looks absolutely beautiful. He has had his hair cut into a very short crop.

'Oh my God!' moans Flo. 'He's like Samson. He'll lose all his strength.'

'Must have got it done this morning,' murmurs Dom.

I'm slapped in the face by a sudden longing for him. What wouldn't I give to be able to clamber over the top of all these people and fling myself into his arms. My stomach fills with butterflies as I watch him settle down behind the table, leaning over to murmur something to one of his colleagues. I'm concentrating so hard on him that I don't notice anyone else coming into the room.

Victoria, the PR girl, keeps giving Simon coy little looks. She teeters around on high stilettos, dressed in a beautiful Jackie Onassis-type suit. I look down at my own outfit. A black crocheted skirt, plum suede boots with a stiletto heel and an embroidered plum-coloured top.

'Oh my God,' mumbles Dom.

'I know,' I whisper back. 'Where do you think she got it from? Whistles?'

I glance over at him and suddenly realise that he's not looking at Victoria. He's looking at someone else. Instinctively I know who it is and my eyes confirm the facts.

'Oh bugger,' I breathe.

Chapter 25

I have no wish to be seen by Rob so I sidle forward and sit down suddenly on one of the chairs. Dom quickly joins me.

'It seems that wherever I look at the moment, Rob is there,' I complain.

'Why is he here?'

'I suppose because he's one of the directors of Wings.'

'Only a non-executive one.'

'Yeah, but he's responsible for all this, isn't he?'

'How are we going to get out of here?'

I look towards the door. We can't possibly leave now without bringing maximum attention to ourselves and making it look as though we're running away.

'We're going to have to sit tight until the end and then slip out with the others,' I say firmly. I can definitely do that. Sit tight, lie low, I repeat to myself. In fact, that's exactly what I would like to do, Bury myself away from all this ghastly business. Someone can dig me up in a few years' time.

The conference kicks off with a representative from the PR agency introducing everyone at the table. I sink lower into my seat. I'm probably quite conspicuous as the only midget in the room. Simon then stands up and talks about what a fine company he thinks Wings could be given the right management, and briefly outlines some of his plans for the company. He explains that the American investors hold the deciding amount of stock and that they would like an extension to the deadline to consider their options.

'So he hasn't managed to persuade them to sell,' Dom murmurs to me. 'He's absolutely stuffed.'

'He might be able to raise the capital from somewhere,' I whisper back. Dom gives me a look. 'Well, he might,' I insist. The people in front of us look round and frown at me. So is that it? Nothing more to be said? It's only another week. But there is the furniture problem, Aunt Winnie *has* to return it today, and the bank is watching the estate like a vulture. Dom is right. He's stuffed.

I slump even further into my chair and frown. I think about all the work everyone has put in to the estate – Monty, Will, Mrs Delaney. Even Aunt Winnie and Dom have played their part. I think what Simon has been through in order to try to keep his home. All for nothing. All because Rob Gillingham wants to keep his place on the board of directors. My eyes suddenly snap up. Rob's looking very pleased with himself, glancing at his reflection in the window and smirking as the American bank outline their reasons for the delay, indirectly citing the newspaper article. He knows that he's won. Everyone can feel it. God, life can be so unfair sometimes.

Questions from the press begin. Simon fields a couple of nasty ones about how many people he would sack as a result of acquiring Wings. Someone then asks what the plans are for Wings if the hostile takeover doesn't go ahead. Rob leaps to his feet.

'I think I can answer this question. Let me start by saying that all of us on the board of Wings are fighting very hard to ensure that this hostile takeover does not go ahead. We believe that a future with the current management team must be preferable to any future at all with Simon Monkwell's company. We accept that our profits have not been those anticipated by our shareholders but hope that our partners in America, who have been with us since Wings was first formed, will stand by us. We have great plans for the company which have been outlined to our shareholders and which we believe will ensure Wings' profits reach acceptable returns. We guarantee we will not be making any staff cuts. I am not alone in thinking that Simon Monkwell would ensure the worst possible outcome for all concerned at Wings – both shareholders and employees. Press accounts have not been exaggerated. He is not a man of his word. He is not a man who keeps his promises.'

'HOW CAN YOU SAY THAT!' I shout. Except that I thought I said it in my head and I can plainly see from all the faces suddenly swivelling towards me that that wasn't the case. I also find I'm on my feet. I hastily try to sit down again. I'm sure we can just gloss over this, I'll distract everyone by pointing out of the window or something. But Dom won't let me sit down. I make frantic swipes at him.

'Go on, Izzy,' hisses Dom, 'go up to the front.' He gives me a shove and I find myself at the end of our row. I vaguely register the faces looking at me; Simon with sharp-eyed interest, Monty and Flo with their mouths open wide. Simon's team look absolutely aghast and Victoria rushes towards me. Is it too late to faint? What the hell am I thinking? Nothing rational, clearly.

I take a look at Rob and my resolve hardens. I am suddenly

furiously angry. I brush Victoria's hands to one side and resolutely march up to the front. Before anyone else can say anything, I announce to the room, 'Rob Gillingham deliberately tried to use me in order to extract any details he could about Simon Monkwell's takeover bid. He knew I would be working in this household and he led me to believe . . .' my lip trembles a little and I look over at Dom who gives me an encouraging nod '. . . that he was very fond of me. He then leaked all the things I innocently told him to the press in an attempt to mislead his shareholders. He is dishonourable and dishonest and the last person on earth to keep his promises. He's a snake.' Snake, Izzy? Snake? 'And Simon Monkwell is the most honourable man I have ever met. He always keeps his promises,' I add for good measure.

I stare at the room for a second until the flash of a camera brings me to my senses. I take one last glance at Simon's amazed face and then try to exit the room with a shred of dignity. Unfortunately, I cannon into the doorway and nearly give myself a black eye. Once out in the hallway, I run to the kitchen. 'Izzy!' Mrs Delaney exclaims, 'what's wrong . . . ?' but I keep on running until I reach the walled garden. I sit down heavily on the ground and look at my hands, which are trembling madly from all the adrenalin rushing around my body. This must be the most embarrassing thing I have ever done. I cover my face with my hands. What will Simon think?

Dom arrives a few seconds later. 'Oh my God!' he says and starts to grin.

'Did I sound absolutely bonkers?' I ask in distress.

'Let's put it this way, I don't think Mrs Delaney will be asking you to look after Harry any time soon. But it was marvellous! The best thing you've ever done!'

'God, Dom. It was awful, simply awful. What on earth was I thinking? Why couldn't I have just kept my mouth shut?'

'Because you were right, Izzy. Everything you said about Rob and Simon was right.'

'Did anyone say anything after I'd left?'

'All hell broke loose. The press started firing questions but then I came after you. Will, Monty and Flo are still there. They'll tell us what happens!' He drops down and joins me on the ground.

'Have you got a cigarette?'

'Izzy, you don't smoke.'

'Just give me a cigarette.'

Dom tuts and extracts a cigarette packet from his pocket. I light up and draw the smoke right down into my boots. It's the most sublime thing ever. Just what I need to get over my rather unfortunate nicotine patch habit.

'Did Simon say anything?' I ask finally.

Dom shakes his head.

'Do you think he'll be cross? Have I ruined everything?'

'How could you have done? Rob is the one in the wrong.'

'This is just what I needed. A little more humiliation and embarrassment. Can we go yet, Dom?'

'We've got to load up the furniture and we can't do that until everyone leaves.'

'How much longer?' I ask pleadingly.

'A couple of hours.'

'I'm just going to stay here and die slowly of embarrassment. If God is merciful, he'll take me right now.'

Dom pats my knee and says, 'Okay. I'll go and get some coffee.'

'See what else you can find out!' I call after his disappearing figure. He raises his hand in acknowledgement.

I sit and stare at the ground, my arms wrapped around my knees, and take a disturbing amount of comfort from my cigarette. When I finish it, I awkwardly swivel my foot on the butt and wonder what they are all up to inside. Dom is right; I should wear little bells to warn people of my approach, or at least take out public liability insurance. I look at my watch – twenty past eleven. The Americans still have forty minutes to accept the offer; my little speech could have been just the catalyst they needed. More likely, they'll just want to wash their hands of the entire affair.

Too nervous to sit still for long, I get up and start inspecting the borders. Moving from plant to plant, I pick off leaves, inspect flowers, even dead-head a couple. I discover a peony being absolutely throttled by honeysuckle and I pull a few tendrils off so the peony can at least breathe. I pace a bit more, discovering rosemary, sage and lemon balm. God! Where the hell is Dom? How difficult can it be to make one sodding cup of coffee? How long is he going to leave me to be Alan Titchmarsh out here before he rescues me with some caffeine?

'Izzy?' I hear a distant voice call. It's not Dom. 'Izzy?' I can see the top of Aunt Winnie's head looking around hopefully for me.

'Aunt Winnie!' I hiss. She doesn't spot me. 'AUNT WINNIE!' I say again. She looks over in my direction and I make furtive waving gestures. This time she spots me, waves back and then does a comical half-run on tiptoes which I think is supposed to convey a level of secrecy.

'Izzy, my dear! Dom said you were outside!' she booms, just in case the pursuing spies had lost her. She reaches me and plants a kiss on my cheek. We both sit down.

'What's happening?' I ask.

'Well, those Purrer girls—'

'PR girls,' I correct.

'That's what I said.'

'No, you said Purrer girls, as though it's a word. It's PR, which stands for—'

'Izzy, do you want to hear this or not?'

'Oh yes. Sorry.'

'Anyway,' she glares at me, 'those Purrer girls are trying to hustle the press out but they're all waiting around, desperate to find out who you are.'

'Where's Simon?'

'He's disappeared into the drawing room with everybody else. One of the Purrer girls wanted to find you to get some sort of statement from you but we've told her we don't know where you are. She's gone to talk to Simon instead.'

'How did he look? Angry?'

'No.'

'Annoyed then?'

'No.'

'A little disgruntled?'

'No, more hassled I think.'

'Hassled?'

'Well it is quite a big story for the press! A director of a company targeted for a hostile takeover uses the caterer for information!'

'I am not a caterer! I am an organiser! I hope that bloody PR girl isn't telling them I'm a caterer! Gerald will kill her! Do you think I'll be in the papers?'

'I think you'll definitely be in the papers.'

'I wonder if Gerald will fire me this time? It's not going to look too good to our clients.'

'No!' Aunt Winnie says cheerfully, 'it's probably not.'

'I haven't even told him about Rob trying to get information from me. I thought he would freak out!'

'Well, he certainly will now!'

I remember writing a list a few years ago of what I wanted to achieve in life. Something about finding a decent man and being successful at what I do. How could I have cocked up so comprehensively on both counts?

'Can we go now?' I ask Aunt Winnie desperately.

'We've got to wait until everyone else has left to get the furniture out, Izzy!'

'Can I wait for you at your house? I don't think I can face anyone.'

'Of course! But don't you want to say goodbye to the family?'

'I'll send them all cards!' I say wretchedly. 'And flowers. And chocolates. Besides, I'll see Monty when he comes over next week.'

'Izzy, I think they're about to lose Pantiles,' she says gently. 'Couldn't you just wish them all well? You needn't see Simon,' she adds shrewdly.

Dom appears in the archway carrying three mugs of steaming coffee. 'Sorry Izzy! People kept button-holing me for information. But I never said a word. I never squealed. Even when they held me down and poked me!' He grins. 'Mrs Delaney sent these.' He produces some broken biscuits with bits of fluff on them from his jacket pocket.

I manage a half-smile back. 'You didn't tell them where I worked, did you?' He shakes his head. 'Maybe they won't find out and then Gerald won't fire me.'

'Um, I think I heard one of the PR girls telling them.'

I stare at Dom in horror. Could this get any worse?

Dom shrugs. 'Maybe Gerald will be okay about it.'

'Confidentiality is supposed to be the hub of our business!'

I stare at the two of them, speechless for a second. On top of everything else I'm going to lose my job, and I don't think I'll get another one in a hurry. Tears spring into my eyes once more and I brush them away impatiently. I'm bored of crying now.

'I'll wait for you at your house, Aunt Winnie.'

They both realise that asking me to stay won't do any good and nod slightly.

I march into the house and up to my bedroom where Meg is waiting for me. I slam the door in an act of defiance that goes completely unnoticed – this household is as accustomed to slamming doors as it is to grasshoppers. I pick up my bags and stagger to the door. Heavily laden, I trudge downstairs with Meg following. My bruised and injured pride is quite a burden in itself. After years of abuse it has finally given up walking.

I successfully make it to the car without meeting any of the family, and then try to find my car keys without relinquishing any of my bags. I finally locate them in my handbag, shove everything in the boot, open the passenger door for Meg to jump in and get into the driver's seat. My hand is trembling so much that I can barely slot the key into the ignition, but I find it eventually, shove the car into first gear and look up. A man and a woman are standing in front of the car. On closer inspection I find they're my parents.

Chapter 26

I stare at them in surprise. Unfortunately my foot slips slightly on the clutch, the car leaps forward and I damn near run them over. Both of them jump back in shock.

I get out of the car. 'God, sorry,' I say as I notice my mother has her hand to her throat and is breathing heavily. 'What on earth are you two doing here?'

They both solemnly and dutifully give me a kiss and a hug.

'What are you doing here?' I repeat.

'Izzy, Aunt Winnie called us,' my mother says. 'We got on the first plane we could.'

I frown. God, Aunt Winnie is taking my love life very seriously indeed. 'I'll be fine,' I say automatically.

'No, that's not it,' says my father. 'Is there somewhere we could go to talk?'

The only place I can think of where we will get any degree of privacy whatsoever is the ruddy walled garden. Meg and I lead the way, treading the well-worn route. Why on earth are they here? Has someone in the family died or something? Thankfully the walled garden is deserted and my parents sit down on the warped old garden bench. I sit on the ground with Meg beside me.

I look at them expectantly. 'Aunt Winnie called you?' I prompt.

They look at each other and then my mother takes a deep breath. 'Yes. She said you and Simon Monkwell were getting quite close.'

'Not any more,' I reply shortly.

My father looks up sharply at this. 'Really?' he says and then looks at my mother.

'What's going on?' I ask, looking from one to the other.

'Well, maybe nothing now,' says my father slowly, staring at my mother as some non-verbal messaging goes on.

'Does this have something to do with Simon?' I ask suddenly. 'Because if it does, I would really appreciate knowing what is going on.'

'*Are* you two close?'

'We have been. I had been hoping that we might be again,' I eventually confess. 'But I don't think so now.'

My parents stare at each other for what seems like an eternity.

'What is it?' I ask. 'You can't not tell me now.'

'She's old enough,' my mother says to my father. 'She'll understand.'

My father nods suddenly as though his mind is made up and then turns to face me. 'Izzy, this is a very difficult thing for me to have to tell you. I had hoped that you would never need to know as it's something I'm very ashamed of.'

'What is it?' I whisper, feeling quite faint.

'I'm only telling you this because, in view of your

relationship with Simon Monkwell, past or present, it would be unfair if you didn't know. We didn't want you to hear it from him.'

He takes a deep breath and continues, 'When we lived at the estate, and you were about eleven years old, I had an affair with Elizabeth Monkwell.' He looks deeply into my eyes and watches the words sink in.

'An affair?' I say eventually.

'Yes.'

'What sort of affair?'

He looks slightly puzzled at this and glances over at my mother. 'Er, the normal sort, Izzy.'

I shake myself slightly and shift position. I stroke Meg's fur and wait for the words to have some effect on me. I'm surprised to find my hand is shaking.

'A long affair?' I ask eventually.

'No,' he says quickly, 'a very short one. Just a few weeks. Izzy, your mother and I were going through a bad patch.' He takes hold of my mother's hand. She smiles at him and nods, as though urging him on. 'Which is absolutely no excuse for what I did. I just want you to know that there aren't any excuses.' This must be very hard for my usually obsessively correct father.

'But what did you do?' I persist.

'Do you remember your mother going away to look after Granny when she had that fall?'

'Vaguely.' I remember eating lots of dinners from the freezer.

'Well, I found it very difficult to manage work and you two children as well. Aunt Winnie was with your mother so she couldn't come and help. I didn't understand why Granny needed the two of them there.'

I nod, wondering when we will be coming to the point of all this.

'So Elizabeth Monkwell came and helped with supper every night and we became close.'

'Right,' I say slowly, feeling some sort of response is expected of me.

'I was up at the main house one day, dropping something off, and Elizabeth and I stood chatting in the drawing room for a few minutes. I don't know how it happened but suddenly we were, er . . . well, kissing.'

I wince slightly. I fervently hope I'm not about to be taken through the whole affair step by step. I might need another cigarette. I wonder if they bought any duty-free and if it would be churlish to ask.

'Where does Simon come in?' I ask suddenly, alarmed by the thought that he may be connected. My time scales are becoming very confused and I start wondering whether we are in fact half brother and sister.

'Well, one day Simon walked in on us.'

'He walked in?'

'Yes. He saw us.'

'What did he do?'

'Simply stared at us and walked out again. We were both distraught. Elizabeth went after him but I don't think she could ever get him to talk about it.'

'What happened then?'

'I told your mother about it when she got back and we agreed that the best thing for all of us was to leave. I took the next post that came up, which happened to be in Italy, and you went to live with Aunt Winnie during term-time.'

'And that was it? The sum total?'

'Yes. That was it.'

'So did Aunt Winnie know about this?'

'Yes. We told her because she was trying to persuade us to stay in England because she was worried about moving you from your schools.'

'What did Simon think? What did he say?'

My father shakes his head. 'We never knew. As I said, I don't think Elizabeth could ever get him to talk about it. It was just before he went away to boarding school. But we thought that if you were to become close to Simon, you ought to know about it.'

I nod, trying to get my jumbled thoughts into some sort of order. 'It must have been the end of a summer holiday then. I remember Mrs Monkwell helping me with my birthday card for you. But you didn't move to Italy until the following year.'

'That was when the next post came up.'

'But that was the autumn that . . .'

My mother leans forward. 'What darling?'

I stare at her, willing myself to think more clearly. That was the autumn Simon started being so horrible to me. The bullying began slowly but by Christmas it had reached a full crescendo.

'Simon was quite unpleasant to me for a while. It was during that autumn. It can't be a coincidence,' I say quietly.

We all frown. My mother says, 'But why would he be nasty to you? Was he nasty to Sophie too?'

I shake my head. 'No. Just me.'

My father suddenly looks racked with guilt. 'Why didn't you tell us? We could have stopped it,' he says fiercely.

'Maybe he was just taking it out on Isabel,' my mother says to my father. My father nods shortly but I can see that he is terribly upset by the idea.

'But why would he take it out on me?' I ask.

'Maybe you should ask him,' my mother says gently. 'After all, you're both adults now.'

I put out a hand to touch my father, who is looking absolutely distraught at this turn of events. He looks up at my touch. 'What a mess, Izzy. I'm so sorry. I had absolutely no idea,' he says softly and takes my hand, which is probably the most physical contact my father and I have had in twenty-six years. It feels peculiar that it should result from something like this.

I get up suddenly. I need to find Simon and talk to him.

'Er, Izzy?' says my mother in some concern. 'Are you okay?'

'Hmm?'

'Izzy? You're not going funny on us, are you?'

'Do you think . . . ? I mean, did Simon think . . . ?' My words trail off as I will my befuddled brain to make some sense of everything. 'What time is it?' I ask suddenly.

'Time for a lie down? It's half past twelve,' my father says doubtfully. 'Are you feeling okay?'

'I've got to go!' I say and walk quickly from the garden.

'Izzy, we're sorry we had to break it to you like this,' my mother shouts after me.

I walk backwards for a second. 'I think it might be the best news I've ever heard!' I shout back. 'I'll send Aunt Winnie out!'

Meg and I jog steadily up to the house, into the kitchen and down the long corridor. 'My parents are in the walled garden!' I call out to Aunt Winnie, who looks amazed. I carry on into the hall and spot Victoria. 'Victoria!' I shout. 'Where's Simon?'

'In the drawing room. But I really don't think you

321

should . . .' Her words are lost on me as I make a lunge for the door and burst in.

A sea of faces stare back at me. I spot Simon as he starts to get up. 'Izzy?' he says doubtfully.

'Simon, can I have a quick word? In private?'

He looks startled by the slightly mad-looking woman in front of him but manages to recover well. Such a professional! 'Er, of course you can. Sam, can you take over? Excuse me, everyone, I'll be back in a moment.'

He leads me from the room and tries the door to the library. Locked. As instructed.

He tries another door. Locked again. As instructed.

In frustration, he drags me past Victoria towards the cupboard under the stairs and shoves me inside, pausing only to turn on the light before following me in and closing the door behind him.

'It's our old den!' I say in surprise.

'Er, yes. Izzy, I hate to drag you to the point but could you possibly tell me what this is all about?' It is a little awkward talking like this. Two adults can't quite stand up in here and our heads are tilted at difficult angles.

'They told me, Simon.'

'Told you what?'

'Everything.'

'Who did? Izzy, my neck is starting to hurt.'

'My parents. They flew over from Hong Kong last night. They told me about your mother and my father.' I try to tone down my elation. 'You didn't want to have to tell me that they were having an affair, did you? Why didn't you tell me?'

'I nearly did but I just couldn't. You might have hated me for telling you.'

We stare at each other for a second. I think he's smiling but it's very difficult to tell at this angle. In one swift movement he bends down and pulls out two old wooden crates from a corner. They might even be the ones we used to sit on. The problem is that I've become a little more fastidious in my old age and I'm worried about spiders, Poppet in particular. I don't get to express my preference for standing because Simon pulls me down to sit on one. Luckily he distracts me by taking my hand.

'In a funny way I hoped you'd never find out,' he says quietly. 'But thank God they told you.'

'Is that why you were so nasty to me?'

'God, Izzy, I don't know what to say. I was only thirteen but I was old enough to know about sex and to realise what was going on when I saw them together.'

'They never actually had a long affair, you know. Just a couple of weeks.'

'I know that now; my mother managed to talk to me about it when I was older. Long after you and Sophie had left the estate though. If she had known what I was doing to you she would have forced the issue earlier.'

'Why did you take it out on me?'

'I think I saw it as being your fault. I mean, at that age it is very hard to blame adults for anything. They are still these God-like creatures who are always right about everything so I looked around for someone else to blame. Then I remembered that you were the reason your family were at the estate in the first place, something about you wanting to ride horses. So I blamed you for the affair, for my unhappiness. It seemed completely rational to me at the time. In my mind the reason they had the affair was because our friendship pushed them together. I've often thought about

323

trying to find you to apologise but I never could have told you the reason for my behaviour. And during these last few weeks, as we've started to get to know each other again, I've found the subject of our childhood increasingly difficult to bring up. I didn't know how to explain my spite away and I couldn't possibly tell you that your father and my mother had had an affair. Izzy, I am so sorry.'

'Simon, don't worry. I know now, that's all that matters. But I've been judging you so harshly for all this time.'

He shrugs. 'I thought it was better that way, better for you to think badly of me rather than your own father. I felt guilty about treating my oldest friend so terribly but I couldn't see what else to do. It was a sort of punishment in a way.'

It's almost painful to see this proud and honourable man in so much distress. 'If it hadn't happened this way, we might have remained friends without ever taking it a step further,' I try to comfort him.

He smiles once more. 'I hadn't thought of it that way. And I suppose this is infinitely preferable?'

'Infinitely. I would go through that dreadful autumn twice if it means I get you at the end.'

'I'll make it up to you, I promise.' I like the sound of this. His smile grows even wider and he moves closer. This is obviously our moment, the part where it all comes right. I am painfully aware of him – the warmth of his hands, those gorgeous eyes looking deep into mine. He moves a little closer, bending his face slowly towards me until . . .

A loud voice interrupts us from out in the hall. '*In* the cupboard, you say? Hell's bells, what are you talking about? What do you mean, in the cupboard? No son of mine would possibly . . .' And with this the door is thrown open. 'Oh, hello Izzy, Simon,' says Monty. 'What on earth are you doing in the cupboard?'

'What does it look like we're doing, Dad?'

'Well, I really don't know. The two of you seem to spend an awful lot of time in small enclosed spaces. Maybe you should see someone about it?' Aunt Flo's face appears next to him. She tugs at his arm. 'Come away, dear. I think they're having a moment.'

Monty allows himself to be led away and Flo quietly closes the door. We can hear him roaring, 'A moment? What on earth is a moment?' all the way down the corridor.

The pause gives me time to gather my thoughts. 'Simon, what's happened with the takeover?' I feel appalled that I haven't thought to ask. I take his hand quickly. 'Have you lost the house? You know, it will be fine. We'll manage somehow and—'

'That was pretty amazing what you did in the press conference,' he says, playing with my hand.

'What? Made a fool of myself? It's something I'm becoming quite an expert at.'

'The only person who looked a fool was Rob Gillingham. At midday the board of directors of Wings lost control of the company.'

'You mean it's all going to go through?' I ask breathlessly.

'It means that the American bank finally accepted our share offer and sold us their shares. I don't think Wings could persuade them not to after your little barrage.'

'So you're not going to lose the house?' I ask.

He slowly shakes his head. 'I hope not. I think I'll be able to persuade the bank to hold off until we have sold parts of Wings and consolidated the rest of the company. Maybe we'll even turn it back into the high-profit company it once was. The Americans have first option to buy back their shares.'

'How long will that take?'

'Twelve months at a push, eighteen at the most. None of this is guaranteed but we'll have some money rolling through the company now from backers. Not a lot but enough to live on and get the furniture back.'

'Are you going to sack lots of people?'

'Izzy, some people are going to have to lose their jobs because the company isn't making any money. But not as many as the current board of directors would have sacked.'

'But Rob said they weren't going to make any staff cuts.'

'He was lying. Let's face it, he's not exactly renowned for his honesty, is he? I'm sorry that I thought you were feeding information to him. I was starting to get paranoid. This takeover meant so much to everyone. I knew as soon as you opened your mouth back there that none of it could be true.'

He grins at me and my heart prances foolishly around. 'Would Gerald let you work here at the estate?'

'If I still have a job.'

'I'm sure you will have when he hears how much there is to be done. I'm thinking about opening the house to the public, a tearoom, some outdoor concerts, that sort of thing. It would be perfect for you. And companies will be queuing up to hold their bashes here after the ball. Then I thought I could retire from the takeover business permanently. Hand over one of the farms to Will.'

'That would be fantastic. I feel a bit sorry for Will.'

'Do we have to talk about him?'

This time he really does kiss me. On and on it goes as we shift position awkwardly on our wooden boxes. He moves one hand to the middle of my back and squeezes me to him. Eventually we break apart and stare at each other. I don't think I have ever seen anyone quite so sexy.

'Simon, what about this lawyer character I've been hearing about? Are you seeing someone?' I ask suddenly.

'Not exactly seeing.' I give him a look. 'Oh come on, Izz, I'm not a monk. I can safely say that since you reappeared on the scene I haven't spoken to her, much less seen her. Come on,' he says, hauling me to my feet.

'Where are we going?'

'I don't know about you but I need to finish a rather large takeover.'

We fall out of the cupboard on top of Mrs Delaney.

We blink in the natural light for a second. 'Mrs D? What *are* you doing?' says Simon as we all find our feet.

'Guarding,' she says fiercely. 'Monty and Flo said you were both in here and he . . .' she points accusingly at Sam who looks petrified '. . . wanted to disturb you.'

'Oh, er, thanks, Mrs D.'

'You're welcome,' she sniffs and marches off back to the kitchen.

'Simon, are you coming?' asks Sam.

'I'll be there in a second.'

Sam scoots ahead of us, blushing furiously.

'You know I had my hair cut short for you?' Simon says, as we wander slowly towards the drawing room, hand in hand.

'Did you?'

'Yes, I remember you mentioning how much you fancied men with short hair.'

'You look gorgeous.'

'Do you think you can put up with my family? I know

they're a pain in the arse but they sort of come with me.'

'I adore your family,' I protest.

'That's lucky because they will be interfering in this from the off. We will be on constant look-out for spiders, have to share the bed with at least seven dogs and then Harry will pop up in the middle of the night asking for bob-a-jobs.' I giggle. 'I gave Harry fifty quid to tape a kipper under Rob's Porsche's bonnet.'

'You didn't!'

'At least he'll win the bob-a-job contest now. We would never have heard the end of it otherwise.'

'Godfrey Farlington was becoming a little annoying.'

'This has probably been a bad time for you to give up smoking then?'

'Actually, I don't smoke.'

'Really? Would you like a cigarette?'

'Have you got one?'

'Ha! Caught you!'

'No, I really don't smoke. I never have. It was Dom.'

On cue, Dominic sidles up to us. He is holding out my mobile phone. 'Izzy, I'm sorry but there's someone who absolutely insists she speak to you.'

'Who is it?' I ask.

'Lady Boswell.'

Simon pauses outside the drawing room. 'Lady Boswell?' he repeats. 'Of the Nordic Ice Feast?'

Our eyes meet. I always said he could read my mind because he takes the phone from Dominic. 'Lady Boswell? This is Simon Monkwell . . .' he says smoothly. He squeezes my hand and then the door clicks quietly shut behind him.